Lowri Turner is a journalist. She made her name as Fashion Editor of the *Evening Standard*, before moving into radio and television presenting. Famed for her wickedly honest views, she was barred entry into numerous fashion shows by disgruntled designers, earning her the title 'Most banned fashion correspondent of all time'. SWITCHCRAFT is her second novel, following the acclaimed STRIPPED BARE.

Switchcraft

Lowri Turner

headline

First published in 2004
by HEADLINE BOOK PUBLISHING

A HEADLINE paperback

10 9 8 7 6 5 4 3 2 1

Cataloguing in Publication Data is available from the British Library

ISBN 0 7553 0260 5

Typeset in RotisSerif by Avon DataSet Ltd, Bidford-on-Avon, Warks
Printed and bound in Great Britain by
Clays Ltd St Ives plc

HEADLINE BOOK PUBLISHING
A division of Hodder Headline
338 Euston Road
London NW1 3BH

www.headline.co.uk
www.hodderheadline.com

For my mother, Shirley, and sister, Catrin,
for having their lives disrupted during
the writing of this book.

Chapter One

'So, do you two ever, like, you know, *go out* with the same bloke?'

There were two things that really irritated Emma and Gill about being twins. The first was the assumption that they were like tubes of toothpaste, permanently on special offer – Buy one get one free! Or a BOGOF, as supermarkets like to call it. Actually, BOGOF was pretty much what Gill and Emma said whenever a guy smarmed up to them and suggested a threesome. In this case Gill and Emma settled for a simple chorus of: 'No.'

The man was persistent. But then, any chap who thought wearing grey slacks was a surefire way to pull women was unlikely to be of a delicate sensibility. He winked in a spectacularly unappealing way. 'Give us a smile.'

'Go away,' said Emma and Gill at the same time.

'You said that together!' he exclaimed. 'Are you telepathic?'

And this was the other thing Emma and Gill really hated about being twins. Non twins, assuming that twins

1

were a bit odd anyway – well, as a twin you only had half a brain, didn't you? – just loved the idea that twins might also have a touch of *The Twilight Zone* about them. In public, Emma and Gill might appear normal. In private, in between setting fire to things, it was assumed they engaged in spots of random levitation, teleportation and getting their heads to spin round and spew green stuff out. No one ever actually said any of this, of course, but all those questions about telepathy were only going in one direction.

As children, other kids had delighted in setting tests. 'Close your eyes and tell me what your sister is holding in her left hand? ... You're right! You should go on *Opportunity Knocks* like Lena Zavaroni!' they'd squeal. As adults, people were transfixed if they saw Emma and Gill shopping in a supermarket together. No, they were driven to explain, they didn't draw their life force from one another. They did, actually, have to buy food.

'No, we are not telepathic,' Emma said, sighing.

'But maybe *you* are,' Gill told the man. She shut her eyes and adopted an expression of extreme concentration. 'Got the message?'

The man looked befuddled. Gill leant towards him, putting her face close to his. She had to make a trade off between appearing threatening and feeling nauseous. 'GO AWAY, YOU ANNOYING LITTLE DWEEB, OR I WILL KNEE YOU IN THE GROIN!'

This finally penetrated his brain and he crept away.

'Thank God for that,' Emma said.

'Yeah,' Gill agreed, picking up her packet of cigarettes. She put one between her lips, lit it with a cheap plastic lighter and inhaled deeply. The lighter landed with a clatter on the wooden slatted top of the picnic table where she tossed it.

Emma and Gill had chosen this pub because it had a garden. Well, that's what the pub called it. Actually, it was a grim patch of asphalt with a few hanging baskets and a smattering of wooden benches and tables speared by spectacularly unstylish brewery-sponsored umbrellas. While Gill had a view of a brick wall, Emma, facing her, was entertained by a view of the pub's grey plastic soil pipe bolted to the side of the building. Their conversation was conducted over the steady hum of the air-conditioning unit and the occasional flush of a toilet two floors above.

Emma watched the smoke plume from the end of Gill's cigarette curl upwards like a grey delicate chiffon scarf. 'I thought you were giving up?'

Gill wrinkled her nose. 'Yeah, I've got the book.'

'Alan Carr?' Emma asked.

Gill nodded.

'Apparently, Mr Carr, or God as I think he's known in ex-smoking circles –'

'Jesus!' Gill exclaimed.

'No, not Jesus, God.'

Gill rolled her eyes in exasperation. 'Yeah, yeah. What

3

I meant to say was I didn't know there were such things as ex-smoking circles. Are they like crop circles? Do they appear mysteriously overnight?'

'Unfortunately, no. They have a depressing sense of permanency about them. Actually, they're like book clubs, only with a fascist undertone.'

'Well, maybe I won't give up after all.'

Emma shook her head. 'I was only trying to say that, if you actually read the book you've bought, it tells you the first step is to get rid of all your smoking-related paraphernalia.'

Gill inhaled sharply. 'Oh, I'd forgotten you did Alan Carr when you gave up. So, do you have to dump *everything*? Ashtrays and ...'

Emma and Gill both eyed the plastic lighter, glinting in the August sunlight like a small strip of green neon.

'Oh, come on, Gill,' Emma said. 'It's hardly an heirloom, is it?'

Gill picked up the lighter and closed her fingers protectively around it. 'I'll have you know this has a rich cultural heritage.'

'Yeah, what?'

'I bought it from a Kurdish gypsy on the Holloway Road. Three for a pound.'

They both laughed.

At thirty-eight, Emma and Gillian Chancellor weren't exactly pretty; more handsome, if that didn't make them sound like they took steroids and called themselves Jeff at the weekends. They had strong physical presences, largely due to their height: five feet ten in bare feet.

Naturally dark-haired, Gillian had overidden Mother Nature's intentions as a teenager and bleached her hair white. Well, that was the aim, but it had actually turned out yellow. Her hair had been short and she'd emerged from the bathroom looking like a human lightbulb. However, over the years, she had perfected the art of hair colouring. She had been blonde, black (for half an hour, which was how long it took to go to the chemist and get some peroxide), strawberry blonde and many, many variations on the above. Currently, she was a redhead.

Emma had remained brunette. It suited her. Emma was capable and straightforward. Even if her hair hadn't been brown, she would have been the antithesis of the wishy washy Timotei blonde. If Emma had been abandoned in a sunlit, leafy glade with only a few flimsy cheesecloth layers to wear, she'd have immediately ground up some leaf, collected a length of spare creeper and tie-dyed herself a couple of changes of outfit.

Still, for Emma there was no danger of going back to nature. She was far too busy. Emma had it all. She was a wife, a mother and had a seat on the board of high-street retailer Smith & Taylor. Others looked on with envy as if Emma had somehow woken up one morning with her life laid out like a row of dominoes standing balanced on a pub table, and all she'd had to do was tip the first one so they all tumbled on command into a satisfyingly neat little pattern. So numerous were the individuals who, on the basis of Emma's apparent good fortune, went puce around the edges, that she had thought of carrying a sign to placate them. Similar in size and shape to those held aloft by lollipop ladies – well, maybe the handle would have to fold to get it in the boot of her car – it would bear the simple but effective message: 'Sorry.'

Gillian was different. It wasn't a case of there being a good and a bad twin – another twin myth – it was simply that their personalities, unlike their genes, weren't identical. Who knew the reason? Nature or nurture? Gillian and Emma's parents had debated that one many times. As children, Gill had been the leader. It was she who rode a bike first and who demanded (and got) first choice of balloon at their twin birthday parties. If her layer of pass-the-parcel newsprint didn't contain a prize, why, she just ripped off another layer and another until she got to the treasure. This alpha female behaviour was partly down to the fact that Gill was older. Yet they had been born by Caesarean, so age was denoted by the place in the queue they occupied rather than actual time of arrival. Even so, Gill claimed first choice of toys, sweets and, later, boyfriends, although, to be honest, they rarely found the same men attractive. Nature or nurture? This time it was Emma and Gill who debated.

Gill wielded her relative maturity like a Star Wars light sabre, which had been another joint Christmas present she had claimed. 'There you are, girls, something for you to share,' Uncle Colin had announced proudly in December 1974 as he handed it over. Emma and Gillian had looked at each other and wanted to beat him to death with it. Now it was Emma who, to the outside world at least, looked like the leader. She was the one with the stable marriage and stellar career. Gill had a rebellious streak that meant she'd never managed to stay in a job for more than a couple of months, let alone build herself a career. As for getting married . . . committing herself to a regular hair colour would have been a start.

Emma sipped her glass of Sauvignon Blanc and stared contentedly into space. She could almost ignore the awful view and worse ambience because she was just happy to see her sister. Gill, too, cherished these shared times, especially since they had become increasingly rare. 'Have they given you an idea of what they're planning?' Emma asked absentmindedly. 'Mum and Dad, that is.'

'No,' Gill answered, sipping her own Bloody Mary and thinking it was more like a Bloody Disgrace. 'They just said they wanted us both at lunch. They've got *an announcement.*'

They both frowned. Then Gill smiled.

'What?' Emma demanded.

'Maybe Dad's decided to have a sex change and Mum's standing by him.'

Emma laughed. 'Yeah, they're going to live together as best girlfriends and give each other shampoo and sets.'

'And argue over who's got the best legs,' added Gill.

They both paused, thinking. 'Dad!' they declared together and laughed.

Gill tipped her head up into the sunshine. It felt deliciously hot against her skin. She was just thinking that it could have been St Tropez, not North London, when she was interrupted by the sound of a slap and then a childish wail. She lowered her chin and opened one eye. Emma's gaze followed hers. A small boy's face was creased into a scowl. 'Waah!' he yelled.

'Shu' up!' spat the woman beside him. She had a mobile phone clamped to her ear and blonde hair extensions that looked about as lifelike as the mane on Gill's old Sindy horse. The woman's nails were so long she could have picked locks with them. 'Jus' the bloody brat,' she said, stubbing a cigarette out into a moulded glass ashtray and lighting another one.

Gillian self-consciously stubbed out her own cigarette. Never mind 'Smoking Kills' on the side of a packet of fags; as a deterrent, a photo of Tracy Towerblock with 'This is you' underneath it would have been much more effective. She really was going to give up. This time, she really was.

Emma, too, felt a pang of guilt. How many times had she told Saskia off in public? OK, she didn't wallop her as well. Even so, the gap between Emma and Ms Mobile Phone suddenly seemed perilously narrow. Inwardly, she shuddered.

Gill folded a frond of red hair behind her ear. It felt hot and brittle like a newspaper left out on a summer lawn. 'Did we ever come to pubs as kids?' she asked.

'God, no. Mum wouldn't have thought it was a learning experience,' Emma replied.

'Oh, I don't know,' smiled Gill, looking back over at the hair-extended mother and son, now silently sulking. 'We'd have been multilingual.'

'The other language being bad, I suppose.'

Gill nodded.

'Come to think of it, it would come in pretty handy at times to be able to speak fluent foul. Some teenage girls pushed past me in the street on the way here. You know the sort, glittery tops and jeans with builders' bottom and about twelve . . .'

Gill nodded. 'Girls in boob tubes are like policemen. They keep getting younger.'

'Well, I tried telling them off and, you know, I'm not totally out of touch. I mean, I've got an Ibiza chill-out CD at home. Anyway, I listened to myself having a go at them and I sounded like Joyce Grenfell.'

'But you are Joyce Grenfell!' Gill exclaimed, laughing.

'And you're J-Lo, I suppose,' Emma said indignantly.

'Oh, no, I'm in far better shape than that old trout, what's-'er-name.'

'We are the same age, remember.'

'On paper maybe, but I haven't been ground down by years of marriage and kids.'

'It's kid, not kids,' Emma pointed out.

'What's that thing about a picture painting a thousand words? Well, one kid can create a thousand wrinkles.'

'Ooh, you . . .' Emma reached across the table and tried to hit Gill, who had shifted her body backwards out of range. She was laughing.

'Only joking! Is it coping with teenage temper tantrums or the lack of a decent sex life, you being married and all that, that's driving you to violence?'

'Neither,' Emma announced, standing up and managing to land a blow to Gill's shoulder. 'It's having a bitter and twisted dried-up old crone for a sister.' She sat down again.

'Less of the old, if you don't mind,' smiled Gill, rubbing her arm and then lighting another cigarette. 'But really, what are Mum and Dad up to?'

'Do you think it might be something to do with their golden wedding anniversary?' Emma asked.

'I can't believe Mum and Dad have been married for fifty years,' Gill said. 'Do you think you and Max'll get there?'

Emma sighed. She had her glass of wine in her hand and was contemplating her reflection in the side of it. She wasn't sure how much of the *Hammer House of Horror* effect was distortion or really her. Maybe she should get Botoxed. 'God knows,' she said.

'At least you're in with a fighting chance,' Gill said.

'You mean in the sense that I'm married and the

closest you've ever come to walking up the aisle was . . .'

'Shagging the vicar at your wedding, yeah.'

'Yes, thanks again for that, although I still think in the vestry *while* we were having our snaps taken outside wasn't the wisest choice,' Emma said. 'Did he stay in the church?'

'I don't know. He was having a crisis of faith.'

'Sounded like he was having a coronary, if I remember rightly.' Emma pretended to disapprove of Gillian's sexual escapades, but they actually provided her with a chance to live vicariously on the wild side. She'd been married for thirteen years and sometimes it felt like fifty.

'Mum and Dad are part of dying breed,' Gill announced.

'Like the Dodo?'

'That's already dead,' Gill pointed out. 'No, *a dying breed* like . . . um . . .' She searched for a suitable example. 'Tom Jones!'

'Dad's nothing like Tom Jones. I don't think he's ever worn leather jeans,' Emma said.

'Jesus, what a horrible thought. Dad in leather jeans. No, what I mean is, Tom Jones is one of a dying breed,' Gill explained.

'Like the Krankies or Emu,' said Emma.

Gill leant across the pub table to Emma and adopted a serious expression. 'I hate to tell you this but Emu wasn't a real bird. He was a puppet. Rod Hull had his hand shoved up an oven glove with feathers.'

Emma smiled again. It was always good to see Gillian. They didn't spend enough time together, what with her frenetic social life and Emma's job and family. When they did, it reminded them how close they were. Throughout the ebb and flow of their lives, they had been each other's one constant. First day at school, first jobs, first relationships, they had shared it all. Those who asked if they were telepathic ignored the fact that in no other relationship did you share experiences so completely. Brothers and sisters were separated by nine months at least. Even the bond between parent and child was pale in comparison to that between twins. As for husbands and wives, they had former lives that didn't include the other, although in the case of Gordon and Charlotte Chancellor that had been so long ago they could barely remember them.

'Fifty years of happily married life. Give it a decade and Mum and Dad'll get into *The Guinness Book of Records*.'

Emma shook her head. 'Oh, no, they'll get the Victoria Cross at the very least.'

Gill nodded. 'Yeah, well, I suppose we'll have to wait till lunch tomorrow to find out what they're up to. You are coming, aren't you?'

'Yeah, you?' Emma asked.

'Yeah,' Gill said. 'I want to remind myself what a nuclear family is like.'

'Is that nuclear in the sense of close or about to explode?' Emma asked.

Chapter Two

The knife cut through the meat with all the ease and elegance of a pair of rounded-end children's scissors through a sheet of foam rubber. It took repeated sawings back and forth to hack anything off the bone. When a chunk of pork was finally dislodged, it fell on to the plate with an exhausted thump, about a quarter-pound of meat to each slice. Juice ran on to the plate also, forming an irregular pool around the piles of roast potatoes and chunks of parsnip.

'Now, who wants crackling?' asked Gordon Chancellor, hopefully. Gordon always did the carving. It wasn't because he was any good at it. When Gordon carved a roast, it disintegrated. Still, at seventy, Gordon was of the generation that stipulated carving as men's work, along with paying the gas bill and checking the back door was closed before bed. For these and his other manly duties, Charlotte, his wife of almost fifty years, offered entirely uncritical praise. It was rule one in the *How To Be a Good Wife* Handbook, 1952 edition. That was opposed to the 1902 edition, although, frankly, there was little discernible difference.

Every week for the past five decades, Gordon had been handed the big knife with the serrated edge and the pronged fork. And every week he had demolished the lunch Charlotte Chancellor had cooked for him.

'I said, who wants crackling?' Gordon repeated.

'Sorry, dear,' said Charlotte. 'I'm sure Max will have some crackling, won't you, Max?'

'Thank you, Charlotte. I'd love some,' said Max.

As if massaging Gordon's ego wasn't enough, Charlotte had taken on the task of tending to Emma's husband as well. It was as if Max were an exotic plant that Emma wasn't watering sufficiently. Charlotte made up for it with her own judicious inquiries as to his health, job and general well-being. Emma and her mother didn't argue about much. She left that to Gill. Still, Emma resented her mother's interference in her marriage. Early on, Emma had discovered that her mum had been calling Max once a week for a little chat to ask him about his day, etc. This was presumably because she, Emma, was not doing a good enough job of stroking his ego. After that, Emma and her mother had had one of their few really big rows.

It wasn't that Charlotte Chancellor disapproved of her daughter. She had wanted her to have a career. She had also wanted her to have a husband rich enough to support her so she could give it up when she had children. Charlotte Chancellor hadn't bargained on her daughter marrying a man with an ex-wife and a daughter who siphoned off his income like someone draining petrol from a tank at dead of night with a bit of hose and an empty can. Now, Charlotte worried for Emma. She had so much on, what with her job and Max and a home to run. Charlotte worried that in all that rushing about, she might forget that a man needs looking after. And, yes, it might be old-fashioned, but if his wife doesn't look after him, then he'll find himself another woman who will, or so Charlotte thought.

'Shall I pour you some gravy?' Charlotte asked Max.

'Max is not a child. He can ask for himself, you know,' Emma said, looking pointedly at her mother.

'I'm sorry, dear,' said Charlotte quickly, realising her mistake. 'I just thought . . .'

Max shrugged, wondering what all the fuss was about.

Max was the physical opposite of Emma. Where she was tall, he was short: five seven on a good day with the wind behind him and if he was stood on a bit of a slope. Where she was rangy, he was podgy. When Emma had first seen Max, all those years ago, she'd been struck by how much he resembled a human doughnut: a funny, warm, intelligent doughnut, but a doughnut all the same. Still, if Max had the cards stacked against him in the sex god stakes, he had cleverly managed to circumvent the system. Max had developed a brand of winning vulnerability that was remarkably effective not just with Emma, but with the whole of the female sex. Old ladies adored him, secretaries worshipped him, the mothers of long-forgotten ex-girlfriends still asked when they were going to see that nice Max Freeman again.

Never mind that Max was a hugely successful lawyer, he always seemed to be the underdog. It was as if he came with a Paddington Bear-style ticket attached to his expensive suits, reading: 'In need of rescue.' And in a way he did, or at least he had done when Emma met him. Max had been abandoned by his first wife, Dominique, when their daughter, Saskia, was just two. He was bringing her up alone. If he'd admitted repairing baby sparrows' broken wings in his spare time, Emma couldn't have been more impressed. Emma's heart melted like a dropped ice-cream cone on an August bank holiday pavement. Here was a bloke, she felt, who understood the concept of commitment.

'Lovely bit of pork, darling,' Gordon said.

'Well, you're doing a great job, Dad,' Emma added.

Gill gave her a look as if to say: 'You crawler.' What was it about being in your parents' house that made you regress? she thought. It was as if your childhood home was a time machine capable of spiriting you back decades. She and Emma had only to walk across the freshly polished doorstep of Number 72 Silver Lane to step back into the 1960s, and it had nothing to do with the original Formica worktop that still adorned the kitchen. Perhaps it was the nature of the relationship between parents and children that however old you got, the balance of power refused to shift. You were the eternal child. Things didn't change until your mum and dad got so dotty and decrepit that they put the cat in the oven and turned the TV so high people could hear it in Basingstoke. Then you became the parent and they became the child and that had to be infinitely more depressing.

Gill looked at Max. For those from outside the family such as him, watching the person they loved in the presence of their parents must be horrifying. Forget taking your potential husband home so your mum and dad could give *him* the once-over, it was the would-be spouse who needed to check out their other half *en famille*. An added plus was that they got to ferret out any obvious genetic weaknesses. A brother with a severely receding hairline at twenty-five and a penchant for the Hawaiian guitar? A sister with fat knees and a parakeet collection? A man could be forgiven for thinking carefully before agreeing to stir that kind of DNA into his own genetic soup. Not that there were any such obvious peculiarities in the Chancellor family; that's if you didn't count a twin sister who had shagged the vicar at the wedding . . .

'Is that a new hair colour, Gillian?' Charlotte asked, handing her a plate.

'Um, yeah, Mum,' Gill replied, taking it. 'Copper red, instead of Titian.'

Hair colour was regarded as a safe Gillian subject by

her mother. She steered clear of work, because Gill frequently wasn't doing any. Boyfriends were also off the agenda. Frankly, Charlotte had given up trying to keep up with the ever-changing cast list for that role. Gill knew that, at thirty-eight, her single status was a source of some embarrassment to her parents. They had never expressed anything other than support for her, but there was a slightly strained edge to their good manners. When describing Gill to friends, they used the word 'single' self-consciously. It was as if they were in a trendy café ordering a café americano, trying to be up-to-date, when all they really wanted was a white coffee.

Gill felt their discomfort and it made her chippy. She watched Emma and thought how much easier a ride she got at these family lunches. She'd done the dutiful thing and got herself a good man, a good job and a gold star. Gillian frequently pondered whether to use one of these lunches to announce she was a lesbian. That would at least have diffused the air of expectancy that always lingered. Her parents were simply dying for her to announce that all this being single malarkey was a huge mistake, wheel in some nice chap in a polo shirt and give them a date for the wedding. She felt simultaneously ashamed for disappointing them and furious with herself that she should still want their approval.

'Saskia, dear, what would you like?' asked Charlotte, glancing over at a vision of depression shrouded in baggy black layers. This was Max's daughter and Emma's stepdaughter. Saskia's face wore a bored expression beneath hacked-at hair that wasn't so much a style as a 'Keep Out' sign. Now sixteen, Saskia was a militant vegetarian who opposed cruelty to all living things except, apparently, humans.

Emma was already regretting her shortness with her mother. As ever, she was now smoothing things over. 'So, Mum,' she said brightly. 'Gill said you and Dad had an announcement to make.'

Charlotte beamed. 'Yes, dear.'

'Well?' asked Gill, impatiently.

'Perhaps, Gordon, you'd like to tell them?' Charlotte said, deferring dutifully to her husband.

Gordon shook his head. 'You do it, love.' He had his half-glasses propped up on his head and was squinting in extreme concentration at the half-collapsed roast as if preparing to defuse a bomb.

Charlotte paused, looking round the table at the expectant faces. 'Well, your father's been looking on the Internet, haven't you, Gordon? Surfing the Web!' Charlotte made surfing the Web sound exotic and slightly shocking, as if they'd both recently attended an Ann Summers party. But Charlotte wasn't the Ann Summers party type. Avon was as close as she'd ever got.

'That's right, dear,' said Gordon. 'Gravy, Saskia?'

'No, no, Gordon. She can't. She's a veg-et-arian.' Charlotte pronounced it slowly, as if she had never heard the word before.

'Bloody silly, in my book,' Gordon pronounced. 'Where would we have been in nineteen forty-five if we'd all been vegetarian? Dead, that's where —'

Ding, dong.

Gordon's lecture on the wartime diet was interrupted by a ring of the doorbell.

Emma got up from the table. 'I'll just get that,' she said. The rest of the table exchanged puzzled glances until, a few moments later, Emma reappeared. Her smile was thin and joyless. She was flanked by a woman with short, flicky blonde hair and too much make-up.

'How lovely to see you, Dominique,' said Charlotte.

Charlotte's impeccable manners could not conceal the frosty reception from the rest of the group for Max's ex-wife. Saskia, in particular, shot her an evil look. For Emma, too, Dominique's arrival was less than welcome. She may have officially abandoned Saskia fourteen years ago but, of late, she had re-entered all their lives. Over the last three years, she had taken to turning up whenever she felt like it and, more to the point, whenever she wanted something.

Emma looked at Max. He had his head down and was forking up Brussels sprouts as if bailing out a sinking ship. He was trying to work out what to do. Whatever they said about having a bird in the hand and another in the bush, having two wives in the same room was a less than ideal situation. Max's normal approach to the multiple-spouse problem was to adopt the precautionary approach scientists used when handling oxygen and nitrogen: keep the two elements apart to ward off a possible explosion. A full-length safety suit of the type mandatory in nuclear power stations when handling highly reactive material might have been useful, too, but Max wasn't sure where he could get one of those.

Max's other tactic for survival was to pretend that Emma and Dominique didn't loathe each other. It allowed him to avoid dealing with the female emotions that bubbled around him like jam in a boiling pan. Instead, he told himself they got on like a house on fire. That is, actually, what Dominique would have liked to do to Emma's home, if she'd thought she might get away with it. But she'd heard they didn't allow trips out from prison to have liposuction, so she'd decided not to risk it.

Dominique was high maintenance in every sense: physically, emotionally and practically. Physically, her face and body were a testament to the artificial. Her hair was highlighted – expensively; her body was honed by visits to the gym. As for her emotional and practical needs, Max propped her up on both counts, alternately delivering pep talks and useful little cheques which he thought Emma didn't know about. Except she did.

'Hmph, hmph, hmph,' Dominique said.

The whole table frowned at this. Dominique wasn't so much speaking as gurgling. Her words bubbled up inside her throat but had trouble getting out of her mouth. That's because the collagen-pumped equivalent of the

Thames Barrier got in the way. Sentences crashed against Dominique's grossly inflated lips and rebounded in again. Dominique was a devotee of lunchtime cosmetic surgery. Emma and Gillian looked closely. Yes, she'd had her lips done again.

Fortunately, Dominique's need to communicate was short-circuited by a crash from the hall. A small human torpedo shot round the corner into the dining room. He was carrying a toy sword, which he was swinging at anything he could reach. One of Charlotte's prized china figurines had already copped it. Now he aimed at another.

'Ah, you brought Kevin,' Emma said, even her thin smile freezing on her face. She jumped to her feet to disarm the small vandal before he could do any more damage.

Being French, Dominique could see nothing wrong with calling a child Kevin. And, indeed, said with a Gallic twang it sounded OK. Emma feared it would mean an eventful time at a London primary, however.

There was a brief tussle between Emma and Kevin before she won. Kevin immediately roared off back down the hall and into the garden. 'Waah!'

'Is it OK if Kevin eats outside?' Emma asked Charlotte.

'Fine, dear,' Charlotte answered

'Toss him some raw meat like they do to the lions at London Zoo,' muttered Saskia.

Saskia's relationship with Kevin was as strained as that she enjoyed with her mother. Kevin was the product of

Dominique's latest *amour fou*. His father was Denzel, Dominique's one-time personal trainer and on-off housemate. Saskia, not unreasonably, resented the knowledge that her mother had chosen to dump her, but was only too happy to play happy families with her replacement, Kevin. Except, of course, there was nothing happy about Dominique's home life. A boyfriend who yo-yoed in and out of her life in cycle shorts, plus a homicidal toddler – Kevin could destroy any environment he occupied for more than five minutes – no wonder Dominique retired to the plastic surgeon's couch. If she hadn't had her face regularly frozen by Botox, it would have been stretched into Munch's *The Scream*.

Or maybe it was everyone else who was doing the screaming. Dominique managed to float above the chaos of her life as if reclined on a magic carpet. This was woven from the shreds of old credit card bills, most of which Max had paid. She didn't work. Well, it would have interfered with her work-outs, her lunches, her shopping trips and her painting holidays in the Dordogne.

'This is a surprise, Dominique,' Emma said. 'To what do we owe the honour?'

'I was in the area,' she said unconvincingly.

Saskia shot out of her chair like a rocket on Bonfire Night. 'If she's staying, I'm going,' she declared.

'Charming!' Dominique exclaimed. 'I come all the way over here and –'

'Well you shouldn't have,' Saskia hissed. Her eyes were blazing.

There was a silent stand-off, then Emma intervened. 'Why don't we all sit down and have some lunch?' she said brightly. As a diplomatic tactic, it probably wouldn't have cut much ice between the Israelis and Palestinians, but it was the best Emma could come up with. Neither Dominique nor Saskia moved.

'Not hungry,' Saskia said, sulkily.

'You don't have to eat anything,' Emma said soothingly. 'That's right, isn't it, Dominique?'

Dominique sniffed disapprovingly.

Emma led Dominique round to the end of the table, facing Gordon, next to Max. Dominique immediately put a hand on his shoulder and began whispering in his ear. 'I was wondering whether you could give me a teensy weensy bit of cash . . .' she began, so solving the mystery of her presence. She wanted to tap Max. Again.

Saskia sat down, mumbling, 'Old cow!'

Fortunately, Dominique's mobile had beeped and she was already pressing keys, so she didn't hear Saskia's comment. A dangerous smile had spread across her face. What was she up to?

'Now, Dominique, what can we get for you?' Gordon asked.

But Dominique ignored him. She was looking at her phone and still smiling as widely as the Botox would allow.

'Dominique? Dominique?' Gordon persisted. 'Something to eat?'

She looked up. 'Have you have got anything without free radicals in it?' she replied, her lips having loosened up a little after a few sips of Riesling.

'Free what, dear?' asked Charlotte.

'Radicals,' Emma said.

Charlotte looked at Max. 'What are those, dear?' she asked.

'Search me,' he said.

Emma looked at Max, too. He had an expression on his face that said: What language are you talking? But then the world of feminine beautification was alien to Max. Emma had once mentioned exfoliation to him and he'd said he didn't think the hedge needed trimming.

'Free radicals,' Emma explained. 'They're –'

'Keep off politics and religion when you're eating,' interrupted Gordon. 'That's what I was always taught.'

'It's not that sort of radical, Dad,' said Gill.

'Is it like cholesterol?' Charlotte offered.

Dominique smiled more widely. Had she taken some sort of drug before she arrived that was only now kicking in? 'Don't worry about me,' she said. 'I'll just have a glass of water.'

'Nonsense, you must eat something. What about an apple?' Charlotte insisted. 'Gordon could slice it for you. Or I could pop it in the oven with some butter and brown sugar. It'd be done in a jiffy.'

'Sugar!' Dominique looked horrified.

Ding, dong.

Dominique stood up. 'I think that's for me,' she announced, before disappearing into the hall.

'Now, who can that be?' asked Charlotte.

'Well, I'm sure I don't know, do you?' said Gordon, frowning and looking expectantly at Emma.

Max looked at Saskia and Saskia looked at Gill and then they too all looked at Emma. 'What am I, the front door fairy or something? How the hell should I know who it is!' Emma exclaimed.

'Watch your language in front of the children, dear,' Charlotte admonished her.

'I'm not a child. I'm old enough to have SEX,' Saskia hissed. 'Not that I want to have SEX if it makes you turn out like all of you,' she said.

'I'll have none of that in my house,' Gordon said.

Emma raised an eyebrow and Max buried his head in his roast potatoes. They strained to hear the conversation from the hall. It was too low to make anything out.

'Do the Jehovah's Witnesses do Sundays?' Gill asked.

The sound of muffled footsteps came towards them. Dominique rounded the corner, pushing a figure before her. 'I think you know Denzel, don't you, Mr and Mrs Chancellor?' she said proudly, as if presenting a pedigree Pekinese to a judging panel at Cruft's. And Denzel did look in peak condition. His skin was glossy and stretched over rippling muscles which were much on display. He was wearing a bandanna, his usual cycle shorts and a vest.

'Yo!' Denzel said as a greeting, aiming a high five in Saskia's direction.

She groaned and looked away.

'Would you like some roast pork, Denzel?' asked Gordon.

Denzel shook his head, a noisy procedure as he had had his hair beaded like a 1980s Stevie Wonder, although Stevie Wonder had at least had the excuse that he was blind at the time. 'Smoothie,' he said, patting his rucksack.

'A smooth . . .?'

'Never mind, Dad,' said Gillian.

'Denzel has just got back from Marbella,' Dominique explained. 'Wasn't due back till tomorrow, were you, sweetie?' She ruffled his strings of hair.

Saskia looked like she was going to be sick.

'He texted me from the car,' Dominique said. 'So I told him to come round. That's OK, isn't it?' She was looking at Max despite this not being his house.

'We're not discussing sex again, are we?' said Gordon, whose house it was but whose hearing wasn't the best. 'In my day —'

'It's all right, Dad,' Emma said.

Dominique had a hand on Denzel's shoulder. The other arm was twisted round his waist. She kissed his shoulder. Saskia groaned.

'Denzel really needs a shower after the flight. Would that be OK, Charlotte?'

'Only a bath here, I'm afraid. If that'll do,' Charlotte replied.

'Sweet,' Denzel said.

'Are we on pudding already?' asked Gordon.

'No, Dad, what he means is –' began Emma.

'Cool,' Denzel announced.

'Oh, are you cold?' Charlotte asked. 'We don't normally have the central heating on in August, but then if you're from a warm country . . .'

'Denzel was born in Peckham, Mum,' Gill said, smirking.

'I think you'll find they call it East Dulwich these days,' pronounced Dominique.

Charlotte smiled in apology at Denzel. 'The bathroom is at the top of the stairs on the left. Fresh towels in the airing cupboard,' she said.

'I'll show him,' said Dominique.

Dominique and Denzel retraced their steps up the hall and climbed the stairs. The bathroom was directly above the dining room. Soon, those left around the table could hear the bathwater running overhead. With Dominique and her toyboy lover – Denzel was twenty-eight to her forty-one – out of the way the atmosphere lightened.

'So, Mum, you were saying Dad had been on the computer.'

'Oh yes.' Charlotte beamed. 'As you know, our golden wedding anniversary is fast approaching . . .'

Splash!

A large object, presumably a person, had landed in the water upstairs. Gordon frowned, but this had nothing to do with the noise from above. Gordon was deaf as a post and refused to wear his hearing aid as it 'ran the batteries down'. The problem was that by now the pork had started to toughen, making Gordon's carving efforts even worse. The vegetables were stone cold too.

Charlotte ignored the interruption and continued. 'Anyway, you know that your father and I have never really had the chance to travel. What with having you and Gordon's work and —' She saw the guilty expressions on the faces of her daughters. 'Not that we minded, of course. Your father was very happy in his work and I was happy to stay at home with you and I won't apologise for that.'

Emma winced. She always felt her mother disapproved of her being a working mother.

'No one's asking you to apologise, Mum,' Gill said.

'It's just life is a bit more complicated now,' added Emma crisply.

Before Emma could elaborate, conversation in the dining room was interrupted by more noise from upstairs. 'No, no, no,' screamed Dominique. *Splash*! Then there was laughter, followed by silence and then quieter splashing. Max looked nervous. Saskia looked furious.

Gill ploughed on. 'So, you said you hadn't done much travelling, Mum.'

'Yes, dear. Well, your father had a look at the Internet and, you know, there are some marvellous offers on holidays on the Web.' Charlotte said this with utter amazement, as if Gordon had discovered a cure for cancer rather than simply stumbled across lastminute.com.

'So, you're going on holiday then?' Gill said.

'Not exactly,' Charlotte replied.

From the garden, they could hear squeals. Either Kevin was being throttled to death or he was throttling something. The former seemed preferable to the latter.

'Should we . . .?' Max began.

Emma shook her head. 'He'll come in when he's hungry.' Frankly, the house was safer when Kevin wasn't in it.

'Oh, oh, oh . . .' went Dominique from upstairs in a suspiciously breathy voice.

Splash, splash, splash, went the bathwater.

This time, even Gordon heard. 'Did someone say something?' he asked.

'No, Dad,' Gill said, raising her voice to cover the acrobatics overhead.

'Yes, yes, yes,' shouted Dominique.

Gordon frowned. 'Did someone leave a radio on in the other room?' he asked.

'No. Never mind, dear,' Charlotte said. Her hearing was better than Gordon's, but good manners demanded she pretend to be deaf.

'No, no, I can definitely hear something –' Gordon persisted.

'It's OK, Dad,' Emma interrupted. 'Any more pork there? You'd like some more, wouldn't you, Max . . .?'

'Um, well . . .' Max said uncertainly.

'Max would love some, Dad,' Emma announced firmly.

Gordon began carving again.,

'So, what are you doing, Mum?' continued Emma gamely.

'Well, as it's our fiftieth anniversary, we thought we'd splash out a bit. You know we're having the golden wedding do after Christmas?'

Emma and Gill nodded.

'Did you decide where?' Emma asked.

'Oh, yes. Your father managed to get a booking at the hotel where we had our honeymoon. Can you imagine it, fifty years on and it's still there? They've agreed to do a sit-down meal. We thought that was better than a running buffet. Well, you don't want to have people standing up for a long time, do you? Not at our time of life, dear.'

'You make it sound like you're a hundred. You're sixty-nine, Mum. That's no age these days,' Emma said. 'I mean Joan Collins is . . .'

'I know, dear. Joan Collins is nearly seventy and she looks marvellous, but then she's a film star, isn't she, and they have all sorts of things done, don't they?'

Emma looked at Max. 'Yes, some women do, I hear.'

'Anyway,' Gill said. 'What about this holiday, Mum, the one you're not taking?'

Before Charlotte could answer, Dominique launched into a renewed bout of bellowing. 'Yes! Oh, yes!' she shrieked from above. 'You feel so b —'

'Vol-au-vents!' Emma shrieked, trying to drown out what was happening a few feet above their heads.

'Yes, dear?' said Charlotte, slightly startled.

'Are you going to have them? Or SALMON PIN WHEELS?' Emma shouted even louder.

'No, dear. I told you. It's going to be SIT-DOWN LUNCH,' Charlotte shouted back, confused as to why they were shouting, but following Emma's lead anyway. It was as if two builders working especially noisy mechanical diggers were having a conversation about canapés.

'Harder! harder!' shrieked Dominique. 'Give it to me!'

There was no possible confusion about what was going on upstairs now. Even for Gordon. His startled expression said he was fully aware of the event unfolding overhead. Saskia was practically under the table with embarrassment.

'I am going to die of anticipation here. WHERE ARE YOU NOT GOING ON HOLIDAY?'

'Sorry, dear,' said Charlotte. 'Your father and I are going on a round-the-world trip. India, Nepal . . .' She was speaking fast, for fear of being interrupted again. 'We're backpacking. I think that's what they call it. Only we're not backpacking. Gordon has got a new suitcase on wheels for us.'

Emma and Gill's faces registered shock. The idea of their parents going off on the hippy trail was like Cliff Richard admitting to sex 'n' drugs orgies in one of the hospitality tents at Wimbledon. It was totally unbelievable. Plus they'd never get that suitcase up the steps of the Taj Mahal.

'It's all right,' Charlotte said, seeing their amazement. 'We'll be back for the party.'

'What party?' Gill said.

'Our golden wedding!' Charlotte reminded her. Gill and Emma nodded.

'So when are you going?' Emma asked, still incredulous.

'Early next month,' Charlotte replied.

The crashing of waves soundtrack from upstairs soared to a *From Here to Eternity* intensity, although Emma and Gill didn't remember Deborah Kerr ever saying, 'Fuck me, big boy,' to Burt Lancaster.

After a final yell, the bathroom was silent. The only sound was the carving knife as Gordon dropped it on the floor.

Chapter Three

'There must be something here you like?' said Emma in exasperation.

'There isn't,' Saskia replied, pursing her lips in disgust at the array of garments surrounding her.

Emma and Saskia were on a back-to-school shopping trip, this being the first week in September, for the new academic year. The aim was to purchase some new clothing before Saskia's old garments fell completely to bits. However, she clung to her favourite almost-black layers – they'd been in the washing machine too often to be truly inky – with the fervour of a religious zealot who thought they had a portion of the Turin Shroud.

Emma sighed. Maybe it had been a mistake thinking that Saskia might be persuaded to branch out, sartorially speaking. She was a girl of sixteen. This made her unpersuadable on a number of issues, getting out of bed in the morning, getting home on time and clearing up her room among them. The notion that her attitude to her wardrobe would be any different had been optimistic at best.

Still, it had been ages since she and Saskia had really spent any time together. Emma looked at the sulky teenager standing next to her and tried to remember the shy two year old she had first encountered. Their first meeting had taken place outside a cinema in Leicester Square. Saskia had been clutching her father's hand. She had looked so small. Emma had been appalled by the clothes she was wearing – white knee-high socks with flowers round the top were the most memorable examples – but had subsequently learned they'd been chosen by a German nanny. Emma had swiftly taken charge of clothes buying after that.

And here she was, fourteen years later. Saskia was a woman; physically, that is. Mentally, she boomeranged from sixteen year old to six year old and back again. The trick was judging where on the Saskia lifecycle she was at any precise moment and targeting requests accordingly.

'Can we go now?' Saskia asked sullenly, edging towards the door.

Emma decided to be tough. She was all for youthful self-expression, but she simply couldn't have Saskia going round like a tramp, or a homeless person, or whatever was the current PC expression. People would start pressing money into Saskia's hand before long.

'No,' Emma said firmly. 'We have to buy something. We've been in seven shops and you haven't looked at anything, not really looked.'

'I have,' Saskia wailed defensively.

'No, you haven't,' Emma corrected her.

At this moment a slight, dark-haired man in a very tight suit with a goatee beard appeared. 'Can I help you, ladies?' he lisped campily.

'No,' declared Saskia, giving him her most withering look. 'Everything in this shop is disgusting!'

'Saskia!' Emma exclaimed. 'I'm so sorry. She's —'

'I know. Hormonal,' the assistant drawled. 'I tell you what. Bring her back when she's a normal person.' He turned on his heel and minced off.

Emma smiled, thinking that might be some time.

Gill had her eyes closed. She was trying to visualise her lungs, or more exactly the black tar that was clinging to them. She was meant to be imagining them getting cleaner and cleaner as her new non-smoking self repaired the damage that had been done to them. The problem was, whenever she thought about the tar, it reminded her of hot fudge sauce and made her want another bowl of ice cream. Since giving up B & H – Benson & Hedges – she had transferred her addiction to B & J – Ben and Jerry's. She had started on one bowl and she was now up to a pint a day. She was already teetering on the brink of breaking into her second tub within twenty-four hours.

Gill's nostrils prickled. Something delicious was wafting in their direction. She opened her eyes. Chloë, her best friend and flatmate, was standing in front of her.

She had the Alan Carr book in one hand and was tipping ash off the end of her cigarette into an ashtray on the coffee table with the other. The smoke smelt fabulous, but Gill waved it away.

'Do not pollute my air with your cancer sticks,' Gill said.

Chloë ignored her. 'It's a government plot, you know,' she declared, not moving.

'What is?' Gill asked

'The smoking-gives-you-cancer thing. They just want an excuse to add loads of tax on to a packet of twenty.'

'You don't actually believe that, do you?' Gill said.

'Yeah, why not?'

'Because it's ridiculous.'

'That's what they said when that bloke said the world wasn't flat.'

'What bloke?'

'I don't know. Columbo?' Chloë ventured.

'I don't think a detective in a mac discovered the world wasn't flat. Do you mean Columbus?'

'No, Archipelago.'

'Archimedes,' Gill corrected her.

'Is that the bloke who sat in the bath, or the one who fired the arrow into the apple? Or maybe that was King Harold?'

'That was an arrow in the eye,' Gill sighed, shaking her head in puzzlement.

Chloë's grasp of history was as firm as her grasp of life

in general. She lived in a sort of bubble, or maybe it was closer to one of those novelty paperweights that you tip upside down and shake so the snow falls inside. Chloë's world was an unpredictable one: bits of her existence swirled around her in crazy directions. Chaos followed her everywhere – or maybe she brought chaos with her. Whatever, she was defiantly single, and her romantic escapades made Gill's look tame.

Gill got up off the sofa. 'Look, I'm going to the kitchen, want anything?'

'If you eat any more ice cream, you'll explode,' Chloë said.

'Yeah, well, a girl's got to get her pleasures where she can,' Gill said over her shoulder as she headed for the fridge.

'Have you thought of sex?' Chloë suggested. 'Calorie free – well, almost . . .'

'A small green salad, yeah, I've heard,' Gill said, as she reached into the icebox.

'And it's aerobic exercise,' continued Chloë.

'Doesn't that sort of depend?'

'If you need to ask that question, you're not doing it right,' Chloë said.

Gill returned from the kitchen with a bowl of ice cream, sat down on the sofa and began to eat.

Chloë put her cigarette out and sat down beside her. She ran a hand through her short, spiky, bleached hair. Her green eyes glittered mischievously. She fixed Gill with a stare. 'Think of all those globules of fat entering your bloodstream and clogging your arteries,' she said. 'Fat cells laying themselves down around your bottom and your thighs and —'

'Do you want some?' Gill asked.

'Yeah,' Chloë said, snatching the spoon and ladling a big mound of ice cream into her mouth. 'Mmm, lovely. Now tell me about this date of yours.'

The little plastic plates of food moved inexorably along the conveyor belt. Each was covered in a clear plastic domed lid. Some were steamed up where the contents were or had been hot. Round and round they trundled. Emma peered into each, trying to identify what was inside. Despite her years in the fashion industry, she had never taken to sushi. But sushi was what Saskia had said she wanted and, since this was the only preference she had expressed that day, Emma had gone with it.

Now, perched on high stools next to each other, in the midst of the culinary mêlée, a thought occurred to Emma. She turned to Saskia. 'Hang on, sushi is raw fish. You're a vegetarian!' she announced.

'There is such a thing as vegetarian sushi,' Saskia replied as if addressing an especially dumb farm animal. She picked a pod off the conveyor with a practised flick of the wrist.

Emma dithered. Should she try the rice with the odd yellow stuff inside or the lurid orange one? Or there was a little dish of what looked like pond algae? No, not the algae. The pressure to make a decision fast was immense. If you were indecisive, your choice whizzed past. Knowing this simply piled on the pressure more so that Emma watched the food go by and found herself frozen in a minor panic.

At work, Emma was Ms Capable. But here, with a hostile teenager around whom she had to walk on eggshells – free-range ones, of course – she was nervous. She'd known Saskia since she was a little girl; she'd basically brought her up. Yet, since Dominique's recent reappearance, Emma had found herself trying to justify her role in Saskia's life. Now that Saskia's *real* mum was back, where did that leave Emma? Dominique wasn't seeking to reclaim Saskia. Perhaps if she had been, it would have been easier. It would have been a straight fight. If Saskia had deliberately transferred her affections from Emma to Dominique, that too would have given Emma some solid ground on which to plant her feet. As it was, nothing was certain.

Emma didn't know if Saskia's hostility was a normal part of teenage growing up, or whether it was specifically directed at her as stepmother. Then again, perhaps Saskia was confused by her mother's return. Emma tried hard to be understanding, to make allowances. She tried to get Saskia to express her feelings – isn't that what the books said you should do? – but that was difficult when faced with an alternately abusive and monosyllabic adolescent.

Would things have been different if Saskia had been Emma's own child? Emma wondered this with a frequency that escalated in direct relation to the speed with which Saskia's behaviour was deteriorating. She felt like they were hurtling down a rollercoaster, only she couldn't yet see the bottom. How low would they go before the slope at least levelled out a bit?

Emma reached for one of the orange swiss roll thingies, missed and ended up with the algae. She sighed and looked back at Saskia. 'It comes to something when you have to catch your own lunch,' she said.

'Sad,' Saskia replied uninterestedly.

'So, are you looking forward to going back to school, seeing your friends?' Emma asked.

'Haven't got any friends,' Saskia replied, between bites of vegetarian sushi.

'What about – now what was her name? Anna. Yes, Anna. You liked her.'

'Boyfriend,' Saskia spat in disgust.

'Oh, well, there must be someone else.' Emma thought for a minute. 'Jake! What about Jake?'

'His family moved away, like two years ago!' Saskia's speech had an upwards inflection at the end of sentences. It was sarcastic and bored at the same time.

Emma tried her algae and then had to discreetly spit it out into a paper napkin. 'Mona, then. Now, I liked her.'

'But you said I wasn't allowed to see any of my animal rights friends. You said –'

'Oh, was she one of them? I must have mixed her up.'

Saskia's interest in vegetarianism had, at one point, tipped dangerously over into anti-vivisectionism. Max and Emma had had to take a firm stand lest the house be overrun by smoking beagles and rabbits with weeping eyes.

'Don't know why you're suddenly taking an interest in my friends anyway. You've never cared before,' Saskia said, removing another plate from the conveyor.

'Oh, Saskia. That's not fair. Your father and I —'

'Don't talk to me about him. All men are rapists.'

'Well, I think that's a bit harsh, not to mention statistically untrue.'

'Truth? You talk about truth!' Saskia exclaimed. 'What do you know about truth? You're a tool of the consumer society, peddling overpriced goods to the masses.'

Emma was used to this speech. A head of Childrenswear for a high street chainstore, her job was, according to Saskia, at best pointless, at worst immoral.

'At Smith and Taylor, our prices are actually very competitive. But that's not the point, Saskia. Your father and I, we work very hard to provide you with the sort of life —'

'I don't want your money,' Saskia said dismissively. 'The wages of conspicuous consumption!'

'You seem to be consuming all right at the moment,' Emma said, eyeing Saskia's pile of empty plates.

'Are you saying I'm fat?' Saskia shrieked.

'No, no —' Emma replied.

'Yes, you are. But then, what else can you expect from someone who works in *fashion*.' Other girls might have been thrilled to have a parent in the rag trade. Not Saskia. 'The fashion industry oppresses women,' she announced. 'It is inhumane and immoral. You are a tool of the patriarchy and you don't even know it!'

'Oh, come on. It's just kids' clothes.'

'Get them hooked young. You're like a drug-pusher. The drug is shopping. I am sitting here with a drug-dealer.' Saskia had begun to shout now. Other people were staring. She was enjoying embarrassing Emma.

'Sask, please.'

'This woman is a drug-dealer,' Saskia shouted even louder.

Emma sighed. 'Why do you have to be like this? Why can't you be —'

'Like the daughters of friends of yours? Nice and normal and boring. That's what you were thinking, wasn't it?'

'No, no . . .'

But it was true. That's what Emma was thinking. She was thinking how lovely it would have been to have had the sort of daughter whom you could take to other people's houses without worrying she might give the host a lecture on the evils of the meat trade or cosmetics research or any one of a long list of, admittedly, worthy causes. It was just Emma wished that Saskia could support them quietly, discreetly, or while wearing vaguely attractive clothing.

Saskia had slipped off her bar stool. This was a task, like programming a mobile or using the interactive button on a TV, that was noticeably less tricky for a teenager than a woman in her late thirties. Emma struggled to follow her.

'You are pathetic and I hate you!' Saskia said coldly, walking away.

Emma couldn't follow immediately because a tiny Japanese lady had appeared. She was totting up the number and type of plates they'd had. She scribbled a quick total on a piece of paper and handed it to Emma. Thirty-seven pounds fifty. Blimey! Is this how much it cost to have lunch with your child these days? If Emma had known she was going to get a side order of total humiliation thrown in, she'd have insisted on the caff round the corner.

'Sask, wait,' Emma said, passing a credit card to the Japanese lady.

Saskia stopped and turned. 'You can't tell me what to do,' she said, scowling. 'You're not my mother!'

The comment was the one Emma had been waiting for since Dominique's reappearance. For three long years she had been braced for the moment when Saskia would use Dominique against her. Now she'd done it and it felt like a hot knife in her heart. The pain was sharp, but did not fade; it was like the sound of a bow pulled across a high-pitched violin. Emma wanted to say: 'I am your mother. I've been your mother for fourteen years. I was the one who sat up with you when you had a nightmare. I kissed your knee when you bumped it and wiped away your tears when you weren't picked for the rounders team. I was your mother through all that. Never mind that Dominique is back: I'm still your mother and I always will be.' Most of all, she wanted to say, 'I love you'. But Saskia was already gone.

'So where did you meet your date then?' asked Chloë, dipping the spoon back in the ice cream.

Gill slapped her hand. 'Oi!' she said. 'It's my bottom we're supposed to be feeding, remember.'

'Your date?' Chloë asked again, handing back the spoon and picking up her cigarettes again. She lit one, then lay back against the sofa, tipping her head up and blowing smoke rings towards the ceiling.

'His name is Michael.'

Chloë took a break from her smoke rings. 'Not bad. Doesn't sound overly gay.'

'How can you possibly tell if a guy's gay by his name?' Gill asked disbelievingly.

'You just can.' Chloë was blowing smoke upwards again.

'Well, what names are gay then?' Gill asked, scraping the last vestiges of ice cream from her bowl.

'Oh, I don't know.' Chloë exhaled. 'Pedro . . . Dirk . . . Hank . . .'

'Hank!' Gill almost choked. 'Hank! Who have you ever met called Hank?'

Chloë continued coolly perfecting her smoke rings. 'I haven't. But it's a gay porn star's name, isn't it?'

'Is it?'

'Yeah. And then there's Cecil and Percy and Octavius.'

'Now you're just being silly.'

'I'm not. I would be very suspicious of going on a date with someone called Octavius.'

'That's just prejudice.'

'No, it's not. It's a wise precaution. A girl's got to look after herself. Did I ever tell you about the time I almost slept with a bisexual? Well, he said he was a bisexual, but I had my doubts.'

'You thought he was straight?'

Chloë sat up and leant forward to tip the by now long sausage of ash off the end of her cigarette into the ashtray. 'Of course not. When have you ever known a straight man pretend to be bisexual? There's nothing in it for him, is there? Not going to get girls that way, is he? "Oh, hello. I'm not sure if I fancy boys or girls but can I shag you anyway?" Not the best chat-up line, is it? Plenty of gay guys try and tell you they're bisexual, though. You're sort of their experiment to see if they really are gay, only you don't know it until you find him in bed with another bloke. That's after you've married him and had his children, of course.'

'So what happened with your bisexual, then?'

'Not much, really. We had a lovely dinner, then during dessert he said he had slept with men and women but he wasn't gay and would I like to come back to his place? I said no and six months later I heard he'd got a boyfriend. It was my own fault really. When I met him he was wearing a Dolce and Gabbana suit.'

Gill sighed. 'Don't tell me, men in D and G suits are gay, are they?'

Chloë smiled broadly. 'Now you're getting the idea. If I were you I'd steer clear of cropped trousers, sunglasses worn on the top of the head, and tight T-shirts, particularly sleeveless ones.'

Gill nodded. 'Now, the T-shirts, I'm with you on that.'

'See, you're getting the idea. Why bother to get to know someone when you can make a snap judgement?'

'There is a snag to all this, you know,' Gill said, getting up to take her bowl to the kitchen.

'What?' asked Chloë.

'It's a blind date. I don't get to examine his T-shirts or anything else about him before I go out with him.'

'Shit! Well, there's always large amounts of alcohol, I suppose.'

'Is that before, during or after the date?'

Chloë thought for a moment. 'On balance, I suggest all three.'

Emma switched on the bedside lamp. It threw a yellowish light across the room as if the bulb were wrapped in old

Sellotape. She sat down on the bed with her back to Max. He was under the duvet, or partly. He was sitting up, having pushed his pillows up against the leather headboard so as to cushion his back, and reading the morning paper, something he always did at bedtime, breakfast invariably being a rushed affair.

'We've got to do something,' Emma said, as she eased one shoe off.

There was no answer from Max. He had taken a bar of chocolate out of the bedside cabinet (where he always kept some) and was peeling back the foil. Chocolate was Max's one real vice. It was the reason his stomach was more beer keg than six pack. Max's chocolate tummy, Emma called it.

When Emma had first discovered Max's chocolate obsession, she'd thought it an oddly female pre-occupation, like watching American made-for-TV movies starring Susanne Summers or having baths with tea lights. But then, there was a strong feminine side to Max. It was one of the things that had first attracted Emma. Max was thoughtful, self-deprecating, almost shy, which was odd for a lawyer, but then he was more a hunched-over-books sort of legal eagle than a court swashbuckler. The flipside to all this adorable vulnerability, however, was Max's emotional avoidance. He had an absolute horror of confrontation, especially with a woman. That's probably why secretaries loved him, because when they asked for a pay rise, or a day off, he just crumbled.

When the going got tough, Max reached for the chocolate, which had been rather charming at first, but over the years had become a source of huge frustration for Emma. Was he getting worse, or was she just noticing it more? Emma didn't know. Still, every time Max didn't tell Dominique to sling her hook, or didn't discipline Saskia, Emma despaired a little more. Tackling him about it was almost worse than doing nothing. Max cowered, literally cowered, as if being told off by a teacher. Afterwards, he was always quiet and crushed and Emma felt like drowning herself in the basin of the en suite. And even then, nothing changed.

Emma sighed. She had no choice. This wouldn't wait. 'Max?' she tried. 'Max? Are you listening?'

'Hmm?' Max answered, either genuinely engrossed or giving a pretty good performance of it.

'Max! We have to talk.' Emma thought she saw a vein twitch on Max's forehead, but he didn't move. So she leant across and put a hand on his forearm. Gently, she pushed down so he could no longer hide behind his paper. At first she met resistance. A surreptitious battle ensued with Max trying to keep the paper at eye level and Emma attempting to push it down. 'Oh, for goodness sake,' she said, letting go.

Max's arms and the paper shot upwards. Max brought them and it down on to the duvet. 'OK, you win,' he said. 'What do we have to talk about?' He said the words as if trudging towards the gallows.

'Saskia,' Emma replied.

'Oh,' Max said grimly.

'She is getting totally out of control.'

Max said nothing.

'Well, don't you agree?'

Still Max said nothing.

'Jesus, Max. It would be easier to have a conversation with a bean bag.' Emma folded her arms in frustration across her chest.

'What do you want me to say?' Max offered. 'She's a teenage girl. She's bound to be a bit, um, tricky.'

'Tricky! Max, she's a nightmare. You'll have to talk to her.'

'But you're so much better at it than . . .'

'No, Max. You've got to take her in hand. She shouted at me today, really shouted. You know what she said? She said I wasn't her mother and she's right. I'm not.'

Max put his arm round Emma's shoulders. 'But you've been a wonderful mother to her. We couldn't have managed without you, you know.'

Emma didn't unfold her arms. 'Maybe we should have had a child of our own, to give her a brother or a sister. Maybe it's being an only child that's made her like this.'

'But we talked about that,' Max replied soothingly. 'You agreed that it would have been nuts to go back to the toddler stage again. I mean, look at Kevin . . .'

Emma rolled her eyes.

'Exactly. And then there was your job. You wouldn't be

where you are now if we'd had another child.'

Emma let her arms fall to her sides. She twisted her body so that she laid her head on Max's chest. 'I know, you're right. But we can't go on like this. Please, Max, will you talk to her? Tomorrow?'

Max kissed the top of her head. 'Can't, darling, remember it's the party tomorrow.'

Emma sat bolt upright. 'Shit, I haven't got my dress ready or anything.'

Max placed a hand on her shoulder and she sank back towards him. 'You'll look lovely. You always do,' he said, picking up the chocolate. 'Now, do you want some of this?'

Emma shook her head. 'Just promise me you'll talk to her.'

Max said nothing. He was too busy chewing.

Chapter Four

The steps were steep and winding. Even if Gillian hadn't been wearing four-inch spiky heels, she'd have been taking her life in her hands. The rain had made the treads greasy. Gill held her umbrella with one hand and clung desperately to the curving wrought-iron banister with the other. Her heels made sharp tap-tapping noises as she descended.

Once at the bottom, Gill sheltered under an awning and folded her umbrella. She slipped it into its cover and put it in her bag. Then she pulled out a hand mirror and examined her cheeks for any mascara that might have run in the rain. Gill squinted. It was dark in the basement, or maybe she needed glasses. But then, the wrong side of thirty-five, she would have needed the Hubble telescope to see really clearly. Anyway, Gill preferred to see herself and life in general in soft focus. If she'd seen her eye bags with twenty-twenty vision, she'd probably never have left the house at all. And, bearing in mind the calibre of the men she'd dated recently – barrel and scraping were two words that came to mind – Gill preferred to approach tonight's date – literally – blind.

She snapped the mirror shut, pulled her shoulders back and prepared to go into battle. She was already regretting tonight. She'd vowed not to do any more blind dates since the one with the bloke who invited her back to his flat and then revealed he had a shrine to Sîan Lloyd in the spare room. She'd told him she suspected there was a cold front approaching, grabbed her coat and scarpered. The reason Gill had agreed to this one date was twofold. Firstly, Michael was a friend of Gus's. Gill worked with Gus at Bliss, a trendy bar; he was the barman and she was a waitress. The second reason was she was desperate.

So, Gill had told Gus to give Michael her number and he'd texted and here they were. Or rather, here Gill was, outside the bar. Michael, hopefully, was inside. Gill was nervous. According to Gus, Michael didn't have either a humped back, six fingers on one hand or any other such obvious defect. Yes, he was single, was not now nor ever had been married, and was in his late thirties. And no, that didn't make him either incredibly odd or a liar. Gill had nodded and decided that he was either another psychotic woman-hater or a bloody miracle.

Not, of course, that being single made you necessarily peculiar. Being single was a positive choice, a statement of freedom – if you were female. If you were a bloke, it meant you were peculiar. If you were male and available, there had to be something wrong with you, didn't there? Single women were unlucky. Single men, well, there was usually a good reason why they hadn't been snapped up.

And Gill was in a position to know, having trawled practically the entire pool of single men in London over the last couple of decades.

In her early twenties, Gillian had been choosy. Potential dates had to be attractive, intelligent and employed. As she hit thirty, she lowered her sights a little. By thirty-five, if he had two arms and two legs she'd give it a go. No longer looking for Mr Right, she was willing to settle for Mr OK In a Bad Light, so long as he could pay half for dinner. What was most annoying was that while Gill's expectations had plummeted, she was now encountering men whose expectations had gone in the opposite direction. Chaps she had rejected when she was younger were now rejecting her. It was those old market forces. As the pool of decent men shrank to a measly little puddle and what had once been a gentle trickle of women keen to settle down turned into a gushing geyser, so ugly blokes wreaked their revenge. They were the ones who could pick and choose now.

Perhaps Gill should just go home now? No, she was determined to give Michael the benefit of the doubt. You never knew when you might meet 'the one', did you? Gill pushed open the door to Tumblers wine bar and went in.

Emma rummaged through a bowl of vegetable crisps like an Open University palaeontologist sifting topsoil. The crumbs at the bottom felt like what you might expect to find lurking beneath the remains of a Jurassic corpse –

gritty, only considerably less exciting. Everything tasted of turnip. Not that Emma had ever been on an archaeological dig. She was possessed of neither a beard, nor an acrylic tank top.

This was Max's boss's annual summer party. It was now evening, and although inside was brightly lit, the garden was shrouded in darkness, but for the flickering of a few candles. Emma was attending as the dutiful spouse. She rested her head on her hand. She was sitting on a sofa at one end of the living room, her elbow propped on top of a pile of cushions and throws so extravagant it added up to a veritable soft furnishing Himalaya.

Emma sniffed the air. What was that aroma? Ah yes, expensive scented candle mixed with the discreet perfume of self-satisfaction. Peter and Tania Kutner's home exuded money (just as they did), albeit tastefully veiled by a gauze of liberal conscience. The floor was stripped, the walls painted white and dotted about were trinkets picked up on travels around the world. Stern African mahogany masks sat next to pretty gilded Thai Buddhas and Indian mirrored pictures. The style was Stakeholder Ethnic: minimalism with a historical and cultural perspective.

Emma could see Tania approaching. Tania didn't work as such. She quangoed. She was chair of various government bodies as well as chairperson of a charity working to eradicate female circumcision. Tania's latest project was a calendar featuring photographs, in arty black and white, of celebrity nether regions. Gail Porter and Christine Hamilton aside, however, she was having trouble drumming up interest from the glitterati, who were somewhat shy of having their pudenda snapped, even if it was by Rankin.

Tania had got hold of the notion that Emma had Donatella Versace's phone number – well, she was in fashion, wasn't she? – and Emma feared a renewed onslaught to release it. Fortunately, Tania swerved off to talk to her husband. Emma breathed a sigh of relief. But not for long.

'All right?' Shreena Diaz had joined her.

'Yeah, fine,' Emma answered. 'Just waiting for Max.'

'You look a bit tired,' Shreena cooed.

Emma shook her head. 'I'm fine.'

Shreena was that most deadly of females: the thinking man's Asian babe. A colleague of Max's, she was bright as well as beautiful, so the chaps in the office didn't need to feel embarrassed about fancying her. Even so, she fitted into all the standard-issue male fantasies about dusky beauties who, for a modest price, would fold your trousers carefully before doing remarkable things with ping pong balls.

Since Shreena had all the men wrapped round her dainty little finger, she didn't bother with cultivating any female friendships. Indeed, she did her best to eradicate any and all female competition that might remove some of the spotlight from her.

'Fabulous piece in the paper,' Shreena continued. 'The *Sun*, wasn't it?'

'No, the *Telegraph*, actually,' answered Emma. Inwardly she cringed.

Emma had been persuaded by Yvonne, Smith & Taylor's head of human resources, to do a newspaper interview as part of a series on high-achieving women. It had come out the previous weekend. Emma had to admit she'd been flattered to be asked. When the article appeared, however, it made her sound like a cross between Boudicca and Mata Hari. Only more irritating.

'Meet Emma Chancellor. She's a wife, a mother, has a demanding, glamorous job in the fashion industry, earns a six-figure salary and still manages to find the time to throw chic dinner parties', the headline had read, underneath a picture of Emma waving a piece of fabric about in her office. Emma had practically committed hara-kiri with a pair of pinking shears when she'd seen it. Let's face it, if she'd been anyone else, she'd have hated her too.

'Who did your hair?' Shreena asked. 'In the picture, I mean.'

Emma coughed. 'Oh, they had someone at the shoot.'

'It's just I was looking for a similar style.'

Emma smiled. 'Well, I'm sure I could get you a number.'

'Oh, it's not for me!' Shreena shrieked theatrically. 'It's for my mother. Or it was. She wanted something easy-care.'

Emma's smile set on her face like jelly in a mould. Shreena, smug at her own bitchiness, had already spotted other prey. 'Clive, darling, congratulations on getting silk . . .' she exclaimed, marching off without saying goodbye.

Emma was alone again. She could see Tania wafting between groups of guests in a haze of African folk art fabric. The guests were collected into little clusters, like pigeons, although without the manky legs. Instead of piles of breadcrumbs, they were pecking at trays of marinated olives and wild mushroom bruschetta. Strange, thought Emma, how rich Brits can't get enough of poor Italian peasant food. Did Italians feel the same? Were fashionable Florentine soirées awash with plates of Scotch eggs and bottles of stout? She doubted it.

In all, there were probably forty people at the party. The vast majority were Identikit middle-class thirty- and forty-something couples. The men, who'd removed their ties but not their jackets, conversed happily together. The women were in flimsy dresses like posh nighties, with handbags they appeared to have mugged a seven year old to secure: all glitter and beading. It was as if they were saying, 'Yes, we've got really important jobs, but don't let that threaten you. We're ickle girlies underneath.' The women alternately laughed politely at their spouses' jokes and admonished assorted children, who were becoming more fractious as the evening wore on. Emma wanted to shriek: 'These children should be in bed!' but that notion would have been as unfashionable as a shellsuit in this context.

'Now, Henry, I don't think we will bang that Cameroon prayer stick on the Native American fertility drum, will we, darling?' cooed one mother.

'Mia sweetie, that's not a potty. It's a Vietnamese birthing stool. Let's put our pants back on, shall we?' whispered another.

What Emma was witnessing was the new version of that seventies stalwart, the Bring-a-Bottle party: the Bring a Baby bash. Instead of some Black Tower, you arrived clutching a sweet, gurgling infant. Actually, any proof that you were a rounded individual with a life as well as a career (i.e. had managed to procreate in between emails), would do. So, while a handful of horrific eight year olds wrestled each other in the hall, and everyone else tripped over a jumble of discarded car seats by the front door, a few sullen teenagers lurked morosely in corners.

Saskia had, of course, refused to come, but for the other parents, the party all added up to pretty effective time management. Why park your little darlings with an expensive nanny at home, when you could spend quality time with your offspring and network at the same time? The downside was that it required that most remarkable of genetic mutations, Maternal Venus Flytrap Arm, to work overtime. While the men were oblivious to the havoc their offspring were threatening to wreak around them, Emma could see women averting disaster at every turn. Female hands were flicking out at the speed of light all over the room and then snapping back in again, having caught regurgitated food falling from a toddler's mouth, saved a priceless artefact toppling off a shelf, or wiped snot off any and all polished surfaces with a surreptitious Wet One. All without so much as a pause in their polite conversation.

At that moment, a waitress approached with a tray of chicken satay. Emma waved her away. There must be a way to prise over-cooked poultry off a burnt wooden skewer with your teeth elegantly, but Emma had yet to find it. She was sticking to her crisps, even if they did taste like something from the Jurassic era.

'Marvellous woman.' It was Peter Kutner, Max's boss. He was clutching a tall glass containing a brown liquid. Bits of fruit bobbed disconsolately about on the surface like survivors of the *Titanic*. Pimm's.

'I'm sorry?' said Emma.

'Rosa, the waitress,' explained Peter. 'From Kosovo. Strapped her entire family to the underside of a Eurostar using nothing but a packet of parcel tape and some Blu-Tack.'

'Goodness,' said Emma.

'Rosa's normally our cleaner. Does a great job on the kitchen tiles and she's incredibly cheap – What I mean is, ahem,' Peter corrected himself quickly, 'we're supporting her application for asylum. Well, you've got to do what you can to help, haven't you?'

The strains of Pan Pipes of the Andes's version of 'Greensleeves' was playing discreetly in the background. Emma found herself wondering if there was anyone left anywhere near the Andes who could so much as get a note out of a recorder. The world seemed overrun with ex-pat pipe players. You couldn't visit a shopping centre in any major international conurbation without stumbling across someone wearing a gentle smile and a pink blanket over their shoulder.

'Been anywhere nice this year?' Peter asked.

'Italy. Sicily, actually,' Emma replied. 'You and Tania?'

'Going next month, as it happens. Brazil.'

'I hear the beaches are lovely. The girl from Ipanema and all that.'

'Oh, no, we won't be on the beach. We're digging sewers in São Paulo,' Peter corrected her.

'I'm sorry?'

'Tania's idea. Got to give something back, haven't you?'

'Well, um . . .' Emma's idea of giving something back was to buy naff, overpriced charity Christmas cards instead of the ones she really liked. It wasn't laying sewer pipes in South America.

'Anyway, as Tania says, it's fabulous exercise and half the price of Champneys.'

'Well, um, it would be, yes,' Emma mumbled, slightly dumbstruck.

Peter changed the subject. 'Saw that piece in the paper, by the way. Max must be very proud.'

Emma was beginning to really, really wish she'd never agreed to do the interview now. Was there anyone who hadn't seen it?

'Not that we get the *Telegraph*, of course,' continued Peter. 'Instrument of the fascist elite, according to Tania. Shreena had a copy in the office. Couldn't see the picture very well, though. Bit of a coffee stain over your face, or some sort of stain anyway. Still, I'm sure you looked terrific.'

They were interrupted by Tania's strident tones, which dissected the air like a machete slicing through endangered rainforest. 'Peter! Peter!'

'Yes, darling,' Peter replied, turning to trot off in her direction. As he went, he turned back to Emma. 'You haven't got a glass for some Pimm's. I'll just nip to the kitchen and get you one.'

Before Emma could say that she hated Pimm's, he had disappeared, and she was left to contemplate her vegetable crisps again. In an attempt to improve her snack experience, she dipped her slice of root vegetable into a container of green dip that was also sitting on the coffee table. Her taste buds registered something vaguely unpleasant.

'Oh, there you are, Emma. Peter asked me to give you this.'

It was Tania. She handed Emma a glass of Pimm's. The pipers had now moved on to 'Morning Has Broken'. Emma looked at the slices of apple and orange, not waving but drowning in their alcoholic sea, and felt a sudden kinship with the fruit.

'Thanks,' she said weakly.

'Now, about Donatella —' Tania began.

'Look, Tania, I think I should clear something up . . .'

But Tania wasn't listening. She had spotted the green stuff that Emma had just sampled. 'Oh, there it is!' she exclaimed. 'Joelly Child's been looking for that every-where!' Tania leant forward, scooped up the gunge and pointed towards a pale, blonde woman Emma recognised as an aristo supermodel – the same as a normal super-model only she didn't have to be as pretty and she probably didn't need the money. This one was clutching a child and was standing with a couple of other breast-feeding mothers. Each one of them had a human lump in the crook of her arm over which she'd draped a pashmina as if putting a budgie to bed.

Joelly Childs was wearing a cropped T-shirt and hipsters so low slung that had she not already obviously given birth, she could probably have done so without undoing her flies.

'It's Sunray's food,' continued Tania, indicating the baby on Joelly's hip and the snot-coloured purée. 'Organic pea and celery, I think.' Then Tania noticed the neat furrow gouged out of the centre. 'You didn't think it was a dip, did you?'.

'No, no,' Emma lied. Jesus, she sounded like a seventeen year old who has scratched her parents' car. 'It was fine when I parked it, honest.' She really must try and get a bit more sleep. It takes a special sort of tired to tuck into baby food and not even notice.

A familiar figure appeared, walking towards them. It was Max. 'Hi,' he said.

'Where have you been?' Emma exclaimed in exasperation.

'Are you enjoying yourself?' asked Tania, gripping Max's shoulders as if wrestling a water buffalo to the ground, only it was Tania who resembled the huge beast more closely. Max looked momentarily panic-stricken, fearful perhaps that he might be crushed to death.

Only when Tania had released her grip did he manage to stutter a reply. 'Yes, yes, great,' he spluttered, turning to Emma. 'Sorry, got chatting. You know how it is.' He lifted one of the glasses of wine towards her as a peace offering. 'Anyway, I've brought some white wine . . . Oh, you've already got . . .' He frowned. 'But you can't stand Pimm's.'

Emma caught Tania's eye. 'Nonsense, darling. I love Pimm's,' she insisted, taking a big gulp. She felt the tart liquid hit the back of her throat. She tried not to gag.

Peter now joined them. 'That's it, Emma, you get it down you,' he said of the foul drink. 'It'll put hairs on your chest.' Then he saw Tania, whose PC antennae were doing an appalled fandango. 'Not that body hair or other such male secondary sexual characteristics necessarily imply improved performance or anything,' he added.

'It's all right, Peter,' Emma reassured him. A piece of orange peel was sticking to the roof of her mouth.

'No, what I mean is –' he began again.

'Really, it's all right,' Emma replied, taking another slug of her punch to dislodge the stray citrus. It didn't work. She now had an apple cube stuck between her teeth.

They all sipped their drinks. Then Tania suddenly turned to Peter and shrieked, 'Oh, darling. I forgot to tell you. Fabulous news.'

Peter nodded in encouragement.

'Moira thinks she can get Joelly Child's vagina for my calendar! Isn't that fantastic!'

'Fantastic, darling,' echoed Peter, without a trace of shyness. Being married to Tania obviously gave you a high pain threshold.

Max and Emma brought their glasses up to their faces and kept them there for a long time. It was the only way to muffle their laughter.

'Bloody Mary, please,' said Gill, trying to smile. Her mouth was dry with nerves and her lips were sticking to her teeth, despite the fact she was wearing so much lipgloss that if Michael did try to kiss her, he would be unable to get even the slightest grip on them.

'A lady who likes her spirits, but are you a spirited lady?' Michael asked, winking rakishly, or in a manner he evidently considered rakish. Gill shuddered slightly and tried to remember why she was doing this. Why didn't she just resign herself to being single? She was turning into the human equivalent of one of those dented cans you see marked down in a supermarket that people pick up and examine but then decide not to buy. Her date stamp was smudged and she had a rusty top.

When Gill had set eyes on Michael she'd thought it was he who appeared to have gone off. He was what used to be called a Hooray Henry. Gill wasn't entirely sure what they called chaps like Michael these days, probably because they didn't make chaps like Michael these days. His conversation was peppered with phrases like 'old girl'. His laugh was too loud and his chin wobbled when he did.

Like Michael, Tumblers, his choice of rendezvous, was something out of another era. It was a wine bar, unchanged from the days when a wine bar was a really exciting thing to be. The curtains were flounced, the menu was chalked up on a blackboard – deep-fried goats' cheese, pâté and French bread – and the tables were so high that if you did manage to clamber on to the wicker seat of one of the accompanying bar stools, you needed a rope ladder to get down again. In the centre of each table was a Chianti bottle encrusted with candle wax. Fresh-ish candles had been shoved into the necks; the one on Gill's table was sputtering. Gill got out a Marlboro Light – she had weakened and bought a packet on the way. The cause of her dramatic fall off the wagon? She'd put on her favourite trousers and found she wasn't able to get the zip done up (all that ice cream), so she'd been forced to purchase a packet of twenty as consolation. She'd give up again tomorrow.

Gill inhaled deeply. She could feel her red blood cells embracing the nicotine as if they were lovers on a train platform after a long separation. She took another look at Michael: the thought of being his lover repulsed her. He was chatting happily to a blowsy woman in a Peter Pan collar behind the bar. Gill sighed. Another evening when she'd far rather have stayed home with a bottle of wine and a clutch of *Frasier* videos.

Crash!

Gill almost jumped out of her seat. She whipped round to see a woman at the next table had knocked a glass clean off her table. A ruddy-faced chap was sitting with her, wiping wine off his sleeve.

'Never mind, Charlie,' he said. (Why did Sloaney girls always shorten their names to boys' ones like Harry and Ollie and Charlie?) 'You can lick it off the rest of me later.'

Charlie guffawed loudly.

Gill turned her head around. The thought of licking anything off Michael was hideous. Still, he was a friend of Gus's so she'd have to stay for at least one drink. She was wondering how quickly she could possibly sink a Bloody Mary when she noticed a flash of light in her peripheral vision.

'Oh, shit!' she screamed. 'I'm on fire!'

* * *

The sky having cleared momentarily, and patio heaters plugged in, Tania herded everyone into the garden. Emma could feel her heels slowly sinking into the wet ground. Indeed, in a bizarre, speeded-up version of the ageing process, the entire group appeared to be shrinking as they too sank into the soggy turf.

Tania addressed herself through the gloom to Emma and Max. 'Now, you two, you should be mingling,' she declared. 'What with Emma and her article in the newspaper, you're our star guests.'

Emma cringed. 'It's fine, really,' she protested.

'Nonsense,' corrected Peter. 'Now, who can we introduce you to that you don't already know?' He squinted into the night.

'Jasmine! Trevor!' Tania boomed, beckoning to a couple who were silhouetted by the French doors, having just arrived. 'Come and meet the most gorgeous people. You're sure to love them.'

They picked their way over to join Emma's little group, Well, he walked. She billowed. She was wearing a silk shalwar kameez and embroidered slippers.

'Mine's a lamb korma and extra poppadoms,' whispered Max.

Emma gave him a look.

'This is Jasmine and Trevor. Trevor heads up one of Number Ten's policy units and Jasmine's in famine relief,' Tania declared. 'There's some chicken satay going round, by the way.' Tania looked about for the waitress. 'Meet Emma and Max. She's a personal friend of Donatella Versace.'

Emma tried to interrupt – 'Well, um' – but it was like trying to stop a herd of stampeding wildebeest with a bow and arrow.

'And Max is an absolute star at Kutner and Schloss, isn't he, Peter?' continued Tania.

Peter nodded as required. 'Absolutely, a star, yes.'

The couples shook hands.

'I feel I know you. Have we met before?' Jasmine said, wrinkling her nose and studying Emma quizzically.

Before Emma could answer, Tania had waded in. 'Oh, well, Emma is our resident celebrity. You must have seen the piece in the paper all about her.'

Emma could feel a hot blush spreading across her neck.

'I think I've got a copy of the article somewhere,' continued Tania.

'No, no, that's all right. I'm sure Jasmine doesn't want to read it,' Emma interjected.

'I think it's in the study,' Tania said. She marched off inside to retrieve the article and Emma took a big swig of her Pimm's. She and Max shuffled awkwardly while Trevor and Jasmine did the same. Trevor picked a handful of pistachios off a nearby tray and then had nowhere to put the shells. He stuffed them in a pocket, so every time he shifted his position, he made a crunching sound like a Labrador on a gravel path.

'I've found it!' bellowed Tania, reappearing brandishing a section of newsprint neatly cut from the newspaper. She passed it to Jasmine and Trevor who tried to study it by candlelight. They made approving grunts.

'Your hair looks nice,' announced Jasmine.

'Yes, I thought that,' agreed Tania.

'Who did it by the way?'

Fortunately, Emma was saved by the sound of her mobile phone ringing.

Beep, beep . . . Beep, beep.

The man in the shop had persuaded Emma to get a phone with a little window in the lid, so she could screen her calls. The slight snag to this marvellous technological advance was that the type was so small, you needed a telescope to read it. Emma squinted, then gave up. She flipped it open. 'Hello?' she said into the receiver. 'Hello? Hello?'

Someone said something on the other end of the line, but Emma couldn't hear them properly. She turned away from her little group and put her other hand over her free ear, so as to muffle the party hubbub.

'Hello?' she said again. 'Saskia, is that you?'

Max looked at her, raising an eyebrow. She shook her head. There was a pause. 'You'll have to speak up,' Emma said. 'I can't hear you.'

There was a longer pause. All the colour drained from Emma's face. 'What do you mean, you've been arrested. Saskia? Saskia?'

* * *

Michael's aim was really quite impressive. All that cricket at school, no doubt. From a distance of a good ten feet, he hurled the Bloody Mary at Gill and managed to get practically the entire glass over her. Unfortunately, by the time he threw it, Gill had already extinguished the flames with a napkin. The tomato juice now dripping down her face was surplus to requirements.

Gill's hair had caught alight on the candle in the centre of the table. When she had whipped round on hearing the glass smash on the floor, her hair had swung outwards and she had inadvertently turned herself into the towering inferno. Now it was smouldering gently. Gill wiped the back of her hand across her forehead. To think she had been worried about a bit of mascara earlier.

Michael had now joined her. 'Been telling Margot she should get rid of those candles for ages. You OK, old girl?'

Gill's face and body were doused in a glass of vodka and tomato juice. One side of her head now sported hair a lot shorter than the other. The ends were charred. No, she was not OK, not OK at all.

Clunk.

The can hit the plate-glass window and exploded, the impact shattering the thin aluminium. Liquid sprayed into the air, creating a dramatic plume effect of the sort you might see coming from the mouth of a stone mermaid lounging in a fountain at the entrance to a stately home. Except this wasn't a stately home and the liquid wasn't water. It was Paddington Green Police Station and the grubby froth now snaking its way down the glass was warm lager.

Emma gave the lurching figure who had fired the alcoholic missile a wide berth. He was staggering and shouting alarmingly. While most of his pronouncements were unintelligible, every so often a word would crystallise. Funny, thought Emma, how the inebriate's diction improves only when pronouncing words beginning with 'f' and 'c'.

Max pushed the door open. Emma followed him through it, dabbing at her collar with a tissue. This wasn't so much a case of shutting the stable door after the horse had bolted as attempting to mount it mid-gallop. The noxious yellow spray that had rebounded off the window and on to her shoulder was already buried in the fabric. She could smell the fumes settling in for an extended stay like unwelcome house guests.

Once inside, they were faced with a long, high desk, topped with the sort of speckly fake granite banks think makes them seem really upmarket, but actually just makes them look as if a customer has had to wait so long to be served he or she has doodled their way across the counter with a biro. Behind the desk sat a woman in a short-sleeved blouse and clip-on tie. The fabric of the blouse was thin and the shadow of her flesh-toned bra was just visible through it. Who came up with the idea of flesh-toned bras? Emma wondered. Obviously the same person who formulated fake tans. Neither bore any resemblance to the colour of any human being Emma had ever seen.

The woman was tapping things into a computer. In front of her, a young man was complaining. 'It's ou' of order. I left i' parked a'side me 'ouse. An' someone 'ad i' away!'

'We might be a bit more sympathetic, Darren,' said the woman, 'if you didn't have twenty-three convictions for taking and driving away yourself. Anyway, we'll let you know if we find it. A Cosworth, wasn't it?'

Darren nodded, then pushed past Emma and Max and headed out of the door, still grumbling. They inched towards the counter. The WPC was now on the phone. 'No, number two is the hot whites wash. You need the delicates cycle . . . No, that's short spin only. Look, I only asked you to put a few socks in . . .'

Emma felt a surge of sisterhood that almost, but not quite, transcended the situation.

'It's not brain surgery, Keith. It's a weekly wash . . .'

Emma took another sniff of her collar. Keith would have a job getting rid of that aroma, even if he did manage to work out how to get the machine working. She smelt like she'd wallowed in a vat of Fosters.

'It could be worse,' whispered Max.

'How?'

'It could have been urine. The last time I went to

Brixton prison, a social worker had a chamber pot emptied over her.'

'My God!' Emma gasped, momentarily distracted from her beer-soaked clothing. 'Did they catch the inmate who did it?'

'It wasn't an inmate. It was an officer. We were doing a role-play exercise to understand the thoughts and feelings of prisoners on remand. He was getting into character.'

'It's amazing that social worker didn't get him into casualty. Was she absolutely furious?'

'She was fine at the time, but now she's been off work for six months and she's suing for post-traumatic stress disorder.'

Emma felt like she was suffering from pre-, during and post-traumatic stress disorder. She had a headache and there was a horrible queasy feeling in her stomach, which had nothing to do with the Pimm's she'd had at the party. She felt as if she were going up and down in a very fast lift. What had Saskia done to end up here? Or, more precisely, what had Saskia done this time? Her record was not exactly unblemished. At fourteen, her pro-Communist phase had netted her a caution for spray painting the words 'capitalist pigs' on the outside of the US embassy and, more recently, anti-globalisation fervour had resulted in an unpleasant incident at a fried chicken restaurant.

Emma thought back again to when she'd first met

Saskia as a tiny toddler outside the cinema. The three of them had piled awkwardly inside and Saskia had scrambled into a seat as far away from Emma as possible. She'd looked terrified. Emma had watched Saskia's miniature legs swinging back and forth nervously, like one of those wooden puppets with a central string you pull to make the legs and arms fly up. She'd seemed shy and terribly vulnerable.

The woman behind the desk was still talking. 'Look, I'll do it tomorrow.' She slammed down the receiver, sighed and finally acknowledged Emma and Max. 'Yes?' she snapped.

Max cleared his throat. 'Um, Saskia Freeman. She called us to say she was here. We're her parents.'

The woman – it said PC Simone Davis on her badge – gave them a confused look. 'Saskia Freeman, no, don't think we've had one of those.' She began looking down a list of names in front of her. 'No, not here.'

'She's sixteen,' Max explained. 'She rang us to say she'd been, um, arrested.'

'Oh, yes. Found it now.' The policewoman looked up brightly. 'Soliciting in a public place.'

'Excuse me?' Max exclaimed, going pale.

'There must be some mistake,' Emma said.

PC Davis checked her admissions book again and rolled her eyes as if to say: 'Silly me.' 'Oops, sorry,' she murmured. Then she read from the book. '"Causing a public nuisance", not soliciting in a public place. Still, easy enough mistake to make, isn't it?' She smiled brightly. 'Well, it's too late to see her tonight. She won't be charged until the morning. Staff shortages – you know how it is.'

'But . . . but . . .' Max stuttered. 'This is outrageous. Saskia is only sixteen. We should have been called immediately'.

'She refused to give her name, initially, sir. We contacted you as soon as we could. Anyway, she's quite safe,' the PC said. 'Can't get into much mischief locked in a cell, can she?'

'She's locked in a cell!' Emma gasped.

'Well, no, actually.' The policewoman corrected herself. 'She's in one of the interview suites. We don't like to put youngsters in cells if we can help it. Even when they have committed a crime'.

Somehow Emma didn't think this suite could be confused with one at the Hilton. 'But . . .' she began.

The PC was unmoved. 'There's nothing you can do. Now go home and come back in the morning.'

Chapter Five

'What's that horrible smell?'

It was Chloë. She was standing in the doorway to the bathroom, holding a pair of strappy high heels in one hand and using the other to massage one of her feet.

Gillian switched off the hot tap and sat down on the side of the bath, looking at her watch. 7.30. She didn't usually get up before noon, but the events of last night, plus the bottle of wine she'd drunk on her own when she'd got back from her disastrous date meant she hadn't slept well. Gill looked at Chloë. 'Seven-thirty. What have you been up to, you dirty stop-out?' she asked.

'Oh, you know, the usual. What about you? As I said, what is that terrible smell?' Chloë asked again.

'I heard you. It could be one of two things,' Gill answered. 'It could be tomato juice or vodka. I kind of got some poured over me last night.'

'Jesus, was the date that bad?' Chloë exclaimed. 'I don't think you've ever had a guy pour a drink over you before. The worst I remember was when that bloke fell asleep face down in his dinner.' She paused, wrinkling her brow. 'You realise if he'd died his family could probably have sued you for manslaughter: asphyxiation in a margarita pizza by reason of boredom.'

'He wasn't bored,' Gill said indignantly. 'He was tired. He worked in the City. He had to get up really early in the morning. He told me.'

'Was that before or after he passed out?'

Gill shook her head and turned on the cold tap. Chloë turned and walked away. As she went, Gill studied her outfit. It was one of her prime pulling outfits: a knee-length silk skirt with a waterfall frill down one side and a tight T-shirt. It was feminine and showed off her body, but stayed just the right side of tarty. According to Chloë, it was OK to behave like a slapper, as long as you dressed like a lady.

When Chloë reappeared, she had a cigarette in her mouth and was carrying an ashtray. Her blue eyes were narrowed in concentration. 'You know, it's not vodka or tomato juice, it's something else. The smell, I mean.'

'Oh, then it'll be burning hair,' Gillian replied, deadpan.

'What?'

'Haven't you heard? They've started burning single women like witches.'

'I know some married women who'd be happy to strike the first match,' Chloë laughed.

'They don't need to bother. They just don't invite us to their dinner parties, hoping we'll wither away from malnutrition,' Gill said.

'As if we'd want their husbands anyway. The moment a man gets married he stops taking care of himself and gets a double chin.'

'And she starts buying his clothes so she makes sure to eradicate every vestige of sex appeal. She starts dressing him like one of her children – maybe that's how she sees him?'

Chloë blew smoke out of her mouth in a determined stream. 'Deck shoes,' she announced.

'Deck shoes?' asked Gillian.

'Yeah, they're what wives buy for husbands to wear on holiday so no woman fancies them. Haven't you noticed? Every married bloke's got a pair in their wardrobe. They are the shoe equivalent of garlic, designed to repel bloodsucking creatures called single women.'

'But we're not bloodsuckers, are we?'

'If he dumps them to marry us, we are. He remarries and bang goes her chances of sending her first-born to private school, that's for sure.'

'But I don't want to get married,' Gill declared.

'No, neither do I,' agreed Chloë. 'Say it loud and say it proud, because the rest of the world will never believe you. Anyway, what really happened last night?'

Gill turned off the cold tap. 'I set light to my own head.'

'I'm all for sexual experimentation, Gill,' Chloë laughed, 'but I think turning yourself into a Roman candle is going a bit far.'

'It wasn't deliberate. I caught my hair on a candle. He threw the Bloody Mary over me to put the flames out.'

'And . . .'

'That's when I left.'

'It comes to something when the most exciting thing that happens on a date is setting your hair on fire.'

'Yeah, perhaps I do want to get married after all.'

'Don't be silly.'

'I need something to strengthen my resolve. Give us a fag.'

'I thought you'd —'

'Yeah, well, I can't deal with a crap date and not smoking all at once, can I?' Gill took a cigarette, which Chloë lit for her. 'You know, maybe I could get a rabbit instead,' Gill said.

'The animal or the rampant electrical item?' asked Chloë.

'The animal. You can housetrain rabbits, you know.'

'Wouldn't the claws be a problem?' Chloë pointed out.

'Our furniture, it's not exactly Chippendale, is it?' Gillian replied.

'Chipboard, more like,' Chloë said.

'You know, maybe a rabbit is the answer. They have those lovely soft ears.'

'And no obvious televisual preferences, I believe. No having to watch *Match of the Day*, that's for sure. But there is a downside, you know.'

'What's that?' Gill asked.

'No sex. But then, who was in Number Ten when you last had a decent orgasm?'

Emma and Max were back at the police station. It was 8.00 a.m. The morning after the night before.

They had been escorted through a warren of corridors, painted two shades of greasy-looking institutional grey. It was as if two horrible snails had slithered all the way along the wall, leaving a pair of grimy trails. Finally, they stopped outside a room with a mahogany-effect door and a spyhole. The door had opened to reveal Saskia sitting, scowling, in a corner.

Emma had taken one look at her and rushed towards her, bending down and throwing her arms around her. 'Are you all right?' she had asked.

Saskia had shrugged her off dismissively. 'Don't make a scene,' she had hissed. 'You're embarrassing me.'

Emma had been brought up short by Saskia's hostility. 'I think it's we who should be embarrassed,' she had stuttered. She had wanted to be soft and supportive but instead she had sounded like – who exactly? Oh, God, she had sounded like her own mother. It could only be a matter of time before she worked her way through those other family favourites: 'What time do you call this?', 'You treat this house like a hotel!' and, 'If you're going to behave like a child then I shall have to treat you like one.' Emma's internal blueprint for outraged parenthood had been formed from altercations between herself and her mum. None of these, however, had taken place in a police station.

That was all last night. Now she, Max and Saskia were sat, not talking, on uncomfortable chairs, waiting for some sign that they could get out of here.

Suddenly, the door opened. A policeman – a sergeant, Emma thought – stepped through.

'Never mind that now,' said Emma, aware of her audience. 'We can discuss it when we get home. Let's just get out of here, shall we?'

The policeman shuffled forwards, pulling out a chair and sitting down. ''Fraid it's not as simple as that. Would you like to sit down, Mrs . . .?'

'Freeman,' said Max.

'Chancellor,' said Emma, sinking back into the seat.

The policeman frowned. 'Well, which is it?'

'Max's surname is Freeman, but I use my maiden name, which is Chancellor,' Emma explained.

'You're not married then?' he asked, scribbling something in his notes, probably along the lines of *feckless hippy parents, no wonder their daughter is a criminal.*

'No, no, we are married,' Max corrected him. 'It's just –'

Emma interrupted him. 'I did think about a double barrel – Chancellor-Freeman – but it seemed a bit –'

'Complicated?' interjected the inquisitor sarcastically. He was wondering why these middle-class women had to make things so difficult for themselves. 'Anyway, what I don't understand is why your daughter's surname isn't Chancellor or Freeman. It's . . .' He read from his notes. '. . . Mont-al-em-bert.' He pronounced the last 't' hard.

'She's not my daughter,' said Emma.

'But I thought you said –'

'She's my stepdaughter.'

The policeman sighed. 'Shall we start again?'

'She's mine, but not Emma's,' said Max.

'But you said your name was Freeman.'

'It is. Her mother's surname is Montalembert. Saskia doesn't normally use it, but, well . . .' He trailed off.

DS Thompson sighed again.

Saskia oozed disdain. The policeman was expressionless. Perhaps that's what they taught them at police school.

He ran his Biro back and forth through his notes. 'OK, let's try and get this straight. Your name is Freeman,' he said, indicating Max, who nodded. 'You're Chancellor.' He pointed at Emma with his pen. She nodded. 'And you're Mont-al-em-bert.' Saskia was impassive.

Max reached for her elbow and stroked it awkwardly as if rubbing Aladdin's lamp in the hope a genie would pop out through the spout and make the whole scene disappear. Saskia shook him off, hissing, 'You're making a show of me.'

'There was a mention of charging her,' Emma ventured nervously.

'Causing a public nuisance is a serious matter,' the policeman proclaimed without looking up.

'Yes, yes, she knows that, don't you, Saskia?' Emma gushed.

Saskia said nothing, preferring to pick at the soles of her ecologically sound plastic sandals.

'Sorry, but we don't actually know what she did that was so serious,' Emma continued tentatively. Securing information from a sixteen-year-old girl made extracting blood from a stone feel like sucking orange juice through a straw. If Emma and Max were to find out anything, Emma knew it would have to be from the man in the uniform.

'Miss Mont-al-em-bert was apprehended whilst distributing certain written material concerning the treatment of livestock in the United States of America outside a branch of Burger Paradise,' DS Thompson read.

'Burgers from Heaven. It was Burgers from Heaven,' interrupted Saskia, sounding bored. 'And it wasn't livestock, it was cows, or rather beef carcasses. Do you know how they're killed? They string them up by their hooves and then they get an electric cable and —'

'I don't think we really need to go into all of that now, do we?' said Emma, glaring at Saskia. 'I was just asking the nice policeman . . .' (Blimey, she sounded like something out of an Ealing comedy now. She'd be saying, 'It's a fair cop, guv,' next.) '. . . so we could get a rough idea of what you might have been involved in.'

The nice policeman ignored both of them. 'There is also the matter of the obscene version of a well-known children's nursery rhyme your daughter was heard shouting at customers.'

Emma and Max stared at Saskia.

'Old MacDonald, I believe,' DS Thompson said. 'The phrase "And on that farm he had some diseased spinal cord" was felt to be particularly offensive to certain smaller children in the vicinity.' He paused again. 'And then there was the blood.'

'Did you say blood?' asked Max, his own draining from his face.

The policeman picked up his notes and peeled back a page. 'Chicken in origin, according to the lab. Your daughter sprayed chicken blood from a water pistol at diners.'

Emma shook her head in exasperation. 'After everything we said after the animal-testing lab thing. You promised, Saskia.'

'I got rid of the balaclava,' Saskia said defensively, her eyes darting sideways at her father, looking for support.

'I don't think this is a knitwear issue,' said Emma firmly. 'Look, just say you're sorry.'

'Sorry,' Saskia said through barely parted lips.

'Unfortunately, madam,' said DS Thompson, 'your daughter is not eight and her crime is not nicking a packet of Smarties.' He rolled the word 'crime' round his mouth with relish. He was warming up for his big moment. 'This is somewhat more serious,' he declared, his chest puffing out self-importantly.

'So, you are going to charge her?' asked Max. 'But that's outrageous. She's guilty of naivety, nothing more . . .'

The policeman ignored Max's tirade. 'Actually, you should consider yourselves rather lucky,' he said. 'We're running a pilot scheme here. It's part of a new government initiative to cut youth crime.'

'Oh, really?' Max said, suddenly eager.

'We are now empowered to enforce so-called Parent Re-education Orders.'

'I've read about those,' declared Max enthusiastically. 'Get the parents to take responsibility for their kids' actions. Very sensible idea.'

'I'm glad you feel like that, sir. The parenting skills workshop is very useful, I understand. Here's a leaflet. Both of you will be required to attend. Now, which of you would like to sign this?'

There was a sharp intake of breath from Max. 'When I said I thought it was a good idea, I didn't mean . . .' he stuttered.

'What, not a good idea for people like you, sir?'

'Well, you know . . .'

'Perhaps you think it is only those who live in local-authority housing who have children who break the law.' He looked pointedly at Saskia. 'Crime crosses all barriers of class and creed.'

Emma and Max both blushed.

'I note this is not the first incident involving Miss Mont-al-em-bert and a fast-food outlet.'

'Well, um . . .' said Max.

'It was Get Clucky last time, wasn't it?'

Max nodded.

'Turkey excrement is, I understand, exceedingly difficult to remove from carpet tiles.'

'She did only get a caution,' Emma interjected.

The policeman caught Emma in his stern gaze. 'Very lucky then, wasn't she?'

Emma gulped.

He was on a roll. 'What is it you do, madam, if you don't mind me asking?'

'Well, um . . .'

'Are you a working mother, I mean working stepmother?'

It was like a farmer asking a fox with a pheasant in its mouth to clarify exactly what was his preferred dish of the day. Emma was acutely aware of her expensive outfit and her nice leather handbag with the electronic organiser in it. Yes, she worked, which, in this bloke's book, clearly made her Wicked Witch of the West. Emma wanted to shout: 'Hey, we can't all be Mary Bloody Poppins, you know!' Instead, she stayed miserably silent.

'Long hours, is it, your job?' he asked snidely.

'Yes, sometimes,' Emma mumbled. 'I work for Smith and Taylor.'

'Really!' He wasn't patronising her now. He actually sounded impressed. 'My wife buys my socks there. Good quality, but, you know, they seem to have stopped doing my favourite type. Diamond check, navy and burgundy. Why is that?'

'Well, I'm in Childrenswear. Socks aren't really my area.'

'You could have a word though, couldn't you? I mean, shops like yours are always interested in customer feedback, aren't they?'

At that precise moment, there was nothing Emma was less interested in than a semi-stranger's hosiery crisis. Still, if socks were Emma's escape tunnel out of here, then she was prepared to start digging with both hands.

'I'll certainly look into it,' she gushed.

He seemed satisfied. He turned to Max. 'And what is it you do, sir?' Before Max could answer, he had started leafing through his notes. 'Oh, wait, I think we asked young Miss Mont-al-em-bert that. It's here somewhere.' He flipped from one page to another, running his finger down the text like an especially slow reader in Braille. 'Ah, yes, it says it here. Father: Solicitor.' He smirked. 'A lawyer in the family. Well, should your daughter intend to continue her criminal career, she won't be short of legal counsel, will she?' With that, he grinned broadly.

'I don't think it's exactly a career. Yet,' said Max, getting annoyed again until Emma kicked him under the table.

'That form . . .' she said.

'Ah, yes. Who would like to sign it?' their tormentor continued.

Max didn't move. So Emma leant forward, took the proffered Biro and scribbled silently. Then they got up from their seats and shuffled towards the door. Saskia joined them as they were led down the long, winding corridor. They were within sight of freedom when they were stopped by the WPC they'd met last night. She looked at Emma. What now?

'Ooh, you just caught me,' she said. 'Finishing my shift, but I wanted to say how much I enjoyed your interview in the *Telegraph*. By the way, who did your hair?'

'Rabbits. Yes, rabbits are definitely the way to go,' Gill said to herself as she switched on the computer. All she had to do was find a website with some especially cute Flospy, Mopsy and Cottontail types and her dating troubles would be over. She'd be curled up on the sofa with a soft bundle of fur and *House Doctor* on cable before she knew it.

The screen flickered into life and the machine began to download. As she waited for the familiar set of icons to appear, she thought about last night's date. On a scale of one to ten of awfulness, it had scored about eleven. The only reason it didn't score higher was the truncated nature of the evening. Perhaps her human Roman candle performance had been a blessing after all. At least it had saved her from having to endure any more of Michael's Hooray Henryisms. If she'd hung about, most likely he'd have started throwing bread rolls or drinking Bolly straight from the bottle, although what with the fall of the stock market it would probably have been Cava.

Gill clicked on the Internet Explorer and then the Outlook Express icons. She'd just check her email before she went looking for rabbits. Since Gordon Chancellor had got a computer and so become the Internet king, he had taken to emailing Gill. If she didn't answer within twenty-four hours, she got an outraged phone call, asking her why she was not online! These days, Gordon viewed not being online at all times as tantamount to not having electricity or being forced to draw water from a village well. There was nothing like a born-again technogeek.

The computer buzzed, beeped and whirred. 'You have twenty-two new messages,' it informed her. Gillian sighed, opened her inbox and looked at the new messages in bold type on the screen. Most of them were spam of the 'men: enlarge your member!' variety. She scrolled down until she found a message from her father. It was a round robin, which irritated Gill slightly. Since when did parents start putting their own children on a list to talk to them? The rot had set in when Gordon and Charlotte had purchased an answerphone. The moment they got that, they stopped being full-time parents and started going out. I mean, that wasn't allowed, was it? Yes, Gill and Emma had been in their thirties, but a daughter was for life, not just for Christmas!

Now it was the computer. Gill read the message.

> Dear all, off on our great trip! See you all next February. Don't forget to RSVP to Emma about the party. See you there! Warmest regards, Gordon and Charlotte.

Gordon was the only person Gill knew who bothered with capital letters and punctuation with email. Still, old habits died hard, she supposed. At least he knew how to vary the type on a computer. Not so a mobile. Emma and Gillian had clubbed together to buy him a mobile a couple of years back. Gill had actually been rather relieved when he gave it back, saying he couldn't get any peace. All his messages had arrived in capital letters. It was like being a child again, being shouted at by your dad, only several times a day.

There was an attachment with Gordon's email. He had only just learned how to send attachments and every message now arrived with reams of them. This one was a picture of Gordon and Charlotte in joky holiday pose. Gill's dad was wearing a safari suit and pith helmet, while her mum had strung some roses from the garden round her neck like a Hawaiian garland. Gill sighed. She suddenly felt rather jealous. Now that was sad, being jealous of your parents.

Gill closed the message from her father and scanned the rest of her list of messages for anything interesting. Among the inevitable 'Get your college diploma now!' and 'Solve your debt problems,' announcements, one caught her eye: 'Ladies – haven't found Mr Right?' Gill sighed. No, she hadn't found Mr Right. Would she ever? Without really thinking, Gill found herself clicking the mouse.

A logo came up on her screen. 'Future Fertility – The Way Forward for the Modern Woman.' Gill read the text underneath.

> Not found Mr Right? Well, don't worry. At Future Fertility, we can provide single women with a safe, easy and fully confidential means to have the baby they want without the need to find a father. For as little as a few hundred pounds, we can provide fully screened fresh sperm for home self-insemination. All instructions are included in the information pack. Click here to read more.

Gill clicked.

> At Future Fertility, we understand that life isn't always perfect. We know that for many modern women the struggle to maintain a career and find a loving, lasting relationship

with a suitable mate is increasingly difficult. But fertility waits for no man, or woman! A woman's peak reproductive years are short. So, don't delay. Act now! If you want a baby but haven't found Mr Right, call Future Fertility. We're happy to help.

We also welcome lesbian singles and couples.

Gillian looked at the screen. She was thirty-eight. She was no expert, but she reckoned her peak productive years were a long way behind her. Her eggs must now be so old, it would take electric shock therapy to spark any life out of them, which, bearing in mind her hangover, was pretty much the way the rest of her was feeling at that moment, too.

Emma looked at Max. He was gripping the steering wheel of the car like Jack Hawkins in a Second World War movie, trying to control a rolling ship in heavy seas, except he lacked the firm chin and resolute manner. Frankly, he could have done with one of Jack's sternly belted macs and a waterproof sou'wester to shelter from what was raining down upon him: female disapproval.

Emma couldn't believe that Max had just got in the car and said nothing to Saskia. Or, rather, she could. During the marriage service, after she promised to love, honour and obey, Max should have chipped in with a supplementary list of all her other marital duties, chief among them being the sorting out of Saskia. She tried to be charitable. From the moment Saskia had been born, Max had been flummoxed. Being an only child, he had no experience of sisters. He hadn't had the chance to observe first hand the ammunition little girls come armed with to pierce the hearts of their daddies. Faced with Saskia's toddler tears or tantrums, he therefore had simply melted.

As Saskia had got older, she had become even more of an enigma to Max. The paraphernalia of girldom, the dolls, the Wendy houses, the pairs of tights that always seemed to go on twisted, were a strange land that Max had no idea how to navigate. When Saskia got to the age where she would march up to him with elastic bands with strange bobbly bits on the ends, demanding he put her hair in bunches, he was totally stumped. He'd have a go, but Saskia would end up with one bunch by her ear and the other on top of her head, and a parting that looked like a slalom track. Emma would have to redo it. Max had been almost relieved when Saskia became a sulky teenager. At least she didn't want to put glittery nail varnish on his toenails any more.

Emma turned and looked over her shoulder at her stepdaughter. She had her DVD player turned up full and was looking out of the window. Now that the fear that Saskia might have been injured had subsided and Emma knew she was OK, she wanted to strangle her.

That's if you could actually kill alien life, which was what Saskia appeared to have turned into: someone from another planet. Emma hadn't noticed when the spaceship had arrived to kidnap the real Saskia and replace her with this person whom she didn't recognise. Perhaps she'd been working late that night. She sighed and wished that ship would come back and beam her up instead.

'A baby? Are you insane!' Chloë exclaimed. 'A minute ago you wanted a rabbit and I had my doubts about you being able to look after that – and now you want a baby!'

'It's not so outrageous a suggestion, is it? I think I'd make a very good mother.'

'You? That plant you bought died because you forgot to water it. And it was a cactus!'

'I know, but . . .'

'You're just hung over. What you need is –'

'A baby?'

'I was going to say a shag, but first things first. Let's get you a drink. A bloody big one. Come on, we're going out for lunch.'

'But . . .'

Chloë wasn't taking no for an answer. She took Gill by the arm and pulled her away from the computer, out of the room and down the stairs.

'Where are we going?' Gill asked.

'It doesn't matter,' Chloë replied. 'So long as the drinks are large and the men are larger.'

'It's not even twelve o'clock, Chloë. We can't pick up men in the middle of the day.'

'Correction,' said Chloë. 'I can pick them up any time. It's just you that is a failure in that department.'

When Emma and Max pulled into the drive, Saskia was already unbuckling her seatbelt and opening the car door, preparing to make a run for it. This was a remarkable show of speed from a girl who could take fifteen minutes just to emerge from underneath the duvet in the morning.

'Not so fast, young lady,' Emma said, eyeing Saskia in the rear-view mirror. 'Max, haven't you got something to say to her?'

Max was mute. His attention had been diverted by the sight of a woman sitting on their doorstep. Emma groaned. What the hell was Dominique doing here?

Chapter Six

The atmosphere over the breakfast table the following morning was similar to that which you might have encountered in a trench during the Battle of the Somme. Max and Emma were huddled together having a tense, whispered conversation which was in danger of being interrupted at any moment by hostilities breaking out elsewhere in the house.

'Well, I couldn't exactly throw her out,' Max whispered. 'Could I?'

'You could have tried,' Emma replied.

'Oh, come on. She had Kevin with her.'

'Exactly.'

'He's not a bad kid.'

'And what exactly is your definition of a bad kid, Max, one who manages to raze our home to the ground on the first attempt, as opposed to the more gradual demolition of the place?'

Kevin had only been in their home for a day and already he had smashed a vase, spilt Ribena over the Persian rug in the hall and tried to stuff Trotsky the cat –

Saskia had been in a Communist phase when they got him – into the microwave. Trotsky had struggled free of his persecutor's clutches and was now sitting outside the kitchen window, refusing to come in.

'Oh, come on, Em,' Max coaxed, putting an arm round her. 'It's not for long.'

'For how long will it be, exactly?' Emma asked.

Max was silent.

'Max?'

'She's on her own. Denzel's done a bunk.'

'Again!' Emma got up to put the kettle on for more coffee. She sometimes wondered if Max secretly liked the fact that Denzel was so unreliable. The more crap Denzel was, the better it made Max look. Currently, Max was enjoying a status not far below that of St Francis of Assisi.

Suddenly, there was the sound of stamped footsteps on the stairs and a loud shriek. A small figure hurtled into the room. 'Yeeow!' Kevin shouted, making dramatic swooping motions with a toy plane in the air. 'Vrooom!'

Emma squinted at the noise. 'Would you, um, like some breakfast, Kevin?'

'Crassssshhhh!' he shouted, swooping the plane towards the breakfast table. Before Emma could stop him, he had knocked over a carton of milk, a cup half full of coffee and a packet of muesli, spraying honey-covered grit over a wide area. Emma eyed Max.

'Well, I must be getting off,' he said, standing up from the table.

'But what about –'

'Dominique will be up in a minute,' Max said, kissing Emma on the cheek and walking to the door.

One thing Emma knew about Dominique was that she was never up for breakfast. It was now precisely eight-thirty. Emma was supposed to be in the office by nine, nine-thirty at the latest. Well, it looked like she was going to be late this morning. Emma had been forced to dash straight out to work yesterday, after returning from the police station. Then she hadn't got back till late. Saskia had therefore escaped the inevitable showdown with Emma. So far. Now was the perfect moment except she couldn't possibly leave Kevin here unaccompanied to go up and see Saskia. If she did, she'd get back down again to be met by fire engines at the very least. Maybe ambulances and a couple of police cars as well.

Emma turned to Kevin, adopting her most patient smile. 'Well, shall we clear this lot up then?'

He looked at her as if she had suggested he unscrew one of his arms and use it to stir her coffee. 'No,' he said.

The interior of Bliss was designer groovy. All the walls were covered in red leather which gave it the feel of a luxurious padded cell. The ceiling and floor were mirrored. This meant by looking up you could see who else was in. It also meant, if they were female, you could simultaneously look up their skirts. Female regulars were wise to this effect and habitually wore trousers. Bliss was so successful it could dictate a dress code.

Gillian slipped off her jacket and went to the bar. Gus was already stocking it. He was bent down behind it, loading bottles of overpriced lager on to the shelves, but his black Hoxton quiff was still visible above it, like the fin of a shark in *Jaws*.

'Remind me never to drink again,' Gill said.

'Did you go out last night?' Gus asked, standing up.

Gill nodded. 'It started off as lunch and sort of progressed.'

Gus winced. 'OK, I'll go easy on you today.'

Gus was boyishly handsome, but studiedly so. His cute hairstyle was matched by skin that was peachy thanks to prodigious cleansing, toning and moisturising. Gill sometimes joked that Gus was a bigger girl than she was and it was true. Gus had begun putting halves of orange in a juicer. He handed Gill a glass of juice. She took it and gulped.

'Did you have a good time, though?' Gus asked.

'I don't remember.'

'Oh, it was one of those nights, was it?'

Gill nodded. 'Still, better than my date.'

'I forgot to ask! How did it go with Michael?' Gus said excitedly.

'I don't think there'll be a date two,' Gill said.

Gus frowned. 'You could have done without that new

haircut. What is that? Is it supposed to be asymmetrical or something? The Human League haven't had a hit in about twenty years, you know.'

Gill tugged self-consciously at her hair. 'Oh, I had a bit of an accident on the date. It, um, caught fire.'

'Where the hell were you?'

'In a wine bar,' Gill replied breezily. 'I was so bored I thought I'd liven things up a bit. No, really though, he was dull. How come he's a friend of yours? I can't believe you have anything in common.'

'Well, when I said a friend . . .'

'What?'

'Um, he isn't exactly a friend.'

'What is he then?' Gill asked suspiciously.

Gus stepped back from the front of the bar so as to be outside hitting rouge. 'I answered an ad in the newspaper for you.'

'You bastard!'

'No, it looked good, that ad. It really did. He sounded perfect for you.'

'Do you think I'm so desperate you have to pimp for me in the small ads?'

'Um . . . yes.'

'Thanks.'

'I'm joking. I thought it would be interesting.'

'Well, it wasn't.'

'Oh, I don't know. He lit your fire, didn't he?'

* * *

The glass doors opened with an expensive swoosh. Emma was hit hard in the face with a blast of hot air from Smith & Taylor's air-conditioning system. This wasn't so much a reception as a tanning cubicle.

Emma shielded her face with one hand and walked towards the lifts. She nodded at the security guard sitting behind a desk in the corner. He had his telly on and her progress was accompanied by a heated row between two invisible but highly vocal individuals. It reminded Emma of the scene she'd witnessed before she left home between Saskia and Dominique, except in the case of the TV at least the combatants were in the same room as they tore each other to pieces. Saskia and her mother had simply yelled at each other through Saskia's locked door.

Dominique had finally appeared at 11.45. Emma could have woken her earlier, but she couldn't bring herself to do so. Being late for work or having to face Dominique before lunch – it was a toss-up which was worse. In the end, Emma had procrastinated and tried to sort things out with Saskia on her own, just as she usually did. So now Emma was late. Very late. She pressed the button for the lift and prayed that she didn't run into Dino, her boss.

When Emma got up to the ninth-floor childrenswear department, the office was already humming. As head of Childrenswear for Smith & Taylor, this was her domain. Emma was responsible for the design, manufacture and import of all items sold in the kids' department. If things went wrong, then she carried the can. Emma surveyed her territory. It had a buzz about it. Desks were arranged into clusters, the gaps between them clogged with rails of clothes. Boards with lines of sketches and scraps of fabric stapled underneath were propped against the walls. The air was full of urgent conversations about shipments from Hong Kong, stitch size and whether you could machine wash the fur collar on a microfibre waistcoat.

Emma navigated a path through the racks of clothes. Outside her office, Jeanette, her deputy, was already at work. But then, if Emma had been in at 4 a.m., Jeanette would still have managed to get to her desk by 3.50 a.m. Jeanette was that most deadly of professional combinations, twenty-something and unattached. This gave her the single-mindedness of a cruise missile. Jeanette didn't actually say anything when Emma had to rush off to one of Saskia's parents' evenings or was late, as she was today, owing to a family crisis. However, on the quiet Emma suspected she poured scorn on Emma and every other woman with kids.

Emma had once been a candidate for the Superior Single Girls Club. But, meeting Max, she'd immediately crossed over to the Knackered Married With Kids Camp. It had felt a bit like joining MI6. The subterfuge required was similar. There were even secret handovers of information, albeit not in dingy Moscow car parks. When Emma let Saskia's existence be known, women she'd barely spoken to before had shuffled over in the Ladies' loo and shoved pictures of their children into her hands.

She'd had no idea they even had kids. At Smith & Taylor you left your womb at the door. Or you did if you wanted promotion.

Emma soon learnt that it was best not to advertise that you had responsibilities at home. When Emma had stuck a picture of Saskia on her desk a few years back, another mum had taken her aside and suggested she remove it. She was making herself too visible. It had felt like being reprimanded by an air-raid warden during World War Two for not closing the blackout curtains properly. She'd allowed a chink of light to illuminate her real existence.

Jeanette was on the phone. Her young face with its carefully applied make-up – no small child wreaking havoc over breakfast to distract her – was cocked to one side. A chunk of glossy, chestnutty hair fell over her cheekbone. She pointed at her watch and held five fingers up, questioningly. Emma nodded. At least she had five minutes before having to endure the onslaught of Jeanette's chirpy enthusiasm. Just the thought of it made Emma feel exhausted.

Emma approached her office. Outside, her secretary Carol was on the phone. 'Yes, Dino. I'm sure Emma hasn't forgotten.' Emma groaned and shuffled past. Carol put down the phone and followed her in. 'That was Dino. We're hot-desking from today. And –'

Emma interrupted her. 'Oh, God! I'd forgotten. I haven't cleared my drawers out. There's stuff in them I haven't seen since about nineteen eighty-two. It'll take me ages.'

'And,' Carol continued, 'the people with the AstroTurf are here.'

'The what?'

'They're . . . um . . .'

'What?'

'They're turning your office into an executive play area to stimulate creative thinking. It's going to be indoor crazy golf in here, hence the AstroTurf.'

'You've got to be joking?' Emma said incredulously.

'Nope. You've got to be out by two. Each member of staff has been issued with one of these,' Carol indicated a trolley at her feet. 'You put your stuff on it and wheel it from place to place. Dino says it's part of a modern, mobile, troubleshooting ethos.'

Emma looked at her trolley. It made her think of the lady who hung about near the local tube station with all her belongings in a shopping cart. All she'd need was a BO problem and a coat that did up with string for the resemblance to be complete.

Carol ploughed on. 'You've also got a conference call to Singapore in ten minutes. Jeanette wants to have a word and there's a new supplier waiting to see you. He's been here for twenty minutes. Coffee?'

Jump leads would have been more apt, but Emma accepted the offer of the coffee instead. Carol disappeared. Emma glanced back at her trolley and considered sitting on it and launching herself out of the window. Then she remembered that, this being an air-conditioned building, the windows were sealed.

'It's OK, I think I've got some money for the cigarette machine in my jacket pocket,' Gill said, walking back to where she'd tossed her jacket when she arrived.

'But I thought you'd given up.'

'Oh, don't you start.'

Gill picked up the jacket and put her hand in the right-hand pocket. Nothing. So she flipped it round and delved into the other side. When she pulled her hand out, there was a big pile of change in it. Gill could always tell how drunk she'd been the night before by the amount of change she found in her pockets the morning after. If there was loads of change it meant she'd used notes to buy rounds, having been too pissed to count out the correct money. Looking at her haul of coins, she must have been blathered last night.

In among the change was a credit-card receipt. Bloody hell, she'd even started buying drinks on tick! The only stage beyond that was being in casualty having your stomach pumped. Gill was about to throw the receipt away when she saw some writing on it: 'Jake 020 7629 1479 Call me!'

'Jesus!' Gill exclaimed.

'What?' Gus shouted over.

'I've got some guy's phone number in my pocket.'

'Whose?'

'I haven't the faintest idea.'

'Just how slaughtered do you have to be, Gillian, to pull and not even know it?'

'Very, apparently.'

'Are you going to call him?'

'I'd have to be crazy, don't you think?'

'Max, why aren't you at work?' Emma asked anxiously.

'Oh, um, Dominique called,' Max answered. 'Bit of a crisis here. Dominique had to, um, go out. I'm holding the fort.'

'What do you mean, holding the fort?' Emma put her hand over the telephone receiver and mouthed, 'Two minutes.'

Jeanette smiled and said in a stage whisper, 'Don't worry about it. You get your domestic problems sorted first.'

There was something about the way Jeanette said 'domestic problems' that irritated Emma. It was patronising, like referring to PMT as 'women's trouble'. Still, Emma ignored it. 'Look, we'll talk about this later,' she said to Max.

There was a bang as the receiver was knocked out of Max's hand.

'Now, Kevin, you know we don't play with knives. Someone might get hurt. Put Trotsky down,' Max said evenly.

'I killing him,' squealed an excited Kevin.

'Well, maybe we won't kill Trotsky today,' said Max. 'Now, if you could just give me that . . .'

There was the sound of a scuffle.

'Ow!'

'Oh, God, Kevin, are you OK?' Max sounded panicky.

'Uncle Max, I bleeding!' Kevin said proudly.

'Um, I'm sure it'll stop in a minute. I don't think you got a major artery,' Max replied.

'I dying! I dying!' shouted Kevin.

'You're not dying,' Max shouted back.

'Waah! Waah!' wailed Kevin.

Max finally picked up the receiver again. 'Sorry, darling. Where are the plasters?'

'Where they always are.'

'And, um, that is?'

'In the box in the bathroom under the sink,' Emma replied, resisting the desire to point out that they had been in the same place for the last seven years, since they moved into the house and she put them there. 'Is Kevin OK?'

'Yeah, well, if I can stem the flow of the blood I think it'll be all right. Keep your arm up, Kevin. Where is the nearest casualty, just in case?'

'St Mary's, but shouldn't you get Dominique?'

'I told you, she went out.'

'God! If she gets any more Botox they'll put her in Madame Tussaud's.'

There was a renewed burst of childish wailing.

'You couldn't, like, take the rest of the day off, could you?' Max wheedled.

'No, I couldn't,' Emma said, deadpan.

'Oh, don't worry,' Max said lightly. 'I just thought –'

'No, Max.'

'Never mind. I just thought, well, you know . . .'

'What, that my job is less important than yours so I can take time off any time I like?'

'No, no . . .' Max backtracked as fast as he could.

Emma was unimpressed. 'I have to get back to my unimportant job now,' she said.

'I didn't say that. Christ, you're so touchy.'

'It must be because I didn't sleep well worrying about your daughter.'

'For God's sake, Em. What time will you be home?'

'I don't know. Got a meeting. Seven-ish?'

'OK.'

There was a pause as Max put the receiver down. Just before Emma heard the click, however, there was a shriek. 'Kevin! Kevin! Put the blow torch down. That's for doing crème brûlée, not for . . .'

Suddenly, Emma heard more shouting, this time coming from the other end of her office. Emma followed Jeanette to the door. She looked out. At the far end of the room, Maureen, Merchandiser: ladies' slippers, was spreadeagled over a desk. Her arms hugged the top, while her body effectively blocked access to the drawers. 'No!

No!' she was screaming. 'You're not taking it!'

'But, Maureen, it's only a desk,' Yvonne, Smith & Taylor's head of human resources, coaxed her.

'It may only be a desk to you!' Maureen exclaimed. 'It's a principle to me. Hitler tried to crush the British spirit in the Blitz, but we stood firm . . .'

'Hitler? What's Hitler got to do with it?' Yvonne asked, confused.

By now there was a large crowd gathered next to Maureen and Yvonne. Emma and Jeanette walked over to join them. Dino had thought hot-desking would bring the staff together, but not quite in this way.

'Maureen,' Yvonne began. 'This isn't right –'

'Right? Right? Was Chamberlain right with his policy of appeasement? And what about Brave Little Belgium?'

'Aren't we getting our wars a bit mixed up here?' Yvonne asked. She took hold of Maureen under the arm and attempted to prise her off the desk. It was like trying to lever a limpet off a rock. Maureen's fingers were clamped round the edge and she was stuck fast.

'Now, now, Maureen, there are lots of nice desks in the office,' Yvonne said, tugging at her.

'But they aren't MINE!' Maureen shrieked. 'An Englishman's home is his castle.'

'Perhaps you'd be better off going home a bit early,' Yvonne suggested.

'We will not falter. We will not flee,' Maureen announced. 'We will fight them on the beaches –'

A male voice interrupted Maureen's heroic monologue. "Scuse me, love."

Emma turned to see a burly bloke with a roll of what looked like carpet over his shoulder. 'Got three rolls of AstroTurf. Where shall I put this?'

'Thank God for texting,' Gill said, pressing buttons on her mobile phone. 'At least I don't have to speak to him.'

'Can you really not remember anything about him?' Gus asked.

Gill shook her head.

'He could be really old or bald, or have bad breath or —'

'Thanks, you're really building my confidence,' Gill said. 'There it is, OK? Casual enough?' Gill handed her mobile to Gus and he studied it.

'Well, it's brief,' he said.

There was only one word on the screen. 'Drink?' it said.

'Well, shall I send it or not?' Gillian asked.

'Oh, go on, then,' Gus said, 'What have you got to lose?'

Emma put her key in the lock. The door swung open. At first, she was unable to fully comprehend what lay in front of her. It looked like she'd been burgled, only that seemed unlikely as she could hear Max's voice coming from the living room. She frowned. The floor was scattered with random items of clothing and toys and little bits of paper. There was a trail of something up the centre of the carpet. Emma knelt down. That wasn't, was it . . .? Yes, it was blood. And the little bits of paper? They were bits of backing from the many, many plasters Max had apparently attempted to apply to the bleeding Kevin.

Emma walked up the hall, collecting debris, and popped her head round the door to the living room. 'Hi, darl . . .' She paused. 'Hello, Dominique.'

Dominique had obviously got back from her urgent trip out, but not early enough to do any clearing up, it seemed. Max scrambled to his feet and came over to Emma. He kissed her on the cheek. 'Hello, darling. Dominique just got back, didn't you?'

Dominique grunted, just as she always did to Emma. She seemed to think if she ignored Emma, she would go away. This was pretty optimistic since Max and Emma had been married for thirteen years.

'Kevin OK?' Emma asked.

'Oh, it was nothing. Just a nick,' Max said.

'From the state of the hall it looks like he was attacked by Freddie Kruger,' Emma said, secretly thinking that Freddie wouldn't have had the guts to take on Kevin.

'Ha, ha, ha,' laughed Max. 'Very good, darling.' He stopped when he realised Emma wasn't smiling.

'I'll just get rid of these,' Emma said, indicating the pile of paper she was holding. 'You eaten?'

'We were waiting for you,' Max said.

Emma sighed. That meant Max was waiting for her to organise something. By the look on Dominique's face, she was expecting to be fed and watered as well. 'I'll see what I can do,' Emma said.

She trudged downstairs to the kitchen and dumped her pile of things on the table. Then she went over to the fridge to look inside. Suddenly, she felt something soft and furry against her leg. She looked down. It was Trotsky. Emma bent down and picked the cat up. She stroked him under his chin and he purred happily. 'Cupboard love, isn't it?' she said, putting him down, but she wasn't angry. 'Let's see what we've got for you.'

Emma stepped sideways to open one of the cupboard doors. Her foot squelched on something. Then her nostrils prickled. A distinctly unpleasant aroma filled the air. She looked down.

'Trotsky!' Emma exclaimed.

A fresh brown turd was sitting on the tiled floor. Trotsky had scarpered. Emma looked over to the cat-litter tray. It hadn't been changed. Had Saskia been shut in her room all day? Why hadn't she been to school? And why hadn't anyone else thought to change it? Emma let out a frustrated sigh. Did she have to do everything? The tinkle of Dominique's laughter floated down from the other room. Emma picked up the cat-litter tray and thought about marching into the living room and tipping the contents into Dominique's lap. Instead she got a bin bag and tipped it into that. Then she took a newspaper off the top of the pile in the corner and folded it flat to reline the bottom of the tray. Emma frowned. She recognised the picture of the woman looking back at her. No wonder. It was her.

'Meet Emma Chancellor. She's a wife, a mother, has a demanding glamorous job in the fashion industry, earns a six-figure salary and still manages to find the time to throw chic dinner parties', it read.

The dinner parties bit was a laugh. The last time Emma and Max had a dinner party, chicken bricks were a new and funky kitchen accessory. Emma grabbed a Biro from the kichen table and scrawled on the newsprint, then stood back to admire her handiwork. 'Meet Emma Chancellor. She's a wife, a mother, has a demanding, glamorous job in the fashion industry . . . and still manages to find the time to clear up cat poo.'

Emma even managed a smile.

Beep, beep . . . beep, beep.

Gill picked up her mobile in a panic. 'Oh, God, it's him, I know it is.'

'What does it say?' Gus asked.

He had to shout as Bliss was packed. They were four deep at the bar and the waving of twenty-pound notes had taken on an aggressive edge.

''Scuse me, darlin', you work 'ere or what?' a man Gill recognised as a premiership football player snarled.

'I'm on a break,' Gill spat back.

She was rigid with fear. All she had to do was press the 'read' button, but she couldn't. What if Jake had turned her down? Or worse, what if he hadn't and then, like Gus said, he was old and bald and had bad breath?

Gus leant across the bar. 'Give it here. If you don't want to find out, I bloody do.'

Chapter Seven

'That chair thingy, or do you want the sofa?' asked Gill, indicating first a hanging raffia bucket seat and then a leatherette bench seat, ripped out of an especially nasty seventies sitting room.

'Let's have the sofa,' Emma said. 'I think I've had enough excitement for one week.'

'Yeah?'

'Dominique's staying with us.'

'What, Ivana Frump again?'

Emma nodded.

'What about the psycho midget?'

'Kevin? Yeah, him too.'

'Jesus, no wonder you wanted a drink. Cheers. Commiserations, I mean.' Gill raised her glass.

Emma clinked hers on the side. 'How'd your date go, by the way?'

'Which one?'

'Was there more than one? I mean the friend of Gus's.'

'Michael? Oh, disaster. Set light to my hair.'

'I was wondering whether your new, shorter hair was a fashion look.'

'No, genuinely, I set light to my hair on one side, so I had to get it all cut. It was on a candle. Eighties wine bars should be banned.'

Emma took a sip of her glass of wine and looked around. She immediately felt out of place. The bar was full of twenty-somethings on the pull. They looked bright-eyed and eager. Here were women unfettered by domestic demands. No lying awake all night worrying about a teenager for them.

'Lambs to the slaughter,' Gill said. 'Give them ten years and they'll be mainlining on Touche Eclat like the rest of us.'

Emma laughed. 'You make us seem ancient. We're not exactly picking up our pensions.'

'No, it just feels like it sometimes.' Gill took a slug of her Bloody Mary. Looking at all these girls, a good ten or maybe fifteen years younger than her, depressed her. Not simply because this was her competition but because it reminded her that her life hadn't changed, hadn't moved on in all that time. Emma had got married. She had Saskia. For Gill, the only thing that had changed was that the hangovers had got worse. She sighed. 'I do sometimes wonder why I still do it.'

'What?' asked Emma.

'Oh, you know, date.'

'It must be very exciting.'

'It's that all right. Some nights more than others. Well, actually, no, it's not really. I've been going on dates for twenty years. Twenty years. That's a lifetime. How many more seared salmons on a bed of mixed salad leaves can one girl eat? You know, it would be so much easier to be settled down, like you; to have the whole matter sorted out. Dating is like having a new house to decorate and you keep buying those little tester pots and painting little patches of wall. Well, my wall looks like a packet of bloody Smarties.'

'Yeah, but you've always said you didn't want to settle down.'

'I know, but we're thirty-eight, Em.'

'I know. Feels more like sixty-eight some mornings.'

'I don't have much time to play with,' Gill said tentatively.

'What do you mean?' Emma said. 'The average life expectancy is –'

'I'm not talking about that. I mean if I wanted to have a baby.'

Emma put her glass of wine down on the table with a clunk. 'A baby! You want a baby!'

'What's so amazing about that? Lots of women have them.'

'But not you, Emma. Think what you'd be giving up.'

'And think what I'd be gaining. You're always telling me how much more rounded as a human being you feel since you met Max and Saskia. Bloody hell, Em, you normally make parenting sound like a religious experience.'

'Well, sometimes you do find yourself offering up a prayer, usually for a decent night's sleep,' Emma said.

'Yeah, but . . .'

'Look,' said Emma, calming down. 'I just don't understand where this has all come from. You always said you didn't want kids.'

'I know and I'm not serious really. Well, most of the time I'm not serious, but I've got to think about it. That old body clock.' Gill smiled and sipped her Bloody Mary. 'Actually, Em, I never understood why you and Max didn't have your own. I mean, I know Saskia's as good as. But, you know . . .'

'I don't know really. At the beginning I really wanted one, but we had our hands full with Saskia and then Max didn't want to go back to nappies and stuff. I suppose I could have made more of an issue of it – fought my corner – but he was so adamant. And now, I do sort of regret it, especially when Saskia is so difficult. I mean, yeah, I look at babies in prams even now and I feel a pang of regret. I'd love to have one of my own. But, well, life is pretty complicated as it is. And now, what with Kevin, well . . .'

'He's enough to put anyone off.'

'Yeah,' Emma laughed. 'Actually, Max almost killed him yesterday.'

'There wouldn't have been a court in the land that would have convicted him. Anyway, where was Dominique?'

'Now, there's a question I ask myself often.'

There was a sudden burst of noise from the bar. A group of office workers were ordering cocktails with rude names. At every mention of a long slow comfortable screw, there was a volley of snorts of laughter. The bar staff were unamused. Gill was suddenly hugely grateful not to be working tonight. She took a handful of pretzels from a bowl on the table and crunched contentedly.

Emma spoke. 'You know it's not that easy being married,' she said.

'What do you mean?' Gill's tone was one of genuine surprise.

'I'm not saying I don't love Max. I do. And I like being married most of the time . . .'

'But . . .'

'It's just it's exhausting. I get up in the morning, go to the office, shuffle pointless bits of paper around for a boss I don't like very much. I get home, we have dinner, we go to bed, then I get up in the morning and do it all over again.'

'Yeah, but you're really successful and –'

Emma interrupted her. 'I know, I know. I'm the woman who has it all. But maybe I don't want it all. Maybe I don't want any of it. Sometimes I don't know whether I can keep doing it. You know I have these mad fantasies about just running away. Getting on a plane and running away.'

'Where would you go?'

'Oh, I don't know. I'd have an olive farm in Tuscany or something.'

'An olive farm? But you don't even like olives.'

Emma sighed. 'It doesn't matter really. It could be Italian olives or a French vineyard or maybe I'd have chickens in a remote part of Spain. I'd just go off on my own for a while. You know, that's what I miss most, time on my own. I don't think there's a moment in the day that is completely mine. And then there's the tiredness. I'm so tired of trying to be brilliant at work and brilliant at home and not being brilliant at either.'

Emma was barely pausing for breath. 'I thought it was bad when Saskia was small. Then there were her piano lessons and the swimming club and, you know, Saskia was invited to twenty-three parties one year.'

Gill nodded, entirely oblivious to the importance of the number of parties Saskia might have been invited to. Gill being single, Emma had always reckoned she wasn't interested in kiddie talk, which she hadn't been up to now, so Emma had resisted the urge to bore her with it. It was the one area of Emma's life that she didn't share much with Gill. It wasn't that Saskia was exactly a wedge between them, but she was a point of difference whose effect they had historically sought to minimise.

The floodgates were open now, however. 'That meant I

had to throw a bash for twenty-three six year olds,' Emma continued. 'It was a bloody nightmare, what with the cake and the juice and the party bags. Do you know you have to spend at least a tenner on each one? That means over two hundred quid before you even get near the children's entertainer or the kiddie disco.'

Gill looked appalled. 'A kiddie disco!'

'You have no idea how withering a six-year-old girl can be if the music isn't up to her standards.'

'Stop! Stop!' Gill said. 'I can't take any more.' She was laughing, but Emma wasn't.

'I thought it would get easier as Saskia got older – you know, that she'd become more independent and I'd get some of my life back, but it hasn't. I mean, the trip to the police station is a case in point.' Emma shook her head in despair. 'There was a woman at work yesterday who went berserk because they wanted to take away her desk,' she said.

'Why were they taking away her desk?' Gill asked.

'Another of Dino's bright ideas. The point is, I sometimes wonder if there are offices all over the country resounding to the sound of women going off the deep end. Men have Road Rage. Women have Work Rage.'

'Or maybe it's just Life Rage.'

'Yeah,' Emma said. 'Whatever Happened To My Life Rage.'

'Perhaps they'd better start putting Prozac in the office Diet Coke machine,' Gill suggested.

'Or perhaps we could start a support group,' added Emma. 'Working Mothers Anonymous. "Hello, I'm Emma and I'm totally knackered."'

'Yeah, why not?'

'If working mothers had time to go to a support group, they wouldn't need one, would they?'

'You may have a point there,' Gill said.

They both laughed.

'You should thank God you don't have the whole kids and work nightmare to deal with,' Emma said.

'Oh, I don't know,' Gill replied. 'My life isn't any less complicated, you know. Yeah, I don't have so many plates on sticks, but I've got the "what ifs" to deal with instead. What if I had a kid? What if I didn't and turned round at forty-five and regretted it? I mean, we're thirty-eight, Em.'

'Stop saying that. Anyway, I didn't know your biological clock was ticking.'

'Well, it isn't, not really. Or I don't think it is. The trouble is, I can't tell whether the ticking is the clock or just my heart beating in panic. I don't know whether I want kids, but I don't want to regret not having them. What do you think?'

'It's hard enough with two of you. You'd be a single mother, or have you got someone lined up that I don't know about?'

'No, although I have got a date later with a new bloke.'

'Ooh, this sounds interesting.'

* * *

Max and Dominique were standing outside Saskia's bedroom.

'Saskia?' he began hesitantly. 'Sask, it's Daddy.'

There was no answer.

'Darling, it's Daddy. Can you open the door?'

More silence.

'You see!' shrieked Dominique, who was standing next to Max with her arms crossed in front of her. 'She is impossible!'

Max could hear the distant sound of squealing coming from the floor below. '*Neeaw*.' Kevin was engaged in one of his normal games of murder and mayhem.

'Darling . . .' Max said to the locked door.

'Tell the old cow I'm not coming out,' Saskia shrieked.

'The old cow' was Saskia's preferred name for Dominique. Emma quite liked it – on the quiet.

'Well,' Max began. Saskia had missed the first day of the new school term. Emma had asked him, well told him really, to 'sort this thing out with Saskia'. He suspected this wasn't the kind of sorting out that Emma had had in mind.

Dominique snorted derisively.

'I'm not coming out. Ever!' Saskia repeated even more vehemently.

Max knew he needed to be firm. But he couldn't be. 'Let's not be rash,' he stuttered.

'I'm not coming out!' Saskia shouted. 'And I'm not going to school tomorrow either.'

Max was the one who was silent now.

Saskia changed tack. Her voice dropped to a plaintive whisper. 'That's OK, isn't it, Daddy? I really don't feel up to it,' she said.

Max melted. 'Well, darling, maybe a couple of days off wouldn't be a bad thing. Shall I bring you up some orange juice?'

'Yes, please. I couldn't have some toast as well, could I? I'm starving.'

Max began to go down the stairs. Then he stopped and turned. 'Shall I butter it for you?'

Gill heard the familiar diesel engine burr of the taxi engine before Jake had even got out. She crept on to the sofa and peered over the top out of the window, which looked on to the street, trying to get a look at her date as he got out of the cab to press the buzzer. If he was a total moose, she wouldn't answer. Given she was on the third floor and hiding behind a pile of cushions, Gill's view wasn't exhaustive. Still, there was no sign of a 666 in his hairline. When the buzzer went, Gill said she'd be right down.

'Right, last-minute checks,' Chloë said as Gill stood in the hall. 'Lipgloss?'

'Check.'

'Mirror?'

'Check.'

'Phone?'

'Which you are going to call in precisely forty-five minutes' time to provide me with an alibi should I want to leave?' Gill said.

'Of course,' Chloë confirmed. 'Tissues, money, emergency cab money, condoms?'

'Condoms! I am not going to sleep with him,' exclaimed an outraged Gillian.

Chloë dipped into her own bag and produced a packet of condoms. 'Have you done your bikini line?'

'Um, yes,' Gill blushed.

'Well then. No use pretending you're intending to be Snow White, is there? Here, take these.' She put the condoms in Gill's bag. 'Now, have a good time. Jesus, I sound like my mother.'

'No, you sound like mine, which is more scary,' Gill laughed, walking down the stairs.

The coin was stuck in the slot.

'The coin's stuck in the slot,' said a morose teenager wearing a polyester company coat.

'I can see that. I was hoping you could unstick it,' Emma said.

The youth didn't move.

'Well, I won't get very far round the supermarket trying to tow all twenty-seven of these things, will I?' said Emma.

Still there was no sound from the teenager. Had he slipped into a cryogenic state without Emma noticing?

'Won't it be a bit of a hazard?'

Finally he spoke. 'Not my problem,' he said.

Emma looked at the youth and realised that she wasn't going to get any joy out of him, so abandoned her pound coin and picked up a basket instead. She trudged round the supermarket, getting milk, bread; all the essentials. As she did so, she saw other women doing the same thing. They all had the same look. They were simultaneously totally exhausted and totally wired.

'What do you mean you've run out of prawns!' one woman was shrieking at the man behind the fish counter. 'You can't have run out of prawns! I have to have prawns, now!'

When not berating members of staff, these scary women were haring round as if on a trolley dash, chucking things into baskets and shopping carts at the speed of light. Other more leisurely shoppers, older couples, single men, flattened themselves against the shelves for fear of being mown down. When they got to the checkout, the packers knew to stand back. These women had a system for packing their shopping and woe betide any spotty adolescent who interfered with that.

One boy, probably new, did offer to help a harassed-seeming female customer.

'Back off!' she shouted, brandishing a cucumber as if it were a Colt 45. Fully loaded.

Emma went to the checkout and was exceedingly polite to the person on the till, suddenly acutely aware of her normal offhand manner. She looked at the woman scanning her goods. She was about Emma's age. Would Emma have swapped with her? Would she have traded her own high-stress lifestyle, with everyone depending on her, for one spent sitting on that chair? Never mind dealing with international clothing suppliers, the most stressful moment that woman had in her day was probably when she couldn't find the right price for a guava.

Emma felt guilty. She knew nothing about this woman or her life. She didn't know if she had children or elderly parents; maybe she was studying applied maths at night school and this job was just a way of funding that.

The checkout lady held up a bottle of Diet Coke and showed it to the woman at the next seat. ''Ere, Carol. 'Ow many litres is this, then?' she bellowed.

'Two,' her colleague shouted back. 'Says on the side, dunnit?'

Well, maybe not applied maths.

'Just bung your bag and stuff on there,' Jake said, walking out of the room. 'I'll get us a drink. Wine OK?'

'Yeah, fine,' Gill answered, looking around. Jake must be doing well as an architect. His flat had that nothing-in-it look that meant the stuff which was must be really, really expensive. The building had once been a glue factory and a certain Evostick-like aroma still lingered. The estate agent probably whacked an extra five K on for ambience. Still, Gill reckoned it was probably worth half a million quid.

The flat was on the fourth floor. Gill was in the living room, or living *space*, as Jake called it. The floor was polished concrete, the walls were exposed brick and right in the centre there were two sofas, set at right angles to one another. A sculpture made out of cubes of broken windscreen glass bonded together sat on a coffee table. Whether this was a reference to the fact that if you left your car outside in this area, that's what would happen to it, Gill didn't know. Jake's flat was in deepest Hackney. Some areas are edgy. This one was positively precipicey. Still, it had lots of old factory buildings so the yuppies could wall themselves into their fabulous loft apartments, like post-industrial Egyptian mummies.

'Sit down,' Jake ordered as he walked across the room and put two glasses down on the table. 'I'll put some music on.'

Gillian had definitely hit lucky on all fronts. Not only was Jake's flat a paean to good taste, he was pretty attractive too. He was slim and dark with an olive skin and brown eyes. Tonight he was wearing jeans, a vintage T-shirt, plus expensive trainers. Gill wasn't quite sure how old he was, but he could have been anywhere from thirty to forty. Jake picked up a remote control and something cool but unobtrusive filled the room. Then he sat down next to her.

'To a lovely evening,' he said, passing a glass of wine to Gill and taking the other himself.

It was smooth, but he carried it off well. Just as he'd carried off everything else this evening. Ordering in the restaurant, which he did, paying the bill, which he did again, there was none of the usual awkwardness. Jake was confident, even a little over-confident, but Gill didn't dislike it. It intrigued, even amused her. There had been a moment in the restaurant before they'd started eating when he'd got out a little packet of wet wipes to clean his hands, which was a little freaky. But then they'd had a lovely meal and, well, what can you expect from an architect? All those clean precise little drawings. They were bound to have high hygiene standards.

Gill was now four glasses of wine and a Bloody Mary on from the wet wipes thing (Jake had barely drunk) and it seemed unimportant. She was sitting in a gorgeous flat with a gorgeous man and it couldn't get any more perfect than this.

Jake propped an elbow up on the back of his cream sofa and stroked Gill's hair. 'So, Gill,' he purred. 'Do you like games?'

'What? Monopoly, Scrabble, yeah, yeah, I love games.'

'That wasn't quite what I had in mind.' Suddenly Gill was aware of the feel of Jake's lips on her neck. It felt good. He brought his head up and looked her deep in the eyes. 'Wait here,' he said. 'I won't be long.'

* * *

The old man was hissing, his breath so hot and angry you could almost see steam escape from the corners of his mouth.

'You're in the wrong queue,' he spat.

Emma frowned and continued unpacking her shopping onto the checkout conveyor. 'What?' she said absentmindedly.

The man was now jabbing a bony finger towards a sign hanging from the ceiling like a geriatric John Travolta in *Saturday Night Fever*.

'What?' Emma repeated, craning her neck to see the sign.

'Five items or less. This is five items or less!' the man exclaimed, his face now puce.

'Yes, I know,' Emma said. 'Five items or less,' folding the handles of her basket down and putting it on the pile.

'But, but, you've got . . .'

Emma looked down at her conveyor. Slowly, methodically, she counted her items. 'One, two, three, four, five, six.' She had six. She had forgotten to count the apples which, in an effort to be ecological, she had neglected to place in a plastic bag. Had she placed them both in one they would have counted as one item. Loose, they were two.

The man was still staring in rage.

'It's only one over,' Emma tried. 'That's hardly a hanging offence, is it?'

'That's not the point,' he hissed. 'Today it's one item,

tomorrow, it's two. By the end of the week every Tom Dick or Harry will be parking in the disabled persons' parking spaces.'

Emma winced inwardly. That's just where she had parked. Well, she'd been in a hurry and if there'd actually been someone in a wheelchair attempting to park a three-wheeled vehicle she would of course have let them have the space, but there hadn't been and there never were, were there? Supermarkets seemed to assume there were thousands of disabled drivers, circling, looking for spaces, and instead there were simply lots of able-bodied people pissed off that they couldn't park anywhere within a mile radius of the front door of the store.

Emma took a breath. 'It's only an apple,' she said.

'It may be only an apple to you, young lady . . .'

Emma hadn't been called a young lady for about thirty years. It felt rather good.

The old man continued, 'But it's a principle to me. You youngsters with your jeans wearing and your bean bags . . .'

'Bean bags? What have bean bags got to do with it?'

'You want to sit on a proper chair. Learn to sit up straight. Get a bit of backbone in you. Don't know the meaning of hard work. You only get out of life what you put in, y'know. In my day . . .'

Emma drifted off. This speech had a familiar ring to it. Was it her father she could hear speaking, or her mother? Jesus, it was neither. It was she herself, Emma, talking to

Saskia. Saskia had said she wasn't her mother. She was right. She sounded like her grandmother.

'Well, say something,' Jake insisted.

'That's a very nice suspender belt. Is it Agent Provocateur?' Gill offered. 'I didn't know they did men's sizes.'

Jake was standing in the bedroom in black satin bra, pants and suspenders. He was wearing stockings and high-heeled shoes. He looked like he should be on stage in *The Rocky Horror Show*, only he wasn't. Jake was here with an audience of one – her.

'You can touch, you know.'

'Oh, I don't think so,' Gill replied, mildly repulsed at the vision of chest hair peeping from a B-cup bra.

'No, no, honestly, you can,' Jake said.

Jake swaggered over to Gillian, took hold of her hand and placed it on his chest, where it sat, stiff and unmoving like a dead pigeon. Gill would have quite liked to have been run over this very moment. She would at least have been whisked away in an ambulance. As it was, she was stuck in a bedroom with a man wearing women's underwear.

'Just got to use your, um, loo,' Gill said.

'Now? Couldn't you have gone earlier?' Jake protested, as if she were a three year old who had announced she wanted to wee in the middle of a long car journey.

'I need to go now,' Gill insisted.

'Second door on the left in the hall,' Jake said finally.

Gill went into the living room and picked up her bag, then walked down the hall, found the bathroom and locked the door behind her. She stood with her back against it and burst into a fit of giggles. She put her hands over her mouth, trying to muffle the laughter, but it was no good. 'Ha, ha, ha,' she laughed.

'Everything all right in there?' Jake shouted from the bedroom.

'Yes, yes, fine,' Gill managed to answer, before giggles overcame her again.

She looked around. The bathroom, like the rest of the flat, was neat as a new pin. Towels were piled up like jumpers in Benetton and the bath looked like it had never been used. Then Gill spotted a window. Did it open? Yes. Gillian looked out and down. There was a sheer drop of four floors. To the right, however, was a drainpipe. If she could get a grip on that, she might be all right.

Knock, knock, knock, went the door as Gill climbed on to the windowsill.

Gill didn't answer, but Jake was persistent. 'Hey, sweetie, Daddy's waiting for you!'

If Jake had been looking for a means to propel Gill down the drainpipe, he had just found it. The hairs on the back of Gill's neck stood on end. If this was what dating was about then, frankly, she'd had enough. She flipped herself over, took hold of the drainpipe and launched herself out of the window.

Chapter Eight

A pair of small seven-year-old arms were folded resolutely over a small seven-year-old chest. One small seven-year-old foot tapped the floor impatiently. 'I don't care. Lilac doesn't suit my skin tone. Haven't you got anything in a warmer palette?'

Emma wanted to say: 'Sod off, you precocious little brat. If you don't stop complaining I'll give your bottom a warmer palette by planting a large smack on it.' Not that she was in favour of smacking. When a man with a beard and a wallpaper table set up outside the post office had asked for her signature on an anti-corporal punishment petition, she'd been only too happy to oblige. Then again, she'd had a clutch of letters in her hand and a man was already emptying the nearby postbox. She'd have agreed to support free gender reassignment operations for confused dolphins if it had got her letter into Postman Pat's sack quicker. Still, in the case of little Tabatha, part-time tweenie fashion model and full-time pain in the neck, Emma was willing to rethink her smacking stance.

Perhaps if Tabatha had been taken in hand sooner she might not now be such a – what was the correct paediatric term? – ah yes, Right Little Madam. Emma studied Tabatha's disapproving expression. She had her lips pursed like an OAP sitting next to a seventeen-year-old leaking speed garage from a Discman turned up too loud. Transforming Tabatha into a pleasant human being at this late stage would take nothing short of a stint in Singapore's Changi prison.

Emma was on a fashion shoot for the spring/summer Smith & Taylor collection. But her mind wasn't really on it. The moment for her and Max to pay their penance for Saskia's arrest had arrived. Tonight was the parenting workshop, the one she and Max were required to attend by virtue of Saskia's picketing of Burgers from Heaven. Emma was dreading it. She just knew she'd be given a lecture by some woman wearing Laura Ashley.

'Well? I haven't got all day,' Tabatha spat. 'I've got a casting for a fromage frais commercial at four.' She was tapping her foot and humming now.

'OK, OK,' Emma said. She scanned the rack of clothes beside her. 'What about this?' she suggested, holding up a little gold leather jacket and leopard-print leggings.

There was a tired sigh. Tabatha shook her red waist-length tresses in disgust. They were teased into the sort of packet of Rolos ringlets Emma had last seen on the Girl's World doll head she'd had when she was nine. This was the doll that allowed 1970s girls to master all manner of complicated grown-up hairstyles. None of these were of any use whatsoever once you actually were grown up because you were too busy getting pissed on Merrydown even to attempt a half-decent French Pleat. Still, as parents used to say about learning to type, it was good to have a skill under your belt.

'Animal prints are so last year,' Tabatha drawled.

The smile set on Emma's face. Her patience was now spent. She wasn't about to be dictated to by someone whose daily reading matter was the back of a Cheerios packet. 'Put them on. Now.'

Tabatha hesitated. Her features were pinched with disdain.

Emma snapped. She leant towards Tabatha and hissed, 'If you don't put them on now, I will tie you to a radiator with your own hair and leave you there.'

Tabatha went pale and scuttled away.

The computer printer made a couple of clicks then whirred into life. Two sheets of paper were sucked into the machine and then spat out of the top, face down. Gill picked them up and turned them over.

'Future Fertility – The Way Forward for the Modern Woman.'

Following last night's awful date, Gill had woken in a bubble of gloom. What was the point of trying to find her Mr Right, if she only ever ended up with Mr Bloody Peculiar? She was thirty-eight. She kept going over that figure in her mind. Thirty-eight, thirty-eight. Her eggs were probably hard-boiled by now. Who knew if she could even conceive?

Ideally, Gill would have liked to have a child within a good, stable relationship. Ideally, Gill would have liked to have thirty-four-inch hips and a yacht on which to cruise the Caribbean. But life wasn't ideal. Right now, through the fog of a hangover, Gill's life felt way, way short of that. And no, she didn't know how she would cope if she actually did get pregnant. She didn't even know if she wanted a baby anyway, but, well, there was no harm in researching the possibilities, was there?

Gillian hadn't told Chloë or Emma. She knew what they'd both say. They'd said it before, after all. You and a baby? Are you mad, blah, blah, blah. Nevertheless, Gill was going to do it anyway. She was printing out the information from Future Fertility and she was going to call them. Well, maybe. She'd have to have a strong cup of coffee first and think about it.

'No, no, no!'

Marco, the art director, was huddled over a Polaroid with Dirk. Dirk was the photographer and, not entirely uncoincidentally, Marco's boyfriend. Emma plodded towards them with a sense of foreboding. Despite spending most of his time arranging cushions for in-store sofa promotions leaflets – Smith & Taylor sold everything from homewares to food and fashion – Marco clearly felt he should have been working on *Vogue*. That he wasn't didn't dent his enthusiasm for staging hissy fits. This one sounded hissier than usual.

'I said I wanted a documentary feel. Gritty, realistic. This is . . .' Marco paused, trying to find the words.

Emma stared at the snap in front of her and was pretty much lost for words herself. The Polaroid featured a dark-haired girl, coif teased into spikes, wearing a Johnny Rotten scowl and giving the camera a one-fingered salute.

'Cute. It's too cute. It needs to be harder!' declared Marco at last.

'Harder!' exclaimed Emma in amazement. Short of doing the entire set of pictures on location at Feltham Detention Centre, she didn't see how they could look harder.

Jeanette had joined them, accompanied by Tabatha, now got up in her gold jacket and spotty trousers, her hair looking as if she had been plugged into an electric socket. 'Remember,' said Jeanette. 'We have got the tattooist on standby.'

Dirk said nothing. His dour Germanic face wore the bored expression of a bloke waiting outside a shop changing room for his wife to stop dithering over which of eight identical skirts to buy so he can get home to watch the football. In his relationship with Marco, Dirk was the straight man – so to speak. Marco did all the flouncing and Dirk just waited for him to calm down. They were the George and Mildred of W9.

Marco cupped a hand to his chin in contemplation. 'Tattoos. Hm . . . Well, maybe a swastika . . .'

Emma knew how touchy Marco could be. Still, faced with the prospect of adorning small children with Nazi symbols, she felt she had no choice but to intervene. 'Marco, forgive me, but aren't we trying to get parents to buy these clothes for their kids?'

Marco nodded.

'Well, I don't feel that kitting them out as the Hitler Youth is going to help, do you?'

'It's sink estate chic. It's very current. John Galliano adores it,' protested Marco.

'I don't care if John Galliano has sold his Paris penthouse and decamped to a Tottenham council flat, our customers won't adore it. They'll hate it and they won't buy the clothes and –'

'But, Emma –'

'No, Marco. I let you and Dirk do that crack chic fashion shoot last season and that was a disaster. We had to ship half the stock to a factory outlet village in Belgium, if you remember.'

Marco's lower lip was stuck out, not unlike Tabatha's had been earlier. 'But at Benetton –'

'Well, we're not Benetton, are we? And don't even think about suggesting an Aids ward, OK?'

Beep, beep . . . Beep beep.

It was Emma's mobile. 'Hello, Emma Chancellor speaking,' she announced.

''Ello, Emma.'

It was Dino. His slight Southern Italian accent was immediately recognisable. He made no attempt to soften it. People heard Dino speak, assumed he was stupid and he could then shaft them with impunity.

'Those glitter T-shirts,' Dino said.

Emma racked her brain. From several hundred items in-store, not to mention those at development stage and the others actually in production, she was trying to locate the source of Dino's inquiry.

'The ten-year-old disco collection . . .' Dino prompted her.

'Oh, yes,' interjected Emma. 'Sorry, Dino, I'm with you now.'

'A mum from Sunderland's been on the phone . . .'

When did Dino have the time to take calls from mums in Sunderland? wondered Emma. Didn't he have a high street giant to run? Dino prided himself on being in touch with the smallest details of his business. This gave the staff at the Stoke-on-Trent branch a thrill when he staged a surprise appearance, but made Emma's life a misery. If there was a dodgy bit of top stitching on a pair of toddler jeans, Dino knew about it and called her, personally, to inform her of the fact. So what was the problem this time?

'It seems her little girl licked the glitter,' Dino continued.

'What, had they run out of Pot Noodle?' Emma said, smiling.

'Little girl had to be rushed to hospital apparently,' replied Dino, gravely.

Emma winced. 'Jesus! Is she OK?'

'Severe stomach pains,' Dino carried on. 'Suspected punctured small intestine.'

'Bloody hell!' Emma exclaimed.

Dino paused. 'Turned out she'd swallowed a pencil sharpener.'

'Thank God,' Emma said. 'I mean, not great for the little girl, but –'

Dino interrupted her. 'The mum's demanding compensation. Says the glitter may have made Dominica – that's the child's name –'

'Dominica?'

'Yeah. Conceived in the Dominican Republic, apparently. Her other three are called Ibiza, Lanzarote and Alicante.'

'Lucky she wasn't delayed overnight at Stansted,' Emma said.

Dino continued. 'The mum says Dominica has Attention Deficit Disorder, brought on by food allergies. The glitter she is supposed to have licked could have made her delirious, so causing her to swallow the sharpener.'

Emma was incredulous. 'You're not serious?' She had heard some stories in her time. Her favourite was the rogue button said to have caused a spontaneous tracheotomy of a twelve year old. According to the girl's parents, this necessitated not immediate life-saving surgery but a free Barbie jumper and dress set 'to cheer her up a bit'. Still, this tale was ridiculous. 'Has the database been checked?' she asked.

Smith & Taylor kept a list of those who had complained in the past so that those making a habit of false claims could be rumbled quickly.

'Yup,' replied Dino. 'The mum's clean.'

'She could have changed her address, or used a false name for the child . . .'

There was silence from Dino.

Emma was desperate. Never mind that the story was laughable, she could hear Dino's brain ticking over as if it were a cab stopped at some lights. She knew what was coming and was trying to head it off.

'I'm considering issuing a recall.'

Emma felt sick. 'But Dino, that'll cost thousands, not to mention the empty shelves and —'

Dino brushed aside her objections. 'Some things are more important than a few empty shelves, Emma,' he pronounced.

It was a fine sentiment, except that the more important thing to which Dino was referring wasn't a sick child, but the potential the situation offered him for self-promotion. Never one to miss an opportunity to polish his public image, Dino had probably booked the photo-op already.

'I put in a call to our PR people. They think I should make a public statement.'

Emma had to think fast. There was no way in hell she could replace an entire line of merchandise just like that. She had no spare stock, no likelihood of any turning up and no time to play with. 'The little girl, you say she has Attention Deficit Disorder?'

'Hmm,' said Dino absentmindedly. He was already mentally picking out his suit for the six o'clock news.

'It's a very worthy cause. Very fashionable right now.'

'Hmm.' Now he was selecting his tie.

'It certainly wouldn't hurt the company image if we were to support it.'

'What?' Dino asked, sounding interested.

'A fundraising effort, even a small one . . .'

'Small?'

'No, big, very big. A really big fundraising effort, a fashion show maybe.'

'Yes?' Dino was sounding excited.

'With a photocall to launch it,' Emma gushed. 'The TV companies would love it. Cute little girl sits on knee of . . . well, who do you suggest? We need someone from Smith and Taylor. Someone who is good in front of the camera. Someone the public trust. Now, who could that be?'

'If it's a big fundraising effort, then it would need input from the very top,' said Dino.

'Oh, yes, Dino, but do you really think you could make yourself available?'

'I'd obviously have to juggle my diary.'

'Obviously.'

'Make a few calls.'

'Yes, Dino.'

'The TV companies would love it, you say?'

'Yes, yes.'

There was silence. Dino had already gone off to consult his PR people.

'Future Fertility, can I help you?' The phone operator had the sort of singsong voice that reeked of fake cheerfulness trying to camouflage abject boredom.

'Oh, hello, yes, I, um, saw your website . . .' Gill began. 'I just called to get some, um –'

'When do you want to come in?' interrupted the woman.

'Oh, I don't want to come in. I was just . . .'

'We can see you tonight at –'

'No, no, I just wanted some information,' Gill insisted. Perhaps the operator had cut her teeth selling time shares. She was un-put-offable. 'You can get all the information you need when you come in. Tonight at six?'

'I don't know –'

'I'll put you in the book then. Name?'

'Gillian Chancellor.'

'Well, we'll see you at six then, Gill.'

Gill put down the phone and wondered what she was getting herself into.

* * *

The cheap metal chair legs scraped across the lino floor with a horrible rasp. Emma and Max sat down behind the table and looked around. The room was half full of people, mostly women in their twenties with too much gold jewellery and no tights. A few were smoking, dragging deeply on full-strength cigarettes and tipping ash on the floor, their bracelets jangling every time they did so. The atmosphere in the room was a mix of boredom and resignation. It was like the queue at Ikea on a Sunday afternoon, only less cheerful.

A man in his mid-forties, wearing jeans and a shirt, slightly crumpled, appeared. He walked to the front of the room and turned to face his audience. 'Hi, I'm Pete,' he said, offering them a hopeful smile. 'First can I say welcome to all of you. I know many of you aren't here entirely voluntarily . . .'

'You can say that again,' whispered Max.

'You're all here because the behaviour of your kids is, um, challenging, in some way . . .'

Well, that was one way of putting it, Emma thought.

'I'm sure if we all work together this can be a really beneficial learning experience for all of us,' Pete continued. Then he noticed the fog of cigarette smoke through which he was attempting to communicate. 'As part of a public health initiative, this building has a no-smoking policy,' he said, pointing to the large signs on the walls.

To Emma's left, a woman with a home-made tattoo on her wrist reading 'Tina' (not her own name, Emma suspected), and legs the colour of cold corned beef, sucked smoke through her teeth. In slow motion she flicked her cigarette on the floor. As a gesture of defiance, she didn't actually put it out, but left it there to smoulder. Emma considered leaning over and extinguishing it for her – well, it was a fire risk – but took another look at her menacing expression and decided against it. Max may have been used to dealing with the rougher end of the human scale through his work as a solicitor, but for Emma it was a bit of a shock. She felt distinctly uncomfortable.

'Now, before we start, I need to get some information,' Pete continued, his eagerness trying and failing to cut a path through the cloud of failure in the room. 'So, could you all fill in the forms you'll see in front of you. There should be Biros there as well. Anyone having problems, we have a literacy outreach officer here tonight. Sadly, the Urdu interpreter is off ill, although I'm willing to have a stab at that.'

Max reached forward and pulled a piece of paper towards him; Emma handed him a Biro from her handbag. The tattooed woman had turned round in her seat and was addressing another woman with a nose ring and bad root regrowth behind her.

'D'they wan' all our criminal convictions?' she asked.

The other woman shook her head. 'Ain't 'nuff room,

is there? Jus' th'last year, I s'pose.'

Max put a line through criminal convictions and another through 'List other children from other relationships (including any on the at-risk register or in care)'.

'Right, all done?' asked Pete. 'OK, if you could pass them up to the front.'

There was a shuffling of paper as the forms were collected.

'Now, if you could all pick up your chairs and put them in a circle,' instructed Pete. 'We'll start with a little get-to-know-you session.'

Emma took another look at the woman with the tattoo and the mottled legs. She was now chewing gum, taking it out of her mouth at intervals, inspecting it and putting it back in again. On a list of people Emma might wish to get to know she came somewhere between General Pinochet and Ann Widdecombe.

The nameplate said: 'Future Fertility Services'. The words were etched into the brass in a confident, official-looking script. It looked surprisingly old-fashioned, considering the ultra-modern service the company was offering, but maybe that was the point. Had they installed a holographic video entryphone, potential clients might have been freaked out about the unnaturalness of what they were about to agree to.

Gill pressed the button and waited.

'Hello?' a muffled female voice said.

'Gillian Chancellor. I phoned . . .'

'Third floor.'

The door buzzed and Gill pushed and pulled frenetically. Managing to get one of these doors open on the first buzz was like trying to catch a leaf falling from a tree. Gillian pressed the bell again, the woman operated the buzzer again and, at the third attempt, Gill fell across the threshold.

The inside of the building was not auspicious. The decorators were in and dust sheets swathed the staircase. The lift, one of the ancient sort with pull-across iron doors, had a hastily written sign on it: 'Out of Order'. Gillian looked up. The stairs wound upwards for four or five floors. She began to climb.

By the third floor, she was so out of breath, she had to stop and wait until she didn't feel like she was having a heart attack. She hid round the corner from the doors to the reception and coughed, so as not to appear quite so unfit in front of the receptionist. She really did have to give up smoking.

The receptionist ticked Gillian's name off a list, handed her a form attached to a clipboard and asked her to fill it in while she waited. Gill took a seat in the corner and surreptitiously observed the other patients. They were all female, all in their late thirties. Jesus, she was a cliché, a social stereotype. The Sad Single Woman.

The form asked her name, age, medical history and credit-card details. Well, there was nothing like cutting to the chase, was there? Gill suddenly felt queasy. This had nothing to do with the climb up the stairs. She stood up. 'You know, I've changed –'

A man popped his head out of an office. 'Chancellor?' he said. 'You're next.'

'Well done, Tammy, good to hear of your progress.' said Pete. 'Crack addiction is a tough one, isn't?'

There were nods and agreeing murmurs from all round the circle.

'Who's next?' Pete continued, looking expectantly at Emma and Max.

Emma cleared her throat. 'Um, I'm, um . . .'

Max took over. 'She's Emma; I'm Max, her husband.'

'Sorry, did you say husband?' asked Pete. 'Don't get many of those,' he said brightly.

All eyes in the room swivelled to study Max as if he were the Elephant Man. He shifted uncomfortably in his seat, although maybe he'd have done that anyway. The textured plastic was beginning to imprint itself on his buttocks.

Pete was smiling encouragingly. 'Well, this is Emma and her HUSBAND Max, everybody. Let's get some background. History of substance abuse?'

'No,' Emma said firmly.

'Alcohol? Amphetamines? Cocaine? Heroin?'

'No,' she said again.

Pete frowned. Clearly this was not a normal

occurrence. 'Solvents? Glue? Lighter fluid?'

'No.'

'Prescription medication?'

'Well, there was that eucalyptus inhaler the doctor gave me last winter for my chest,' Max offered helpfully.

'The sperm is delivered in one of these,' Keith explained. 'It's really very simple.'

'But it's a . . .' Gill spluttered.

'Yes, a Thermos flask. We find they do the job just fine.'

The flask was tartan, eerily similar to the one Charlotte Chancellor had always produced on whatever chilly beach they were spending their summer holiday as children. Usually, it had been Prestatyn, but one year they had branched out and headed for Charmouth in Dorset. The sea hadn't been noticeably warmer. The collision of this childhood memory with the notion of buying live sperm was faintly horrifying.

Gill looked at Keith. She wasn't sure he was a doctor. He wasn't wearing a white coat, but maybe that was just post *ER* modern practice. Still, he certainly seemed to know his way around a syringe. He was holding it up to the light, pushing the plunger in and out and admiring it, as if it were a priceless piece of Baccarat crystal. Considering the price the company were charging, it might as well have been.

If Gill wanted to go ahead, there was a two-hundred-pound registration fee, following which her name would go on to the website. Then any man who fancied earning seventy-five pounds could access it and the company would 'manage' the match. For this they charged a further two hundred pounds. Then they added the cost of ensuring the donor had up-to-date tests for Aids, hepatitis and a whole host of other unappetising sexually transmitted conditions, some involving the word wart. It all meant Gill wouldn't get much change out of a thousand pounds.

'But you can't put a price on a child,' Keith said, ignoring the fact he had just done so.

Keith's shiny suit was off-putting, as was his habit of over-using her name. 'So, Gill, when was the first day of your last period, if you can remember, Gill?' Gill didn't particularly want to discuss her menstrual cycle with a total stranger in a shiny suit, but he was persuasive. And so what if he was a bit slimy? That didn't mean the father of any child she might possibly have would automatically be a slimeball too.

Gill's sperm donor could be a hugely intelligent but penniless brain surgeon looking for a quick and easy way to raise some cash. Was there such a thing as a penniless brain surgeon? Probably not. Well, maybe he was a Bavarian prince whose castle needed a new roof, Bavarian princes not being as flush as they once were. More likely he was a penniless student who wanted some beer money. Still, if his sperm could swim in the right direction, who was Gill to argue? Not, of course, that she was going to go through with it.

'So, Gill, is it Access or Visa?'

Chapter Nine

'Tell me we never have to do that again,' said Max, sitting up in bed.

Emma was already by the window, winching up the blind. The early morning sunlight flooded into the room, throwing a shaft of brightness across the duvet cover as crisp and clear as a newly painted yellow line on fresh tarmac.

Emma turned back to Max. 'We never have to do a parenting workshop again,' she said. 'Unless Saskia ever gets herself arrested again, I suppose. Then we'd have to.'

'No, no, not the woman with the tattoos, please,' Max groaned, pulling the duvet over his head.

Emma laughed and walked over to the bed. 'Actually, I was thinking of getting one, so I fitted in better next time. What do you think about a bunch of cherries on my right hip? Or maybe a swallow on my shoulder? Then again, I could just have "love" on one set of knuckles and "hate" on the other.'

'Ooh, sexy,' Max said, emerging from the duvet, putting his hands on her hips and pulling her to him. He buried his head in the softness of her T-shirt-covered tummy.

Emma stroked his hair and kissed the top of his head.

'Come back to bed,' he coaxed.

'Max, I've got loads to do and . . .'

Max pulled Emma on to the bed. She rolled on to her back and he climbed on top, pinning down her arms. 'Now you're all mine,' he said, kissing her.

'But what about . . .?'

'Oh, I forgot to tell you.' He gave her a broad grin. 'We came in so late last night and, well, I forgot.'

'What?' asked Emma.

'Dominique's gone.'

'Gone!' Emma would have done a jig if Max hadn't been sitting on her legs. 'What do you mean, gone?'

'I had a word with her and suggested she patch things up with Denzel and . . . well, I don't want to take too much credit, but . . .' Max said, clearly waiting for as much credit to come his way as possible.

'Oh, Max.' Emma sat up and hugged him. Then she froze. 'Has she taken Kevin? Say she's taken Kevin.'

'Of course she has. She wouldn't leave him behind, would she?'

Emma pulled her head back so she could see Max's face. 'Well, she's done it before, Max.'

'That was years ago. She's much more mature now.'

Emma could have argued with Max on this point, but she decided not to. She was far too happy. 'Whatever you say,' she agreed, smiling.

'So, we've got the house to ourselves,' Max said, pulling at her T-shirt.

'Apart from Saskia,' Emma pointed out.

Max glanced at his watch. 'Seven o'clock – should be having breakfast by now, so she isn't late for school.'

'School?'

'I had a word with her too.'

Emma kissed Max, then she put her arms up. He pulled her T-shirt clean over her head.

When Gill got to work at 10.00 a.m., her head was still full of her trip to Future Fertility. Of course she'd given Keith her credit card – well, she could always cancel it, couldn't she? But she knew she wouldn't. Her name was probably at that moment being posted on the website. Unshaven students with one hand down their pyjamas were no doubt scrolling through it. Yuk! That sounded horrible. But still, she hadn't called Future Fertility to tell them she'd changed her mind. She hadn't done anything. She was leaving it to fate.

Gus looked serious when Gill got to the bar.

'What's up?' Gill asked.

'Boss's in,' Gus explained. 'He's in the back. I tried to cover for you . . .'

Gill heard a voice with an all-too-familiar plummy accent coming from behind her. 'How nice of you to join us.'

It was Alex Bonnington, owner of Bliss. Alex was the

son of Lord Somebody-or-other. Dad stayed in the country, minding the family seat. Son, who reckoned he had an entrepreneurial streak, ran Bliss.

'Sorry, I um . . .' Gill began.

'Sorry you're late?' Alex asked. 'We start at nine-thirty. But you're always late, aren't you, um . . .'

'Gill.'

'Yes, Gill.'

Gill and Alex had only met once before. She'd been late on that occasion too. Alex had seen her around, of course, but Alex Bonnington didn't fraternise with the staff. And Gill was very definitely staff. Gus was hiding behind the bar, out of the line of fire.

'I wonder, Gill,' Alex continued, 'whether you see your future in the area of entertainment and leisure?'

'Well . . .'

'Or whether, since you seem incapable of dragging yourself out of bed, you might prefer to seek employment in another mileu?'

'Meel what?' Gus whispered.

'I think this milieu suits me just fine, actually,' Gill said defiantly. 'I don't think you'll find the customers complaining. I'm very popul –'

'Well, now you come to mention it . . .' Alex took a step towards Gill. He was average height, about five feet ten, with short blonded hair and skin bronzed from long summers in St Tropez. His eyes were the pale blue of old-fashioned air-mail envelopes. Gill was close enough to see his pale eyelashes. 'Not all our customers are as enamoured of you as you seem to believe.' He paused. 'A footballing acquaintance of mine was in the other day with a rather important table and you refused to get him a drink.'

Gill frowned.

'Apparently you were too busy talking to the barman. Now, who could that have been?' Alex turned to look at Gus, who ducked even lower behind the bar. 'When he asked if you were a member of my staff, you uttered the immortal phrase: "I'm on a break."'

Gill thought for a minute, then she remembered the night she'd discovered the piece of paper with Jake's name written on it. There'd been that aggressive guy who'd marched up to her asking if she worked there and she'd told him to get stuffed. So, he was a friend of Alex's. 'Oh, sh –' Gill exclaimed.

'Quite,' Alex added crisply. 'Your attitude is clearly not sufficiently work-oriented. The next thing you'll be telling me is you want to run off and have lots of babies and I'm supposed to ban smoking from the bar and give you bloody maternity leave!'

Gill coughed but said nothing.

'Right,' continued Alex. 'I hope I've made myself clear, um . . .'

'Gill.'

'Whatever. Now, get on with your work.'

Alex went back into his office and Gus popped up

from behind the bar. He had his head tipped to one side with his tongue stuck out at an angle. One hand was raised as if holding the other end of the noose from which he was being hanged.

'Blimey!' Emma exclaimed. She was standing at the hall table, holding a piece of paper. Max was downstairs in the kitchen, sorting through post.

'What now?' he shouted up.

'It's Saskia,' Emma replied.

'Oh, God, we aren't going to have to go back to that class, are we?'

Emma had begun to walk down the stairs. Max could see her feet as she spoke. 'No, no, it's good news,' she said, her body gradually coming into view.

Max frowned. Good news? That didn't sound very likely.

When Emma got to the bottom she handed Max the piece of paper.

Hands Across the Ocean: a multi-faith (and no-faith) celebration of global empathy [it read]. Dove Community School invites you to an evening of music and dance. The programme will include demonstrations of traditional Sikh sword dancing by year 2, Inuit igloo construction by year 3 (warm clothing recommended) and Masai body

piercing by year 5. Mrs Warman is still
looking for volunteers for this. Anyone
interested, please contact the staff room.

'Is this a joke?' Max asked.

'Do you mean the igloo-building or the fact that
Saskia appears to have left it out for us?'

'Both.'

'The igloo thing is, I fear, all too serious. As for Saskia,
I can't see how she would have left it on the hall table by
accident. It was propped up.'

'But she didn't go to school yesterday, so how?!'

'She must have had it for ages, been hoarding it.'

'So why get it out now? When is it, by the way?'

'Harvest Festival – end of the month.'

Every year, Saskia's school mounted a Harvest Festival
celebration, except they didn't call it that because that
would have been to predicate the event upon a date in
the Christian calendar, which wasn't PC. So they called it
a celebration of global empathy or some other wishy-
washy twaddle. Whatever they called it, however, Emma
and Max were never invited. Saskia always managed to
lose the letter so effectively that if they did ever find it,
it was two months late.

'Do you think she wants us to come?' Max asked
gingerly.

'That's what it looks like,' Emma said. 'Maybe that
whole scene at the police station did actually achieve

something, after all. Maybe the last few days with her mother have persuaded her that we're not so bad after all. Maybe she's . . .'

'Turning over a new leaf?' Max offered.

'Is it too much to hope for?' Emma sounded scared.

Max put an arm round her. 'Well, her hormones had to stop swirling about at some point, didn't they?'

'I suppose so. It's just . . .'

'I know,' Max said soothingly. 'Let's face it, after the week we've had, it's time for a bit of peace and quiet round here, isn't it?'

'Fucking Alex fucking Bonnington,' Gill fumed. 'I hate him. He can't even remember my fucking name.'

'Jesus!' Chloë exclaimed. 'What happened? Something at work?'

Gill had just come in and, having thrown her jacket on the sofa, was now mixing herself a Bloody Mary, a large one, by the fridge. Chloë had got out of the shower and had a towel wrapped round her. Her wet hair was dripping on the tiled floor, making a *rat, tat, tat* noise.

'I was only a little bit late, but he has to make a big deal out of it . . .' Gil took a long gulp of her drink.

'Shall I put that on an intravenous drip for you?' Chloë asked. 'Slow down and tell me what happened.'

Gill put the glass on the worktop. 'I was late and Alex was there and Gus, lord love him, had tried to cover for me, but it's the second time Alex knows I've been late . . .'

'As opposed to the truth, which is that you're always late?'

'Yeah, so is that a crime now?'

'No, but it is a sacking matter. Anyway, what did Alex say?'

'He said I had a problem with my attitude and, get this' – Gill laughed hoarsely – 'that I'd better not run off and have lots of babies.'

'Well, you're not going to run off and have lots of babies, are you?'

There was no answer.

'Gill? What have you done?'

'Nothing, I just . . . Well, you know . . . that website.'

'Oh, Jesus, Gill. Let me get a towel for my hair. I'm creating Lake Victoria here on the floor. Mix me one of those and you can tell me all about it.'

When Chloë got back, Gill was sitting on the sofa. A drink was waiting on the coffee table. 'Thanks,' Chloë said, taking a sip. 'Now, what exactly have you done?' She lit a cigarette, offering one to Gill, who took it.

'I just rang up that website,' Gill said, inhaling and blowing out smoke nervously.

'And . . .?'

'I went to see them.'

'And . . .?'

'I can always get my money back.'

Chloë threw her head back and groaned. 'Oh, Gill, you gave them money. Why? What have you agreed to?'

'They've just put my name on the website, which, um, men who want to donate, um, sperm, can, um, access.'

'Look, are we agreed that I've been around the block a few times?' Chloë asked.

'You've been round the block so many times, you've worn a groove in the pavement.'

'OK, no need to be rude.'

'Sorry.'

'Well, one thing I do know is that only a fool would set out to be a single mother. Yes, we all have our wobbly moments when we think what is the point of all this, but then we look at the alternative – which is smelly nappies and sleepless nights – and realise how bloody lucky we are.'

'I know, but . . .'

'There are no buts. Our mothers didn't have this choice, Gill. Mine had three kids by my age. She was finished. No career. No job. She even had to ask my dad for money if she wanted to get her hair done. I don't want that life, do you?'

'No, but . . .'

'And my mum and yours, well, they had husbands to help out. You'd have no one to ask for money even if you could bear to do it. You would be on benefits, Gill.'

'I'm sure my family would help.'

'Are you? Are you really? Your mum and dad are away on this trip, aren't they? Don't you think they want to enjoy their retirement? What makes you think they'd be happy to do the night feeds at their time of life? It wouldn't be fair even if they did agree. And Emma, she's got her hands full, more than full from what you tell me. Face it, Gill, it's impossible.'

The end of Gill's cigarette was damp from the tears that were now flowing. 'I know, I know,' she sobbed. 'And if I was like you and was happy having a different man every night . . .'

'Thanks.'

Gill put her sodden cigarette in the ashtray. 'You know what I mean. If I was a . . .'

'Slapper?'

'No, no, I was going to say a more happy-go-lucky person, then maybe it would be OK, but I'm not happy, Chloë.'

'And you think having a baby is the solution to that? Come here.' Chloë hugged Gill as she sobbed. 'Look, give me the number of the clinic and I'll call them and cancel, OK?'

Gill nodded.

'And that'll be an end to it.'

When the phone rang, Emma was clearing out a drawer in the kitchen. It was the sort of job she never normally had time for. But it was Saturday and she fancied playing Domestic Goddess for once. 'Hello,' she said cheerfully into the receiver.

''Ello, Emma, is Dino.'

Emma's heart sank. Couldn't Dino leave her alone for twenty-four hours? 'Hello, Dino, how are you?' she said as breezily as she could manage.

'Never mind me, how is fashion show?'

Emma gasped. She'd forgotten all about the fashion show she'd promised to organise. To be honest, she'd hoped that Dino might forget about it too. Apparently, that had been a vain hope.

'Oh, yes, fine,' Emma said.

'Naomi Campbell,' Dino announced.

Emma frowned. 'What about her?'

''Ave we got 'er?'

'I know supermodels are slim, Dino, but I don't think even Naomi Campbell can get into children's clothing.'

'Oh.' He sounded downcast. 'Britney Spears?'

Dino clearly had an inflated idea of the importance of Smith & Taylor's childrenswear collection.

'Why don't we really push the boat out and get Christina Aguilera, Robbie Williams and Michael Jackson? Well, perhaps not Michael Jackson,' Emma corrected herself.

'Christina Aguilera? Do you think we could?'

'No, Dino, I don't. I was joking.'

Dino was suddenly angry. When he was angry, his accent was stronger. 'Well, I no' joking. Thees fashion show gotta be good, OK?'

'Yes, Dino.'

'I no be happy if rubbish.'

'Yes, Dino.'

'And if I no' happy, you no' happy.'

'Yes, Dino.'

There was a loud click as Dino slammed the phone down.

Gill ran a finger along the ribbing around the collar of a cashmere crew neck. It felt as soft as the down on a new chick. 'Bloody hell, Em. One hundred and eighty quid!' she said. 'It's for a four-month-old baby, not Pava-bloody-rotti.'

'It's not the size, it's the effort that goes into it,' Emma pointed out.

'I've heard that before and I didn't believe it then either,' laughed Gill.

Little Angels was a children's clothing emporium. That was emporium as opposed to shop. Emporia sold things, but they were much, much more expensive. So there were cashmere jumpers at almost two hundred pounds a pop, as well as designer bibs, bottles and other trinkets. It catered for mothers who, having seen their social life and bosoms wither post childbirth, were desperate to spend money on something, anything.

Emma was here on an industrial spying mission. It was part of her job to keep abreast of the competition. Smith & Taylor might have trouble shifting a baby's bib fashioned from hand-tooled leather, but they might get away with a PVC version, so long as it was easily wipeable and she could get it on the shelves for £1.99.

Gill was depressed. After her bollocking from Alex, she knew that any idea of having a baby was out of the question. She'd lose her job for a start. She'd come on the shopping trip with Emma because she needed cheering up. The fact that they were in a baby shop wasn't making the outing quite as cheerful as she had hoped. She picked up a sheepskin Babygro in lilac and brushed it across her cheek. It felt divine. 'Don't tell me, second mortgage time,' she said, dropping it down to waist level, finding the tag and turning it over. 'Shit! Four hundred! Do they still send kids up chimneys?'

'Not in one of those they don't,' Emma said. 'It's dry-clean only. Actually, the people who shop here don't have to put their kids up chimneys. They put them in *Hello!* instead. It pays much better and there are no grubby hand prints to worry about afterwards.'

'Well, my kid is going to have to beg money on the tube if this is how much things cost,' Gillian said.

'Your kid?'

'My hypothetical kid.'

'Is that like an invisible friend?'

'Similar, but you don't have to set a place for it at dinner.'

Emma and Gill rounded the corner of a circular clothes rack and began looking at miniature combat pants.

'Anyway, how're things?' Gill asked.

'Oh, work's a bit busy, got this fashion show to

organise. Other than that, things are pretty good,' answered Emma.

'You certainly seem a lot happier,' Gill said.

Emma laughed now. 'I think the last time, you got me on a bad day,' she said. 'Dominique's gone.'

'Oh, thank God. I thought she'd stapled herself to the carpet.'

'What's even more amazing is Saskia seems to have seen the error of her ways.'

Gill was holding a miniature lizard-skin cowboy boot with gold spurs. She was momentarily stunned. When she pulled herself together, she managed to splutter, 'Saskia has what?'

'Seen the error of her ways.'

'Teenagers never see the error of their ways. Well, not until they're at least thirty-two, anyway.'

'Well, that's what it looks like. Max and I went to this appalling parenting workshop and maybe that made her feel guilty. Now she's invited us to her school concert.'

'Invited you? But I thought . . .'

'Well, not exactly invited. She left the piece of paper from school all about it on the hall table, so that's pretty much the same thing, isn't it?'

'I suppose.' Gill sounded doubtful.

'I can't believe it. After five years of hormone hell, she may finally be turning back into a human being.'

'If you say so.' This time Gill sounded even more doubtful.

A woman in leather chaps and a suede jacket trimmed with fluffy marabou hovered near Emma. 'Would you mind?' she asked.

'No, no, sorry,' Emma replied, stepping to one side so she could pass. The woman had a baby balanced on one hip and she was talking on a mobile. Emma vaguely recognised her. Then she remembered. She was the aristo supermodel who'd been at Max's boss's party. She looked even thinner close up. It was like standing next to an anorexic giraffe.

'Joelly Childs,' Gill whispered. 'Comes into Bliss sometimes. Her brother's . . .'

'Oh, but I really need a new handbag . . .' Joelly was shouting into her mobile. 'No, that one's too big. I just need to be able to get a bottle in it . . .'

Emma raised an eyebrow. She was looking at the baby. Poor little mite. Mother out nightclubbing when she should be at home breastfeeding. Gillian was wondering why Joelly Childs needed to bring her own bottles into nightclubs. Surely she could afford to buy a round of drinks, even at Bliss's prices.

'No, not a bottle of vodka!' Joelly laughed. 'A bottle of milk! Look, I'll see you later, bye.' She picked up the lilac sheepskin Babygro without looking at the price tag and went up to the counter.

Gill, watching her, thought how easy it must be to be that rich. She was sure Joelly Childs hadn't had to consider whether her boss would give her maternity leave. She probably had so much money she could afford to take the rest of her life off if she wanted to. She felt a surge of envy.

Emma turned back to Gill and saw her frown. 'Anyway, what about you?' she said. 'You look tired.'

Gill stopped looking at Joelly, turned back to Emma and smiled weakly. 'Oh, I'm OK, just got a bit of a bollocking at work. It's nothing.'

'Are you sure?'

Emma looked so happy, Gill didn't want to spoil the atmosphere by telling her about the fertility clinic, especially as now she wasn't going to go through with it. Emma would give her a lecture and Gill wasn't really up to that. Gill changed the subject. 'Well, good luck with the school concert. What's Saskia doing? I take it she's passed the playing "Au Clair de la Lune" excruciatingly badly on the recorder stage?'

'Yeah. I don't know what she's doing. I think she's going to surprise us.'

Chapter Ten

The car park was like Sainsbury's on a Saturday afternoon. Max edged the car past the massed ranks of Espaces and Scenics in vain.

'Look, why don't you get out? I'll take the car round the corner and meet you inside.'

Emma undid her seatbelt and climbed out. As she did so, she almost collided with a woman whose vision was impeded by the fact she was wearing a burka. She was with three demure little girls in headscarves. She looked like a Dalek duck with a trio of Dalek ducklings paddling around the side of a lake.

'Sorry,' said Emma.

'Bollocks,' said the smallest duckling.

Well, that's what you get for sending your child to school in Islington, thought Emma.

This school had actually been Saskia's choice. When she was eleven, Emma and Max had experimented with allowing Saskia self-determination. This was before she became determined to cause havoc for herself and everyone else. Max had expressed concerns about the

SATs results. However, the headmistress showed them the fully functioning tropical rainforest eco-bubble on the roof and Saskia was hooked.

Thanks to extra government funding for 'improving' schools, otherwise known as ones that would be closed down if they didn't stop being completely crap, they also had twenty-first-century electronic whiteboards in every classroom. Max was rather impressed with this, although Emma had noted that none were ever in use because the twentieth-century teachers hadn't the slightest idea how to work them. Still, at least they didn't get chalk on their maharishi pants.

Emma followed the crowd shuffling towards the front door. It was flanked on one side by two pupils taking tickets and on the other by someone dressed as a hamburger. He was standing underneath a banner which read: 'Burgers from Heaven. Divine intervention that delivers success in schools!'

'Would you like a Heavenly Study Snack?' asked a teenage boy in a Burgers from Heaven sweatshirt and baseball cap. 'Packed full of essential nutrients and brain-boosting vitamins and minerals, it's the snack that's made for success!' He was holding a hamburger and a carton of chips.

'Isn't that a hamburger and a carton of chips?' Emma asked, bemused.

'Well, yes,' the boy whispered. 'But we've been told to call it a Heavenly Study Snack and anyone who doesn't gets detention for a week. Please take one,' he pleaded.

Emma mutely accepted her limp burger and limper fries.

'Ah, there you are,' said Max, joining her. 'What's that?'

'A Heavenly Study Snack,' Emma replied.

'Looks like a . . .'

'I know, but suspend your disbelief or the kid gets it. Detention, that is.'

Max shook his head in confusion. 'Any sign of Dominique?'

'No,' replied Emma. 'Or Saskia. I do hope tonight goes well for her. She seemed genuinely excited this morning. You know she actually asked if we were coming?'

Max bent forward and took a bite out of Emma's hamburger. 'Hallelujah!' he exclaimed.

Gill stared at the motorcycle messenger. 'Yes, that's right. Gillian Chancellor.'

The messenger handed her his clipboard, clammy from the wind and rain, and a pen. 'Sign at the bottom,' he ordered.

'But I didn't . . .'

'I just deliver the packets, lady. You're Gillian Chancellor. Sign at the bottom.'

Gill did as she was told. The messenger took the clipboard back, rifled through the box on the back of his bike, and pulled out a large brown Jiffy bag.

'Here,' he said, handing it to her. 'Good luck.' Gill was sure she saw him wink.

Gill shut the door and sat on the bottom step of the stairs. She pulled at the top of the bag where it was stapled. The bag opened and she peered in. She could see something round and plastic. Gill squinted, but couldn't make out any more in the gloom of the bag. She reached in and pulled something out. It was a Thermos flask.

When Emma and Max got inside, they spotted Dominique immediately. She was lying down on the stage, being attended to by two St John Ambulance volunteers. Kevin was unrolling bandages at her feet. Max rushed over. 'My God, what's happened?' he asked, appalled.

'Stand back, sir, stand back. Nothing to see,' said one of the ambulance men.

'No, she's my, my . . .'

'Cross to bear?' muttered Emma.

'My ex-wife. She's my ex-wife,' Max said.

'Oh, Max,' said Dominique, sitting up. 'I had a body wrap this morning and now I've come over all weak.'

'What's a body wrap?' Max asked.

'It's where they . . .' Dominique began.

'Shame they didn't wrap her mouth,' one of the ambulance men whispered. 'She hasn't shut up since we got here and as for the kid . . .'

Kevin had now discovered the splints and was attempting to jab Max in the leg with one.

'Thank you, Kevin,' Max said, trying to protect himself.

'Sorry, guv, but we need to clear the stage,' the other ambulance man said to Max officiously. 'Can you take over now?'

'Good luck, mate,' the first one said, rolling his eyes.

Max climbed up on to the stage, thereby escaping Kevin momentarily, and helped Dominique down the steps at the side of the stage. Then they all looked round for some spare seats. The room looked like the backstage area before the national dress section of a Miss World contest. Every national costume was represented, from African loincloths to Austrian dirndl skirts, through saris, kimonos and exotic Caribbean garlands.

'You can feel the world coming closer together, can't you?' said a middle-aged woman in a Moroccan djellaba standing beside them.

At that moment, a small child in an Albanian gypsy outfit closed a fist round the handle of Emma's handbag. She wrenched it free. 'Closer, yes, absolutely,' she said.

'Over there,' Max said, pointing at three free seats. As they approached, the lights began to go down.

A stout woman in a velvet maxi-skirt and Paisley blouse climbed on to the stage. It was Mrs Marshall, the headmistress, or team target facilitator, as she was now officially known. 'Ladies and gentlemen, mums and dads, carers and court-appointed guardians,' she began. 'Thank you all for coming tonight. Later, of course, there is the Inuit igloo-building demonstration on the netball pitch, so I hope you've all brought your woollies. Sadly, the Sikh sword dancing has had to be abandoned. For those who were asking, Mr Thompson is now in a stable condition and off the ventilator. So, well done to him.'

There was a spontaneous round of applause. Max squeezed Emma's hand. 'So nice to be here as a family,' he said.

'So tell me, why have you got me here?' Gus said.

'And me,' Chloë agreed. 'I was meant to be on a date tonight. I only cancelled because I'm not feeling great.'

'You're always on a date,' said Gus.

'About the only man Chloë hasn't been on a date with is the Archbishop of Canterbury,' Gill said. 'And that's only because –'

'She doesn't like men in dresses?'

'Men in women's clothing is more your line, isn't it, Gill?' Chloë said mischievously. 'Anyway, what's the big mystery? What's going on?'

Gill, Chloë and Gus were all in the kitchen of Gill and Chloë's flat. They were sitting round the table. Either the floor was uneven or the table had one leg much shorter than the others, because it wobbled like a child's rubber dinghy in a choppy sea. Gill got up and went to the fridge. She took out the Thermos.

'No thanks, I've eaten already,' Gus said.

'It's not soup, idiot,' Gill said.

'Well, what is it, iced coffee, tea? Are you thinking of going on a long journey?'

Gill unscrewed the top and put it on the table, then, carefully, she took out a syringe and a sample jar.

'Oh, my God!' Chloë shouted.

'My reaction entirely when I got this.'

'Jesus, Gill, I'm sorry. I meant to make the call, I really did. It's just . . .'

'Would someone tell me what's going on?' Gus demanded.

Gill picked up the pot and held it up to the light. 'I'm surprised you don't recognise this, Gus. It's sperm.'

'Sperm?'

'Yes, and I ordered it over the Internet, only I thought I'd unordered it, or rather that Chloë had unordered it, only she forgot, didn't you?'

'God, I'm so sorry, Gill, I really am. But I don't know why you left it to me. You know I'm crap at organising things.'

'You offered!' Gill exclaimed.

'I know, I know.'

Gus took the pot from Gill and studied it. 'There isn't very much, is there?'

'Typical bloke,' said Chloë. 'Quantity over quality every time.'

'You don't know if it is quality, do you, Gill?' asked Gus. 'Whose is it, by the way?'

'Well, it's mine, now.'

'Yeah, but whose was it?'

'I don't know. The donor is anonymous.'

Gus put the pot down and frowned. 'I still don't get it. Why did you order sperm over the Internet?'

'To have a baby,' Gill said. 'I wanted to have a baby, then I decided I didn't, but I've got the sperm anyway.'

'So what are you going to do?' Chloë asked.

'How the hell should I know?' Gill replied.

'Now, before we start,' Mrs Marshall continued, 'I'd like to thank Burgers from Heaven for all their support. Brad Zimmerman, marketing director for Burgers from Heaven, is with us this evening.'

A man so scrubbed he appeared to have been peeled, stood up, turned and saluted the crowd. He was wearing a Burgers from Heaven tie.

Mrs Marshall carried on. 'The new canteen has proved a huge success and the soft-drink vending machines now installed in every classroom are running at eighty-three per cent of target spend. So keep up the good work, everybody, and remember, Burgers from Heaven puts the fizz into the study day.'

There was another spontaneous round of applause.

'Now, we begin this evening with the Sixth Form singing a truly inspirational song.'

The curtains behind Mrs Marshall opened jerkily to reveal several rows of teenagers all dressed in Burgers from Heaven sweatshirts and baseball caps. Saskia was in the second row in the middle.

'Is she . . .?' asked Max.

'Yes, smiling,' Emma answered, equally amazed.

A few dads bobbed to their feet with camcorders. A man in a beige corduroy jacket – a relic from a former time: the man as well as the jacket – began hammering a tune out of a half-dead upright piano at the side of the stage.

Then the kids began to sing.

> 'Burgers from Heaven, you are tops,
> Making sure that we aren't flops.'

As all the children sang, Saskia reached down and began to pull her Burgers from Heaven sweatshirt over her head. Emma and Max exchanged puzzled glances. It didn't seem especially warm in the school hall, so why was Saskia undressing?

> 'Commercial rivals, can't you see'

Saskia now had the top above her head. Fortunately, she was wearing another T-shirt underneath. Something was written on it.

> 'Burgers from Heaven helps us academically.'

Saskia threw the Burgers from Heaven shirt to one side

and pushed her way to the front of the stage. As the singing died, she extended her arms outwards. 'MEAT IS MURDER!' she shouted, a sentiment echoed on the front of her T-shirt.

There was a horrified silence, broken abruptly by a shriek. Brad Zimmerman, Burgers from Heaven's UK marketing director, vaulted on to the stage and rugby tackled Saskia. 'MEAT IS MURDER!' Saskia bellowed again as she went down.

Brad had his arms round her waist. Saskia took hold of his tie and began to strangle him with it. 'Why, you little shit,' he shouted, his voice sounding increasingly constricted. 'I'm only five per cent away from my bonus and no silly little girl is going to stand in my way.'

By now, the other kids had taken up Saskia's chant. 'Meat is murder!' they shouted. 'Meat is murder.' Some were tearing off their sweatshirts and stamping on them.

Mrs Marshall now climbed back on to the stage, one hand genteelly picking up her velevet maxi-skirt as she went. 'Children, please,' she said, spectacularly ineffectually. 'This is no way to treat our sponsor.'

There was a whizzing sound as the massed ranks of parental camcorders zoomed in on Brad Zimmerman's now purple face. He wrenched himself free of Saskia's grasp, loosening his tie as he sat up. Mrs Marshall put out a hand to help him up. 'I'm so sorry, Mr Zimmerman,' she said.

'You'll be hearing from the company about this,' Mr Zimmerman replied.

The pianist had carried on playing throughout, like a plucky band member at an East End dance hall during the Blitz. There might have been doodlebugs overhead but he was getting to the end of the song if it killed him. In this case, it was Burgers from Heaven sweatshirts that were raining down upon him, but he carried on regardless, a tangle of sleeves now decorating his head and shoulders.

Mrs Marshall swivelled her head to look at Mr Corduroy. 'Oh, shut the fuck up,' she said.

'What I don't understand is how it got here so quickly,' Chloë said, looking at the Jiffy bag. 'Bearing in mind how long it took my holiday postcards to arrive.'

Chloë had retired to bed. She was beginning to feel quite ill. Period pains, she said. Still, Gill had made her a hot-water bottle and she had that pressed to her stomach. Gill and Gus were sitting on top of the duvet.

'They biked it,' Gill said, shaking her head in disbelief. 'This stuff has a use-by date, you know.'

'How long is that?' Gus asked.

'I don't know,' Gill said. 'You've got the instructions.'

'Typical,' Gus said. 'Expect the bloke to be able to understand the instructions. We're not building a flat-pack here. We're making a baby.'

'Are we?' Chloë asked.

'I don't know,' Gill said. 'I need a cigarette.'

'Bad for the baby,' Gus chided her.

'There isn't any baby. Not yet. Maybe not ever.'

Chloë tossed Gill a packet of cigarettes. Gill was still enough in denial of her smoking that she was refusing to buy her own cigarettes except in a dire emergency – that is, if she wasn't with anyone she could borrow one off.

'Of course, you know what'll happen,' Gus said to Chloë. 'If she does get herself up the spout, she'll turn into one of them.'

'One of who?' Gill asked.

'One of the Boring Mummy Brigade. You'll give up alcohol, stay in all the time and become addicted to the soaps.'

'And she'll have dinner lady arms,' Chloë added.

'What?' asked Gill.

'Those flabby arms women who never go to the gym have,' explained Chloë.

'When was the last time you went to the gym?' Gill said.

'I've been too busy.'

Gus was hunched over the instructions. 'I never was any good at Airfix kits,' he said. 'Now, give me a Barbie to dress and I'm fine.' He held up the syringe and played with the plunger. Then he picked up the pot and studied the measurements on the side.

Chloë shuffled her bottom up the bed, closer to him. 'I

don't think it's that complicated,' she said. 'That goes in there and that goes in there and –'

'Ooh, it's like *The Krypton Factor*,' Gus said.

'Well, I'm glad you two are enjoying yourselves,' Gill said. 'This is supposed to be a deeply meaningful moment. The moment of conception.'

Chloë and Gus exchanged glances.

'She really is turning into one of them, isn't she?' Gus said.

'Yeah,' Chloë agreed.

'Dinner lady arms,' Gus said solemnly.

'What's this with the dinner lady arms? I do not have dinner lady arms. I'm not going to get dinner lady arms.'

Gus shook his head. 'And this is how she is before the hormones have kicked in.'

'And the sleep deprivation.'

'Shut up, both of you,' Gill said. 'And give me the instructions.'

'So, are you going to do it, then?' Gus said breathlessly.

'Maybe the fact you didn't cancel it, Chloë, maybe the fact it's here is fate. Maybe I'm supposed to do it. It's just . . .'

'What?' asked Chloë.

'It seems so clinical.'

'What do you want? Candles and a Barry White CD?' asked Gus. 'This is what it boils down to.'

'I think if you boil it, it definitely won't work,' Chloë said.

Gill picked up the sample jar, the syringe and the instructions. 'I'm going to my room for a while. Are you OK on your own, Chloë?'

Chloë nodded.

'Go home, Gus. I'll talk to you tomorrow.'

'But are you . . .?'

'Go home, Gus.'

Chapter Eleven

The morning after the school concert, Max was lying in bed with a pillow over his head, while Emma remonstrated with Saskia downstairs. Remonstrated was a polite word for what was actually going on, which was Emma and Saskia shouting at each other through her bedroom door.

'Saskia! Open this door at once,' Emma ordered.

'No. It's my bedroom and you can't come in,' Saskia shouted back.

'Open this door, Saskia. I want to talk to you.'

'No. Go away. I hate you!'

'You don't hate me, Saskia.'

'Yes I do.'

'No you don't.'

'Can't you even allow me to have my own opinions? Do you have to run my life all the time? You are such a control freak.'

'I am not a control freak. I just want the best for you.'

'Your idea of what's best for me. What about what I want?'

Emma sighed. 'What do you want?'

'I want you to go away.'

Emma looked at her watch. She was late for work again.

Buzz, buzz . . . Buzz, Buzzzz.'

Whoever was pressing the buzzer was jolly persistent.

'Sorry, Chloë, I think I'd better get that,' Gillian said, getting up off the bed.

Chloë nodded weakly. She was still not feeling well. The period pains were, if anything, worse.

'Hello, who is it?' Gill said into the intercom.

'Well, it's about bloody time,' Gus answered. 'Let me in.'

Gill pressed the door-open button and waited for Gus to climb the stairs.

'So, did you do it then?' asked Gus, eagerly.

Gill could hear Chloë moaning from the other room.

'Um, can we talk about this later? Chloë's not well. I mean, really not well,' she said.

'How not well is that?' Gus asked, concerned.

'Come and see.'

As Gus and Gill walked up the hall, they heard a horrible sound from Chloë's room. It was half scream, half sigh. 'Jesus!' Gill shouted, pushing the door open and rushing in.

Chloë was half out of bed. Her skin was waxy and very white and covered with a fine dusting of sweat. It glittered in the light from her bedside lamp. Gill had closed the curtains and put the lamp on, thinking it would be more soothing than daylight. Now it gave everything a dramatic film noir glow.

'Christ!' Gus said, kneeling down beside Chloë and taking her wrist in one hand. 'Call an ambulance.'

Gill was rooted to the spot. 'Is she dead?'

'No, I don't think so. I think I can feel a pulse,' Gus said. 'Ring nine nine nine now! *Do it*, Gill.'

Gill ran up the hall into the living room where the phone was kept. She dialled and waited. As she waited, the vision of Chloë, half slumped out of bed, kept flashing into her mind. Gus had said she wasn't dead. She wasn't dead. Not dead. Not dead.

'Which service do you require: fire, ambulance or police?' the operator asked.

'Ambulance!' Gill shouted, as if by speaking loudly it would get to them quicker.

When she got through to the ambulance operator, the woman was very polite and very calm and Gill was neither. She wanted to wring the woman's neck. She asked all sorts of questions like was it a one-way street and was there access to the front or rear of the building? And were there any hazardous chemicals stored nearby? Gill just wanted them to get there.

When Gillian had given all the details she needed to, the lady said she should stay on the line while she got an ETA. 'Are you OK, love?' she asked, while they waited.

'It's my friend,' Gill said. 'My friend Chloë, you see. She looked so terrible. Please tell me she's not going to die.'

The clock above the boardroom table said ten-thirty-five. Dino drummed his fingers on the desk impatiently. This was the weekly progress meeting for all heads of department. An assortment of men and women in smart suits sat silently round the table. In front of them they had folders and flip charts and any paraphernalia they thought might save them from Dino's wrath.

'Emma didn't say she would be off today, did she?' asked Dino.

Jeanette, sitting opposite him, leant forwards, her blouse falling open just enough for Dino to catch a hint of her bra. 'She's probably just running a bit late. I think she may have a few domestic problems,' she said.

'Domestic problems?' Dino asked, annoyed.

'Oh, I'm sure it's nothing,' Jeanette replied, propping her chin on her hand and tipping her head to one side to give Dino a better view of her breasts. 'But then it must be really hard when you've got other responsibilities. Family and that kind of thing.'

There were nods and murmurs of approval from around the table.

'Hard, yes, really hard,' agreed Adrian from ladies' blouses.

Dino looked nonplussed. His family was run along Victorian principles. They were seen in publicity pictures but not heard of otherwise. They certainly didn't cause him any problems that might make him late for an important meeting.

There was silence round the room, broken by Jeanette. 'You know, they say a woman's brain shrinks during pregnancy,' she said.

'Really? That's fascinating,' Dino said. Those breasts really were rather good.

'I'm not saying it doesn't go back, but you never know, do you?' continued Jeanette, conveniently ignoring the fact that Emma hadn't actually ever given birth, Saskia being her stepdaughter.

'And then, of course, there is the lack of sleep,' added Michael, gentlemen's knitwear.

A nasty little alliance was forming. Smith & Taylor's very own axis of evil was cranking itself into life.

'It must be almost impossible to give one hundred per cent when you're tired,' Jeanette continued.

'Impossible,' echoed the others.

'Not that Emma isn't marvellous. She is the most fantastic person to work with.'

'Fantastic, yes,' everyone agreed.

Dino swivelled his chair round to face Jeanette. He gave her a long look up and down. 'Well, we'd better get started without Emma, I suppose. Jeanette, perhaps you could fill us in.'

'No problem, Dino,' she replied.

* * *

Gus and Gill were sitting on plastic chairs in a side room, just off casualty. It said 'Relatives' Room' on the door, but the nurse had told them it was OK since there were no relatives here. Chloë had a mother, but she was on holiday in the Canaries with her third husband. Chloë had said hello to him at the wedding, but that was about as far as their relationship went. There was a brother Callum, but Chloë hadn't seen him in years. He was married with two kids and lived in Bishop's Stortford.

Gill traced one of the stripes making up the orange check on the seat of her chair with her fingernail. The material was worn, faded and frayed in places. An effort had been made to make the room bright and welcoming. The skirting boards and architrave round the door were painted bright yellow and there was a picture of sun-flowers on one wall, but the atmosphere was depressing, as if the walls and soft furnishings had absorbed the grief of the people who spent time in this room like cigarette smoke. The room also smelt of that. The hospital was a no-smoking area, but this room was given an unofficial amnesty.

They'd been shut up in here for two hours, ever since Chloë had been brought in. With tubes in her arm and a mask on her face, she didn't look like the Chloë Gus and Gillian knew. She wasn't talking or laughing. She was so quiet; all the quieter, it seemed, because of the noise around her. People were shouting and machines were beeping and the trolley wheels squealed as she was pushed though the swing doors into the resuscitation room. As soon as the doors had banged shut after her, Gus and Gill had been shown into this room and, pretty quickly, a nice nurse had been in to see them. Suspected ectopic pregnancy, she said. A fallopian tube may have ruptured. Chloë had gone into surgery and 'might be a while'. But how long was a while? It felt like hours and hours. People died from ectopic pregnancies. Gill had read about it happening. She wasn't religious, but she put the palms of her hands together, closed her eyes tight and prayed: 'Please, please don't let Chloë die.'

Gus was silent. The two of them were much of the time. It was as if they believed that if they didn't say what was on both their minds then it wouldn't happen. Neither of them had the strength to talk anyway. All their energy was put into willing Chloë to keep breathing. So they sat in silence, Gill picking at her chair and Gus staring at the sunflowers.

Suddenly, there was a creak and the door swung open. Gill peered through her hands. She saw a flash of white coat. The doctor had arrived to give them the news. How many times had Gill seen this moment on TV? This was the bit where the TV doctor smiled triumphantly and said: 'I have good news. The surgery was entirely successful.' Only it wasn't always that way. There was the alternative scenario where the TV doctor looked grave and simply uttered the words: 'I'm very sorry.'

But this was real life, not TV. Gill could hardly bear to

look up at the doctor's face, but she knew she had to.

'Sorry,' said Emma to Carol, her secretary. She rushed towards her office, taking off her coat as she went. 'Domestic problems, you know what –' She saw Jeanette's face and didn't finish her sentence. Was that triumph she could see? Carol followed her in.

'They had the meeting without you,' she said. 'Dino wasn't very happy.'

'Oh, shit. Yeah. I did my best but . . . stuff at home . . . Did Jeanette fill in for me?'

Carol raised an eyebrow. 'Oh, yes. She did that all right.'

'You gave us a bloody fright, you know,' Gus said, kissing Chloë on the cheek.

Chloë smiled weakly. 'Sorry,' she whispered.

'Don't take any notice of him,' Gill smiled. 'We're just glad you're OK. You know, there was a moment there . . . But never mind. All you've got to do now is get well.'

Chloë had been given her own room at the hospital. According to the nurse who showed Gus and Gill to it, Chloë was lucky. Wait until winter. If it snowed over Christmas they'd be full up with OAPs with flu and broken hips. Chloë didn't look very lucky. Some of the colour had returned to her face, but she was weak and still a bit woozy from the anaesthetic.

Gus had opened the door of the bedside locker and was looking inside.

'Oi, nosey. Stop that,' Gill said.

'Just seeing what's inside. I've never been in a hospital before – well, not properly. Not exactly the Ritz, is it?'

'No. It's a hospital, Gus. They don't have mini-bars.'

Gus shut the door to the cupboard and fixed Gill with a questioning look. 'Talking of hospitals, what about you? We never did find out if you might be needing one of these in nine months' time. Well, did you do it?'

'I really don't think this is the time, Gus.'

'Just a simple yes or no will do.'

'Oh, all right, no. I didn't do it.'

'I knew you wouldn't have the guts.'

'It wasn't a question of guts. I just didn't think it was the right way to have a baby.'

Gus and Gill had been so intent on their conversation they hadn't realised that Chloë had begun to cry. She did so softly, as if trying not to bother them. When they saw her tears, both were immediately contrite.

'Oh, Chloë, what's the matter?' Gill asked. 'Are you in pain? Shall I ring for the nurse?'

Chloë shook her head.

'Well, what is it?' Gus asked more gently.

Gill took a tissue out of a box on top of the cabinet and handed it to Chloë, who blew her nose, a tube stuck to one of her hands wobbling. 'The doctor said . . .' Chloë began, but couldn't finish.

'What did the doctor say?' Gill asked.

'He said . . . I . . . I . . .'

'Yes?' Gus said.

'After the ect . . .'

'Ectopic pregnancy, yes?' Gill prompted.

'I might not be able to . . . have children.' Chloë collapsed into tears again.

Gus frowned. 'But you never wanted children.'

'Oh, shut up, Gus.'

Emma looked at the mountain of paperwork facing her. She was exhausted. She wanted to go home. Max had already been on the phone asking her when she would be there. But after Jeanette's little performance in the meeting this morning, Emma knew she had some ground to make up. Carol had filled her in on Jeanette's sparkling display in front of Dino and his approval of it. Emma knew she was going to have to watch Jeanette. But how was she supposed to do that and do her job and be a wife and a mother and . . . and . . . and . . . Emma's list of responsibilities seemed to get longer every day.

Emma took a sheet of paper off the top of her pile. It was an invoice from a fabric supplier. She turned to her computer and accessed the correct file. It was the start of another long night in the office.

Through the hospital window, Gill could see the dark spindly shadow of trees, their jagged branches swaying in the wind. Through them, the lights from the windows of the tower block next door shone like Hallowe'en lanterns.

Each time the trees moved, the lights were alternately revealed and obscured, making it look like they were flashing a sort of Morse code. What were they saying? Hello? Help? Maybe both.

Gus had gone home and Chloë was asleep. Gill was alone at her bedside. The night sister had done her round in the ward outside. The voices and clattering – wards at night, Gill had discovered, can be noisy places – had now faded into silence, interrupted only by the occasional snore or cry. Gill listened to Chloë sleeping. She was wheezing. Maybe that was an effect of the anaesthetic. Still, she looked peaceful enough.

Gill couldn't sleep. One of the nurses had brought in a cushion and a blanket, so she could sleep in the chair, but she was quite unable to drop off. There was too much on her mind. What the doctor had told Chloë was going round and round in Gill's head. She might never be able to have children. Gill had tried to comfort Chloë when she'd said it, but what was there to say? How do you comfort a woman whose future has suddenly been curtailed in this way?

Gus was right, Chloë had said she never wanted children and so had Gill. The difference was that Gill and Chloë's glib dismissal of the maternal instinct was made in the belief that it was their choice. For Chloë, it might not now be a choice, but a medical certainty. In the past, a tiny part of Chloë might have reserved final judgement, given herself just an infinite sonal space within which to change her mind. Now that space might not exist. To Gill, it was terrifying.

What if it had been Gill who was in Chloë's situation? What if she hadn't had children and then, one day, out of the blue, the option was taken away? Part of her wished she had gone ahead with the insemination. At twenty, having children had held no appeal. At thirty, Gill still wrinkled her nose at the very idea. She hadn't wanted to become, as Gus put it, one of 'The Boring Mums Brigade'. Now, though, time suddenly seemed so short, her chance to be a mother too precious to leave to providence.

Sitting on her uncomfortable plastic chair, watching the night creep towards dawn, Gill listened to the blackbirds as they greeted the first rays of light. They did so loudly, joyfully, with raucous cries and squeaks. They embraced the new day. It made Gill think about herself. Could she honestly say that she woke each morning eagerly anticipating the twenty-four hours ahead? Not likely, she was usually too hung over.

Gill glanced at Chloë. She loved her. Gill loved Chloë's energy and her wit and the fact that her life was even more chaotic than Gill's own. But did she want to be where Chloë was in a couple of years' time? Did she want to have missed the opportunity to have children? It didn't have to be an ectopic pregnancy that ruined her chances, she might just leave it too late. Even if, ultimately, Gill decided against the idea, the mere fact of having a choice offered the option of another sort of life. And without that, what was there? Perhaps it would have been different if Gill was in a good relationship, one that filled the emotional space in her that wasn't filled by children. But she wasn't. Was she going to spend the next forty years going out and getting drunk and dating dodgier and dodgier blokes? She'd look bloody silly falling off a bar stool when she was pushing eighty.

Chloë stirred in her sleep. Gill put a hand on her shoulder and she relaxed again. Gill kept her hand there. It felt like the least she could do. Then she looked outside again. Some of the curtains had been drawn in the tower block. People were getting up to start their day. Gill was ready to start the next phase in her life too. She wasn't sure what that phase would be, but she knew something had to change.

Chapter Twelve

'I can't believe we're doing this now. It's a month till Christmas,' grumbled Gill.

'Shut up and look,' Emma insisted.

'OK, OK, so whose Christmas presents are we looking for again?' Gill asked as she turned over a mirror with a jewelled frame to look at the price on the back.

'Well, there's Max and Saskia, obviously,' Emma replied, eyeing a vibrating foot massager. 'And then there's you . . .'

'Is that when we go to Tiffany's?'

'No, it's when we go to Woolworths.'

Gill had called Emma suggesting they meet up. Emma wasn't quite sure why, but she'd been glad of some company on this, her last-ditch attempt to complete her Christmas present list early. They'd come to Goddess, a shop full of completely pointless and utterly overpriced bits of tat. It was packed with other people also trying to get their Christmas shopping done early. A woman barged past Gill, almost spearing her with a candlestick in the shape of a cherub.

'You know, I've heard of women who do their Christmas shopping in January,' Gill said. 'I've read articles about them.'

'These are presumably the same women who make their own marmalade and rotate their shoes so they last longer?'

'Are there women who do that?' Gill was flabbergasted.

'Apparently,' Emma sighed. She only had three pairs of shoes that she actually wore. At any one time, two of them would need reheeling. These sat in a plastic bag at the bottom of the stairs in the hall for about two months before she remembered to take them in, by which time the third pair needed doing too but she couldn't take them because then she'd have to go into the office barefoot. Jeanette would definitely have curled her lip at that. Emma had only nipped out. She had to get back to work by two as later she had the office Christmas do to go to. Emma was dreading it.

'What do you think about this?' Emma asked, holding up an aromatherapy pillow.

'Who for?' Gill asked, flinching. This time it was her eye that was almost taken out by a harassed-looking shopper clutching a pair of garden flares and an inflatable pig.

'Dominique.'

'Are you thinking of using it to smother her?'

Emma smiled. 'No, it goes in the microwave, you know.'

'Yeah, yeah, but hang on a second. Can you explain to me why you are buying your husband's ex-wife's Christmas present? Shouldn't he be doing that?'

Emma laughed dryly. 'No, no, silly, didn't you know? Men are genetically incapable of doing the Christmas shopping. It's like working a washing machine or making dental appointments. They don't possess the bit of the brain you need for that. Actually, I did let Max have a go at the Christmas shopping one year. We were still paying off the credit-card bill in August.'

'Doesn't it piss you off, though?' asked Gill.

'Yeah, but that's marriage for you.'

A woman carrying a popcorn-maker in the shape of a farting hippo and a pair of huge mushroom-shaped beanbags was bearing down on Emma. Emma tried to flatten herself against a life-size replica of Elvis, which immediately began belting out 'Heartbreak Hotel', but without success. There wasn't enough space for the woman to get past. She and Emma eyed each other, like two wildebeest in a clearing.

'Shall we get out of here?' Gill said, breaking the deadlock.

Emma nodded and she and Gill plunged into the outside air with relief.

'There's a coffee place on the corner,' Emma said, leading the way.

When they got to Beanz Meanz Us! Emma went up to the counter to order two lattes and Gill bagged a corner banquette. The place was filled with other shoppers. They had the battle-weary appearance of ground troops pulled back from the front for a brief respite, before heading back into the war zone. Expressions were tense but determined.

Gill saw Emma returning. She shuffled up to make room for her. 'Thanks,' she said as Emma put her coffee on the table.

They sipped in silence for a few moments.

'Well?' Emma asked finally.

'What?' Gill replied.

'Why did you want to meet up?'

'Oh, no reason.'

'Come on.'

'Well . . .'

'Yes?'

Gill put her cup down and stared into it, watching the milky liquid swirl round inside. 'Chloë had an ectopic pregnancy.'

'Oh, God, is she all right?' asked Emma.

'Yeah. It was pretty scary though. She collapsed and . . .' Gill looked up. 'She looked terrible, Em. She was such a funny colour and I thought she was dead, I really did. Gus was great.'

'Gus was there?'

'Yeah, thank God. He felt her pulse and came in the ambulance and then stayed with me in the hospital.'

'Strange, isn't it,' Emma mused, 'how some people

surprise you in a crisis. I'd have thought Gus would have gone into a flap.'

'No, not at all,' Gill explained. 'He became weirdly heterosexual, sort of I'm-the-man-so-I-must-take-charge, which sounds really annoying, but was actually brilliant.'

'How long was she in hospital?'

'She's still there. Comes out tomorrow.'

'Well, send her my regards.'

There was silence, broken by Gill. 'I had an email from Mum and Dad.'

'So did I.' Emma smiled.

'The picture of Dad in the sarong?' Gill asked, grinning too. 'Wild, eh?'

Emma nodded. 'They seem to be having a good time, but, you know, I miss them.'

'Never thought I'd say it, but I do too.'

Gill scrabbled about in her handbag, found her cigarettes and put them on the table.

'You're not still smoking?' Emma exclaimed.

'Give me a break, Em, it's been a tough time.'

'There's always an excuse to smoke, Gill.'

'Thank you, Sigmund Freud.'

'Did you read that book – the Alan Carr one?'

'What do you think?'

Emma shook her head.

'Anyway,' Gill continued. 'The thing is, Chloë, well, the doctors say she might not be able to have children any more.'

Emma closed her eyes and sighed. 'Is she devastated?'

'Pretty much.'

'How old is she again?'

'A couple of years older than us.'

'Well, I suppose she might have left it too late anyway.'

'Thanks,' Gill said.

'Sorry, but you know what I mean.'

'Yeah, I do.' Gill took a slow drag on her cigarette and blew out the smoke very deliberately. 'Which is why I've got to make a decision, Em, and I thought you might be able to help me.'

Emma frowned. 'Yes?' she said uncertainly.

'Remember what we used to do as kids – you know, swap.'

'Swap what – Barbies? Cigarette cards?'

'Identities.'

'I don't get it,' Emma said, confused.

'When we were children, you and me, we used to change clothes and pretend to be each other, remember?'

Emma nodded.

'And no one ever twigged, did they?'

'No,' Emma agreed.

'Remember when you sat that test for me?' Gill asked.

Emma laughed. 'Oh, yeah, spelling and I got ninety eight per cent and Miss Armitage said –'

Gill interrupted her, ' "If only your sister Emma could have as good a command of the English language, Gillian." '

'Yeah, and I was really ticked off so I said —'

'"I'm not Gill I'm Emma."'

'And we both got bloody detention.'

Gill and Emma laughed warmly at the memory. When their laughter had died down, Emma said, 'But that was just a joke. We were kids.'

'I know,' Gill said. 'But, don't you see, it could solve my problem.'

'How?'

'I've got to decide if I want children and I'm terrified.'

'What of?'

'Of making the wrong choice. Of having them and regretting it or not having them and regretting it.'

'But we all have to take that gamble.'

'Yeah, but I've got an advantage – you. You could be my dry run. Don't you see? If I pretended to be you I could see if I'm really cut out for this motherhood malarkey.'

'Oh come on, Gill. Don't be ridiculous. How could you possibly make a decision based on being me for a day?'

'I'm not talking about a day.'

'Well, how long then?'

'Oh, I don't know, two months, maybe three.'

'Three months!' Emma was shaking her head. 'No, no. I couldn't possibly walk out on Max and my job and everything for three months.'

'But you wouldn't be walking out on them. I'd be there and you'd be around to make sure I wasn't doing a totally rubbish job. I'm not talking about you going off to Peru or something.'

'But we'd get found out. I know we're identical, but we're not that identical. Max for one would be sure to spot it.'

'Are you sure?' Gill asked.

'Well, actually, no. It takes him about three days to notice when I've had a haircut,' Emma admitted.

'Well, then.'

'Mum wouldn't be fooled for a minute.'

'But she's away, remember. That's what makes now such a perfect time to do it.'

'Perfect for you, maybe. What about me? What about my job? Things are tricky enough at work at the moment without you fucking things up for me.'

'Thanks for the vote of confidence.'

'I'm sorry, Gill, but you're not exactly the most reliable person workwise, are you? I have a whole department depending on me, millions of pounds worth of orders. There's no way you could just walk into that and carry it off.'

'You could give me a bit of coaching.'

'I've spent twenty years working my way up to doing that job and you think you could do it in five minutes?'

'I didn't mean it was easy. I just meant . . . At least think about it.'

'Why? I can see what's in it for you, but what's in it for me? I'd have to leave the husband I love for a start.'

'But you're always moaning about how tired you are. You were only saying the other day that you were feeling burned out; well, this would give you a complete rest.'

'Unless you bought a yacht when I wasn't looking, Gill, I wouldn't spend my time lying about doing nothing. I presume I would have to do your job.'

'Well, yeah, but it's not difficult. You could do it standing on your head.'

'Wouldn't I spill the drinks that way?'

They smiled at each other, then lapsed into silence. They were both thinking.

'It would be fun, wouldn't it?' Gill said.

'Yeah,' Emma agreed, then sighed. 'But we have to get real.' She shook her head sadly. 'Even without my job, there's Max to think about. How do you think he would feel when he found out, and he *would* find out, that I'd abandoned him to go off and pretend to be a single girl? It's a bit of an insult, isn't it? I mean, I'd go mad if I thought he was trying to pass himself off as a single man.'

'Oh, but just think, Em. No teenage angst to deal with,' Gill offered. 'And no nightmare ex-wives or horrible three year olds.'

'But that's the thing. Dominique and Kevin aren't being horrible at the moment,' Emma explained. 'We haven't seen them in ages. If we'd had this conversation months ago, I'd have probably bitten your hand off at the wrist, but things are fine at home.'

'But . . .'

'No, Gill. I've got too much to lose and not enough to gain.'

Carol, Emma's secretary, popped her head round the office door. 'You coming then?' she asked.

'Oh, I don't know if I'm in the mood,' Emma replied.

'Go on. You can't say no to a free sausage roll and a glass of warm Rioja.'

Emma sighed. 'You make it sound so tempting.'

When Emma got to the boardroom, the festivities were in full swing. This translated at Smith & Taylor as everyone standing around shuffling their feet as one of the more daring boys from the post room fired a streamer canister.

'Can I interest you in a mincemeat sushi roll slice?' asked Colin from food development. 'They're part of our new festive fusion line.'

'Well, um . . .' Emma replied, eyeing the plate with considerable suspicion, 'I'm not terribly hungry.' A growl from her stomach – she and Gill hadn't got beyond coffee – gave her away. She put her hand there in a pointless attempt to muffle the sound.

Colin smiled. 'Or we've got Thai turkey stuffing balls with a hot and sour dipping sauce?'

'Sounds, um, delicious, Colin, but I think I'll wait till supper,' Emma said, moving away from him as fast as possible. 'I think I'll just have a mineral water.'

'Tulip and nettle root with extract of St John's wort?' asked Jane from non-alcoholic beverages. 'Or we've got guarana/holly infusion flavour?'

Emma frowned. 'Got any, um, water flavour water?' she asked.

'Oh, we don't do that any more,' Jane replied dismissively.

'Really?' Emma said.

Jane turned to a colleague and sighed. 'Sarah, sweetie, could you run to the Ladies and put a cup under the cold tap?'

Emma searched the room for some friendly faces. In one corner, a group of men were gossiping. All between thirty and forty, every one of them had his hair shorn so short he looked like a skinhead. How peculiar, thought Emma, that the male of the species now prefers looking like a Nazi to displaying an even slightly receding hairline. With their round, polished heads bent together, they looked like skittles waiting for a big ball to knock them all over.

Emma looked over to the other corner of the room. Jeanette was talking to Dino. Actually, she was flirting with him. She was doing the female equivalent of tickling a trout. As with fish, this worked better when the man was old and bloated and a bit slow. He was so stunned by the attention he went into a hypnotic state and she could haul him out of the water whenever she pleased.

Still, it was a dangerous game. Jeanette had to go so

far, but no further. She had to tease and flirt, but not so much that Dino demanded a follow-through. Her power relied upon the implied possibility of her sleeping with him, not the actuality of it. Indeed, the moment she did remove her underwear her hold over him would disappear. He'd be on to the next bit of office crumpet before she could say P45.

What was even more dangerous for Jeanette, however, was the reactions of the other women in the room. While making a point of not looking at her, they were all actually studying her every move. The beams of hatred being directed at Jeanette were almost visible, they were so acute. It was as if Jeanette was the centre of an old-fashioned laser light show, only she didn't know it. She was basking in the glow of power coming off Dino, enjoying its warmth. Everyone else was waiting for her moment in the spotlight to pass. Women have long memories, as any bloke who's ever admitted to fancying a character on TV or film will testify. Said once, reminded of it for ever. Emma knew the minute, the very minute Jeanette fell out of favour with Dino, to be replaced by a younger, firmer rival, all those other females who had watched her sucking up to him would simply stand back and watch her tumble from grace. No one would help her. No one would cushion her fall.

For now, though, Jeanette was using her femininity as if it were a battering ram to get to the top. Dino was loving every minute of it. He was sticking out his chest and running his hand through his hair as if he were a peacock strutting up and down in front of an interested peahen. Emma almost felt sorry for him. Didn't he know it was his power, not his penis she was interested in?

When Dino saw Emma, he beckoned her over. 'Emma, Emma, glad you're here,' he said excitedly 'How's the fashion show going?'

Inwardly, Emma groaned. Not the fashion show again? Didn't Dino have anything else to think about, like perhaps running his billion-pound empire? The truth was, apart from making a call to Britney Spears's agent – the answer was a firm 'no' – Emma had done nothing about it. She had been hoping the whole thing would just go away. Emma pasted a smile on her face.

'Fine. It's all going just fine,' she said.

Fortunately for Emma, at that moment there was a distraction. Yvonne from human resources began to push what looked like a fish tank on wheels across the room. There was no lid, but there were a lot of what looked from a distance like balls floating about in it.

'Right then, everybody,' Yvonne announced, clapping her hands to attract attention. 'It's time for the party games. Who's going to blow up the balloons?'

Party games? No one had mentioned party games. Must be another of Dino's team-building exercises, Emma decided. She hated any sort of group jollity. When Saskia had been tiny, Emma had been persuaded to attend a playground with her one morning a week. This had entailed wearing a name badge – parents, not children – and acting out nursery rhymes in front of the group. Emma had an abiding memory of herself warbling 'Here we go round the mulberry bush', while holding a potted plant.

Yvonne now had a balloon in her hand. 'The idea is you put the balloon between your legs like this . . .' She clasped it between her thighs. 'And you have to pass it on to the next person like this.' Derek from accounts (expenses division) thrust his pelvis towards Yvonne and there was much hilarity around the room.

'Don't tire yourselves out, though,' Yvonne continued. 'There's apple bobbing later,' indicating the fish tank. 'And then we're playing sardines in the ground floor loading bay area.'

Oh, God, thought Emma.

'Do you think you can manage the stairs?' Gill asked anxiously. She had an arm looped under one of Chloë's and clasped round her back.

'I'm OK, really,' Chloë said. 'Don't fuss.'

'Perhaps I ought to carry her?' Gus suggested.

'Carry me? Chloë snorted. 'You couldn't carry a half-pound of potatoes up a slight slope, let alone me up these stairs. No, really, I'm OK.' Chloë grasped the handrail and started to climb, one step at a time.

Gus and Gill had picked Chloë up from the hospital in a taxi. It was a week since her operation and the doctors said she was ready to go home. Still, Gill was nervous. It seemed a big responsibility, looking after Chloë. Chloë was normally the one who looked after her. She was the tough, resilient one. But events of the last week had proved that Chloë could be frail too. They had shown Gill how easily Chloë might have been taken away from them. She would never appear quite so invulnerable again.

At the top of the stairs, Chloë paused.

'See?' said Gus. 'I should have carried you.'

'Just get me a drink,' Chloë ordered.

'Didn't the doctor say you weren't allowed –' Gill began.

'A drink of water!' Chloë exclaimed. 'Not that I couldn't have vodka if I wanted. Jesus, am I living with Marie Bloody Osmond now?' She walked into the living room and slumped down on the sofa. While Gill got her the water, Gus swung her legs up on to the cushions.

'Do you need anything else?' Gill asked.

Chloë shook her head, then she looked round and smiled. 'Oh, you've put the decorations up. Bit early, isn't it?'

Gill and Gus smiled proudly. The room was festooned in gaudy tinsel. In the corner there was a Christmas tree whose branches were barely visible under layers of silver foil icicles and multi-coloured baubles. Lights twisted in and out of the other decorations, flashing on and off.

'We did it last night,' Gus explained. 'Do you like it? We thought you might like a bit of bling.'

'Oh, yes,' laughed Chloë. 'Very minimalist.'

Gill sat down next to Chloë. 'We're going to look after you, Chloë. It doesn't matter how long it takes. We're here for you.'

'Thanks, but . . .' *Buzz*. Chloë was interrupted by the front-door buzzer. She frowned.

'Who's that?' Gill asked no one in particular.

'Oh, that'll be my mum,' Chloë said. 'I called her from the hospital to come and pick me up.'

'But you hate your mum,' Gus said.

Chloë swung her feet on to the floor and stood up. 'I don't hate her. I just haven't seen eye to eye with her over a few things,' she said, walking down the hall, speaking over her shoulder. 'But when I was in hospital I had time to think and, you know, I reckon if we spend a bit of time together over Christmas . . . Well, she is my mum.' Chloë picked up the entryphone handset. 'Hello, Mum, come up.'

'Have you met her?' Gus whispered to Gill.

She shook her head. The only thing Gill had ever heard about Chloë's mum was that she'd split up with Chloë's dad when Chloë was five. After that, there had been a succession of 'uncles', each of whom Chloë disliked more than the last. When Chloë had got to sixteen, she couldn't wait to leave home.

'Gill, Gus, this is Veronica, my mum,' Chloë said.

Standing next to her was a woman in late middle age.

It was difficult to tell exactly how old she was because she was what is often called well preserved. Her make-up was immaculately applied, if a little thick, and her hair was 'done'. It was dyed a dark brown and puffed up like the cloud from a nuclear explosion.

'Pleased to meet you, Veronica,' Gill said, extending a hand.

Chloë's mother shook it with a well-manicured one of her own and did the same to Gus. 'Traffic's murder,' she said, turning her attention back to Chloë. 'Had to come off the M1 at Birmingham and do A roads all the way. My back is killing me. As Peter always says [Peter was her latest husband], "Veronica, you're a martyr to your back."'

'Still, you're here now,' Chloë ventured, her smile a little forced. 'Would you like a cup of tea before we set off?'

'I'd love one, but I can't take the tannin these days, dear. Plays havoc with my irritable bowel syndrome. Plus, tea's bad for the skin, you know, Chloë.' She peered at Chloë's face. 'You could do with thinking about that, you know. You're not as young as you used to be. Comes a time when a woman's got to start taking care of herself —'

'Right,' Chloë said, interrupting her mother. 'We'll be going then.'

Chloë kissed and hugged Gus and Gill. 'How long will you be away?' Gill asked.

Chloë shrugged. 'Dunno. A fortnight, a month? I need a break.'

'Well, you'll need these then,' Gill said, retrieving two quickly wrapped boxes from underneath the tree. She had bought them on her shopping trip with Emma and was glad she had done.

'Sorry I haven't got you anything,' Chloë said.

'You've been a bit busy, we know,' Gill reassured her.

Veronica hovered at the top of the stairs. 'Peter's waiting outside in the car,' she informed them.

'OK, OK, I'm coming,' Chloë said, walking down to meet her. She turned and looked over her shoulder.

'Have a good rest,' Gus said.

'Yeah, see you, you know – whenever,' Chloë replied.

The rolls of wrapping paper tumbled out of the carrier bag and on to the carpet, swiftly disappearing under the sofa. Emma got down on her hands and knees and fished about underneath until she could grab hold of a cylinder of snowflake-print paper and pull it back towards her. Then she put it on the coffee table along with some Sellotape. Next to it sat a jumble of carrier bags.

Emma had brought a bottle of wine and a glass with her from the kitchen. She poured herself a drink and started. This was her annual task: wrapping the Christmas presents. She cut, folded and stuck, tied ribbons and wrote gift tags. 'To X, love Max and Emma.' She didn't even bother to fake Max's signature. Everyone knew no man ever wrapped presents, unless he didn't have a woman to do it for him, in which case he visited the gift-wrapping desk at a department store.

Max was upstairs in the office emailing or something. Emma suspected he was just staying out of the way in case she asked him to do anything. She put a CD of Christmas carols on to get her in the mood.

It would be strange this year without Gordon and Charlotte. Emma had had them over for Christmas lunch ever since she and Max moved in together and she officially became a grown-up. Still, it would be nice to have a small, family Christmas. Who knew, maybe even Saskia would rise to the occasion and decide to be a human being?

Emma could smell cinnamon coming from the kitchen. The Christmas cake was in the oven. She was sure the kind of woman who did her shopping in January would have had her Christmas cake cooked many, many weeks back, allowing the flavour of the whisky or cognac, or whatever it was you were supposed to douse it in, to develop. Indeed, wasn't there a whole ritual to do with stirring it you were supposed to do sometime back in August? Or was that Christmas puddings?

Ding, dong.

It was the doorbell. Probably someone selling tea towels, Emma supposed. She got up, walked down the hall and opened the front door.

'Vroom,' screeched a shrill voice, and a small child pushed past Emma and ran up the hall, pushing the wheels of a toy car in a grubby trail all the way up the formerly nice, clean, white walls.

'Max in?' said Dominique, also pushing past her.

The pair of them disappeared into the living room, leaving Emma on the doorstep. She paused. Criminal thoughts were flooding through her mind, evil fantasies of what she'd like to do to Max's ex-wife and her devilish spawn. When these had receded somewhat she began to make resolutions. No, Dominique was not staying and neither was Kevin. No, she would not allow Max to persuade her. No, no, no.

'Hello, darling. Did I hear the door go?' Max asked. He had come to the foot of the stairs.

'Dominique's here,' Emma said evenly.

'Max? Max? Is that you?' Dominique trilled from the living room.

'Ding dong merrily on high,' went the hifi, exuding a festive jollity that now jarred somewhat with Emma's mood.

Max headed in to see her.

'Just promise me she won't be staying,' Emma said as he went. 'Max? Did you hear? Max . . .?'

Chapter Thirteen

Other people might have been woken on Christmas morning by the gentle *tweet, tweet* of a robin, the excited crunch of snow under a child's wellington boot as he or she put the finishing touches to a snowman, or just the mournful chime of a distant church bell. For Emma, the sound that jolted her awake was that of a sixteen year old shouting, 'Fuck off. I hate you!'

Max had gone up to coax Saskia out of her bedroom for a festive family breakfast. He had singularly failed to spark any enthusiasm in her for such a gathering.

'But, darling, please,' Max begged.

'Leave me alone,' Saskia bellowed back through her firmly closed door.

Emma put her head under the duvet and considered staying there for the rest of the day. Then she looked at the travel clock on the bedside table. Seven-forty-five. She sprang out of bed with, if not quite the agility of a young gazelle, then not a bad attempt at it for a thirty-eight-year-old. 'Just nipping in the shower,' she said as she brushed past Max in the bedroom doorway.

'I thought we could . . .'

'No time. Got too much to do. Then again, maybe Dominique would like to give me a hand?'

Max looked uncomfortable.

'No, I thought not.'

Since Dominique's arrival many, many weeks ago, she had become a fixture in Emma's home. Emma begged, argued, cajoled, but there was always a new excuse. First, she'd broken up with Denzel, then the central heating wasn't working, then there was dry rot, wet rot, rising damp . . . The list of excuses went on and on. In the end Emma had become too exhausted to argue. She had to be Ms All Powerful at work; she didn't want to come home and give orders as well.

Now it was Christmas morning and Dominique and Kevin were still here. They'd become like stains on a carpet that you shifted the furniture to cover but that lurked anyway. A large chest of drawers on top of Dominique was an appealing prospect. Emma dashed downstairs to begin the Christmas cooking marathon.

At Gill's flat, things were more laid back. With Chloë away at her mother's, she and Gus were on their own. They'd started the celebration early, staying up drinking until the early hours. Gus had crashed out on the sofa and Gill had somehow managed to crawl into her own bed. Now, she lay under the duvet only semi-conscious. Suddenly, her door was flung open.

'OK, get out of bed, you old tart,' said Gus, smiling. He didn't get hangovers, which made him both hugely cheerful and hugely irritating this morning.

'Who are you calling an old tart?' Gill replied.

'All right. Get out of bed, you young tart, then,' Gus said. 'It is Christmas, after all. The season of good will and all that.'

'I think I had enough good will last night. Come back in, oh, about three days.'

'Oh, come on, misery guts. Cheer up. It's Christmas. Here, I got you a present.' Gus put a small rectangular package impeccably wrapped in aubergine crêpe paper with black ribbon on top of the duvet.

'I would say, you shouldn't have, but since I have to work with you, I reckon I deserve a present,' said Gill, now smiling too.

'Bloody charming,' Gus said, sitting down on the corner of the bed. 'Open it then.'

Gill ripped the paper and pulled out a book. *Fifty Ways To a Sensational Sex Life.* 'I haven't got a sex life!' she exclaimed.

'Exactly!' Gus said. 'Happy Christmas.'

Emma stared at the space on the shelf in the garage where the turkey should have been. This was the turkey she was supposed to be about to put in the oven. The one they were all going to eat for lunch. Her brow was wrinkled. The plate was there, but it was empty of the expected deceased fowl.

'Max?' she shouted.

'Yes,' he answered cheerily from the kitchen where he was making coffee.

'Where did you put the turkey?'

'What turkey?'

'The one we're having for lunch.'

'I don't know what you mean.'

'The turkey you took out of the freezer to defrost, where did you put it?'

There was silence.

'Max? You did take the turkey out of the freezer, didn't you?' Emma walked over to the freezer and opened the door. She slid the bottom drawer towards her. It felt heavy. That was because sitting inside it was a ten-pound turkey resting contentedly as if still in its coop. Except the turkey was dead, obviously. 'Oh, Max . . .' she wailed.

Max wasn't listening. He was reading a note left on the kitchen table.

Dear Max,

I've tried, I really have, but I don't think this motherhood thing is really working out for me. Some people, like Emma for instance, seem to enjoy the humdrum, day-to-day stuff, but you know me, Max. I need to be free. I'm like a butterfly and you can't cage a butterfly, can you? The reason I came

back is Denzel has been offered a permanent
job in Marbella and I'm going with him. I
didn't tell you as I knew you'd try to stop
me. Look after Kevin. He's better off with
you, anyway.

Love Dominique xx

Oh, no, not again! How was Max going to break this to
Emma? And what about Kevin?

'Max, Max,' Emma was shouting from the garage.

Max picked up the note and put it in his pocket, then
trudged to the garage. When he got there, he peered over
Emma's shoulder at the chilly fowl. 'Aah,' he began.

'Oh, Max, how could you have forgotten to get it out
of the freezer?'

'I'm really sorry. I meant to do it. I really did. It's just
Dominique . . .' Max saw Emma prickle at the mere
mention of Dominique's name. It didn't seem an
opportune moment to mention that she had gone off
leaving her three-year-old son for them to look after.
Would Emma notice if he housed Kevin in the garden
shed and popped out there a couple of times a day to feed
and water him? Max looked at Emma's expression. It was
thunderous.

'It's the only thing I asked you to do,' Emma wailed.
'I've done all the shopping for the food and the presents.
I've written all the Christmas cards and I've put up the
decorations. All on my own. Christmas is not like PMT,

Max. It doesn't only affect women. You're part of it too.'

Rather than simply accepting the blame, Max then made the fatal mistake of thinking he could use rational argument to save himself. 'Never mind, darling,' he coaxed. 'At the end of the day, none of it matters really, does it?'

Emma exploded like a liquidiser whose top has not been put on firmly enough before an attempt is made to make a strawberry milkshake. 'At the end of the day!' she shrieked. 'At the end of the day! What day is this, exactly? Oh, yes, it's CHRISTMAS DAY! Christmas Day, Max, the day when the British traditionally sit round a table and eat roast turkey –'

'Actually, turkey's not quite traditional,' Max said, interrupting her. 'Goose is much more traditional. Turkey is an American import –'

'I don't care if the turkey is from fucking Kathmandu. Ours is frozen solid.'

Max went to put an arm round her shoulder. 'Never mind. It's only a turkey. What's really important is that we're together as a family,' he cooed.

Emma ignored him. 'Maybe that's what's important, Max, but it's the turkey and the bread sauce and the bloody chipolatas that stop us from killing each other.'

Max was thinking that she would kill him when she found out about Dominique. He tried to calm her down. 'Don't you think you might be getting this a teeny bit out of proportion?' he said. 'It's only a turkey.'

'Stop saying it's only a turkey!' Emma bellowed. 'It isn't only a turkey.'

'Oh, come on, Em,' Max persisted. 'It's not that bad.'

'It's all very well you saying it's not that bad. You're not the one who's supposed to be Delia bloody Smith for the day. I ask you to do just one tiny thing. Just one, Max.'

'I know. I'm sorry.'

Emma was tearful now. 'I work hard. Really hard,' she wailed. 'And I do all this stuff on top of that.'

'I know.' Max was finally sounding guilty.

'No, I don't think you do, Max. I don't think you have any idea how I feel. How exhausted I feel.'

Max couldn't meet her eyes. But: 'It's only a turkey,' he repeated.

'If you say that one more time I won't be responsible for my actions,' Emma said.

'Well, cheers,' said Gus.

Gus and Gill raised their glasses of eggnog slightly half-heartedly. Gill had, of course, been invited to Emma's, but without Chloë, Gus would have been on his own, so she refused. They were two singles trying to summon up some festive spirit. The sound was thin and hollow. There was silence as they sipped their drinks. The eggnog had been Gus's idea. Gill had only ever had it out of a bottle, but Gus had made it from scratch. To Gill it felt like drinking alcoholic custard.

'Shall I put some music on?' asked Gus, trying to stir up some enthusiasm. Gill lit her seventh cigarette of the morning. It was only eleven a.m.

Gus went to the CD stack and began rifling through the available albums. 'Have you got any carols?' he asked.

'No,' Gill said. 'I hate Aled Jones.'

'*The Snowman* is not a carol,' Gus said. 'Anyway, he's grown up now.'

'You know what else I hate?' Gill asked

'Well, this is a cheerful festive subject,' Gus replied, 'but, OK, what else do you hate?'

'Enya,' Gillian said with feeling. 'She's the musical equivalent of loft insulation.'

Gus found an old Wham! CD and put it on. 'Wake Me Up Before You Go Go . . .' warbled in the background incongruously. Gill got up and went into the kitchen.

'What are we having for lunch?' Gus shouted after her.

'Turkey with all the trimmings, of course,' Gill shouted back.

'Oh,' Gus said, surprised. 'I didn't know you could cook. Are you doing the Gary Rhodes or the Jamie Oliver Christmas dinner?'

'Actually,' said Gill, who had appeared at the door holding a packet. 'It's the Findus Christmas TV dinner. Do you know whether, if you put more than one thing in the microwave, you have to double the time?'

* * *

'Right then,' announced Max. 'Let me at it.' Max was holding a power drill.

'I asked you to get the legs off the turkey, not put up some shelves,' Emma said.

'It's all I could find in the shed,' Max said, aiming the drill bit at the top of the turkey's legs. 'I think if I can puncture it in a few places the legs should just . . .' Max had actually found the drill in the shed as a side effect of secreting Kevin in it with a new Scalextric set and a pound of Dairy Milk. This was a holding pattern until he could explain to Emma where Dominique was, or rather wasn't. He switched on the power and the drill connected with the frozen poultry. It slid straight off the bird without leaving a mark and skittered across the worktop, gouging a jagged trench all the way across.

Gus had the TV guide from the newspaper spread out flat on the carpet. He was running his finger down the columns. 'Right then, what do you fancy?' he asked. 'What about a film?'

They'd finished their lunch. Without the need to pass the gravy boat, spoon out the cranberry sauce or bicker over who had the last of the bread sauce (or other such traditional family pastimes), lunch for Gus and Gill had taken approximately twelve minutes. Now they had the rest of the afternoon to fill. They hadn't yet got to the desperate stage of getting out the Monopoly – they'd have to be a lot drunker for that – so it was TV for now.

Gill picked up the plates from the table. She had taken the trouble to serve the microwaved food on plates, rather than leaving it in the little compartmentalised tray. Well, it was a special occasion, wasn't it? 'What's on?' she asked.

'Well, later there's *The Great Escape*, of course,' replied Gus.

'Of course.'

'Now there's either *Police Academy 4, Flubber* or, oh yes, *The Sound of Music*. Oh, damn, it's started.' Gus pressed the remote and the TV flicked on. He jumped on to the sofa.

Gill stopped listening. She was thinking how pointless Christmas was when you were single. There was that creaky old maxim about Christmas being for children, but actually it was true. From the age of about fourteen until you had your own children, Christmas was just a day when the shops were closed. It was a minor irritation enlived by the opportunity to get drunk in the middle of the day.

Gill wondered what she would have felt if she'd gone ahead with the insemination. She might have been looking forward to having a child of her own. This made her think of Chloë. She hoped she was OK. They'd had a couple of phone calls. Chloë had sounded cheerful, if a bit stilted. But then maybe she'd had an audience. Veronica hadn't seemed the warmest of individuals. As for Peter, since he couldn't be bothered to get out of the car, he hadn't seemed that welcoming either.

Julie Andrews was singing. 'Me, a name I call myself . . . Dum de dum de dum de dum . . .' Gus was singing along. He was as happy as a gay man listening to Julie Andrews can be. Well, he could have been happier. That's if it had been Judy Garland, but *The Wizard of Oz* wasn't on until later.

The Raj Vogue Tandoori on the ropier end of Caledonian Road was empty, so empty Emma and her family's voices would have echoed off the walls and ceiling had it not been for the flock wallpaper the thickness of shagpile carpet in which they were covered. The walls were further festooned with tinsel, and plastic Father Christmases were posted at intervals along them.

Max had driven and driven until they'd found somewhere that was open. Their home-cooked Christmas dinner having been scuppered by him, he was determined to find a replacement. 'It'll be fun,' he said as they went through the door.

Bizarrely, 'The Girl From Ipanema' was playing loudly on the in-house stereo. This was a curry house where no one could hear your scream over Astrid Gilberto at full throttle. Still, Emma had had to admit defeat with the turkey and it was the only place open. The staff pushed a couple of smoked glass tables together and they sat down. They were handed menus. The mood was strained/jovial, which was better than downright depressed but still a long way from the warm cosiness of an Andy Williams Christmas special.

A waiter, his manner the cloying side of unctuous, appeared. 'Drinks?' he said expectantly.

Max turned to Emma first. Her good nature being the most fragile, he felt it wise to oil it with some alcohol as fast as possible. 'Would you like a glass of white, darling?' he asked. Emma nodded.

'What white wine do you have?' Max asked the waiter.

'Sweet or medium sweet,' the waiter replied.

'Yes, but what I mean is, what sort of wine: Chardonnay, Pinot Grigio, Sauvignon Blanc?'

'One moment, please,' the waiter replied, before disappearing behind the bar. When he reappeared he was holding two bottles. He passed them to Max. One said 'Sweet White Wine' on the label, the other 'Medium-sweet White Wine'. That was it. There was no mention of a country of origin, let alone a grape variety. They'd probably been mixed in big chemical vats in some industrial estate in Loughton. Emma sighed. They'd managed to find the one totally ungentrified Indian restaurant in London.

'I think we'll have the medium-sweet,' Max said.

'Coke! Coke! Coke!' chanted Kevin. 'I want Coke!'

Emma was frowning,

'Orange juice,' said Max, looking at Kevin.

'Vodka,' Saskia said.

'I don't think that's a good idea,' Max declared. But,

seeing her murderous expression, he relented. 'Well, maybe just a little. It is Christmas, I suppose.' He turned to the waiter. 'One very small vodka with lots of orange juice, please.'

Saskia glared at the waiter. 'Make it a double and I'll have it straight.'

The waiter looked from Saskia to Max and back again. Saskia being the more menacing he nodded at her and went off to get the straight vodka. A basket of poppadoms and some pickles appeared on the table. Kevin fell upon the poppadoms like a starving hyena. He broke one in two, stood up on his chair and immediately began jabbing a sharp shard of deep-fried snack in Emma's direction. She batted him away.

You wouldn't have thought poppadoms could be an offensive weapon. When you checked your luggage in on a plane there wasn't a sign with a picture of a poppadom with a red diagonal line through it. They didn't ask you if you were carrying knives, scissors, aerosols or Indian hors d'œuvres. Still, Kevin had the unique ability to turn even the most innocuous of materials into a potentially lethal weapon. Kevin's poppadom connected with Emma's eye.

'Ow!' she shrieked.

Kevin immediately dipped what was left of his poppadom into some lime pickle and popped it into his mouth. His face began to go the colour of an aubergine. He began to wail. With Emma groaning in pain and

Kevin shouting in anger, even Astrid Gilberto was having a tough job making herself heard.

'Max?' Emma said when the pain had subsided a little.

'Hmm?' he said, trying to force water down Kevin's throat.

'Max!' Emma was insistent now.

'Yes, darling?'

'I've just noticed. We seem to have left Dominique behind. Should we go back and get her?'

Max was silent.

Emma frowned. 'Actually, I don't think I've seen her all morning. Have you?'

Still Max was silent.

'Max? What's going on?'

'Well . . .' he began. He had hoped, somewhat naively, that Emma wouldn't notice Dominique's absence.

'What?'

'She . . . um . . .'

'What, Max, what? Where is she?'

'She left a note.'

'A suicide one, hopefully,' Saskia spat.

Kevin had now recovered from lime-pickle poisoning, had got down from his seat and was running up and down the carpet, flicking the waiters with a napkin. Max made a half-hearted attempt to calm him down. 'Now, Kevin, are you going to sit down like a big boy?' he said.

'Don't want to be a big boy,' Kevin answered.

'What did the note say, Max?' Emma asked.

'She's, um, gone,' Max replied.

'Gone? Gone where? For how long?'

'Marbella. Apparently Denzel's got a job out there.'

'How nice for him. When's she coming back?'

Max didn't answer.

'When, Max?'

Max still didn't answer.

'What about Kevin? Oh, Jesus, she's done it again, hasn't she? Well, hasn't she? Max?' Emma pushed her chair back from the table. 'Not again, Max. Not again.'

Gus had fallen asleep on the sofa. After consuming his own body weight in Quality Street, plus numerous glasses of eggnog, he had passed out. It was a shame really. Dorothy was following the yellow brick road on the telly and he was missing it. Gill sighed. After the first sip of eggnog, she had switched to Diet Coke. She was, therefore, stone-cold sober. So this is what her Christmas had amounted to: a microwave lunch, a book pointing out what a crap sex life she had and an evening spent listening to her best friend snore in front of the TV. She broke off another slice of Terry's Chocolate Orange and put it in her mouth. Oh well, it could be worse, she thought, lighting a cigarette. She could have given up smoking as well.

At first, Emma didn't know where she was going. She felt claustrophobic, so she pointed the car north, as the quickest way to get out of the city, and just drove. Pretty soon, the narrow streets and small houses, kebab shops and minicab offices gave way to dual carriageway and then motorway. She chose the MI. It was the road she and Gill had watched out of the car window as children, the road her parents had taken to get to North Wales for their summer holidays. There was no sunshine now, however. The weather outside was cold and grey, the clouds ominously plump with rain.

The road was empty. There were no cars with over-loaded roof racks or towering, rickety caravans. No other children to wave to. Emma could almost hear her mother: 'I spy with my little eye . . .' She put the radio on, finding a station that was playing Christmas hits of yesteryear back to back. She turned it up to fill the silence. Soon, the streetlamps were flashing past with a comfortingly rhythmic regularity. The speedometer said fifty-five, but Emma could have been flying. She could have been driving Chitty Chitty Bang Bang. Here on her own, in her car, with her phone off, the radio up and the gas pedal down, she felt light, free, happy. Sealed inside her tin can, Emma was shut off from responsibility. No one could reach her and that felt good.

She saw a sign ahead. 'Watford Gap. Blue Boar Services.' She smiled. This was the same service station they'd stopped at as children. They'd had a machine which tumbled orange liquid, in a plastic tank before pouring it out. It was rumoured to be squash but was a much more unlikely colour. When you got to the end of your cup, there were gritty bits in the bottom.

Emma indicated and pulled off the motorway on to the slip road. She fancied a trip down memory lane and she needed to make a phone call anyway.

The Blue Boar, as Watford Gap Services used to be known, had been renamed, or rebranded as the marketing men no doubt called sticking up an alternative plastic logo and getting the same staff to wear different coloured house coats. It was now called the Resteezzee and it was empty. Almost. A solitary cleaner dragged a recalcitrant vacuum cleaner across the peanut-shaped patch of carpet on which was parked the French Pâtisserie cart. Quite how, indeed why, Monsieur le pâtissier might have got this example of rural kitsch across the Channel was a mystery. Perhaps he had paused in his faux peasant smock and thumbed a lift from a passing Seacat at Calais.

Emma watched as the cleaner, whose efforts to collect croissant crumbs were singularly ineffective, was berated by a man with a nametag on his lapel and a burning ambition to become area manager. He was met with a brick wall of indifference from his employee, or maybe it was a language barrier. He appeared to be from the further reaches of the Thames Estuary. She looked like she hailed from Costa Rica.

Emma picked up a mahogany-effect plastic tray and trundled past the hot food counter. A dumpy woman in an apron stood listlessly behind it.

'Café latte, please,' Emma said.

'Coffee what?' the woman replied as if Emma were speaking an entirely different language.

'Um, café latte,' Emma repeated. 'Do you do it?'

'Just white or black. Or we've got Ribena,' she said, waving in the general direction of a machine behind her.

Emma reviewed her options. 'White coffee, then,' she said. She paid at the cash desk then slid her bottom on to one of the white plastic seats, which were padded slightly with a bright patterned fabric. The fabric choice was evidently something to do with jolting weary drivers awake. Certainly, one look at that and she wouldn't be falling asleep at the wheel, or indeed anywhere else.

One hour and forty minutes later, Emma was still sitting at her plastic table, nursing the same coffee. Ordering another one didn't seem a good idea. She'd fetched a magazine from the kiosk by the front door and was filling in a questionnaire. 'How safe is your marriage?' So far, she wasn't scoring well.

'Hi.'

It was Gill. Emma smiled warmly, relieved to see her. 'D'you want a coffee?'

'No, I'll get them,' Gill said. 'What is it, cappuccino?'

'You'll be lucky. No, actually, I'm fine.'

When Gill had got the phone call from Emma, she'd been surprised. Still, something strange in Emma's voice had got Gill into her car and up the M1.

Gill didn't press Emma immediately. She went to get

herself a coffee. When she got back, she shook her head. 'It's like *The Time Tunnel* in here. I asked for a cappuccino and she looked at me like I was talking Serbo-Croat.'

'Yeah, sorry. If I'd planned to run away from my family, I'd have chosen a more chic spot.'

Gill looked shocked. 'Is that what you've done? Jesus, why – and why here?'

'Don't you remember?' Emma said. 'This is where Mum and Dad always brought us.'

'With the gritty orange machine, yeah,' smiled Gill. 'That seems to have gone.'

Emma nodded.

'So?' Gill was waiting for an explanation. 'What's going on?'

'I don't know. I had to get away and I suppose this place reminded me of happier, simpler times. Things really were simple for Mum and Dad, weren't they?'

'What do you mean?'

'Well, they got married, had us, Mum gave up work and that was pretty much it, wasn't it?'

'I'm sure they had their ups and downs, Em. Don't you remember the silences sometimes?'

'I'm not saying there weren't rocky patches, but they didn't have ex-wives and stepchildren and jobs and the whole bloody shebang to deal with.'

'So, you've left the whole shebang, have you?'

'Not really. I'm just having a break. I left them in an Indian restaurant.'

'An Indian . . .'

'Yeah, well, the Chinese was closed and the Thai looked a bit ropey.'

Gillian frowned. 'But it's Christmas. You're supposed to do the big family roast thing. You always do the big family roast thing.'

'Max forgot to defrost the turkey.'

'Oh.'

The row between the cleaner and the man with the nametag had started up again. It was pretty one-sided. He was shouting and she was saying nothing. Finally, she snapped. Her English wasn't good but she had clearly mastered a few key phrases. 'You, little man,' she spluttered. 'You stick it up your arse.' Then she turned on the heel of her cheap trainers and marched off. The man stood, stunned, as the vacuum cleaner hummed next to him like the engine of a car in neutral while its owner nips to the cashpoint.

Gus rubbed his eyes, squeezing the flesh above the bridge of his nose to release the tension. 'Gill?' he called.

There was no answer.

He got up off the sofa and stumbled over to the table, more chocolate drunk than anything else. He had so much sugar in his blood, he couldn't walk in a straight line. On the table he found a note scrawled on the back of an envelope. 'Back soon, Gill,' was all it said.

Gus thought Gill must have gone for a walk. Maybe

she was missing Chloë. He decided to go to the kitchen to make a cup of tea. As he did so, he glanced at the TV. Gill had turned the volume down. The credits at the end of *The Wizard of Oz* were scrolling soundlessly up the screen.

'Damn!' Gus exclaimed, as he kicked over a tin full of empty, screwed-up Quality Street wrappers.

'OK, so Mum and Dad's lives are easy. And yours isn't. What's new about that?' Gill asked.

'Dominique's left Kevin. With us, I mean.'

'She's dumped him on you?'

Emma nodded.

Gill shook her head. 'That woman. She doesn't change, does she? What does Max have to say about it?'

'You know Max.'

'Can't criticise the ex-wife, can he?'

'No, just expect the current wife to clean up her messes. But I can't do it. Not again. I've given Saskia everything I've got and it's still not enough. I haven't got anything left to give.'

'So what are you going to do?' asked Gill.

'That's why I asked you here,' Emma replied.

Back at the Raj Vogue, the food was arriving. 'Chicken jalfrezi?' the waiter said brightly, holding a steel dish with something radioactive-looking inside it.

Max nodded. 'That's for me.'

'Pilau rice?'

'Yeah, me too.'

'And the prawn tikka?'

'That's for my wife,' Max said. 'Just put it down there.' He indicated the space in front of Emma's seat.

Next to Max, Kevin had picked up a naan bread and was attempting to suffocate himself with it. From the gasping sounds coming from behind it, he was being at least partially successful. Max reached across and tore a hole in the middle. Kevin took a lungful of air. He quickly lost interest in that game, picked up an empty Cobra bottle and whacked Saskia in the stomach with it.

'Why, you . . .!' Saskia shrieked.

'Children!' Max admonished them. 'Play nicely.'

'I told you, I'm not a child!' Saskia protested, before turning back to Kevin. 'Evil little beast.'

Max was just thinking that perhaps it hadn't been wise to allow her that second vodka on an empty stomach when she raised her glass in the air. 'Another when you're ready,' she instructed the waiter.

'Your wife, sir, is she coming back?' the waiter asked.

When Emma had left, Max had assumed she'd popped to the loo, but she'd been away a very long time. You were supposed to get the runs after not before an Indian, weren't you? 'I hope so,' he replied. 'She is freshening up, I think. You couldn't . . .?'

'Have a look for her? Of course, sir,' the waiter said. 'We wouldn't want the lady's food to get cold, would we?'

* * *

'I don't understand. When I suggested doing a swap, you were dead against it!' Gill exclaimed.

'I know, but I've changed my mind,' Emma admitted. 'You say you'd like to find out what it's like to have kids, well, here's your chance. You've got an extra one, a three-year-old child, thrown in for good measure.'

'Sorry, did you say child, or small human incendiary device?'

'He's not that bad.'

'Oh, come on, Em, you're always saying how awful Kevin is.'

'All right, but maybe you'd make a better job of looking after him than I would.'

'On what basis?' Gill asked incredulously. 'My huge experience of bringing up children?'

'Well, you'll never get experience if you don't give it a go,' Emma pointed out.

They both stared into their coffees.

'Do you really think we wouldn't get found out?' Gill asked.

'I don't know. I don't think so,' Emma answered.

'What about Max?'

'I told you, I could shave my head and run round naked and he'd just ask if I'd got anything in for supper.'

'And Saskia?'

'She doesn't make eye contact if she can help it.'

'So we could do it then,' Gill said, beginning to sound excited. 'In theory, I mean.'

'Yeah, we'd have to think about the way we look,' Emma said. 'Your hair's different for a start. Especially since, you know, you set it alight.'

Gill touched her hair self-consciously. 'It's OK now, isn't it?' Emma nodded.

'But we'd have to swap everything, you know?' she said. 'Not just hair.'

'Jobs and . . . husbands.'

'You haven't got a husband,' said Emma.

'I know, but you have. What about Max? How do I get out of, you know, sleeping with him? I mean, he'd think I'm you.'

'You've talked enough men into bed, I'm sure you can talk one out of it.'

'Not that many . . .'

Emma raised an eyebrow. 'We're married, remember, we hardly ever have sex anyway. But if the matter is, um, raised, just tell him you've got cystitis. That should do the trick. Women's problem: he'll run a mile.'

'Well . . .' Gill was uncertain.

'Trust me, I'm a doctor.'

'No, you're not.'

'Well, no, I'm not, but you'll have to trust me anyway.'

'I haven't said I'll do it yet.'

* * *

In the Indian restaurant, Max frowned. 'Say that again,' he ordered.

'She's not there, sir,' the waiter informed Max.

'What do you mean, she's not there?' he asked.

'Your wife, sir. She's not in the Ladies.'

'She must be.'

Saskia now had Kevin in a half nelson, his head pushed down on the table and his arm behind his back. He was squeaking like a musical soft toy that is being stood on.

'Well, have you checked . . .' Max began

'The Gents. Yes, sir. She's not there either.'

'Well, where the hell is she?'

'So how long would we swap for?' Gill asked.

'Well, you suggested three months, remember?' Emma answered.

'Did I? Jesus. That sounds a bit long.'

Emma nodded. 'Yeah, it does, doesn't it? What about if we set a deadline of . . . um . . .'

Gill interrupted her. 'Mum and Dad's golden wedding. That's two months. Eight weeks.'

'Well, it's academic anyway,' Emma said. 'We're sure to get found out long before that. I give it a day before Chloë spots me.'

'You're OK, for now anyway. She's away. Gone to her mum's.'

'But I thought she didn't get on with her mum.'

'She doesn't; I mean, she didn't. They've had some sort

of rapprochement because of the op. Gave Chloë a bit of a scare, I think.'

Emma nodded. She was thinking. 'The thing we haven't talked about is my job. How could you possibly do that?'

'I reckon I could have a stab at it.'

Emma shook her head. 'That fills me with confidence.'

Gill sighed. 'You're changing your mind, aren't you?'

'No, well, yes, sort of. Look, I was the one who got you here, but now we actually think about it clearly, it's not tenable, is it?'

Gill looked disappointed.

'Well, is it?' Emma persisted.

'I suppose not,' Gill said wistfully. 'It is a good idea, though, isn't it?'

'I don't know, maybe I don't really want to run away anyway. I'm a grown-up, for goodness sake. Grown-ups don't run away. I love Max and Saskia. Well, some of the time.'

'Yeah, I know,' said Gill.

Emma smiled. 'Why don't we drive back in convoy? I've just got to call Max. He'll be wondering where I am.'

Emma turned her phone back on and dialled the number and waited for Max to answer. She was nervous. She wondered if he'd called the police, perhaps scoured local hospitals worried she might have had an accident. She'd been away a good three hours now. She felt a wave of guilt wash over her.

'Where the hell are you?' Max's voice was angry. More

than angry. He was furious. Emma was slightly taken aback. She had expected concern, relief, even tears, but not anger.

'I've been coping with everything here,' Max barked. 'And you just disappeared and —'

'I thought you might be worried about me,' Emma stuttered.

'Well, yes, I was. I am, but . . . Hang on. Kevin, please don't swing off the fairy lights . . . Where are you, anyway? I thought you went to the loo?'

'I'm sorry. I just needed a bit of a break.'

'A break! I haven't had a break. I tell you what, if I'd known Christmas Day was going to be this hard work, I'd have stayed at the office.'

Emma thought about all the Christmas dinners she had cooked. All the presents she had wrapped and all the decorations she'd hung. She thought about all the times she'd looked after his daughter. On her own. Now, she'd left him in charge for a couple of hours and he thought it was the end of the world. Suddenly, it was she who was angry She looked at Gill, who was reapplying her lipstick after her disgusting coffee.

'Look, Max. I'm sure you're capable of holding the fort for a while longer. I'm not ready to come straight back. Actually, I'm not coming back tonight. I'll see you in the morning.'

'What do you mean —?' he spluttered.

Emma pressed the end-call key before Max could

finish his sentence, and switched the phone off. 'Right, do you think there's anywhere round here we can get a pen and paper?' she asked. 'If you're going to do my job, we've got a lot of homework to do.'

Chapter Fourteen

In *The Great Escape*, British soldiers only got into the tunnel once they'd had German lessons and had been provided with brand-new outfits, run up by Christopher Plummer. Yes, he was half-blind and kept banging into things, but that was hardly the point. They were prepared. They had a plan. Gill and Emma sat on the bed in their newly rented hotel room and tried to work out theirs.

'So, Jeanette is your deputy. I think I've met her. Remind me what she looks like?' Gill asked. She had a notebook in front of her and was scribbling things down.

'You have met her. At that charity ballet thing that Smith and Tayler sponsored.'

'Oh yeah.'

'She's late twenties, brown hair, sort of eager,' replied Emma.

'Oh, God! Now I remember – annoying, human Chihuahua.'

'My feelings exactly. You'll need to watch her though. She's got very friendly with Dino.'

'OK. Anything else?'

'Well, there is this fashion show. You'll need to find a location.'

'How do I do that?'

'There's a file on my computer, marked Events – all the details are in there.' Gill scribbled and Emma frowned. 'Stick Marco in charge of the staging.'

'Marco?' Gill asked.

'Art director. Batty old queen, but he'll love it. Get the PR department to do the guest list and Jeanette can sort the samples, which just leaves models. Dino wants Naomi Campbell.'

'Well, I've heard models are much smaller in real life,' Gill said uncertainly.

'Yeah, well, not that small. We need an angle, a gimmick. I tell you what, why don't you set Jeanette that as a task, a sort of hoop you expect her to jump through. She'll be sure to come up with something because she can't bear to fail, especially not in front of Dino.'

'What about Dino?' Gill asked nervously. 'How do I handle him?'

'Just nod a lot and go along with his stupid management wheezes. They don't achieve anything, but they keep him happy.'

Gill sat up and put down her pen. 'Right then, my turn.' She picked up a paper bag next to her and pulled out a box of hair dye and a pair of scissors. They'd had to drive miles to find a chemist open on Christmas Day. When they found one, the person behind the counter clearly couldn't understand why they would have come out just to buy dye and scissors.

'Hair emergency, nee, naa, nee, naa,' Gill had announced, waving her hand above her head to indicate a spinning blue light.

However, since the shop assistant was only about seventeen and therefore had never heard an old-fashioned Z-Cars-style police siren, she had absolutely no idea what Gill was going on about.

They went into the bathroom. Gill put on the clear plastic gloves. They crackled as she took hold of the dye container and cut the nozzle off the end. 'Here goes,' she said, squeezing bright orange gloop on to Emma's head.

'I want sausages,' Kevin insisted.

'But we haven't got any sausages. Will ham do?' Max asked.

'Sausages . . . sausages . . . sausages,' Kevin chanted, banging his knife and fork on the table.

'THERE ARE NO SAUSAGES!' Max exploded, snatching the knife and fork out of Kevin's hand. Kevin immediately began to cry.

'Don't look at me,' Saskia snorted. 'I never said the little brat could stay. Anyway, I'm going to bed.' She stomped off upstairs and Max glanced at the clock on the cooker. Eleven-forty-five p.m.

'Uncle Max?' Kevin said through his tears. 'I'm starving.'

'Well, why didn't you eat more in the restaurant?' Max declared in exasperation.

'Uncle Max?'

'Yes, Kevin.'

'I'm starving. All over.' Kevin's eyes were like saucers. His lip quivered. Had his pudgy arms and legs not been plain for the eye to see, Max might have been persuaded by his waif-and-stray act. Max opened the ice box.

'Ice cream! What about ice cream?' he offered.

Kevin looked suspicious. 'What fwavour?' he asked.

'Chocolate?'

'Chocowit, chocowit, I want chocowit!' Kevin squealed excitedly. 'Can I have it in da tub, Uncle Max?'

'Of course you can,' Max replied.

Max watched Kevin eating ice cream out of the tub with a serving spoon – somewhat inadvisably he'd let Kevin choose the spoon – and sighed with relief. He wished Emma were here. He couldn't believe she'd just gone off like that. What was she thinking of? A terrible thought struck him. Perhaps Emma was having some sort of mental breakdown. Oh, God, he hoped not. Then he'd have to deal with Kevin and his supper every night.

At the hotel, they had reached a crucial point, hair dye-wise. Emma was about to see herself as a redhead.

'These towels aren't very absorbent, are they?' said Emma.

'Keep your head still, or you'll drip all over the floor. I'm doing my best,' Gill replied.

Emma had her head bent over the hotel bath. Gill had taken the shower attachment off the wall and used it to rinse Emma's scalp. Now she was rubbing Emma's head with a towel about as thick as a J-Cloth, only, as Emma had pointed out, considerably less absorbent.

'OK, I think you can look now,' Gill announced.

Emma straightened up, put a hand through the front of her hair and combed it back off her face. 'Oh, my God. I look like Fergie.'

'No, you don't,' Gill insisted. 'Well, actually you do a bit, but don't worry. It'll fade down.'

'Thanks.'

'It's fine.'

They studied the reflections in the mirror. It was weird. Even though they knew they were twins and had even been known to walk up to mirrors and greet the other, they still didn't usually think they looked alike. It was only when other people reminded them of their similarity to each other that they acknowledged it. They were only identical when reflected in someone else's gaze.

Emma and Gill had spent their teenage years taking it in turn to try things on in changing rooms – well, why should they both try something on? If it suited one it would suit the other – and even when they shopped alone frequently returned home clutching the same garment. Now, they stared at the mirror in wonder. Having altered just one aspect of themselves – Emma's hair colour – they had become clones. It was a shocking reminder of how little really divided them.

'Right, now your turn,' Emma said. 'How do you fancy going back to your natural colour?'

'What colour's that then? I can't remember. I haven't seen it in about twenty years.'

'Brunette, Gill. Or it was – it's probably grey by now.'

'My hair is not grey!' Gill declared, outraged.

'All right, all right, don't get your knickers in a twist. Shall I cut it after we've dyed it?'

Gill took a handful of long red hair and studied it. 'Don't cut too much off,' she said.

'I've got to make it the same length as mine, haven't I?'

'I suppose so.' She took one last look at herself in the mirror as a redhead. 'Right, boring brunette here I come.'

'Thanks,' Emma said.

'Uncle Ma-ax?' shouted Kevin from the spare room upstairs.

Max ignored him. It was two-twenty-five a.m. and he was exhausted.

'Uncle Ma-ax?' Kevin tried again.

Max still ignored him.

There was an ominous silence, followed by a squeak and then more silence. Max lay in bed listening, trying to identify the source of the sounds he was hearing. It was like some peculiar parlour game: 'Guess what the child from hell is up to?' A bit like charades only you had sound and no picture to work on. Suddenly there was a bang and then another, accompanied by a scream.

Bang, bang, bang . . . 'Argh!'

The banging was getting nearer. Now, what was that? Max sat up with a start. Something was coming down the stairs. Max ran to the door and opened it in time to see Kevin sailing towards him on a micro-scooter. His speed had built now so that he no longer bumped down the steps. He was practically flying over them. Kevin was screaming and hanging on.

Fortunately, something was in Kevin's path to prevent any further descent. Unfortunately for Max, it was himself. Kevin smashed into him, sending him careering backwards into the bedroom. Max landed on his back with Kevin on top of him, still astride the scooter.

'Uncle Max?' Kevin said.

'Yes, Kevin,' Max managed to reply from his prone position.

'Can we do that again?'

'My fringe is wonky,' Gill said, pulling at it

'It's not that bad,' Emma insisted.

'Nicky Clark's job is safe, I reckon,' Gill said, giggling.

They felt like teenagers, trying out new looks in one of their bedrooms before a party. All they needed was a bottle of cider and the scene would have been complete.

'If our breasts were more perky, I'd say we were fifteen again,' Emma said.

'You speak for your own breasts. Mine are perfectly perky, thank you,' Gill replied. She walked over to the wall-mounted hand-dryer and put it on her face to blow away any loose hairs. 'There is one thing we haven't talked about,' she said. 'My work. We've talked about yours, but not mine.'

'Well, I know Gus.'

'Yeah,' Gill said. 'That's a start, but there's more to it than that, you know. I tell you what, open the mini-bar and get everything out. We'd better give you a lesson in drink preparation.'

Emma went to the mini-bar and began pulling out bottles and cans.

'I don't think the peanuts are going to help us much,' Gill said as she joined her in the bedroom. Gill studied her reflection in the mirror at the end of the bed. Emma glanced over too.

Gill's hair wasn't quite the colour she'd been hoping for. It looked like the sort of stain they put on cheap pine beds to make them look like mahogany.

'It's bad, isn't it,' Gill said in an anxious voice.

'No, no. It's fine,' replied Emma, unconvincingly. 'Look, the office is shut over Christmas, and I've taken some extra days off, so you've got a breathing space before anyone there sees you. I don't know whether Max'll be fooled though.'

'You said he never notices your hair.'

'He doesn't, but, well, if he does, you'll have to tell him you went to the hairdresser's.'

'On Christmas Day?'

'Well, I don't know,' Emma said in exasperation. 'Tell him you booked yourself into a spa for a special pampering package or something and the hair came as part of it.'

'Will he go for that?' Gill asked.

'Sound stressed and he will. You know, rant a bit. He won't argue if he thinks you're having a mental breakdown or something. Men think women are mad half the time anyway.'

Gill nodded and turned away from the mirror to survey the collection of beverages on the bedside table. She sat down on the bed, next to Emma. 'OK, let's have a test. If someone asked for a whisky and soda, which of these whiskies would you serve them?' She held up a teeny bottle of Glenfiddich and one of Kentucky bourbon.

'The Glenfiddich?' Emma tried.

'Wrong. The answer is neither. When serving whisky with a mixer you don't use premium quality, you use a blended one.'

'Oh,' Emma said.

'Tequila sunrise. What are the ingredients?' Gill asked.

'Tequila, obviously,' Emma answered. 'Orange juice and, oh, what's that red stuff called?'

'I'm not helping you.'

'I give up.'

'Grenadine,' Gill said. 'Jesus! We haven't even got to prices yet.'

'I'm sorry if I haven't spent the last decade in a cocktail bar,' Emma said, disgruntled. 'I've been rather busy.'

'OK, OK, but it looks like it's not only me who's got to do some cramming.'

In Max and Emma's bedroom at home, all was quiet. Max and Kevin lay in a tangle of arms and legs across Max and Emma's bed. The duvet was littered with small sharp pieces of plastic from the box of Kerplunk! Max had managed to find on the top of the wardrobe. It had been an act of desperation at about four a.m. to get it down. But Max had been exceedingly desperate. And it had worked. Fifteen minutes of Kerplunk! and Kevin had finally conked out. Max had followed a couple of minutes after. His last thought as he went to sleep was how much he was looking forward to getting back to the office. At least at work, he got the occasional break. He also vowed to be nicer to Emma. This full-time childcare lark was a bloody nightmare.

'You'd better have these then.' Gill handed Emma the keys to her 1982 Mini Mayfair. 'The door is a bit stiff and the accelerator pedal tends to squeak in wet weather.'

'I know,' Emma said. 'I've been in it, remember.'

'Oh, yeah,' Gill said.

In turn, Emma gave Gill her house, office and car keys. 'For the office, wave this,' Emma pointed to a small black stick hanging from the fob, 'at the door to open it.'

'Very high tech,' Gill said.

They each studied their unfamiliar keys. They were the keys to their new lives.

After a minute's silence, Emma took the lead. 'Right then, shall we go?' she asked.

Gill nodded. 'You follow me.'

'Always have to be first, don't you?' Emma laughed.

'Not any more. You're me, remember,' Gill said, also laughing.

Emma climbed into the Mini and Gill into Emma's Audi. They both thought how strange it was that the seats were already adjusted just right for each of them. They started the engines, met at the exit to the car park and, after a cheerful beep of the horns, headed off down the motorway. As they drove, each sealed in her own little capsule, they thought about what they were giving up and what they were taking on. They each felt nervous but excited.

At the outskirts of London, Emma swung her car alongside Gill's. 'OK, well, call me if you need anything,' she said.

'Yeah,' Gill nodded.

They hovered side by side as other cars beeped in

frustration around them. They wanted to hug, but there were two sheets of metal and several feet of air between them. All they could do was clasp each other's hands.

'Good luck,' Gill said.

'Yeah, you too,' Emma said. 'Do you think we can really pull this off?'

'God knows.'

With that, Gill let go of Emma's hand and the two cars and their drivers started off in different directions.

When Gill arrived at Emma's street, she parked the car and got out slowly. It was just getting light. She looked down at her clothes. They were Emma's. They felt unfamiliar; grown-up. Gus would have said they were wife clothes and that's exactly what they were. Gill was wearing a grey zip-up velour top and grey tweed flares, plus low-heeled black boots which needed reheeling. Is this what you were supposed to wear when you were thirty-eight? Gill usually shopped in Top Shop. She was invariably the oldest person there by a good decade. Indeed, she often joked with Chloë that a security guard might accost them at any moment and escort them out. 'Could you please leave the store, ladies, you're frightening the other customers.'

Gill stroked a hand over her tweed trousers. Her middle-aged-wife tweed trousers. She was no younger than Emma, but she felt as if she were. That was the thing about being single. It allowed you to inhabit a permanent teenage state. Gill and Chloë and Gus and all the other thirty-somethings she knew who were unattached were in a sort of limbo where they got to behave like children but on adult wages.

Gill opened the gate and walked up the path towards Emma's front door: Emma's grown-up navy front door. She felt like she was stepping into the adult world for the first time.

Emma looked down the line of bells. She'd never really noticed before, but there were six. Distinguishing between them was difficult. Attempts to slip new names inside the little clear plastic compartments had been abandoned long ago. The plastic was now milky with age and covered in layer upon layer of paper and Sellotape. The names themselves, scrawled in different coloured Biro, had faded, or had been rendered illegible by rain.

These were all rented flats, hence the quick turnover of occupants. People came and went. Emma was entering a world of impermanence, one where your name could be Sellotaped over in a few moments, your existence wiped out as easily as dirt on a window – speaking of which, the windows could have done with a bit of a going over. On Emma's street, she knew her neighbours, most of whom had been there for years. If you so much as put your rubbish out a day early, someone from the conservation society – they were Grade Two listed – would be round. When she'd had a man in to paint the front a couple of years ago, a lady from four doors down had come to inspect the paint pots to ensure he was using the historically correct hue, known as gull wing.

On Gill's street, Emma doubted anyone cared what colour the front door was painted, or indeed if it was painted at all. Emma smiled. This was her chance to be anonymous. It was as if she were moving to a strange country where no one knew her. More importantly, it was one where no one expected anything of her. Emma felt as if she were going on holiday. Not quite sun, sea and sand, but teenager- and toddler-free, which was almost as good.

The bells may have been indistinguishable, but Emma knew Gill was the third down.

She'd pressed it so many times. This time she didn't. She used the key to open the door and immediately trod on a mountain of pizza restaurant flyers and minicab cards. She bent down to pick them up, then stopped herself. She didn't have to clear them up. She wasn't responsible for ensuring a clean and tidy house. Emma stepped over the pile of waste paper and began to climb the stairs.

Gillian looked around. She had never studied Emma's hall before. She had just walked through it. Now she took in every feature. This was her hall, the hall she would be walking through for the next, well, who knew how long? It was tall and narrow. There was a glass console table with a vase of twiggy things in it. Gill wasn't big on twiggy things. The kind of people who had twiggy things also had kilim-covered footstools and wicker laundry baskets. They designed their homes rather than just living in them. To be able to do that, you had to be settled and Gill had never been settled enough even to think about a laundry basket. She just piled her things on the floor and when she couldn't find anything clean she stuffed the lot into the washing machine.

But now she was Emma. Gill had to get used to the idea that she was now a twiggy-thing and laundry-basket sort of woman. She had a husband, a teenager and a three year old to look after. Jesus, never mind the laundry basket, she'd need a skip for all the washing there must be.

'Hello?' Gill said it tentatively. She hoped no one would answer. She needed to get used to the idea of being Emma before attempting to pass herself off as her in front of an audience. 'Hello?' She said it again just to be sure.

Still there was no answer. Gill walked up the hall and into the kitchen. It was huge, with a stainless-steel cooker and extractor and the kind of fitted cupboards that don't come from MFI. She'd been here a hundred times but as guest, not owner. She didn't actually know how anything worked. Gill bent down and began opening the doors on the base units. She attempted to memorise the contents. Well, you never knew when someone might demand an egg poacher, did you? She needed to know where everything was. It reminded her of a game she and Emma used to play as children. Their mother would bring a tray of items: a jug, a ball, a knife etc., into one of their bedrooms. Then she would take it away and cover it with a tea towel. They had two minutes to write down everything that had been on the tray. Emma had always been better at it than Gill.

Next Gill studied the line of switches above the work surface and began switching them on and off to work out which operated what. So that was the dishwasher, that was the cooker, the washing machine. What had started out as a joke was turning into a cross between *Mastermind* and a Duke of Edinburgh's Award Scheme event. Your task tonight: Orientate your way round your twin's kitchen without the use of a compass or a map.

Grrrrrrrm.

Gill jumped a foot across the kitchen. She had switched on the waste disposal without realising. She promptly leapt the foot back again so as to turn it off. If there was anyone else in the house, she didn't want them disturbed by that noise. Gill fumbled for the switch and rocked it back into the off position. When her heart rate had dropped to mere panic, she went back into the hall. Staring at her were the stairs. Up those stairs was the bedroom and in the bedroom was Max.

This was the really tricky bit about the swap. She'd deliberately played it down in front of Emma. She didn't want her to think she couldn't manage it, but, secretly,

Gillian was terrified of how she was going to handle Max. The mere thought that he might try and have sex with her – well, she was his wife, he thought – made her stomach turn over in fear. And what if he rumbled her? Maybe Max was asleep. She hoped he was.

There was only one way to find out.

Emma sighed. Gus was asleep on the sofa. Next to him was a plate scattered with crisps and chocolates and the TV remote. Other plates and glasses were strewn around the room as were sweet wrappers, halves of pulled crackers and the multi-coloured remnants of party poppers. Emma felt a terrible déjà vu. This was Saskia's bedroom, only the devastation was on an even larger scale. The telly was still on. It was showing *National Velvet*. Elizabeth Taylor was riding to victory in the Grand National. Emma had loved that film as a child. So had Gill. She wondered how Gill was doing.

Gus snorted and turned over. Emma was startled, but he was soon sound asleep again. She breathed out. She was a bit depressed. After all the excitement of the swap, now she was faced with either going to bed or joining Gus on the sofa, pigging out on chocolate. She could have stayed at home to do that. Well, she might have had to take a phone call, deal with a three year old and unload the dishwasher at the same time as stuffing chocolate in her mouth, but the end result would have been the same.

Emma consoled herself with the thought that the exciting part of being single might start when Chloë got back, whenever that was. Secretly, she'd always been slightly jealous of Chloë's relationship with Gill. She knew that, in a way, Chloë was a replacement for her. She'd left a hole in Gill's life when she met Max and became too busy with him and Saskia to be Gill's playmate. Now she had a chance to do the things with Chloë that Gill told her about. She was rather looking forward to it.

Emma was startled by the sound of a key in the front door.

'Hello?' she said tentatively.

'Get the vodka out, then.' The door swung open. It was Chloë. Emma stiffened. Would Chloë realise she wasn't Gill? She tried to look relaxed, but hadn't the slightest idea where the vodka was.

'You're back, um, early,' Emma managed to stutter.

'Yeah, a hundred and twenty quid for a cab.'

'Of course, no trains today, I suppose.' Chloë nodded. 'So why didn't you wait till tomorrow?'

'I realised something,' Chloë said.

'What?' Emma asked.

'I can't stand my mum. Now get the vodka out. I'm gasping. And by the way, have you cut your hair again? You look like Fergie.'

The door squeaked as Gill pushed it ajar. As her eyes

adjusted to the early morning light, she saw a lump on top of the duvet. Or rather, it was two lumps. Kevin and Max were fast asleep.

Gill took off her shoes and walked to the side of the bed. Her foot stepped on something sharp. 'Ouch!'

Max stirred and Gill froze. 'Please God,' she prayed. 'Don't let him wake up.'

But she needn't have worried. He was comatose. Gill tiptoed round to the far side of the divan and peeled back the duvet as if it were a section of a Jenga tower. She moved it inch by inch, pausing every so often to rest, before her whole body tensed again as she renewed her peeling action. Finally, it was back far enough for her to slip underneath.

She laid the quilt down and began to take off her clothes, or rather Emma's. Gill sat down on the bed and realised she was sitting on something. It was a T-shirt. She was hugely grateful for this layer of privacy. She pulled it over her head and slid herself under the duvet. There wasn't much room, what with Max and Kevin on top, but she was glad for the padded wall between her and them.

Max stirred again. Gill stiffened. He turned over and threw an arm across the top of the quilt. Gill felt it across her stomach. She was rigid with fear. Her twin's husband's hand was lying on her hip. She stared at it. Gill had been in bed with plenty of men she didn't know very well before and had felt perfectly comfortable. With Max, a man with whom she had shared Christmases and birthdays, she felt paralysed. His arm thrown across her was part of the easy intimacy of marriage. This was an entirely alien state.

Max snuggled himself closer. Gill could feel his breath on her face. Every sinew of her stiffened in embarrassment. What the hell had she got herself into?

Chapter Fifteen

'Good morning,' Emma shouted cheerfully from the kitchen. 'Toast?'

Chloë was still in bed, but Gus was stirring on the sofa.

'What . . . what time is it?' Gus said. He managed to tear his head off the sofa cushion, only to let it fall back down again. He might not have suffered from hangovers, but he was not an early riser.

'Eightish, I think,' Emma answered brightly.

'Eightish? Eightish!' Gus said, aghast. 'The only eightish I'm getting up for is the eightish that's actually nearer elevenish. What planet are you on, Gill? It's the crack of dawn and it's Boxing Day and you're never normally up before noon!'

Emma realised her mistake. Her sleep patterns had been blown to smithereens by a combination of bringing up Saskia and always having work to finish early in the morning because of being up all night with a small child. Eight simply wasn't that early to her. Looking at Gus, however, she realised that she was not normal. 'Eightish. Did I say eightish? Oh, I meant elevenish. That's what time I thought it was. I must have got my times mixed up. Hungover, I suppose,' Emma said.

'You and your hangovers, Gill. I swear they're getting worse.' Gus frowned.

Emma changed the subject. 'Chloë's back.'

Gus smiled. 'Great. Is she OK?'

'Seems fine. Well, better, anyway.'

Gus was staring at Emma's head. 'What have you done to your hair?'

Emma put a hand up to her newly red hair, the red hair Gill had dyed for her. Gill's hair was normally a bit longer. 'Oh, I gave it a trim and boosted the colour a bit,' she blurted out nervously.

'When?'

'Last night, after I came in. You'd passed out. I was . . . um . . . bored.'

'It just goes to prove,' Gus pronounced, lying back down on the sofa and closing his eyes, 'you should never make a hair decision when you're not sober.'

Bang, bang, bang, bang, bang . . .

'Ohmygod!' stuttered Gill, sitting up in bed with a start. It sounded as if the house were under heavy bombardment from a succession of Scud missiles. The floors were shaking and even the pictures on the walls were rattling.

Bang, bang, bang . . . it started again.

Gill cowered against the leather headboard.

Bang, bang . . .

'You couldn't see to that, could you?' said a calm male voice from on top of the duvet beside her.

Gillian's heart leapt again. She'd forgotten she wasn't on her own. Now she had rocket fire and Max in bed with her to deal with.

'See to what?' she said.

'You couldn't see to *that*, could you,' Max said again.

How? Gill wondered. Was she supposed to go out on the lawn waving a white flag? Was there a foxhole in the garden which she was supposed to man? Or maybe there was a fixed gun emplacement on the roof from which she could lob hand grenades at the enemy?

Bang, bang, bang . . .

'Em. You weren't here last night. I reckon it's your turn with Kevin.'

So that was what that terrible sound was. Kevin had obviously risen early, small children having a Margaret Thatcheresque ability to survive on almost no sleep, and was now wreaking havoc somewhere in the house. Gill looked at the alarm clock on the bedside table. 'It's eight-forty-five!' She bellowed the words into the semi-darkness.

'Yeah, a bit better than Saskia used to be,' Max said, turning over.

Better than Saskia used to be! Gill shivered more in horror than cold. What bloody time had Saskia woken them?

Bang, bang . . .

'OK. OK,' she said, before Max could remind her again. 'I'll go.'

When Gill got downstairs, she discovered Kevin had a football and was kicking it against a wall. *Bang!* it went as it ricocheted off a picture. *Bang!* it went again as it hit the picture rail.

Gill went up to Kevin and attempted to remove the football. Kevin resisted, running to the other side of the room, dropping it and kicking hard. *Bang!* it went as it bounced off her head.

Yes, this married-with-kids thing was turning out to be a real blast.

'Got any coffee on?'

Chloë was standing groggily in the doorway to the living room. She frowned. 'You know, that hair really is a bit extreme.'

She was one to talk. Chloë's hair was so bleached, you could have scoured pans with it.

'I've already told her,' Gus said, deadpan. He was lying on the sofa with his eyes closed.

'Well, I suppose it's better than after you set light to it.'

'Are you sure?' Gus asked sarcastically.

'I'll just get that coffee,' Emma said, escaping to the kitchen.

Well, they were both now sober and they hadn't spotted that she wasn't Gill. Emma reckoned she was doing pretty well. She wondered how Gill was doing with Max and Saskia. And Kevin. Now that would be an eye-opener. Emma had never actually said to Gill: 'You don't know you're born,' but she did think that Gill took the simplicity of her life for granted. She also felt Gill didn't give her enough credit for managing to juggle all the competing bits of her life. As much as Emma wanted a rest, this swap was a way for her to get Gill to understand more clearly the pressure she was under. Emma fully expected, when they swapped back, for Gill to go down on her knees and say: 'I am not worthy. You are super-woman.' Well, she didn't actually expect her to do it, Gill being the older twin and everything, but she hoped she might think it.

'Where's my caffeine?' Chloë shouted from the other room.

'Just coming,' Emma answered.

Gill pulled the chocolate-brown cashmere sweater over her head and fed her arms through the sleeves. She pulled on a pair of brown boot-cut trousers and slipped her feet into the only shoes she could find, the black boots from yesterday that needed reheeling. She looked in the mirror. Seeing herself as a brunette was still a bit of a shock, but the total effect wasn't bad. She'd have to remember to go easy on the make-up, as Emma did. Unlike Emma, who wore the bare minimum, Gill had a very definite approach to make-up. As far as she was concerned, if you were going to take the trouble to put it on, then you wanted to see some proof of your efforts at the end of it. As Emma had pointed out on more than one occasion, her sister's favourite cosmetic tool was a trowel.

Gill listened to the sounds of the house. There were none. Max had gone to get a paper and there wasn't a sound from Saskia's room. Having prevented Kevin replaying the cup final in the living room – Gill had removed the football – she had got him dressed, given him his breakfast and he was now in the living room painting with a watercolour palette she'd found in one of the kitchen cupboards. Admittedly, it had taken Gill three hours to accomplish this task, but she was still rather proud of herself. Her first morning of being a mother and she had short-circuited an attempt to destroy the house and given Kevin something creative to do.

Kevin had wanted to watch a video. But Gill felt that she should start as she meant to go on. She was not going to use the TV as a babysitter. No, she was going to stimulate Kevin's young mind with all manner of useful enterprises. When he'd finished his painting, Gill reckoned he could do some cake-making and then maybe it would be papier mâché masks this afternoon. Gill didn't actually have any firm idea how you made papier mâché masks: she just had a vague memory from her school days of newspaper and wallpaper paste. However, she supposed that once you came into contact with a child, such knowledge was gleaned by osmosis. Have a child in the morning; be an expert in handicrafts by the afternoon.

Emma was always moaning about how difficult it was to be a working mother and how exhausted she felt. Frankly, how hard could it be? All you had to do was keep children amused. Emma had said that Kevin was a handful. All Gill reckoned he needed was a bit of attention.

Gill picked up a hairbrush and began to smooth the tangles out of her newly shorn hair. The quiet was delicious. The house, which only a couple of hours ago had seemed to be under attack, was now serene. Had Gill had a more practised maternal ear, she would have heard alarm bells in that silence. Instead, as she finally decided to wander downstairs to survey Kevin's artwork, she congratulated herself on her own cleverness.

When Gill reached the living room, she smiled to herself. This was going to be a doddle. She opened the door and her mouth dropped open. Every wall was daubed with coloured smudges. Quite how Kevin had managed to reach above the picture rail was a mystery. At only three feet tall, his determination, at least, was to be applauded. As was his concentration. Having covered the walls, Kevin was putting the finishing touches to a splatter effect on the coffee table.

'What . . . what . . . what have you done?' Gill screamed.

'Graffiti!' Kevin announced proudly.

* * *

'I'm going back to bed,' Chloë said, walking out of the room, carrying her coffee.

'Again!' Emma exclaimed. 'But you've only just got up.'

'I didn't sleep much in the cab,' Chloë insisted. 'Anyway, who are you? My mother?'

Emma felt a twinge of maternal guilt. She was a mother; one who had abandoned a daughter, not to mention a husband.

'Yeah, me too,' Gus said, snuggling himself further into the sofa. 'I could do with some more sleep.'

'Oh, right,' Emma said, unsure what to do next. She didn't know quite what she had expected, but the single life wasn't turning out to be quite as glamorous as she'd hoped. To someone as married as Emma, the idea of singledom was tinged with sparkle. She had assumed it would be wall-to-wall nightclubs and chic cocktail bars. Instead, it appeared to be at least fifty per cent lying in bed. She was actually rather missing the freneticism of her life. She was also missing Max. Her anger of yesterday had receded and she felt homesick. She decided to call Gill.

Emma crept into Gill's bedroom. She was paranoid that someone might hear, so she put her head under the duvet and dialled the number.

'Hello? Gill?' she whispered when Gill picked up. 'It's me. How's it going?'

Kevin had picked up a paintbrush again and was

heading out into the hall to continue his graffiti theme. Gill threw her body into the doorway to bar his exit. He dropped down on to his hands and knees and began to try to head-butt a way through her legs.

'Ow!' Gill said.

'What's that?' asked Emma.

'Oh, nothing. How are you?'

'Fine, yeah. Just calling to see how you're getting on.'

Gill ran her gaze over the grafittied living room. 'Fine. Just, um . . .' She searched for some suitably wholesome image with which to impress Emma, rather than the squalid one that actually was the case. 'Admiring Kevin's handiwork. He's been painting.'

'Painting?'

The image worked. Emma was stunned.

'And, um, we're going to do papier mâché masks this afternoon,' Gill continued. 'He's very, um, creative, isn't he?'

Emma was even more stunned.

Kevin was now wedged between Gill's knees. His face was starting to go a funny colour. Would Emma mind if she killed Kevin? Gill loosened her knee lock and Kevin slumped to the carpet, spattering yet more paint on the furniture as he did so.

Emma didn't hear the scuffling. Panic had overcome her. Papier mâché? They were doing papier mâché now? They'd be off on a bloody nature walk next. She felt a surge of anger. Just because Gill was new to the motherhood thing didn't mean she had to go out of her way to make Emma look crap.

'I thought we'd have a walk later,' said Gillian. 'Is there a park nearby?'

There was a sudden kerfuffle. Emma heard a series of thumps, followed by wailing. Kevin had got to his feet and made a lunge for the sofa. Gill had caught him by the ankle and he had fallen, hitting his head on the coffee table.

'What's that?' Emma asked.

'Oh, nothing,' Gill lied.

Kevin had passed out cold, which meant at least he was quiet.

'How are you?' Gill asked.

'You already asked me that,' Emma said suspiciously. 'I'm doing fine.'

Gill wasn't really listening. Kevin still wasn't moving and Gill began to wonder if she had indeed committed murder. 'Look, I've got to go,' she said hurriedly.

'Are you really all right?' Emma asked.

'Oh yes, doing fantastically well. Talk to you soon.'

Gill put down the phone. Kevin was moving and had started to sob. She sat him on her knee and gave him a hug. When she looked at the walls again, she wanted to sob too.

'Right then, hold still.' Chloë peeled back the corner of the waxed strip and pulled hard.

'Yeaow!' Emma screamed.

'What? What?' Gus said, running into the room. He was presented with the sight of Emma lying on Chloë's bed, which had been covered with towels. She was naked from the waist down and Chloë was stirring a pot of something as if she were a witch casting a spell.

'Hubble, bubble, toil and trouble. A smooth bikini line so the wax will bubble.'

Gus took one look and recoiled. 'Too much information!' he screeched, covering his eyes.

'There's many a man would pay good money to see this,' Emma said.

'Well, I'm not one of them,' Gus said. 'I thought you were killing her. I'll be in the other room. Shout when you get to the nail varnish stage.'

It was now mid-afternoon and Chloë and Gus had finally risen again. Short of things to do, they had taken it upon themselves to give Gill, or the woman they thought was Gill, a makeover. Emma was trying to enjoy it, but kept being distracted by the excruciating pain.

In between her ministrations, Chloë was reading aloud from the sex book Gus had given Gill. 'It says here that you shouldn't sleep with a guy until the fifth date. Fifth!' Chloë was incredulous. 'I don't think I've ever got to the fifth date. Now, are you ready?' Chloë had peeled the edge of the wax strip and was preparing to pull it off.

Emma winced. 'Can't we go straight to the pedicure?' she asked plaintively.

'No, we can't,' Chloë said, ripping off the strip. 'Anyway, what are you on about? We've done this loads of times before and you've never made this fuss.'

Emma stiffened. 'Yeah, of course,' she said. She only ever had her bikini line done before a holiday. The thought of other people on the beach looking at her was the only thing that got her through the pain. She hadn't put on a swimsuit for a good six months.

'Ow!' she squealed as the strip came off.

'It's no wonder you're such a dating disaster if this is how you look after yourself. It's like the bloody Amazon down here, there's so much undergrowth.'

Emma felt faintly queasy at the idea that Chloë was examining her pubic hair.

'We need to get you on the market,' Chloë said. 'And you don't put a house on the market with peeling wallpaper, do you?'

'No,' Emma agreed weakly.

'Well then, think of yourself as a house. We're doing you up.'

Doing me in, more like, Emma thought.

At Emma's home, Gill and Saskia were surveying the wreckage inflicted by Kevin who was loitering guiltily nearby. 'It's a bit of a mess, isn't it?' Saskia declared.

'Yeah, well, perhaps you'd give me a hand? With two of us it wouldn't take long to repaint,' Gill added.

Saskia's expression changed to one of chilly

condescension. 'Like that's going to happen,' she snorted.

'No, I mean, can you give me a hand?' Gill asked, thinking Saskia must be joking.

'I heard you the first time. He's not my kid!' Saskia spat.

'Actually, he's not mine either,' Gill said, eyeing Kevin.

'No, he's the old cow's.'

Gill was exasperated. 'Look, we're going to have to roller these walls. Do you at least know if there's any white emulsion in the house?'

'No.'

'Well, do you know if there's a cardboard box knocking about? We're going to have to put all the pictures and ornaments and stuff away so they don't get damaged while we paint,' explained Gill.

Saskia didn't move.

'I think I may have seen a box in the kitchen, if you wouldn't mind bringing it,' Gill said.

'You'd be better off bunging the brat in it and leaving him in a telephone box,' Saskia said. 'That's what people do to unwanted children, isn't it?' She looked straight at Kevin. He looked defiantly back. Gill thought how alike they were, each trying to get the upper hand over the other.

'Oh, come on, Saskia, he's only little,' Gill said.

'Little monster. I'm going up to my room and HE and YOU had better not follow me.'

'Aren't you going to . . .'

Saskia stomped off.

'Aunty Em?' Kevin said. 'Can I have some ice cream?'

'No,' Gill replied.

Chapter Sixteen

Max chewed on a piece of toast, reading the paper at the same time. He was still a little sleepy. Every time he picked up the toast and took another bite and then put the toast back down again on his plate, he left a marmalade smear on the newsprint, except he didn't notice. Gill sat opposite him, sipping coffee and listening to the sound of Power Rangers playing upstairs. Her vow not to use the TV as a babysitter had lasted about a day and a half. Now, she was just delighted to have some time to herself.

Things had soon settled into a pattern for Gill at Emma's. Two weeks into the experiment and Max didn't seem to have spotted a thing. Gill rose early, invariably woken by a small child banging something he shouldn't have against something he shouldn't touch. After struggling with Kevin for an hour or so, there was breakfast with Max. Following the initial panic that he might suspect she wasn't Emma, Gill had relaxed. She now chatted over the newspapers, they swapped plans for the day and then he headed off to the office. Emma had taken Christmas and New Year weeks off. The plan had been to spend more time with Saskia. For Gill, this meant she was spared having to pass herself off as her sister at work, for now, at least.

Still, Gill knew it was coming. The day when she would have to walk into Smith & Taylor and issue orders to a team of staff was not far away. In the meantime, she had a problem. A big problem: Kevin. What was she going to do with him while she was at work? If Charlotte and Gordon hadn't been gadding about the world, Gill might have asked them, but that wasn't an option. There seemed only one solution.

'Max?'

'Hmm . . .' he replied.

'We need to talk about Kevin.'

Max hid behind his newspaper, as if barricading himself against invasion by for marauding savages. Well, one anyway.

'You know I have to go back to work next week?'

'Yes,' Max said tentatively.

'Well, we need someone to look after Kevin, don't we?'

'I suppose so.'

'We need a temporary nanny, Max – just to tide us over till Dominique gets back. She is coming back, isn't she?'

Max said nothing.

'Max! A nanny?'

Max groaned. He remembered the nanny nightmares

he'd had before he met Emma. 'Do we have to?' he asked, like a small child who is told he has to go to the dentist.

'I don't see any alternative.'

'She won't have to, um, live in, will she?' He sounded horrified.

'Hadn't thought of that. An au pair might be cheaper,' Gill mused.

Max put down his newspaper on top of his toast and marmalade so it was now sticky on both sides. 'Oh, God. We'll be living with some grumpy teenager who clears out the fridge.'

'I think we already live with one of those, don't we?'

Max smiled grimly. 'How much do au pairs cost?'

'Dunno. Eighty, maybe a hundred pounds a week?'

'Do we have to feed them as well?'

'I don't think we can ask her to grow her own vegetables in the window box, Max. Or perhaps you'd like her to rifle through the neighbours' bins for sustenance?'

Max sighed. 'It's just I don't want someone else living in our house,' he said.

'Little do you know it's already happening.' Gill said under her breath.

Max took Gill's hand and squeezed it. She felt massively uncomfortable. 'I just want us to be together as a family.'

'There's no other way to manage, Max,' Gill said, gently but firmly retrieving her hand. 'So, shall I set up interviews?'

'If you like,' Max said, resignation in his voice. He folded the newspaper, unsure why it was covering him with a sticky residue. He got up, went to the sink and rinsed his hand and the cuff of his shirt which had acquired an orange rim of marmalade.

'So when's good for you?' Gill asked.

'Sorry, I don't follow,' Max answered.

'For the interviews. When is the best time for you?'

Max looked stunned. 'You want me to be there?'

'Well, of course,' Gill said, frowning.

Max took his jacket off the back of the chair and slipped it on. 'Nonsense. You don't need me,' he said, taking a couple of steps towards Gill and planting a kiss on her cheek. 'You know you're so much better at all this kid stuff than me. Anyway, I'm far too busy at the office to take time off. See you later.'

Gill watched Max walk out of the room.

Emma and Chloë were in Chloë's bedroom. Chloë was holding a leather jacket against herself and looking in the mirror.

'So, where are we going tomorrow night?' Emma asked.

'Oh, I thought we'd hit a few places,' Chloë answered. 'You know, see how it goes.'

Emma nodded. It had been years since she'd been out 'on the pull' as Chloë insisted on calling it. She was half excited, half terrified at the prospect. When Emma had decided to do the swap with Gill, she had thought she'd just have a rest from being everybody's mother – Max's included. She had thought that pretending to be single would give her a chance to be on her own for a while. Emma hadn't bargained on actually going out trying to pick up men.

But Chloë was adamant. She had fully recovered from the operation. Indeed, she refused even to discuss it now. Chloë seemed a tad hyper, but maybe that was her way of coping.

'Right then, what're you wearing?' Chloë said. 'What about this?' she suggested, dropping the jacket and holding up a very short silk skirt.

Emma took it and immediately felt guilty. What was she doing? She was married. She couldn't go out on the pull with Chloë. What was she thinking?

'You know, perhaps we could just stay in,' Emma suggested.

'What, and play Scrabble?' Chloë said.

'That would be nice,' Emma said, relieved.

'Bollocks to that,' Chloë announced. 'Get an early night tonight because tomorrow we're hitting the town, whether you like it or not.'

The nanny agency had lined up three possibilities for Gill to see. She hadn't the faintest idea what she was supposed to ask in the interviews, but she agreed to them anyway. She tidied up the living room. Kevin was watching *Shrek* for the fifth time in a row, Gill having abandoned any pretension towards creative play. Neither she nor the house could take any more attempts at papier mâché or even plasticine. Anyway, if they got a nanny, Gill would make that her responsibility and she could clear up the carnage that resulted.

Ding, dong.

Gill went to the door to answer the bell. When she opened it, she stood, speechless for a moment. In front of her was a vision of teenage loveliness the like of which was not normally seen outside a video on MTV. The girl on the doorstep was about nineteen. She had hair as long as her dress was short. It was sleeveless and her arms poured out of it like streams of oil from a can. They were smooth and shiny with youth and health.

'Meessus Freeman?' she said.

Gill frowned, then remembered that Freeman was Max's name. She'd given it to the agency. 'Oh, yes, sorry. Come in,' she said. 'Call me Gi— I mean Emma.'

Gill was still getting used to using Emma's name and she was constantly in danger of giving herself away. The silky teenager followed her down the hall into the living room. Gill beckoned her to sit down on the sofa. 'Can I get you a coffee, um . . .'

'Vonya,' the girl answered. 'My name ees Vonya. From Russia.'

'Russia, really? Wow! Anyway, pleased to meet you,

Vonya,' Gill said. 'I'll just go down to the kitchen and get the coffee.'

Gill shook her head as she went out of the room. She hadn't actually said to the agency 'Give me the ugliest girl you've got,' but she hadn't expected to be confronted by Miss World. Had she been given the option of dumpy legs or facial warts, she would have gone for it. It would be way too depressing to confront Vonya every morning. Still, Gill told herself not to be prejudiced against her. Maybe she was a very nice girl.

When Gill got back upstairs, Vonya was ensconced on the sofa. Sitting down, her skirt seemed even shorter. Surely there weren't still fabric shortages in the former Eastern bloc? Couldn't they have rustled up something with a bit more coverage? This was London in January. Goodness knows how Vonya had managed at home. Either she was the human equivalent of a Thermos flask, or she had found other ways of keeping out the free market chill.

'Are you warm enough?' Gill asked, putting the coffee on the table. 'I could turn up the central heating.'

Vonya shook her head.

Gill sat down, aware of the silence. She suddenly felt like an employer, which was a distinctly new sensation. 'Well, Vonya,' she began. 'I suppose I should start by telling you about the set-up here. There's me and my, um, husband Max.' Saying that felt odd. 'Saskia is sixteen, so we don't see much of her' – not if we're lucky, thought Gill – 'and then there's Kevin.'

'Keveen?' Vonya said enquiringly.

'Yes, he's three. He's a typical three year old, you know, bundle of energy, but lovely, really.'

Could you get done under the Trades Descriptions Act for misrepresenting children to a future nanny? Gill hoped not, but for some reason she felt the need to sell herself, Max and the children to Vonya. Why? Gill was the employer and Vonya the potential employee. Shouldn't it be the other way around? Shouldn't Vonya have been grovelling to her? If this was how the hierarchy was going to be, Gill was beginning to have her doubts about contracting out childcare after all. Perhaps she'd just give up her job – well, Emma's – and look after Kevin herself? Then she thought about it. Maybe not.

'Anyway, that's us. What about you? You're from Russia?' Gill prompted.

Vonya nodded. 'Much experience with cheeldren,' she said in her halting English. 'My mother, she have eight.'

'Eight, really?' Gill said. 'Goodness. She must have had her hands full.'

Suddenly, Vonya burst into tears. Then she began to wail, rocking back and forth on the sofa. Gill didn't know what to do.

'Vonya, are you OK?' she asked, when it was patently obvious she was not.

'My mother's hands,' Vonya wailed. 'Her beautiful hands . . .'

'Yes, what about her hands?' Gill said.

'After accident . . .' Vonya began.

Gill winced. She had a feeling she was not going to like what was coming, but she felt she had to ask anyway. 'The accident?' she said.

Vonya looked up at Gill through her tears. 'The factory. My mother, she work for forty years. She . . . she . . .'

'Yes?' Gill said.

'She do extra shift cleaning machine and . . .' continued Vonya.

'Yes?

'Not easy to cook borscht with only one hand.'

Oh, blimey. Now Gill knew why that comment about her mum having her hands full had caused such an emotional explosion. Her mum had lost a hand in an accident!

'That's terrible,' Gill stuttered. 'Still, presumably the rest of the family rallied round. Your father, for instance?' She immediately regretted this suggestion as it triggered more loud sobbing from Vonya. Gill braced herself.

'My father, he was painter. Socialist realism, you know?'

'Oh, yes, marvellous,' Gill nodded.

'He paint Gorbachev, Mikhail Gorbachev, esteemed Soviet premier . . .'

'Yes . . .'

'My father fell from scaffolding . . .' She was weeping loudly now.

Jesus, all Gill needed now was for one of Vonya's family to be arrested by the KGB and sent to the salt mines and she'd have the full Soviet sob story.

'My brothers, they help,' Vonya stuttered. 'Before taken away by KGB . . .'

Gill got up and went over to the sofa. She sat down, putting an arm round Vonya's shoulder as it shook with her sobs.

One interview down, two to go.

'How many calories are there in a Mars bar?' Chloë asked.

'Dunno.' Emma shrugged. 'Too many, probably.'

'Yeah, better have the Crunchie.' Chloë handed the money over the counter and she and Emma walked out of the shop. Chloë unwrapped her chocolate bar. 'I hate Crunchies,' she said, inspecting it.

'Well, why did you buy it?' Emma said, surprised.

'No pain, no gain.'

'What?'

They were walking along the street now. Chloë had decided that nothing in her or Gill's wardrobe was suitable for tomorrow night. So they were out shopping looking for something new, ostensibly for Emma, but actually for Chloë. She had stopped to look in a shoe-shop window.

'If we're on the pull tomorrow, I need a flat stomach.

I'm still reeling from the food at my mum's.'

'You were only there for the flash of an eye,' Emma said.

'Yeah, well, you've heard of how they fatten up geese for foie gras? I'm not saying my mum actually forced a tube down my throat, but . . .' She broke off and beckoned Emma into the shop, pointing at a pair of pink mules.

'Do you need . . .?' Emma started.

Chloë gave her a look that said: 'Don't even go there.' She attracted the attention of a member of staff, a feat which, given that no shoe shop assistant has ever willingly served a member of the public, ever, was pretty amazing. Still, Chloë was practised. She simply marched up to one on the phone and took her by the sleeve until the girl couldn't ignore her. Then she and Gill sat down and waited for her to be brought a size six.

'Anyway, your mum's food can't have been that bad; I thought she was obsessed about her weight?' Emma said.

'She is.'

'So why was she fattening you up?'

'What am I, her therapist?' Chloë exclaimed as her shoes arrived. She slipped one on and hobbled towards the mirror. 'She's always been like it. Maybe because she doesn't eat herself, she wants everyone else to.'

'Or maybe she's jealous of you?' Emma suggested. 'You know, a daughter is her mother's biggest competition. She still wants to be able to say, "Mirror, mirror on the wall, who is the fairest of them all?" and the answer be her.'

'She was always on about my weight as a teenager. She was more obsessed with mine than she was with hers, which is saying something,' Chloë said.

'You'd have thought with, you know . . .' Emma trod carefully '. . . The *hospital thing*, she might have softened.'

'Yeah, well, maybe some women shouldn't have children. And maybe some women can't and . . .'

Gill watched Chloë. She was looking at herself in the mirror, only it wasn't her shoes she was studying. She was staring at her own face: sadness rippled across it like a pool of water into which a stone had been tossed.

'And maybe it's a shame they're not always the same women,' Emma said. 'But sometimes it's the most unlikely people who make good mothers. I mean, I didn't expect I'd –' Emma realised her slip immediately. She corrected herself. 'What I mean is, don't you believe in the redeeming power of a mother's love for her child?'

Chloë shook her head. 'I believe in a mother's ability to fuck up her child. That's what I believe.'

'Oh, Chloë, that's terrible . . .' Emma began, but she was interrupted by the arrival of the assistant again. Funny how when you wanted some service you couldn't get it, and then when you didn't they were all over you.

'OK?' the assistant asked.

Chloë wrinkled her nose. 'Don't think so,' she said. 'Don't really need pink mules, do I, Gill?' And she smiled.

'So, Tara, do you have any hobbies?'

Gill was on round two of her nanny interviews. Tara was a New Zealander who had come highly recommended. Girls from the New World were, according to the lady at the agency: 'So full of beans, don't you think?' Gillian looked at Tara in her shorts, with her thighs the width of tree trunks, and wondered if she could crush a can of beans between them.

'Well, o'course, there's m'rugby,' Tara explained.

'Sorry,' Gill said. 'Did you say rugby?'

'Course.' Tara nodded. 'An' m'weight trainin'. I c'n lift three times m'own bodyweight. Would y'like to see?' Tara got up from the sofa and advanced on Gill.

'Well, um, I'm sure . . .' Gill didn't get to finish her sentence because Tara hoisted her over her shoulder in a fireman's lift. Gill's head was dangling the wrong way up down Tara's back. Her voice was understandably a little strangled. 'Well, thank you very much, Tara. I think that's all I need. I'll let the agency know,' she said.

The water was so hot that, under it, Emma's skin was as pink as a lobster. Every time she moved, it stung. Emma shifted herself a little lower, wincing as the water lapped her shoulder, and closed her eyes. She could smell the heavy, slightly soapy scent of the candle she had lit and put on the shelf near the door. This was the only light in the room.

After four hours of going in and out of shop changing rooms, trying things on, Emma was exhausted. A pile of crisp carrier bags was now sitting on her bed, while she enjoyed an uninterrupted bath. The last time Emma had bathed alone had been when she was away on a business trip about three months ago. She disliked travelling these days, the novelty having worn off when she visited Hong Kong for the twenty-second time, but one boon was the opportunity her stays in hotels offered her to take baths alone. Still, even then she could guarantee that the phone would ring and there'd be some crisis at the office or at home, or frequently both.

In Gill's world, the one Emma was currently inhabiting, however, a bath alone meant just that. Emma inhaled the silence like a cigarette.

'Oh, shit!' She sat up bolt upright in the bath.

Emma had forgotten that Gill smoked. If she smoked at home, Max would be sure to spot it wasn't her. Emma grabbed a towel and wiped her hands, then she picked up her phone and dialled.

'Hello?' she whispered.

'Em, is that you?' Gill whispered back. 'You sound as if you're in –'

'The bath. Yes, I am. Look, I've just realised. You smoke.'

'Yeah, so?' Gill said.

'And I don't.'

'You're stating the obvious, Em.'

'What I mean is, since you're me, you can't smoke. Max will spot the smell immediately and –'

'Don't worry. I've already taken precautions.'

'What do you mean?'

Gillian patted the nicotine patch she had stuck to the top of her arm. 'I've got some patches,' she explained.

'Oh.' Emma relaxed. 'Thank God. Do they work?'

'No, not really. I'm desperate for a cigarette, but –'

'You can't!' Emma exclaimed.

'I know, I know. I tell you what, though, this nanny business is enough to drive you to drink, let alone fags.'

'Nanny business?'

'Oh, sorry. I forgot to tell you. I thought we needed a nanny to look after Kevin when you, I mean, *I* go back to work. That's OK, isn't it? Obviously, ideally, you'd do the interviews, but, you know . . .'

Emma was slightly annoyed by this 'we need a nanny' business. She felt her life was being organised without her consent. Still, she couldn't really complain about the nanny.

'What does Max say?'

'He's not very keen.'

Emma smiled. 'I can imagine. Has he been going on about having to feed them?'

'Yeah. How did you know?' asked Gill.

'Whenever I've talked about an au pair before, that's what he always says: "Do we have to feed her?" Maybe you should hire a vampire and she could find her own food source?'

'Isn't there already a bloodsucking monster in the family? Name of Dominique?'

Emma laughed. 'Talking of work, are you feeling OK about it? You've only got a couple of days.'

'Thanks for reminding me,' Gill replied. 'I think I'll be OK.'

'Just remember to watch your back,' Emma said. 'Smith and Taylor can be a real nest of vipers. Still, I'm sure you'll be fine.' She didn't sound that sure.

It was Gill's first day as Emma at work, and already she was nonplussed. Was it usual for Emma's office to be like the *Marie Celeste* at ten a.m.? Emma had led Gill to believe that, at Smith & Taylor, it was nose to the grindstone pretty much twenty-four/seven. Gillian scanned the office, however, and there was nobody. Not a soul. She could see some handbags on desks and a scattering of abandoned mobile phones. So, people were in, but where were they? Then Gill heard something coming from the far end of the office. That couldn't be singing, could it?

She picked her way through the desks, stepping over piles of clothes and fabric samples. She had on one of Emma's suits. It felt oddly buttoned up. Gill followed the sound until she saw a group of people inside a meeting room. The Venetian blinds were only half closed. Through them she could see what looked like a gathering of an evangelical church. People were standing and, yes, they were singing. Gill frowned. Emma hadn't said anything about her office being especially religious. Gill pushed the door open to hear the singing.

> *'Smith and Taylor, we love you.*
> *· And our customers, they do too.*
> *We come to work happy every morning;*
> *If we worked elsewhere, we'd still be yawning.*
> *Every night when we go home by train,*
> *We just can't wait to come back again.*
> *Smith and Taylor, we love you . . .'*

A smallish plump man with an unwise moustache clapped loudly. Gill recognised him as Dino Marconi, Smith & Taylor's boss. 'Excellent, everybody!' Dino exclaimed. 'Same time tomorrow.'

There was a just audible groan from the Smith & Taylor employees before they filed out. Gill was on the point of following them, when Dino collared her. 'Ah, Emma,' he said. 'You missed the new company song. It's been written by the man who did the *EastEnders* theme.'

Gill resisted the urge to say: 'You woz robbed!' 'Great,' she commented.

'I'll get Yvonne to email you the lyrics,' Dino continued. 'You can learn it in time for tomorrow's early morning yoga session.'

'Early morning what?' Gill asked.

'Oh, haven't you heard? Six a.m. Sting's trainer's coming.'

Gill shuddered, but her mind was elsewhere. She'd left the new nanny in charge of Kevin. Her name was Barbara. She was a no-nonsense older lady from Nottingham and despite a slightly totalitarian edge – she had looked at the kitchen and asked Gill in a disapproving voice if she was familiar with Dettox spray – she was the best of the ones Gill had seen. Gill had no time to do more interviews and, besides, Kevin wasn't exactly a delicate flower. It was the nanny Gill should be worried for, not Kevin.

Dino was still talking. 'Anyway, I'm glad you're here,' he said. 'I was expecting a memo.'

'A memo?' asked Gill, who, never having worked in an office, wasn't aware that if cars ran on petrol, offices ran on memos.

'Yes, yes. I . . .' Dino's voice trailed off, interrupted by some more singing. Only this time, it wasn't coming from the boardroom, but from the room next door. It was the Gents lavatory, but it adjoined the boardroom and hadn't been soundproofed properly. High-level meetings were routinely interrupted by running taps.

'Smith and Taylor, we hate you,
You are just a pile of poo.
We only come to work to earn the cash;
Dino's face we'd like to smash . . .'

'Yvonne! Yvonne!' Dino shrieked.

Yvonne cantered up the office on command. 'Yes, Dino?'

'Find out who's doing that singing and sack them immediately,' Dino declared.

Yvonne nodded and turned to leave, when Dino stopped her. 'And whoever had the stupid idea of a company song, sack them too,' he said.

'I think it was your idea, actually, Dino,' Yvonne said tentatively.

Gill saw the back of Dino's neck turn pink. He then turned back to her. 'Right, I'll expect that memo tomorrow morning,' he barked. 'I want details of the fashion show. Do we have a date yet? I must say, I don't understand why it's taking so long.'

'Well, um.' Gill flim-flammed. Dino persisted.

'Why couldn't it have been at Christmas?'

Gillian nodded, trying not to look too scared. She thought quickly. 'Not high profile enough. Too many other big events on. By doing it in February, we get a clear run at the papers.' All that time listening to celebs in Bliss had come in useful after all.

Dino seemed satisfied. 'A clear run, you say?'

'Yes, Dino. Absolutely.'

Now it was Emma's turn to palm herself off as Gill at work. She'd begged a fortnight's holiday from Bliss just as she had done for Gill at Smith & Taylor. She reckoned they both needed some breathing space to get comfortable in their new roles. Now that time was up, ready or not.

Emma was nervous. She told herself not to be so silly. Being a waitress had to be easy after the job she normally did. At Smith & Taylor, Emma led a team of a dozen people. She was responsible for sales running into millions of pounds. All she had to do now was try to remember the price of beer and then not spill it over a customer.

'Gill? Table five,' shouted Gus from behind the bar.

Gus had arrived early. He was now in full flow. With one hand he was opening a beer, with the other he was pouring a spirit. He wasn't trying to be Tom Cruise in *Cocktail*. He was just bloody busy.

Emma looked around. Bliss was packed and this was only lunchtime! What was it like in the evening? All the tables were taken and they were four deep at the bar. Emma's attention was caught by a couple in the corner. He looked vaguely familiar. 'Oh, my God! It's Bob Beresford,' she exclaimed under her breath.

Bob Beresford was a hugely famous American talk-show host in his late fifties. His sinewy hand was placed on the thigh of a woman significantly younger than himself, who had breasts unfeasibly large considering the tiny size of the rest of her body. She was sitting beside him on the banquette that ran along one wall. Her legs were crossed and her knees were turned towards him. She kept leaning into him, whispering and giggling.

'Gill!' Gus shouted again. 'Table five.'

Emma didn't hear him. She was fascinated by the scene going on in the corner. The young girl – she couldn't have been more than nineteen – was now sitting on Bob Beresford's knee. She had her arms wound round his neck and they were snogging. His cheeks were going in and out as if he was in an oxygen tent. Bearing in mind his age and her enthusiasm, Emma thought that if they had sex an oxygen tent is where he might end up.

Actually, to be fair, he was quite attractive, thought Emma. But why did old guys have to get themselves young girlfriends? Did they think it made them look young, too? It didn't. The effect reminded her of what happened when you painted a room. The next door one, which had seemed fine, immediately looked dowdy. In comparison to the girl's extreme youth, Bob appeared decidedly scuffed.

'Gill!' Gus was getting impatient now.

Emma finally registered he meant her. 'Oh, sorry,' she said. 'Just coming.'

When Emma got to the bar, Gus was shaking his head. 'You're on another planet at the moment. Didn't you hear me shouting?'

'Yeah, but I didn't think it was for me.'

'Is there another person called Gill here?'

Emma blushed. 'No,' she said, picking up two glasses and putting them on a tray. 'Table five, right?' she said.

Gus nodded.

Emma began to make her way across the room. It was so packed that every foot she had to say, 'Excuse me,' or 'Would you mind?' Every time she squeezed through a narrow gap, she spilt a bit more of the drinks. It was like a more chic version of the old *It's a Knockout* game where contestants had to navigate an assault course carrying a container of water on their heads – only they managed to arrive at the end with more of it left than Emma. However, when Emma got to table five, the man there simply handed her a twenty-pound note. He didn't mention the short measure he had received: Emma wondered why she'd worried.

As she turned to make her way back to the bar, she was facing Bob Beresford again. The girl on Bob's lap whispered into his ear, then threw her head back, allowing her hair to tumble down behind her and him to get an eyeful of her cleavage. She was laughing uproariously. She wrapped her legs round his waist and he began to stand up. However, halfway, he wobbled. A hand that had been on her bottom was transferred to the small of his back. He groaned, paused, then collapsed on top of her, on the floor.

'Ow!' she shrieked.

Emma and everyone else in the bar gasped, but no one moved.

'Oi, get off me!' she squealed.

Bob was as immobile as a beached whale. He simply

lay there and whimpered. With a show of strength that belied her wire-hanger physique, the girl managed to roll Bob off herself and stood up.

'Call my osteopath!' Bob wailed.

'Call 'im yourself,' the girl snapped.

'Please. I'm in pain,' Bob pleaded.

The girl was towering over him in her high heels. She was attempting to wipe a dust mark off her white denim mini with its fringed hem. 'This is new, this is,' she said, giving him a disparaging look.

Emma watched and wondered at the cruelty of the young. One minute that girl had been sitting on the lap of Bob Beresford, TV star. The next, he was just some old guy lying on the floor. The girl gave herself a final dust down. 'See ya!' she said, turning on her heel and marching across the bar. Still no one else went to help Bob.

Emma put her tray under her arm and went over. 'Are you OK?' she said. 'Can you stand?' She took him under one armpit and, using the table to push himself up, he came to a vertical position. He groaned.

'Let's get you sitting down,' Emma instructed. She felt like she was working in an old people's home, helping one of the residents back to their chair after an arduous effort at line dancing. Once Bob was safely back in his seat, he smiled.

'My knight in shining armour,' he said.

'Well, I'd better get back to work,' Emma said.

'D'you have to?' he asked, his eyes twinkling as he switched on the full talk-show charm.

Emma blushed.

'You in trouble?' asked a tall, blond man, who had just joined them. He looked tanned and confident.

'Alex! Good to see ya!' Bob declared. 'How ya doin'?'

'Well, I better, you know . . .' Emma scuttled away.

Alex watched her go, then turned back to Bob. 'More to the point, how are you doing, Bob?' he asked.

'Fine,' he grinned. 'Thanks to that little lady. You should give her a raise. What's her name, anyway?'

Alex looked at Emma again. She had almost disappeared amidst the throng at the bar.

'Jane,' he said. 'No, no. Gill. That's her name. Gill.'

Gill took a deep breath. 'Jeanette?' she said. 'Could you come in for a moment?' Then she went back into Emma's office and sat behind a desk. She had already seen Marco. As Emma had suggested, she had put him in charge of staging the fashion show. Marco had been delighted, just as Emma had said he would be. He'd started going on about a circus theme and big tops and trapezes, which had worried Gill a little, but she'd decided to leave him to get on with it. He must know what he was doing, mustn't he?

'Hi,' said Jeanette, poking her head round the door.

'Come in,' Gill said, sounding as official and in charge as she could. She really, really wanted a fag. 'The fashion show,' she began.

'Yes?' Jeanette said.

Gill noticed Jeanette's clothes. They were immaculate, businesslike, but sexy. On her blouse she had undone one more button than she strictly needed to, and her heels were a good inch higher than was really practical, but the whole effect had a polish that was frankly frightening. No wonder Emma was concerned about her. This girl was trouble. If Gill had met her in the Ladies at a bar, she wouldn't have been lending out her mascara, that's for sure. Gill needed to use psychology.

'I know how keen you are to progress at Smith and Taylor . . .' Gill began. That was good. Appeal to her ambition. 'So I'd like to offer you the opportunity to have your input into the show.'

Jeanette took the bait. 'Yes,' she said enthusiastically.

'I'm putting you in charge of the models. Do you think you can manage that?' This was tactic number two: appeal to Jeanette's innate sense of superiority over Emma.

'No problem,' Jeanette said confidently.

'We need a gimmick,' Gill said, repeating what Emma had told her. 'An angle. What do you reckon?'

Jeanette smiled broadly. 'Oh, I'm sure I can come up with something.'

Chapter Seventeen

The Winchester Hotel was a 1930s baronial extravaganza. Made of stone the colour of custard, the front sported turrets and medieval-style battlements. The windows were divided into myriad tiny diamond shapes by lines of black lead. Gill and Chloë walked up the front steps on their way to beginning their big night out. A porter in a navy uniform covered in gold buttons and bits of superfluous satin rope opened a glass door. They walked through and approached the lifts.

'I'm sorry, ladies, can I help you?' Another member of Winchester staff, wearing full morning dress – what was this, a hotel or a Gilbert and Sullivan operetta? – was blocking their path.

'No, I don't think so,' Chloë answered. 'We're going to the bar.'

Ting! the lift went as the doors opened.

The man in the silly outfit didn't move. 'I'm sorry, ladies, but we don't allow unaccompanied females in the bar,' he said.

'You're joking, right?' Chloë said.

'No, madam, I am not joking,' he replied. 'It is hotel policy.' He ignored the lift doors, opening and closing behind him like a hungry crocodile's jaws. 'Now, if you wouldn't mind leaving,' he added pompously.

The reality of what he was suggesting hit Emma – that she and Chloë were prostitutes! The concierge thought Emma was a lady of the night rather than one who normally got an early one! It would have been funny if it weren't so insulting.

'I know what you think I am,' Emma said defiantly. 'And I think it's outrageous.'

'I'll handle this,' Chloë said. 'Now, my good man . . .'

The concierge was unimpressed. 'I'm sorry, ladies. Would you please leave?' he repeated, taking a step towards her.

'No, no, you don't understand –' Emma began.

'I understand perfectly, madam.' His lip was really curling now.

There was a short stand-off with Emma and Chloë and the concierge staring each other out. Then, in one deft manoeuvre, he hooked an arm under both their armpits and began to shuffle them towards the door – fast. The doorman swung the door open again and Emma and Chloë were deposited on their bottoms on the pavement. It felt cold against Emma's thin skirt. She found herself wishing she'd worn her usual knickers rather than one of Gill's G-strings. This supposed night out on the pull was not turning out quite the way she had imagined.

The concierge and the doorman looked at Emma and Chloë with contempt. The concierge swept the palms of his hands together as if brushing nasty dust off them.

'Just wait till I get my lawyer on to this,' Chloë shrieked.

'Have you got a lawyer?' Emma whispered.

'Of course not,' she hissed back.

At that moment a shiny limo pulled to a stop opposite them. The concierge and the porter stood to attention. Emma and Chloë watched from their lowly position on the pavement as the limo driver hopped out nimbly and opened the rear passenger door. A slightly gnarled hand took the handle and then a man got out.

'It's Bob Beresford,' Chloë hissed excitedly. 'The talk-show guy, you know.'

Emma nodded.

Bob saw Emma and smiled. Chloë looked at Bob and then at Emma and then back to him again. 'He's smiling at you,' she said in amazement. 'Do you know him?'

'Not really,' Emma muttered back. Then she froze in fear. Bob was coming over.

'My turn to be the knight in shining armour, I think,' he said, extending an arm. First Emma took it, then Chloë as he helped them both to their feet. 'What are you doing here, if you don't mind me asking?' he said.

'Sitting in the gutter. Haven't you heard? It's the latest thing,' Emma said.

'Ha, ha, ha. You English girls. Very funny,' Bob said.

'We haven't met,' Chloë announced, fixing Bob with her gleamiest smile. 'I'm Chloë.'

'Very pleased to meet you, Chloë. Shall we go in?' Bob offered Emma and Chloë each an arm and they cruised past the doorman.

'Mr Beresford,' he said, tipping his cap.

'I think I owe you a drink, don't I?' Bob asked as they approached the lift.

'Do you?' Emma said.

'Champagne, I think?' Chloë said, giggling.

'Champagne it is,' Bob confirmed.

'Well, I'll be off then, Mrs Freeman,' Barbara the new nanny said, buttoning up her sensible mac. It was nine p.m. and Gill was back from work.

'Sorry again about me being so late,' Gill said.

'Never mind.'

'I'll pay you overtime, of course.' Barbara nodded. She was in the hall, near the front door. They'd agreed that she should live out, at first anyway, largely as a sop to Max who was still unhappy about the whole notion of a nanny. Barbara hadn't actually spoken to Max. She treated him as if he were the family gerbil, of occasional if vague interest, but not actually to be consulted about anything. Indeed, Barbara believed that childcare was a matter strictly between mother and nanny. She stepped through the open front door. 'I'll see you in the morning,' she added. 'Seven-thirty sharp.'

'Yes, it's G—Emma, I mean, call me Emma, please, Barbara.'

'No, no, that's all right, Mrs Freeman. I prefer to keep things on a professional footing,' she insisted. 'If you don't mind.'

'Well, I suppose if you prefer . . .' Barbara was a nanny of the old school. Her thoughts on childcare were as rigid as her grey perm. Frankly, she terrified Gill, but she reckoned Kevin would cope.

'Speaking of which,' Barbara added, 'I hope you don't think I'm talking out of turn, but I did have a little glance in your daughter's room earlier . . .'

Gill frowned. 'Daughter? Oh, you mean Saskia.'

'And, well, if you let these things progress, you never know where you are. Spare the rod and spoil the child, I say.' Barbara's lips were pursed.

'I hope you're not advocating corporal punishment, Barbara?'

'I was speaking figuratively, Mrs Freeman, but there are many ways to skin a cat . . .'

Jesus, so she wasn't just a potential child-beater, she was a would-be cat-torturer too! Gill told herself not to be so silly. Barbara had come with excellent references. Gill had rung one of the mothers listed and her recommendation had been glowing. There had been just one phrase, 'You have to let her get on with it,' which Gill had been nervous of, but that didn't mean she was a Nazi, did it?

Barbara was still talking. 'What I mean is,' she was saying, 'if I'd had her from birth, things wouldn't be as they are. Children are like dogs, Mrs Freeman. They need regular feeds, a lot of walking and discipline. Well, I'll leave it there, Mrs Freeman.' She smiled. 'See you in the morning.'

The bar at the Winchester was on the top floor. The view was spectacular. Emma, Chloë and Bob had a table right next to the window. The London streets were laid out beneath like tangled strings of Christmas fairy lights. In the bar, the decorations were now gone, holly and ivy replaced by vases of trumpet lilies and weird jungle flowers that were so ugly they must have been incredibly expensive.

Chloë and Bob were getting along famously. They were chatting about New York, which was where Bob was based. Chloë had been there a couple of times shopping and they were swapping the names of bars and restaurants. Emma left them to it. She was looking down at the scene below and thinking about home. What would Max be doing now? And Saskia? She even missed Saskia. She hadn't thought she would, but however much of a nightmare Saskia was, Emma still missed her. And loved her.

Emma had been unsure of her feelings towards Saskia when she had agreed to this swap with Gill. She'd felt so ground down by Saskia's behaviour and Max's refusal to deal with it that it had obscured the reality of how she felt. Now that there was some space between them, the fog had cleared. It was one positive thing that had already come out of the swap. The other was how she felt about Max. Yes, he had his faults, but Emma now knew that without him, her life was meaningless.

The traffic snaked along far below and Emma wondered if Max, on his way home from work, was in one of those cars. She wished she was the one waiting for him.

'So, are we going on to a nightclub then, or what?' Chloë asked.

Gill stared at a dirty coffee mug. She had been on her way down from putting Kevin to bed when she spotted Saskia's door open. So this is what Barbara had meant. The room looked not dissimilar to the aftermath of a hurricane. Clothes were scattered on every available surface. Grubby crockery covered the few remaining sections of floor not draped with fabric. She knew she and Chloë weren't very tidy, but even by her low standards, this room was an unbelievable tip. She bent down and picked up a plate with some unidentifiable remains on it. Then she gathered up a mug and a glass. She was just considering whether to sort through the sartorial rubble to try to work out what might need washing when she heard footsteps behind her.

'What are you doing?' said an outraged Saskia, standing with a towel round her, wet hair dripping on the carpet.

'Isn't it obvious? I'm trying to clear up,' Gill replied.

'Well, you can't.'

Gill frowned. 'If I don't do something, we'll be able to supply the local hospital with all the penicillin it needs,' she said, indicating the plate of food.

'God! You don't understand anything,' Saskia said, snatching the plate back and stomping into the room. 'This is my room. I can have it any way I like and I like it untidy. It's not up to you. Daddy said.'

Gill turned round. She had her back to the door. 'Saskia, please . . .' she began.

Saskia advanced on her. She took hold of the edge of the door. 'Leave me alone,' she shouted.

'Are you going to come downstairs and have some dinner?' Gill asked.

'I am on a fast in solidarity with the oppressed people of Tibet,' Saskia announced.

Gill looked down at the plate Saskia was holding.

Saskia blushed. 'I only started the fast today,' she mumbled. 'Anyway . . .' She thought for something generically horrible to say and came up with: 'You're not my mother. You can't tell me what to do.'

'But, Sask . . .'

The rest of Gill's sentence was lost as Saskia slammed the door in her face.

Emma and Bob waited at the table. Chloë had gone to the Ladies and Bob was waiting for his credit card to be returned by a waiter.

'Quite a gal, Chloë,' Bob said.

Emma nodded and smiled. She would miss her when she swapped back.

'You coming with us?' Bob asked.

'Oh, I don't think so,' Emma said. 'Two's company and all that . . .'

At that moment an English voice rang out. 'Bob, you old goat, what are you up to?'

Emma followed Bob's gaze across the room.

'Alex!' Bob exclaimed, smiling broadly. 'Haven't you got a bar to run?'

Alex walked over to meet them. 'Oh, hello – Jane, isn't it? No, Gill. Yes, Gill, sorry,' he said, surprised to see Emma. He looked at Bob. 'Well, you didn't waste any time.'

'Hi. You've got the wrong end of the –' Emma began.

'It doesn't matter,' Alex said, turning back to Bob. 'Can you stay for a drink?'

Bob shook his head. 'Off to a nightclub.'

'Oh, well,' Alex said. 'Good to see you, Bob, and you, um, Gill. See you soon.' And he walked off.

'Who was that?' Chloë said, rejoining them.

'Oh, nobody,' Emma replied. 'Just my boss. Anyway, you know what, I think I will join you at that nightclub.'

'Really, um, Jane?' Bob said, smiling.

'Very funny, Bob.'

Gill stood on the back-door step into Emma's home,

looking out at the garden. The house was quiet. Max had gone to bed. Saskia was locked in her bedroom and Kevin was asleep in his. Gill inhaled deeply. The end of the cigarette glowed an intense orange as she pulled air through it. It tasted fantastic.

So, how was she doing? On the plus side, no one had rumbled her. As far as Max and everyone else was concerned, she was Emma Chancellor. And she had to admit that she was even beginning to feel a bit like Emma. She was wearing Emma's clothes, living in her house. On the negative side, Gill was disappointed. She hadn't expected a rerun of *The Waltons*, but the companionship she had expected had failed to materialise. Emma's home seemed to consist of lots of little compartments. The inhabitants of each met up occasionally, only to separate again.

There was also a cloud on the horizon – the fashion show. Despite Emma's advice, Gill was really nervous about it. Jeanette had come up with the idea that, since the fashion show was in aid of children with Attention Deficit Disorder, it should feature them as well. Dino loved the idea because it was also bloody cheap. Gill had got Jeanette to put a call in to Christina Aguilera's agent, but they had said she didn't appear for less than a hundred thousand dollars and Gill didn't think that Emma's budget would run to that.

Gill took her phone out of her pocket. Maybe Emma had an idea. She dialled the number. She and Emma had swapped mobiles like everything else so it was her own number she dialled. It clicked straight on to answerphone.

'Hi, you've reached Gill, leave a message and I might call you back. No promises though, so make it interesting!'

It was weird listening to her own voice.

'Hi, it's me,' Gill said into the phone. 'Just called, y'know. Call me, if you can.' Then she added as an afterthought, 'I miss you.' And she did. She missed Emma. She also missed the person whose voice was recorded on the answerphone message. The woman she used to be.

It was the day before the fashion show and rails of clothes snaked round Emma's office like an express train in a siding. Gill looked at them and tried not to panic. 'Um, so how many outfits do we need?'

Jeanette popped her head between a pony print coat and a pair of glittery jeans. 'A hundred and twenty. That's fifteen models, eight changes. Anyone would think you'd never done a show before. Are you sure you're OK?'

'Yeah, of course. I'm fine.' Gill was terrified, but she didn't tell Jeanette that.

All the samples for the new season had arrived from Hong Kong and the invitations had gone out. They'd had acceptances from almost everybody. All the top newspapers and magazines were coming. The caterers had been confirmed. The hairdressers and make-up artists were all organised. Everything was ready, so why did Gill feel so scared? Oh, yes, it was because she didn't have the slightest idea what she was doing. Gill yearned to go outside for a cigarette, but she didn't. Instead, she checked her lists one more time. Just for luck. Then she looked at her watch. Half past ten.

'Oh, shit!'

'What?' said Jeanette. 'Have we forgotten something?'

'For the show, no. But I was supposed to leave the nanny some money to get Kevin some pyjamas. That's Max's ex-wife's son. He's staying with us.'

'Well, I tell you what,' Jeanette offered. 'If you need to nip off, I can finish off here while you sort out your *domestic problems*.'

There was something about the way Jeanette said 'domestic problems' that Gill didn't like. 'No, no, it's fine. She can get them tomorrow. Hadn't we better pack these up to go over to the venue?'

'Well, if you're sure?'

Gill nodded.

Chloë waved the airline tickets in front of Emma. She squinted. It was midday, but she was still hungover from last night.

'Look! Look!' Chloë ordered. 'Bob sent them over. Isn't it fantastic?'

'What, he sent you a ticket to New York, just like that? You only met him last night!'

'Yeah, so some of us know how to make an impression.'

'Oh Chloë, you didn't.'

Emma had left Bob and Chloë in the club and Chloë had rolled in at 4.00 a.m.

'Does it matter?' Chloë said defiantly. 'I got a trip out of it!'

'New York, yeah, great,' Emma said. 'Have a good trip.'

'No, silly. He's sent two tickets. For you and me.'

'Two? But why does he want me there?'

'I don't know, there was something in his note about knights and chivalry or something. Oh, it doesn't matter. We're off to New York tomorrow!'

'Tomorrow! But I can't go tomorrow!'

'Why not?'

'Well, there's the packing to do . . .'

'What's to pack? A pair of high heels and some lipgloss.'

'What about work?'

'I've already cleared it with Gus. He's fine about it.'

'You woke Gus up?'

'Yeah, well, it was an emergency. Anyway, he says you've been acting really odd lately and thinks you need a holiday.'

'Yes, but . . . what about you and Bob? I don't want to play gooseberry.'

'Don't be ridiculous. No one's going to play gooseberry.'

Gill loaded her shopping into the boot of the car. It was extra heavy as it consisted entirely of ready meals. Gill had concealed her inability to cook behind excuses that the fashion show was taking up too much time for her to come home and whip up a cordon bleu supper. And it was true. She was tired, so tired she'd quite like to have lain down in the boot of the car as well. And shut the top over herself. She didn't. She got into the front and drove home. On the way, her phone rang. It was Dino. He had big news. 'Liberty Honeywell is coming to the show,' he said excitedly.

He'd pulled some strings, had a word in a few ears. Gill tried to sound impressed. 'Really, Liberty Honeywell? The soap star? That's great, Dino.'

'Obviously, she'll have to go on my table,' he said. 'Next to me.'

'Fine,' Gill said.

Then a thought struck her. She'd have to tell the caterers that there was one more than they had bargained for, food wise. The chef was a nightmare. He'd throw an absolute fit. Then again, this was Liberty Honeywell they were talking about. She was so thin she could be mistaken for a clothes hanger. Gill would get them to put an extra glass of water on the table.

When Gill got home, she found an envelope on the kitchen table. It was addressed to 'Mrs Freeman'. Gill dumped the bags on the floor and opened it.

Dear Mrs Freeman,
I am sorry to inform you that I can no

longer work under these conditions. Your
children are messy, rude and entirely
undisciplined. As I have not completed my
trial period of employment, I am not under
contract. I am therefore leaving forthwith.

It was signed 'Barbara Thompson'. She'd been sacked by
her own nanny.

Chapter Eighteen

Emma and Chloë got out of the taxi at Heathrow and turned to face the automatic revolving glass door. They approached gingerly, hovered uncertainly, then leapt into an empty compartment. 'This is what it must feel like to be a hamster,' Chloë said as they shuffled round in their little portion of glass wheel.

When Emma and Chloë got to the other side, they were tipped out into a cavernous space dominated by ranks of check-in desks. They stretched out ahead of them and to their left and right too. Huge letters hung from the ceiling, denoting the different sections. Everything was outsized. Even the luggage being wheeled around them seemed huge. But then, Emma was acutely aware that she had almost none.

Normally when Emma travelled, she did so with Max and Saskia and they had lots of luggage. When Saskia had been three or four they'd virtually needed to charter an extra plane to cope with all the clothes and toys she'd insisted on bringing. Now here Emma was with just an overnight bag – and it felt great.

'I'll just go and see where we check in,' said Chloë.

Emma nodded. 'OK.'

All around Emma people were trundling purposefully along, criss-crossing the concourse with their wheely suitcases, expertly avoiding each other like skaters at a roller disco, only without the body glitter. They knew where they were going and they were in a hurry to get there.

''Scuse me,' said an annoyed female voice from behind her.

Emma turned to see a large woman in a one-shouldered T-shirt. Her bikini-strap mark was glowing super white against her otherwise tandoori flesh like a pair of white knickers under an ultraviolet disco lamp. She was pushing a trolley loaded with bags and suitcases. An assortment of surly children were tagging behind. One climbed on to the trolley. 'Oi, Sean, I told ya. Ge' off!' the tandoori woman said, clouting the boy. The flesh on the top of her arm kept wobbling long after the blow had landed. It was like the aftershocks of an earthquake. Emma stepped out of the way lest she catch the final reverberations of upper-arm flab – it would have been like being slapped in the face by a piece of raw haddock.

'I'm so sorry,' Emma stuttered.

The woman steered her trolley past Emma and headed for the door. 'Dozy cow!' she grumbled.

Emma was acutely aware that the passport she had in her bag wasn't hers. It was Gill's. Although she told herself no one would know, *she* knew. She felt conspicuous and dishonest and not a little nervous. Perhaps her nerves would give her away if her passport didn't.

Chloë had been studying the big departure board. 'Come on. It's over here,' she said, making Emma jump.

The two of them negotiated a path through the other travellers, but when they got to the check-in area, the queue for the flight was already snaking back and forth behind a succession of metal posts joined together by tape. Emma half expected to hear a starting pistol and then a commentary on the Tannoy: 'And in aisle two, we have Emma Chancellor. She's the favourite, but has been looking a little peaky of late . . .'

A man in a kingfisher-blue tie approached Emma. 'Ticket?' he asked expectantly.

Emma looked blank.

'Have you got your ticket?' he asked again.

'It's all right. I've got them,' Chloë said, handing him a cardboard wallet.

Emma's heart was thumping. What if he asked to see her passport? He handed the tickets back. 'Have a good holiday, ladies,' he cooed.

While Emma and Chloë were jetting across the Atlantic, Gill was facing her toughest challenge yet. It was the day of the fashion show and Emma had arrived at the location. Marco was already in full flow.

'Higher, higher', he shouted, pointing at a swing suspended from the ceiling.

'No, not that high. She's supposed to hover above the crowd, not dive-bomb it. Have you never seen *Moulin Rouge*?' Marco sighed and crossed his arms over his chest. He turned to Gill, tipping his head towards the workman who was suspending the swing. 'Great pecs, but he hasn't got much upstairs, has he?'

Gill and Marco were standing on a makeshift catwalk set up in a former DHSS office in Elephant and Castle. The new owners had converted it into a trendy restaurant. They'd installed a bar where the enquiry desk had been, but had left the booths down one side. Especially favoured diners could now sit either side of a piece of scratched plate glass to enjoy their linguine with shaved truffles (£25). As a further gesture towards irony, the TV bolted high up to the wall was set to show daytime TV with the sound turned down on a permanent loop. Richard and Judy alternated with *Watercolour Challenge*, with occasional excerpts from *Can't Cook, Won't Cook*.

It had been Jeanette's idea for Smith & Taylor to hire Sign On to stage their fashion show. She'd seen something about it in one of the gossip columns and had decided it was the 'in' place. In just a few hours, the venue would be packed with people who had stumped up £250 for a ticket (all proceeds to Attention Deficit Syndrome charities) to have dinner and rub shoulders with whatever celebrities the PR department had managed to rustle up. So far, the list ran: Barbara Windsor and Dale Winton, a handful of It Girls and Liberty Honeywell.

Gill looked up. She was beginning to wonder if leaving the planning of the show to Marco had been a good idea. The swing was dangling perilously.

'Marco, I take it you're not planning to put a small child on that?'

'Yeah, I've had a sequined bodysuit just like Nicole Kidman's made up in an age six to seven, why?'

'Because she might plunge to her death, that's why.'

'But . . .'

'No, Marco.'

'But —'

'I said no, Marco.'

'But no one's going to notice if there is a little accident. They'll all be pissed on champagne. As long as we have a few little girls who are the same size we can keep restocking the swing, can't we?'

Gill ignored him. Were people in the fashion industry completely insane? The answer appeared to be: yes. She gave her attention to the workman instead. 'Hello?' she shouted up.

He paused and looked at her.

'Sorry to bother you,' Gill said, 'but can you take that thing down, please?'

He didn't move.

'I said —' continued Gill.

'I heard what you said,' he answered. 'I just wanna

know who's in charge here. Is it you or Larry Grayson down there?'

'Larry – I mean . . .' Gill began.

Marco sucked in his cheeks in annoyance.

'Can you just take the swing down, please.'

'Well, make up your bloody mind,' the workman muttered, starting to dismantle his handiwork.

Marco looked at Gill.

'What?' she said suspiciously.

'Nothing,' he answered. 'Just don't expect me to cancel the . . .'

At that moment, there was a knocking sound from the other end of the restaurant. A woman in a Barbour and wellies popped her head round the door.

'Hello, there,' she said. 'Edwina from Barry Buttle's Circus. Where do you want these tigers then?'

When Emma and Chloë got to the gate, there was a commotion going on up at the desk. A man was arguing with the airline steward in the kingfisher jacket, the one who'd checked their tickets earlier.

'Whaddya mean, you won't let my wife on the plane?' he shouted. He was wearing surf shorts and sandals and was holding his partner up, as she was clearly unsteady on her legs. Her head was lolling on his shoulder.

'Well, Mr Baines, your wife is . . .' the tie man began.

'What? Fat? Ugly?' the man said, grinning. 'I could have told you that myself.'

The woman's glazed expression cleared briefly. 'Oi, Shane, leave it out,' she muttered. Then her head tipped back and slowly rolled round to its former diagonal position, propped against his shoulder.

'I was going to say she was inebriated, sir.'

'Well, yeah, she has had a couple of drinks. But we're on our honeymoon and she's afraid of flying, see. We just got married.'

'Congratulations, sir, but she is now unfit to fly.'

The woman's ankles buckled. If she really had only had two drinks, they must have been laced with horse anaesthetic. The man at first attempted to keep her standing, then abandoned his efforts and let her slump to the ground at his feet. She stayed there like a handbag at a disco. The back of his neck was turning pink with anger. 'I know my rights,' he said, his voice rising. 'You can't stop us. We've got tickets.'

'Correction: you did have tickets,' said the steward, snatching them from the man's hands. Then he leant into a microphone in front of him and pressed a button. 'Security. Gate twenty-eight,' he said briskly, his voice booming round the airport.

'You can't do that,' the man said, outraged. He lunged for the microphone. 'You bastard, I'll have you.'

The flight attendant picked up the mike and stepped deftly back. 'There's no need for that, Mr Baines.' He spoke into the mike again, with a renewed sense of urgency. Since his voice had started off pretty camp, this meant it was rapidly elevating to a bat squeak. 'Security, gate twenty-eight,' he said. 'Security, gate twenty-eight.'

The furious would-be passenger clambered on to the luggage conveyor at the side of the desk and made another swipe for the microphone. Then he lost his balance and came down like a felled oak, albeit one wearing bad sportswear and swearing. As he landed, two security men rounded the corner at a gallop. They took hold of him and hauled him back upright. He and his wife were led away. He was still shouting, 'Just you wait till *Watchdog* hears about this.'

The steward ripped the tickets in two. 'Next, please?' he said smartly, his voice beginning to slide back down the vocal scale.

'OK, so we've got three no wheat, five no dairy, two no sugar and one in an oxygen bubble,' announced Vera, the lady from the Attention Deficit Disorder Association.

'Did you say oxygen bubble?' asked Gill.

'Yes, poor Tarquin. Pretty severe case,' Vera replied. 'After he had chewed his way through the bedroom carpet, a kitchen table and a three-piece suite, it was decided that perhaps the Ritalin wasn't working. His parents are now experimenting with total environmental exclusion.'

'Is it working?'

'Well, they haven't had to visit DFS for a week or so.'

Gill had managed to dispose of the tigers, dispatching

them back whence they came. Now she had a room full of hyperactive kids, one of whom looked like Buzz Lightyear. Not to mention Kevin. Gill had been forced to bring Kevin with her. Well, she reasoned, no one would notice him in the midst of a gaggle of other children. With any luck, he might actually behave better than some of the others. Gill looked round for him. She spotted him in the corner. He was wearing a tutu on his head and spinning round and round. Every so often he fell over and laughed hysterically.

Marco was shaking his head. 'Well, no one mentioned an oxygen bubble to me.'

'It'll be OK,' Gill soothed.

'No, it won't. You tell me how we're supposed to get an Edward Scissorhands costume over that helmet.'

'A what?'

'Edward Scissorhands. It's part of the Hollywood theme. Still, I suppose the Freddie Kruger mask might just stretch.'

'Cheers,' said Chloë, raising her glass of champagne.

'I still can't believe you blagged that off the steward. You don't get it in economy, you know,' Emma said.

'You don't ask, you don't get,' said Chloë, smiling. 'Now, are there any decent blokes on the plane?'

'Oh, Chloë. You are incorrigible.'

'You don't ask, you don't get,' she laughed. 'Anyway, let's just have a great night.'

* * *

The lights dimmed. It was the signal for the fashion show to start. A few dogged diners attempted to shovel the last mouthfuls of white and dark chocolate mousse with a rasberry coulis into their mouths in the pitch dark, and there was the odd startled cry as mousse missed mouths and slid down cleavages. Apart from that, the room was silent, expectant. Suddenly, the voice of Ethel Merman filled the restaurant. 'There's No Business like Show Business,' she rasped.

Backstage, Marco signalled for the first tiny tot to take to the catwalk. Gill was standing nearby, making last-minute adjustments to outfits. She had decided to let Marco have his Hollywood theme, albeit minus *Moulin Rouge* swing and *Born Free* lions. A seven year old dressed as Julia Roberts in *Pretty Woman* stepped on to the stage. She was the image of Julia, except she lacked the air of winning naivety.

Next, in a sudden burst of light, Kevin tottered towards the audience. He had proved a surprising hit in rehearsal. Amazingly, considering he was wearing four-inch heels – Gill couldn't fight Marco on everything – Kevin managed a half-decent sashay. Gill peered round the side of the backdrop. She could see Dino at the head of the table at the end of the catwalk. A small child was sitting next to him. Gill hadn't realised that Dino was going to bring one of his kids. Poor thing looked only half fed. Gill peered closer. Oh, no, that wasn't a child. It was Liberty Honeywell.

Dino looked happy. Emma felt relieved. Kevin retraced his steps and made it back without falling, and two more mini-models took to the catwalk. They were dressed as Joan Crawford and Bette Davis in *Whatever Happened to Baby Jane*? The audience looked mildly startled by the effect, but clapped anyway. Then a pint-sized Marlon Brando from *The Wild One* and James Dean in *East of Eden* joined them to wild applause.

Gill began to relax. After all her fears, things weren't going badly after all. She had expected these kids to be bouncing off the walls, but they weren't. In fact, they were behaving beautifully.

Suddenly, there was a loud crash. A clothes rail had toppled to the floor. Behind it, two women were locked in a tug of war over a piece of fabric. A pair of little girls in just their pants stood at their hips. They watched, mute.

'You take your hands off that dress before I snap them off at the wrist,' shouted the first woman, a tall brunette in a Chanel sweatshirt.

'But can't you see how much better it will look on my Gemma?' the other shouted back. She was smaller and blonder, but no less terrifying. 'Better than it does on your ugly little gargoyle,' she screeched

'Don't you call my Ellie a gargoyle.'

'Well, let's face it. She's no oil painting, is she?'

'Why, you . . .'

Gill had been so focused on the children's behaviour, she hadn't considered that it might be the parents who caused the trouble. Now, as if in slow motion, she watched as the small blonde mother took hold of the tall brunette mother's hair and pulled it. Hard. The brunette broke free and made a run towards Emma, carrying the disputed frock. The blonde followed her, clutching a handful of brown hair.

'Sssh,' said Marco, turning to face the warring pair. 'You're interrupting Liza Minelli.'

The women ignored him. To the strains of 'Cabaret', they made grabs for each other. Gill had managed to get herself in between them and was attempting to restore some order. 'Now, if we could all just calm down,' she said.

They ignored her.

'Come here, you bitch,' shouted the blonde.

The brunette waved the dress, taunting her enemy with it. 'What're you going to do about it?' she sneered.

By now, the noise had reached the audience. Some were straining to see backstage to locate the source of the rumpus. Dino's smile was looking thin.

Liberty Honeywell turned to him and whispered, 'Is this part of the show?'

Dino laughed nervously.

Gill was desperate. 'I tell you what, why don't both your daughters wear the dress, one after the other?' she suggested.

The women paused, eyeing each other.

Gill held her breath.

On warbled Liza.

'Well, my Gemma's wearing it first,' announced the blonde.

–'No, she's not,' said the brunette.

'Yes, she is.'

And with that, the brunette pushed past Emma and ran on to the catwalk, waving the frock like a flag of victory. The blonde followed her. 'Come back here with that, you old witch.'

Gill had no choice. She scrambled after them. 'Now, ladies,' she began. Her words were lost in a mêlée of decidedly unladylike language as the female foes fought each other all the way up the catwalk. Small children were scattered in their path. When they got to the end, they continued to trade blows and insults. They were about a foot from Dino and Liberty when Gill caught up with them. She positioned herself in front and addressed the crowd with as much dignity as she could muster. 'Ladies and gentlemen, I'd like to apologise for this slight interruption to the show,' she said. 'Normal service will be resumed as soon as –'

Gill felt a shove from behind. The two women had hold of each other and were wrestling. One had the other in a half nelson and was attempting to get her down on the ground. In the process they had careered in Gill's direction. Gill felt herself being propelled forwards. For a moment she appeared to be flying. Then she hit something hard and landed with a bump. She was temporarily stunned. When her vision cleared, she saw

Dino's face. It was surprisingly close up. Gill looked down. She was sitting on his lap. To his left, Liberty Honeywell's face was wearing a shocked expression and half a white and dark chocolate mousse, not forgetting the raspberry coulis. An empty plate sat in her lap where it had deposited itself after Gill had inadvertently launched it.

At the back of the restaurant, Jeanette Adams was smiling.

When Chloë and Emma arrived at Kennedy airport, their eyes were assaulted by the harsh fluorescent bulbs overhead. Emma felt nervous as they joined an endless queue for passport control. The fact that she was technically committing fraud by travelling on Gill's passport still weighed heavily upon her. She was also excited.

She shuffled forward and finally got to the booth. Chloë went first, then, when it was Emma's turn, she put her visa form on the counter and tried to appear calm. A man with a bullet-proof vest stood nearby.

'I'm sorry, ma'am, I can't accept this,' the man in the booth said.

All the blood drained from Emma's face. 'I'm sorry. I didn't mean to . . .' she began.

'You haven't signed it, ma'am,' the man said, pushing the paper towards her.

Emma blushed and searched her handbag for a pen.

The man offered her his and she took it and signed, trying to stop her heart from beating so fast. She handed him the form again, he typed things into a computer screen and she waited. When he finally handed her documents back to her, she walked away as quickly as possible. She had only got a few steps however when she heard his voice ringing out over the arrivals lounge again. 'Ma'am, ma'am.'

Emma froze. Maybe he wasn't calling her. She took another step.

'Ma'am, ma'am.'

Emma turned to see him waving at her. The muscles in her cheeks twitched with nerves. She tried to smile, but her face felt like iron.

'My pen?' he said.

'You've got his pen,' Chloë shouted over.

Relief flooded through Emma. She searched her pocket, found it and walked back to give it to the man. 'Sorry,' she said.

He nodded and she retraced her steps.

'Jesus. I can't take you anywhere, can I?' Chloë said. 'We'd better go or we'll be at the back of the taxi queue.'

Emma and Chloë walked out of the arrivals door and into the main hall of the airport.

'So where are we staying?' Emma asked.

'Haven't quite worked that out yet,' answered Chloë.

Emma stopped dead. 'We've flown all the way here and we haven't got anywhere to stay? What about Bob?'

'I don't think his wife would approve.'

'He's married!' Emma exclaimed.

'Of course. Didn't you know?'

'And you've slept with him anyhow?'

'Yeah – so?'

'But that's . . .'

'Wrong! Oh Gill, you're so *Blue Peter* sometimes.'

'But what about his wife?'

'You don't need to feel sorry for *her*. She gets a New York apartment, a house in Connecticut, a villa in the South of France. Do I need to go on?'

'That doesn't change the fact that she's been betrayed.'

'Yeah, well, life ain't fair, you gotta take what you can. I learned one thing in the hospital, Gill: it was that life is too short, you know?' Chloë looked serious for a moment. Then, just as quickly, the moment was gone. She smiled.

Maybe Chloë was right. What was the point of pretending to be single if you didn't take a chance or two? They were in New York and Emma decided to just go with the flow. 'All right, but where are we going to stay?'

'Something'll turn up. Come on,' Chloë said.

They began to walk again. To get out they had to follow a little cordoned-off path. People were banked up either side as if it were a horse race. They were a mix of limo drivers holding hand-written signs and eager relatives holding children. Emma scanned the signs casually. She wished her name was up there. How lovely it would be to stretch out in the back of a limo.

Suddenly, Chloë nudged Emma. She pointed at a sign. 'Baines, London', it read.

Emma shrugged.

Chloë pointed again. 'Baines, London,' she said.

'Yeah?' Emma said.

'It's the couple they wouldn't let on the plane.'

'The drunk ones?'

Chloë nodded. 'Come on.'

'Come on where?'

Before Emma could argue, Chloë had walked up to the driver. 'Baines. That's us,' she announced.

'Gee, I thought it was a honeymoon couple,' he said.

'Yeah, well, change of plan. Tragic story. She was jilted at the altar.' Chloë indicated Emma.

'Hang on, I . . .'

'Still a bit sensitive about it, actually,' continued Chloë. 'I'm trying to help her get over the trauma.'

The driver took their bags from them and they followed him out of the airport.

Chapter Nineteen

Emma poked her head and shoulders up through the sunroof of the limo. She tipped her head back and took a great lungful of New York air. It smelt great – a mix of exhaust fumes and the warm, yeasty aroma of fresh pretzels. It was always the same when she came to New York: the sound, the smell. New York was one of the few cities to which she came on business that she didn't get bored of. A police siren screamed in the distance. Behind her there was the hooting of car horns as the lights changed and the vehicles up ahead didn't react quickly enough. The car lurched and she was jolted.

'Ow!' said Chloë, who had chosen that moment to join Emma in the open air. She was holding two glasses.

'More champagne?' Emma said, taking her glass. 'We'll be plastered even before we get to the hotel.'

'Oh, for God's sake, just get it down you,' Chloë said, smiling.

The car swept smoothly through the traffic. The wind was blowing Emma's hair. She put a hand up to keep it off her face. She didn't want to miss a minute of the view.

The rush of people and cars, the shouted arguments, the *beep, beep* of horns: the sheer wall of noise swirled around Emma. It was as if she were in a whirlpool and being corkscrewed downwards. Rather than trying to climb out, however, she let herself be spun down. She was happy to drown in the glorious, delicious atmosphere.

Then she suddenly felt a sharp stab of guilt. She shouldn't be here, or rather she shouldn't be enjoying herself here. What about Gill and Max and Saskia? Emma fantasised that they were having as good a time as she was to make herself feel better. She looked at her watch and wound the time forward to London time. It was about midnight now. She hoped the fashion show had gone well. Still, she'd given Gill as much help as she could. She was sure it would have been fine.

'Ma'am, ma'am.'

The car had stopped and the driver was standing holding the door open. Chloë and Emma looked at one another and scrambled back down through the sunroof. When they got out, they stood on the pavement as their driver carried their bags up some stone steps. A good-looking young man in a charcoal floor-length coat nodded at him and opened a pair of huge metal doors, the type you might find on a fashionable gaol. He went through.

Emma and Chloë exchanged glances. 'What do we do now?' Emma hissed.

'Just leave it to me,' Chloë answered.

'But . . .'

Chloë launched herself up the steps. Emma followed. When they got to the door, the young man in the coat smiled at Emma. 'Welcome to the Majestic,' he said.

The Majestic Hotel had featured in every article on chic New York Emma had ever read. She had always wanted to stay there, but Smith & Taylor wouldn't run to the cost, which was considerable. She looked up at the handsome stone carving over the door and walked slowly up the steps.

The lobby was the size of an aircraft hangar. A cherry-wood shelf ran all the way along one wall. Lined up on it at precise intervals – did the staff use a tape measure? Probably – were identical glass vases. Each contained an orchid wired with a tiny lightbulb in the centre. The other wall was mirrored. It reflected the hustle and bustle as people walked up and down the strip of grey carpet that formed a walkway between clusters of tables and chairs. Waiters with tiny trays bearing huge plates with almost nothing on walked purposefully back and forth. Guests sat or stood and chatted to one another with an ease that suggested they didn't need to read their credit card bills each month. The whole place smelt of money.

'Come on,' Chloë said.

She was already halfway up the grey runway. Emma struggled to catch her up. When she did, she caught Chloë's arm. 'We can't possibly afford this,' she whispered urgently, her eyes darting furtively around so as to take in her surroundings without actually catching anybody's eye and thus exposing her own fear.

'I said, leave it to me,' Chloë answered.

They arrived at a huge curved sweep of cherrywood. It was the desk. Two women in size six charcoal suits stood expectantly behind it.

'Yes, ma'am?' said one.

Chloë cleared her throat. Emma held her breath. 'Baines,' Chloë said.

'I'll just have a look for you,' the woman in grey said, tapping the keys on a keyboard. 'Ah, yes, Baines. We have a booking, but . . .' She looked up. 'It's supposed to be for a Mr and Mrs Baines.'

Chloë leant across the desk and cupped a hand over one side of her mouth, before whispering conspiratorially, 'Bit of a hitch with the wedding. He was shagging the bridesmaid.'

'Shagging?'

'Oh, you know, bonking, sleeping with . . .'

'Gee, that's awful,' said the receptionist, casting Emma a pitying look.

'Actually, got her pregnant . . .'

'Oh, my.'

'And then there was the bridesmaid's mother . . .'

'No!'

Chloë nodded.

Emma could barely believe what she was hearing. In

the airport she'd been jilted. That was enough of a whopper. Now her husband had got anther woman up the duff and done goodness knows what with her mother. Give Chloë another couple of hours and who knows what else she might invent.

Chloë saw Emma's disapproving look. 'She's still very fragile, you know. Better not mention it to her,' she instructed the woman in grey.

The woman nodded sagely. 'Men, huh!' She sighed.

'Yeah,' agreed Chloë.

As this conversation had been going on, the woman had continued to tap things into her keyboard. 'If I could just have a credit card for the swipe,' she said brightly.

Chloë said nothing and Emma froze. A credit card! Of course, they'd need a credit card. But neither she nor Chloë could possibly cover the cost of even a weekend at the Majestic. Emma sighed. It had been a nice fantasy while it lasted.

'Didn't Shane give you his credit card details when he booked' – Chloë dropped her voice to a stage whisper – 'the honeymoon?'

'Well, no,' said the receptionist. 'The holiday was actually the prize in a competition. He didn't pay for it. It is usual to take a swipe as well, though.'

'Bloody cheek!' Chloë exclaimed. 'Using a free holiday as a honeymoon.'

Emma winced. Chloë put an arm round her. 'She's holding up quite well, but she is devastated. Don't you think the hotel might like to make the minibar complimentary as well.'

'Well,' the receptionist said, sounding doubtful. She was looking at Emma's expression which was horrified, but came across as traumatised. 'Hell, yeah!' she said. 'We girls gotta stick together.' She slipped a sliver of plastic into a paper wallet and handed it to Chloë. 'The Penthouse Suite,' she said.

Chloë smiled. 'You know, it's not the cheating – it's the lying that you can't forgive, isn't it?'

It was the morning after the fashion show. Dino towered over Gill. He hadn't so much gone pink as trans-mogrified into a human radish. He was luridly red. 'Liberty Honeywell is suing,' he shouted. 'Do you understand?'

'Well, yes, suing is what happens when –' Gill began.

Dino ignored her. 'She is suing Smith and Taylor for damage to her professional reputation . . .'

'Well, um . . .'

'Pain and suffering . . .'

'Oh, dear . . .'

'And the cost of a Gianni Versace evening gown. A couture one!'

In contrast to Dino, all the colour now drained from Gill's cheeks. 'Bloody hell!' she exclaimed. Gill wasn't exactly sure how much a Versace couture dress cost but it had to be a shed load.

'Exactly,' Dino said, puffing out his chest. 'I'm glad you now appreciate the seriousness of the situation.' He gestured to Gill to sit down in the chair on the other side of his desk. Up to now, he had preferred to bellow at her from a standing position. Gill sheepishly lowered herself on to her seat and waited for a renewed onslaught, but Dino seemed calm. 'What I can't understand is why you used real kids rather than models in the first place,' he said sadly. 'You must have known that their parents would be difficult.'

Gill frowned. It had been Jeanette's idea. She'd said she'd cleared it with Dino. She'd said he was delighted.

'Anyway, I've decided that perhaps we both need to consider our positions. Apparently, you have domestic problems.'

'Domestic what?'

'That's the thing with women who have children. Only have one eye on the job.'

'Hang on a second . . .'

'I am giving you gardening leave.'

'But I don't like gardening.'

'Fortunately, we already have someone who can stand in for you.'

'Who?' Gillian was stunned.

'You know I like to promote from within. I feel it motivates the entire staff,' Dino said.

'It also saves the cost of a recruitment agent,' whispered Gill under her breath.

'What was that?'

'Nothing.'

Morning in New York. Light flooded into the Penthouse Suite of the Majestic Hotel.

Emma was standing in the middle of the room. She was wallowing in New York. Windows surrounded her on all four sides. Her feet were sinking into cream shagpile. It ran across the floor and stopped about a foot from the windows. A border of slate then filled the gap. To Emma's left a huge slab of glass stood on two metal spheres. The dining table. A dozen more metal spheres sat around it. The chairs. On her right, a sheet of wall hung from the ceiling. A plasma screen was set into it. Light washed up the windows, periodically changing colour from floor lights set into the slate.

'So where are we going tonight?' Chloë asked, clambering on to the grey suede sofa and pulling back the blinds.

'But we can't stay!' Emma announced.

Chloë turned round. 'What do you mean?'

Emma insisted, 'We can't stay.'

'Are you mad? It's fab,' Chloë said, collapsing on her back on the sofa.

'I know it's fab, but it's not ours, is it?'

'The woman on reception thought it was ours.'

'That's because you lied to her.'

'Yeah, so?'

There was a knock at the door. Chloë jumped off the sofa and jogged to open it.

'Your complimentary honeymoon breakfast basket,' said yet another good-looking chap in grey, wheeling in a trolley. Chloë signed for it and the man left.

The London drizzle prickled Gill's face. She turned the collar up on Emma's coat to shield herself, shifting her position on the park bench. As she did so, the clammy wooden slats clung to her bottom like a greasy-haired teenage boy at a school disco slow dance. Gill shivered and went to push her hands into her coat pockets. Then, she realised she couldn't. Emma had kept them sewn up, presumably to prevent sagging. Such fashionable niceties now seemed a spectacular irrelevance.

Gill had escaped from the office, round the corner. She needed to be on her own. She'd have to go back, of course: they'd be delivering her things in a cardboard box to reception in half an hour or so. But, for now, she sat on her own, wallowing in her depression. She had messed up. Big time. How was she going to explain to Emma that she had more or less lost her her job? It felt like having been asked to cat sit, and having let moggy out by accident only for it to be run over. When Emma and Gill swapped back, Gill was going to have to hand her back the career equivalent of a deceased feline.

It was lunchtime, but it could have been dusk. The light was grey, even without the drizzle. The only other people in the park were a handful of dog lovers in thick jumpers and boots with socks folded over the top and two old Japanese ladies doing t'ai chi under the relative shelter of a horse chestnut tree. Gill had always quite liked the idea of doing t'ai chi. She studied the ladies more closely. They were short and dumpy, an effect not helped by their attire: black trousers and anoraks with the hoods up. They were standing on one leg which made them look less like elegant storks than plump penguins. They were moving their hands in front of them in slo-mo. It reminded Gill of watching an inept barman make a cappuccino really, really slowly. She wanted to rush up to the zen twins and shout: 'For God's sake, get on with it!' Perhaps it was fortunate she'd never got around to doing t'ai chi herself. Maybe she wasn't quite cut out for it.

Gill's nose was running in the cold. She reached inside her handbag, or rather Emma's, for a hankie. She rootled about, scrabbling among discarded Biros, old super-market receipts and crushed Polos. Her hand connected with something cool and smooth. She pulled it out. It was Emma's passport. She carried it everywhere just in case she had to get on a flight. That was the mark of a 'jet-setting' executive, Gill decided. In their case, an ex-jet-setting executive. Gill ran the tips of her fingers over the Euro burgundy cover of the passport – she still preferred the old British blue ones – and then peeled the back open. A picture of Emma stared back at Gill. She looked closer.

Yes, it was definitely Emma. When she looked at childhood snaps of herself and Emma she often couldn't work out which one was her. It felt strange to study your own history and be unable to work out if it was really yours or that belonging to someone else: your sister.

But then, even now, Gill could chat to her mother on the phone and Charlotte would suddenly ask: 'How's Gill?' Gill would be forced to say, 'You've been talking to her for the last ten minutes.' Charlotte would be mortified. But Gill didn't really mind. She was used to correcting people, even her own parents, as to her identity. She'd had thirty-eight years of it. This picture was definitely of Emma, however. It had been taken six, maybe seven years before, when her hair was shorter.

Gill smiled. She remembered the first ever passports she and Emma had got. They'd had them done for a French exchange when they were about thirteen. Emma had been paired with a girl called Valérie who was a former ice-skating champion and whose parents had a flat in Paris. Gill had been partnered with Héloïse who had a face like rice pudding and who lived in a grim Paris suburb. Had Gill known that she was to spend a fortnight in the French equivalent of Reading, she might not have bothered with the passport.

As it was, Gill and Emma had read an article in a newspaper that said if you wanted a good snap of yourself, you had to use a foil-covered tea tray to reflect light up on to your face. They'd duly snuck into their local Woolworths with a tray covered in Alcan. Gill had pulled back the orange curtain, Emma had wound up the seat and put the tray under each of their chins. They'd had to swap seats halfway through because they could only afford one set of pictures. People had passed as they did it and thought they were mad.

Gill wiped moisture off the clear plastic covering to the snap of Emma. The foil she'd used this time didn't seem to have significantly narrowed the gap between Emma and Cindy Crawford. Still, she did look different. Younger. Her lips were parted in a half-smile and her eyes looked a bit surprised. It was the sort of look you had when you had just opened a parcel containing a really nasty jumper knitted by a distant relative and the distant relative was there. You were trying for pleased and you were giving off panic instead. But overall, the expression was optimistic.

Gill shivered. It really was cold. She looked at her hands. They were pink and puffy, like Bill Clinton's face. She had the ex-President of the United States's hands. Gill rubbed them together. It didn't help. Maybe if she walked a bit it would keep her warm. She didn't want to go home. To whose? To her own? To Emma's? Then she remembered she had to pick up her stuff from the office. She got up off the bench. The back of her coat felt soggy against her calves as she stood up. She walked towards the park gates then turned out through them.

* * *

'You're weird, you are. We come all the way to New York and we could go to any of a hundred nice cafés for lunch, but no, you want to go ice skating.' Chloë laughed as she laced her boots up. 'This is not the sort of footwear they sell in Saks, you know.'

Chloë stood up unsteadily and clumped towards Emma. Emma smiled. She'd never skated in Rockefeller Plaza. She'd seen the rink many times; had passed it in a cab on the way to and from business meetings. Now she was actually going to skate on it. Emma double-knotted the bow on her laces and stood up. She'd forgotten how awkward skates were off the ice. She and Chloë stumbled towards the gap in the wall that led to the rink itself with all the elegance of wind-up robot toys. As they approached the ice, the air became colder. Emma watched as she breathed a cloud of smoke out of her mouth. Chloë's cheeks were pink.

'OK, after three,' Chloë said, clambering on to the ice and grabbing the wall to prevent herself slipping. Emma did the same. 'One, two, three.'

Chloë grasped Emma's hand and the two of them pushed off. They glided forwards, the push giving them enough momentum so they didn't need to move their feet. They simply swooshed along. 'You know, this is quite fun,' Chloë said.

Gradually their speed decreased until they glided to a stop.

'So what do we do now?' Chloë asked. 'I could do with

a tow. Why is there never a handsome AA man around when you need one?'

Emma shook her head and laughed. 'Come on.'

Emma pushed her right foot forward. Her centre of gravity immediately shifted backwards. As her right leg extended in front of her, her left grappled for a hold on the ice. Soon her feet were spinning wildly until she landed on her bottom. Chloë stood looking at her. 'Do you need a hand?'

Emma rubbed her bum. It felt wet, cold and a bit numb. She nodded. Chloë lowered the top half of her body and held out a hand. Emma caught it and began to pull herself upright. But then Chloë started to move. Her feet slid from under her. She let go of Emma's hand and cartwheeled her arms wildly. 'Oh shi . . .' she wailed and she too landed with a thump on the ice.

The two of them looked at each other and laughed. Emma felt as if she'd known Chloë for ever. They were sitting on a patch of ice in the middle of one of the most exciting cities on earth. Above them the sky was crispy blue. The coolness and stillness of the ice against the hustle and bustle of the street just a few feet away felt at once peaceful and exhilarating. Chloë had begun to shuffle on her bottom towards the wall of the rink. Emma followed her lead. When Chloë got to the side, she hauled herself to her feet. Emma managed to stand up too.

'Shall we give it another go?' Emma asked.

Chloë shook her head. 'My arse can't take the pounding.'

'Oh, go on . . .' Emma pleaded.

Chloë shook her head again. 'You're on your own.'

Emma looked around. The man from the ticket office was clearing rubbish from between the benches. He would soon pull the plastic sheeting over the rink. There were only a couple of other people skating. They were the last of the die hards. 'OK, just for five minutes then.'

Emma positioned herself parallel to the rink wall. She held on with one hand and pushed out with one leg. As she moved forwards, she swiftly brought her feet together and tried not to wobble. With each attempt, she got a little steadier, until she let go of the wall altogether. Emma looked for Chloë to show off to, but there was no sign of her. She'd probably gone to give back her skates. Emma went a bit faster, then a bit faster. She was soon speeding along, the crisp sound of her skate blades cutting through the ice in her ears and the wind in her face. Her limbs were buzzing from the cold and the exercise. Her smoky breath stood out against the darkness. She felt a surge of happiness.

Suddenly, Emma was aware of clapping coming from the side of the rink. She looked for Chloë, but could only see a blurred male figure. She peered closer, losing her balance as she did so. In a blur of arms and legs, she crashed to earth on her back, her whole body sliding across the ice until it collided with a wall of the rink. *Bang!*

She briefly blacked out. When she regained consciousness, a figure was standing over her.

'Oh, thank God. I thought you were dead,' he gasped.

'I'm not dead,' Emma said.

'Well, now I know that. But you gave me a hell of a fright.'

Emma sat up and her vision began to focus. The face looking at her was tanned and handsome, with a pair of bright blue eyes. It was framed by blond hair.

'Do you think you can stand, Gill?'

'Alex, what are you doing here?' Emma asked.

'I could ask you the same question,' Alex said.

Gill stood on the doorstep of Smith & Taylor, trying to get up the courage to go in and collect the box. As she hovered, she was accosted. 'Can you spare a few minutes to talk about poverty in the developing world?' an eager beaver with a clipboard asked her.

Chuggers were a pain in the bottom at the best of times, but right then they were the last thing Gill felt she could stomach. She was only a whisker away from stuffing his clipboard down his throat, when she realised she had an audience. A cluster of smokers were skulking round the corner, guiltily puffing away.

'No thanks,' Gill said with a fixed smile.

'Oh, come on,' coaxed the chugger. 'It'll only take a moment.'

'No, thank you,' Gill repeated, her smile fading.

'Did you know that for just one pound a week you can bring fresh water to an entire village —'

Something snapped inside Gill. She took hold of her tormentor by the collar of his sweatshirt and pulled his head towards her. 'Did you know that a chugger dies each day and no one ever finds their bodies?' she hissed.

A terrified look passed across the young man's face. When Gill loosened her grasp, he scuttled away like a daddy long legs behind a skirting board. Gill leant back against the wall, feeling the marble cladding cool against the back of her skull. She was losing it, she really was. Then she heard clapping. She turned her head. The smokers were giving her a round of applause. Gill walked towards them. 'You don't have a spare fag, do you?'

Alex wasn't how Emma had expected. On the basis of her meetings with him back in London, she'd thought he was snooty and standoffish. Now, though, as he helped her walk over to a bench at the ice rink, he seemed different. Nice. He bent down and helped her unlace her boots.

'Aren't you going to introduce me?'

Alex stood up. It was Chloë. She had an amused look in her eye. Emma prayed she wouldn't say anything to embarrass her.

'Oh, Chloë, this is Alex, owner of Bliss, my boss.' Emma said the last bit pointedly, in an attempt to make Chloë behave. She understood.

'Very pleased to meet you,' she said. 'I'm Gill's flatmate.'

Alex shook her hand. 'Delighted to meet you too,' he said. 'But ignore all that stuff about me being Gill's boss. Bearing in mind how often she's late, I reckon I work for her, not the other way round.'

Chloë laughed and Emma blushed. 'It's not that often . . .' she began.

'Yes, it is!' Chloë and Alex said together, before laughing again.

Alex took Emma's boots back to the booth. While he was gone, she was grilled by Chloë. 'So, what's going on?' she asked.

'Nothing,' Emma replied.

'He's cute . . .'

'Sshhh, he's coming back,' Emma said.

Alex handed Emma a twenty-dollar bill. 'Your deposit,' he said.

'Ooh, I'm rich,' Emma crowed, waving it.

'Well, you can buy the drinks then,' Alex said.

'A drink?'

'Thanks very much. I thought you'd never ask,' Alex said.

Gill put her key in the front door.

'Hello?'

It was Max. What was he doing home?

Gill walked into the kitchen. 'Hi,' she said.

'Kevin's in bed and I'm cooking dinner,' he said.

'Did he have a good time?'

'Yeah, seemed to.'

Kevin and the boy in the oxygen bubble had formed something of a bond at the fashion show, mainly because Kevin probably couldn't do too much damage to Tarquin, what with his head being protected by a sheet of glass. Tarquin's mummy was so delighted that her child had made a friend, that she had offered to have Kevin for the day.

Max was bent over a cookbook. His face was blotched with flour and his hands were sticky. The kitchen was a mess. Every surface was covered with bowls and saucepans and jugs. Every single gadget appeared to have been used to prepare this meal. 'You look whacked,' he said.

'Yeah. Dino called me in this morning. I've been . . .' Gill burst into tears, unable to finish her sentence.

'Oh, darling.'

Max folded her into his floury arms. His chest smelt of butter and sweat and it felt softly comforting. His pastry hands made prints all over the back of Gill's jacket. She didn't care. She sobbed into his chest. This was the closest they'd been. In the weeks they'd been sharing the house, Gill had managed to avoid any sort of physical contact. She'd used the cystitis excuse, as Emma had suggested, and it had worked a treat. Now, though, Gill yearned for human contact. She wanted someone to forgive her for making such a mess of the fashion show. The person she really wanted to do that was Emma. But she wasn't here, Max was.

'It doesn't matter, darling,' he said.

'He's put me on gardening leave,' she sobbed.

'But you hate gardening.'

'I know.'

'Well, maybe it's not so bad,' Max said.

'But how am I going to explain it to –' Gill stopped herself just in time.

'Who, darling? Explain it to who, darling?'

Gill thought wildly. With her head in Max's chest, he couldn't see the panic in her eyes. 'To . . . to . . . myself!' she said. 'How am I going to explain it to myself?'

'You are a funny one,' Max said, stroking her hair, now getting flour in that too. 'You're too hard on yourself. We can't always get everything right all the time.' Then he wrinkled his nose. 'Have you been smoking?'

Gill stepped away from him, suddenly aware of how she must smell of tobacco. 'Oh, um, well, the stress and everything,' she said.

'But you haven't smoked in years,' he said.

'I know. I'll stop tomorrow. Anyway, what's cooking?'

'Salmon en croûte with dauphinoise potatoes and a watercress sauce. Plus apple strudel and cream.'

Gill raised her eyebrows.

'What?'

'There must be about four million calories in all that.'

'You don't need to worry about that,' Max said. 'You look beautiful. You always look beautiful.'

Emma and Alex took a booth in the corner of a dimly-lit bar, unpeeling coats and scarves and putting them in twin piles facing each other. Chloë had excused herself, saying there was an urgent shoe sale she needed to attend. Emma didn't believe her, but was grateful anyway. She and Alex ordered hot chocolates and toasted sandwiches, which were the only things the bar said weren't 'off.' Then they waited.

They were both a little shy. Alex stared out of the window and Emma pretended to read the cocktail drink menu, but actually peered at Alex over the top of it. He intrigued her. It wasn't simply that as the boss she'd expected him to be snooty, and he wasn't, there was something about his face that didn't fit. On the surface he was a good-looking man in his late thirties/early forties, Emma reckoned. But there was more going on than that. The lines round his eyes were beginning to creep across his cheeks and there was a worry furrow between his eyebrows. This wasn't the face of a moneyed aristo playing at being a bar owner.

Alex glanced back from the window, catching her looking at him. They were both embarrassed. Fortunately, at that moment, the food and drinks arrived. The chocolate was good, hot and thick. Emma wiped froth off her top lip with a paper napkin from a chrome dispenser on the table. The sandwiches weren't so enjoyable. The bread was like cushion stuffing, the cheese utterly tasteless.

'This is disgusting, isn't it?' Alex said, putting his sandwich back on his plate with a perfect single bite taken out of the side.

Emma nodded, also putting hers down.

'Sorry,' Alex said.

Emma shook her head. 'It's not your fault. You didn't cook it.'

'No, but, well – will you let me make it up to you? Will you come out with me tomorrow?'

'That really was delicious,' said Gill.

'Glad you liked it. Have some more wine.'

Max and Gill were sitting at the table. They had just finished the meal Max had cooked for them. They were on their second bottle of wine. Emma had that slightly woozy, happy, contented feeling.

'You know, you could see this gardening leave as a blessing,' Max said.

'Oh, I'd forgotten about that. You're depressing me now.'

'No, I mean it. You're always saying how tired you are.'

'I am?'

'Yes, you know you are. This will give you a chance to slow down a bit. Look at Gill. She doesn't work anything like as hard as you do and she seems happy.'

Inwardly, Gill tensed. 'Gill, happy? Why do you say that?'

'Don't you think so?' Max sat back in his chair. He folded his arms behind his head and knitted his fingers together.

'Well, I think she might be wondering about children,' Gill said cautiously.

'Oh, I thought she liked the freedom,' Max said.

'I'm sure she does, it's just . . . Well, maybe she looks at, you know, you and, um, me, and maybe she's a bit envious. I'm just guessing, you know.'

'Envious of what?'

'Oh, of the fact that, um, we're, um, settled.'

Had she been entirely sober, Gill would still have had trouble with the multilayered nature of this conversation. Through the fog of alcohol, she was struggling to refer to herself as Emma and remember that Gill was another person entirely.

'But she's not the type to be settled down, is she?' Max asked.

'Well . . .'

'I can't imagine her with children.'

'Why not?' Gill said defensively.

'Well, she wouldn't be interested, would she?'

'She could be.'

At that moment, there was a shout from upstairs. 'Mummy,' said a plaintive three-year-old voice. 'Mummy!'

Kevin was calling for Dominique. But Dominique wasn't there. Neither was Emma. 'It's OK. I'll go,' said Gill.

When she got upstairs, Kevin was sitting up in bed

looking confused. 'Mummy?' he said, his eyes squinting in the half darkness.

'No, it's not Mummy. It's Aunty G – Emma. Aunty Emma,' Gill said, sitting down on the corner of his bed.

'Oh,' he said. 'Dropped Dinosaur.'

Gill looked round the foot of the bed for Kevin's favourite toy. She saw a tail protruding from underneath the bed, bent down and retrieved it. 'There you are,' she said, handing it back to Kevin.

He clasped it to his cheek with one hand and put the thumb of the other hand in his mouth. Then he flopped his head back down on the pillow. He lay there, half covered by the dinosaur. Gill put a hand out and stroked his hair. It was warm and slightly sweaty. She bent her head and kissed his hot cheek. He was already asleep.

'They look angelic when they're asleep, don't they?'

Gill jumped. She hadn't heard Max come up the stairs. 'Jesus. You scared me,' she said, putting a hand to her throat.

'Sorry,' Max smiled.

Gill had never taken much notice of Max. He was Emma's husband. Her safe, dependable husband. That was pretty much it, as far as she was concerned. Now she found herself looking at him in a new way. His very dependability seemed comforting. His behaviour over dinner had shown her other qualities she hadn't been aware of before. He was kind. He had a gentleness that was appealing. And there was something slightly wounded about him, too. He seemed to need saving in some way.

Max was looking at Kevin. 'Difficult to believe he could be a monster, isn't it?'

'Yeah,' Gill nodded.

'You know, maybe what he needs is . . .' Max said.

'A mother?'

'I was going to say a mother and a father,' he said. 'He might really blossom if he was part of a proper family.'

Gill wondered if that's what she needed, too. So far, her experiment at being married with kids had been a bit of a disaster. But maybe she hadn't given it enough of a go. Now that she had been put on gardening leave, it would give her a chance to spend some time with Saskia and Kevin. And Max. He put a hand on her shoulder and slid it towards her neck, which he stroked. Gill found herself bending her body into his. Max leant forwards and kissed her neck, then gently turned her round.

Before Gill really knew what was happening, she and Max were kissing. His lips tasted of wine and watercress sauce. He drew his head back and put an arm round her shoulder. 'Shall we go to bed?' he asked.

Gill nodded.

Max touched her cheek. 'It's going to be all right, you know,' he said.

'Is it?' Gill asked.

Max smiled.

Chapter Twenty

The light glowed around the blinds as if they were the moon and there was an eclipse. They were fringed with light. Gill frowned. Her head hurt. What time was it? She propped her body up on her elbow and reached over to see the alarm clock. Her fingers brushed something cold. It was a wristwatch, a man's wristwatch. 'Oh, shit!' Gill exclaimed.

'Sorry, darling? What was that?' Max said from the en suite bathroom. He stepped into the doorway.

'Oh, Jesus!' Gill exclaimed again.

Max was naked. As Gill was in bed and he was standing, her head was on a level with Max's groin. Gill was presented with an uncompromising view of her sister's husband's nether regions. After the initial shock, she calmed down. Not bad. Gill gave said nether regions a closer appraisal. Quite nice really. She felt a sort of affection for them. She wanted to wrap them up in a tea towel and put them in front of a fire like a new-born puppy. Then she realised why she was feeling such affection for the contents of the Y-fronts he was not wearing. They were familiar; not quite old friends, but certainly she was on cordial terms with them. The events of last night began to come back to her. They hadn't had sex, had they?

'Oh, fuck!' Gill exclaimed one more time.

'What is the matter, darling? You look as if you've seen a ghost.'

Gill wished it was a ghost. She wished Max was an apparition. Then this would be a nightmare instead of an awful reality. She had slept with her sister's husband. In parts of East Anglia this might qualify as practically normal. In North London, it wasn't the done thing. Christ, she'd be wearing white stilettos and an ankle chain next.

'I thought I'd take the day off. We could take Kevin out somewhere,' Max said, walking back into the bathroom.

'Oh, um . . .' was all Gill could manage.

'I've put in the hours lately and now you're, well, you know . . .'

Gill remembered the other startling event of the last twenty-four hours: her gardening leave. She threw her head forward, then picked up a pillow and covered herself with it. Inside her pillowy prison it felt soft, warm, dark, almost womb-like. Perhaps she'd just stay like this. For ever. There was a squeak and Gill felt the bed bounce. Then there was a gentle knocking on her pillow. She lifted it to see Kevin peering in at her. His head was at an angle.

'Aunty Emma?' he said. 'Can I come in the house, too?'

Gill smiled. 'Come on, then.' She held the duvet up and Kevin scrambled underneath. She slid her body down and pulled the duvet over the top of them both. Kevin lay next to her sucking his thumb and holding his dinosaur. After a minute or so, he turned to Gill.

'Where's Mummy?' he said quietly.

Gill was flummoxed. She didn't want to lie to Kevin, but she couldn't tell him the truth. 'She's . . . um . . .'

'Is she coming back?'

'Um. Well . . .'

'Did she go away because I'm naughty?'

'No, no.'

'She did, didn't she? I'm a bad boy.' Kevin's eyes were big and teary. They were brimming at the corners. His bottom lip was quivering. Gill felt a switch inside her click on. Was this what the maternal urge was? There was that phrase: 'Her heart melted.' Gill felt just that. The inside of her turned to liquid. She was like a human cherry truffle chocolate, warm and fluid at the very centre. Gill put her arm out and Kevin snuggled into her shoulder.

'You're not a bad boy. You're . . . you're . . . you're my boy,' she said.

Even as she said it, Gill felt guilty. He wasn't her boy. He wasn't even Emma's boy. He was Dominique's – not that she seemed to have noticed recently. Gill's whole situation was fraudulent. She was playing at being a mum. And last night, she'd played at being a wife. But she couldn't stop herself. She knew she was going to have to switch back, so in the meantime, who did it hurt? The floorboards creaked. Gill peered under the corner of the duvet.

'Can I come in the house, too?' Max asked.

The cheese sauce formed a silky puddle round the bottom of the golden muffin. Spinach was piled on top of that, and then, at the very top, was a perfect poached egg. The skin was a delicate, translucent white, as fragile as mother of pearl. It wobbled, but refused to give up the runny yellow yolk until spiked with a fork. Then the yolk poured out, leaving the white wilted but succulent.

'Are you sure we don't have to pay for this?' Emma said, taking a mouthful of spinach and cheese and egg and muffin.

'Stop worrying,' Chloë replied, chewing her salt beef sandwich enthusiastically. 'I had another chat with that very helpful woman on reception.' Emma rolled her eyes. 'You want a free breakfast or not? Anyway, considering ONE of us went out to dinner last night, I'm surprised you're hungry.'

'Sorry. You're not angry, are you?'

'To think *you* were worried about being the gooseberry.'

'I know, but there's nothing going on. Alex and I –'

'Oh, it's "Alex and I" now, is it?'

'That's his name.'

Chloë raised an eyebrow and took another bite of her sandwich.

'What?' Emma asked.

'Nothing.'

'Look, it's not as if I'm going to sleep with him or anything.'

'Which means you're going to sleep with him.'

'It does not.'

'Yes, it does. The moment you say something like, "I'm not going to sleep with him," it proves you're thinking about it.'

'I am not!'

'Yes, you are.'

In truth, Emma was thinking about it, but she was doing her best not to. Just a few hours ago she'd been missing Max and now she was thinking about another man. It didn't make sense. She loved Max. However, she felt a tingle with Alex she hadn't felt in years with her husband. Maybe it was inevitable that some of the excitement waned once you'd been together a while. Add their jobs and Saskia and, well, they didn't have much time for each other.

'Your knickers are twitching,' Chloë declared.

'What did you say?' Emma said incredulously, wiping her mouth with a napkin.

'Twitching. Your knickers are twitching.' There was mustard at the corner of Chloë's mouth. She wiped it away. 'I can tell. Go for it, girl, I say. What have you got to lose?'

Now that was a question. Emma had more to lose than Chloë could ever have guessed. She had a good husband and a good marriage and a good life. One that she wanted to go back to. If she let anything develop with Alex, she was putting all that in jeopardy. And yet she was tempted, very, very tempted.

Chloë had finished her sandwich. 'So, what are we doing today?' she asked.

'Well . . .'

Chloë sighed. 'You're going out with him, Alex, aren't you?'

'You don't mind, do you?'

'I suppose not, but you know you're not supposed to dump your girlfriends for a guy. That's the first rule of the sisterhood.'

'What's the second rule?'

'If you do sleep with him you have to tell me EVERYTHING!' Chloë laughed.

'Thanks,' Emma said.

'You're welcome,' Chloë replied.

'Ow!' said Max. 'Keep your feet still. You're kicking me.'

'They're my wheels,' Kevin shouted happily. '*Peep, peep.*'

'Are you Thomas the Tank Engine?' Gill asked. He was about the only train she could think of.

'I'm Gordon!' Kevin corrected her.

'Sorry. Hello, Gordon.' Gill was clearly going to have to work on this train thing if she was going to communicate with a three-year-old boy.

'Can we open the door to the house?' Max said. 'I'm boiling.'

Gill peeled back the duvet and they all lay still, gratefully breathing in the cool air. Max turned on his side to face Gill. He smiled. 'So what do you think about a trip out, all of us. A sort of family outing?'

Gill was in turmoil. She was still feeling guilty after last night, but she was also happy. She was happy to be lying in bed with Max and Kevin and that made her feel even more guilty. Kevin made up her mind for her. 'Can we go on a train?' he asked breathlessly.

'Yes,' Max said, eyeing Gill. 'We can go on a train.'

'*Peep, peep*!' Kevin tooted.

Max sat up and put his feet on the floor. He seemed happy too. 'I'll just go and try and muster some enthusiasm from Saskia,' he explained.

'Good luck.' Gill smiled.

Max put his face very close to hers. 'Oh, ye of little faith,' he said laughing. Then he kissed Gill and jogged out of the room and up the stairs.

'*Peep, peep*!' Kevin tooted again.

Alex picked Emma up in a yellow cab. He held the door open and she scrambled across the vinyl-covered seat.

'So, how are you today?' Alex asked.

'Fine. You?' Emma replied.

'Yeah, good. I thought we'd go up to SoHo, but first I need to get something.'

'Oh, yeah, what?' Emma asked.

'Just a present for someone,' he said. 'It won't take long.'

When they came out of the train station at Brighton, the air hit them like a cold, wet flannel. It wasn't actually raining, but the air was damp. It clung to Gill's face and hands and worked its way under the cuffs of her cagoule. Still, she didn't mind. It was good to get out of London. She looked at the sky. 'You know, I think it might cheer up,' she said hopefully.

'Yeah, right,' said Saskia, putting her hood up and tying it tight around her cheeks.

Max had Kevin on his shoulders, Kevin was oblivious to the damp. He was laughing and kicking Max, still excited by the train. 'Did you see the wheels, Uncle Max?' he chirped. 'Thomas has blue wheels! *Peep, peep!*'

'*Peep, peep* to you too,' Max said, glancing behind him at Saskia trudging along. 'Oh, come on, Sask,' he said. 'It's not as if we go to the seaside every day.'

'It's cold,' she grumbled. 'Don't know why I had to come anyway.'

'Because we're going out as a family,' Max said. 'Anyway, you got a day off school, didn't you?'

Saskia sniffed derisively and continued to kick her toes against the uneven paving stones as they headed downhill towards the seafront.

'I love Brighton when it's like this,' Gill said. 'It's sort of depressed, if that doesn't make it sound . . .'

'Depressing?' offered Max.

'Yeah.' Gill laughed. 'I mean it's good in the summer when it's full, but I like it better when it's quieter.'

Max nodded.

'Ice cream! Ice cream!' shouted Kevin, pointing at a swinging metal sign with pictures of cornets and lollies on it. The wind and sea air had rusted the edges and faded the colours.

Max peered to see if there were any lights on in the shop. Many of them were shut out of season. There was a dingy lightbulb and the door was open. He winked at Gill. 'Do trains eat ice cream?' he asked.

'No, no,' Gill said seriously. 'Only coal.'

Kevin's face was panic-stricken. 'Trains do eat ice cream,' he said. 'Not only coal.'

Gill smiled. 'It's OK, sweetie, it was only a joke. Of course trains eat ice cream. What would you like?'

Max lifted Kevin down from his shoulders and he ran in through the open doorway of the kiosk. 'That one!' he announced, pointing at a lurid rocket-shaped lolly that must have contained so many chemicals, Kevin would probably launch into the stratosphere after a couple of licks.

Gill pushed the glass door on the top of the fridge back, reached in and, despite reservations, pulled out the rocket lolly. As she picked it up she glanced at Max. 'You want one?' she asked.

'Ninety-nine,' he requested.

Gill nodded. 'Me too. Do you know why they call it that?'

Max shook his head.

'One of life's great mysteries.'

Kevin was now leaping up and down trying to reach the lolly in Gill's hand. 'Mine,' he shouted. '*Zoom*!'

'OK, OK. We've got to pay for it first,' Gill said.

'I'll have a ninety-nine, too,' Saskia said as she joined them. 'With two flakes.'

'I thought you were on a fast in solidarity with the people of Tibet,' Gill laughed.

Saskia said nothing.

'Only teasing. We're here to have fun, remember?'

Saskia managed a weak smile.

They all went up to a high counter at the other end of the shop. The soft-scoop ice-cream machine was behind it.

'Three ninety-nines, one with two flakes, please, and this rocket thing,' Max said, taking a handful of change from his pocket.

A teenage black girl with the kind of hair that hasn't so much been cut as chiselled, turned round. Maybe her hairstyle was a precaution against the bracing sea air.

Much of it pointed vertically, as if it had been caught in a force ten storm. Were she to be genuinely assaulted by a strong wind, not a hair on her head would have moved. She picked a cornet out of a pile and pulled down the lever on the ice-cream machine. It whirred into life and a smooth sausage of white ice cream came out of the spout. She moved the cone so it corkscrewed on to the top.

Meanwhile, Gill was tearing the wrapping off Kevin's lolly. 'Now, don't drop it,' she advised.

'I'll hold on to it very tight,' Kevin said seriously, his eyes as big as a lemur's. Within seconds his tongue had been turned entirely purple and his face was wearing a smile of pure joy.

'Here,' said Max, passing Gill her ninety-nine.

Max paid and they all wandered outside eating their ice creams. Gill bit the point off the bottom of her cone. She then held it up and began to suck the ice cream down the inside of the cone.

Max laughed. 'I haven't seen you do that for years,' he said.

The glass front of FAO Schwarz soared upwards. The cab, waiting outside, seemed small and tatty in comparison.

'You don't mind, do you?' Alex said. 'I'll only be five minutes.'

'No, no, you go ahead,' Emma said.

Alex climbed out of the cab and walked purposefully inside, threading himself neatly through the other shoppers. He had soon disappeared among the jumble of people and toys Emma could see though the window. Emma gazed at this temple to childhood. She'd often passed it while she was in New York on business, but had never been in. She'd always been too busy. Saskia was too old now for anything in it. And Kevin? Emma was tempted, but then discounted the idea. She didn't want to have to explain to Alex why she wanted to buy a present for her sister's husband's ex-wife's son. She was having enough trouble remembering not to drop herself in it as it was.

Emma watched the shoppers and the commuters bustling down the street past the cab. They were wrapped up as much against each other as the weather. They were wearing woolly armour. Their heads were down and they were forging ahead, somehow managing not to bang into each other. It was as if each was surrounded by their own don't-even-think-about-it force field. This repelled panhandlers and leaflet-giver-outers or simply anyone who wanted to make eye contact.

The taxi driver had some sort of Eastern European folk music on. A woman was wailing in a foreign language from the dashboard. Even through the glass screen, Emma could hear it. It filled the cab with melancholy from a far-off place. Emma considered tapping on the screen, getting the man to open it and asking him where he was from, but then she saw the cardboard Christmas tree hanging from the rear-view mirror. If the screen opened, she might be asphyxiated by air freshener. She sat back in her seat and waited for Alex.

When Alex returned, he was clutching a small carrier bag.

'What did you get, then?' Emma asked him.

He put the bag on his lap and pulled out a brown suede monkey. The monkey had a smile and ears like Prince Charles. Emma grinned. She took the monkey from Alex and instinctively hugged it. Then she sat it facing her and stroked the monkey's tail. 'It's cute,' she said.

Alex leant forward and put his mouth close to the only areas of the glass partition that was perforated. 'SoHo,' he said. He turned back to Emma. 'I thought we could have a decent meal.'

'Can we go home now?' Saskia moaned. 'This is boring.'

'No, it's not,' said Max, annoyed.

'Yes, it is. I want to go home. I didn't want to come here anyway.'

Gill rolled her eyes at Max. Kevin was now asleep on his shoulder.

'I vote we get some lunch,' Max said.

Saskia brightened, just a little. 'Fish and chips?'

'But I thought you were on a fast in solidarity –' Max began, laughing.

'Sshh,' Gill said. 'I'm sure we can find some fish and chips.'

Gill had been wrong when she said the weather would improve. The sky had turned dark. Large drops of water began to fall, swifly turning into a downpour.

'Come on,' said Max. 'I saw a fish-and-chip shop up the hill.' He began to run. Kevin wobbled on his shoulder like a rag doll, but didn't wake, the excitement of the train ride and the lolly having put him out cold. Gill ran too. Only Saskia refused to break out of a walk.

'Come on, Sask,' Gill shouted. 'Last one to the fish-and-chip shop has to pay.'

'I haven't got any money,' Saskia shouted through the rain.

When they reached the fish-and-chip shop, Gill and Max piled inside. Saskia was still trudging up the hill behind them. Kevin woke, the smell of vinegar in his nostrils rousing him more effectively than being joggled up a hill. 'Chips,' he pronounced sleepily.

Gill ruffled his wet hair and smiled, watching Saskia scowling as she approached.

'What?' asked Max.

'It's nothing.'

'No, what?'

'I was just thinking that we're like a proper family. Not a perfect one. Just a normal, dysfunctional one.'

Max frowned. 'What are you on about?'

'Alex, good to see you.' A large bear-like man with a beard was shaking Alex's hand. 'And who is this?' he asked, looking at Emma.

'Oh, sorry. How rude of me,' Alex said. 'This is Gill. She's a friend of mine.'

'Hello,' Emma said, putting out a hand. The bearded man took it in one of his own, which was the size of a shovel.

'Frank is the owner of this place,' Alex explained. 'Been running it for years.'

'You should know. You used to work here,' Frank said.

Emma frowned.

'The best busboy I ever had,' Frank said. Alex was blushing. Frank put an arm round his shoulder. 'Not a busboy any more, are you, Alex? Now let me find you a table. A good one.'

Frank led them into the restaurant. L'Auberge de Saint-Jacques was an American's idea of a ritzy French eatery. The tables were round with multiple tablecloths; the chairs were carved and painted white with gold twiddly bits on. Frank pulled one out and waited for Emma to sit down. As she did so, he pushed the chair in. Emma always hated it when waiters did that. It made her fear they'd whip it away and she'd end up on the floor. Frank then did the next thing she hated waiters doing. He unfurled her napkin and placed it across her lap. There was something unpleasantly forward about it that always embarrassed Emma. Still, Frank was the owner of L'Auberge de Saint-Jacques and Alex's friend, so she said nothing. Just smiled.

'I can recommend the sea bass,' Frank said. 'But the duck I don't know about. We've got a new chef. His mind is not always on the job. I think he may be' – Frank leant forward conspiratorially – 'seeing the barman, if you know what I mean.'

Frank glanced over to the bar. Emma and Alex followed suit. The barman appeared actually to be a woman.

'Volatile relationship,' Frank commented.

They both nodded.

'The sea bass, then,' Alex said. 'If that's OK with you, Gill.'

'Fine, yeah,' Emma said.

Frank went to the kitchen to place the order and Gill and Alex were left alone. 'Frank used to be a professional wrestler,' Alex explained. 'Bought this place when he retired. Bit of a character.'

Emma nodded. So Alex had been a busboy. He hadn't simply opened a bar with Daddy's money. He'd served his time at the bottom of the pile, after all. Now she was really intrigued.

'So, Gill,' Alex said. 'I don't know much about you. Apart from being a useless ice skater, what else is there to know about you?'

Before she could answer, they were interrupted by the sound of voices coming from the kitchen. One of them was Frank's.

'Whaddya mean, there's no sea bass?' he boomed in his broad New Jersey accent.

'I do not – how you say? – feel like cooking sea bass today!' a man with a heavy French accent shouted back. 'We geev them sole. Sole meunière. *Magnifique!*'

'But they ordered sea bass, buddy!' Frank shouted.

'Zey 'ave sole meunière.'

'I told 'em we had sea bass!'

'Zis is intolerable! I am artiste, not grocer! I cook what I feel and I feel like sole meunière.'

'I tell ya how *I* feel . . .'

A slight man in a chef's hat backed slowly out of the kitchen and into view. '*Non, non, non!*' he exclaimed.

Frank was advancing on him, holding a frying pan as though about to hit him with it.

'*Chérie! Chérie!*' the chef squealed.

The lady barman abandoned the drinks she was mixing and vaulted over the bar. She pushed the chef behind her to protect him. 'You heard him, bud, he's an artist,' she said to Frank.

'Artist, my ass!' Frank answered, swinging the frying pan.

The chef was cowering. 'I 'ave 'ad enough! I quit!' he squeaked.

'He quits,' echoed the bar lady.

'Why, that little squirt!' Frank exploded. 'He can't quit on me.' He put the frying pan down on a nearby table, put out his arms in what was obviously a well-practised wrestling pose and advanced on the chef and his girl-friend.

'Y'know what? I quit, too! Y'can stick yer lousy job where the sun don' shine!' the bar lady said. With that she picked up the chef and slung him under one arm like a small clutch bag, then jogged out of the door. As she went, the chef squealed, '*Chérie, chérie!*' Frank was left standing in the middle of the restaurant. He straightened up. At that moment the door swung open again and a crowd of people entered, giggling.

'Bergman,' said a man with a carnation in his lapel. 'We booked. Wedding party?'

Frank sighed. 'Sorry, bud,' he said. 'Chef and barman just went AWOL.'

The giggling died down. A woman, evidently the bride, stepped forward. She was wearing a blue suit and carrying a bouquet of cornflowers. 'But we booked,' she said. 'You see, we had our first date here.' She looked tearful.

'Sorry, ma'am, ain't nothin' I can do 'bout it.'

Emma and Alex had been watching this whole scene from their table, as had the three or four other tables who were also waiting for food that would now not be arriving. Emma looked at Alex. 'How are your chefing skills?' she said.

Alex frowned. 'Well, now you come to mention it, I did do a year at the River Café.'

'Good,' said Emma, standing up. She put her napkin on her table and walked over to the bar. She found the section that lifted up and went underneath it. Frank watched her, nonplussed. Alex was still sitting at the table. 'Well, come on,' she said to both of them. 'We can't let these people down. Chop, chop. We've got a wedding breakfast to do, haven't we?'

Gill and Max were sitting on the train, opposite each other. Saskia was across the aisle, asleep, the sea air having got her in the end. Kevin was perched next to Gill. He was running a cheap toy car they'd got out of a machine on the prom up and down the little table in front of them. '*Brrrrm*,' he said.

Gill was trying to wipe her trousers with a napkin: Kevin had just managed to spill a whole cup of orange juice down them. The sticky juice was now all over her hands and had even worked its way up in between her fingers. Whenever she put her fingers together, she had trouble separating them again. They remained partially stuck, as if she were an alien saying hello to the crew on *Star Trek*.

'Is it coming off?' Max asked.

'Not really,' Gill replied. 'Never mind. We'll be home soon.'

But Gill wished they weren't going home. Away from the house, Emma's house, she could forget that this wasn't real. She could just enjoy it. The moment she crossed the threshold of the home Max shared with Emma, however, Gill would feel the guilt. There would also be the small matter of what happened when Gill and

Max went to bed. Would she? Could she repeat the events of last night?

Max reached across and took Gill's sticky hand. 'It's been a lovely day,' he said. 'We should do this more often.'

Gill nodded, looking down at her hand resting in Max's soft palm.

'So that's five tartes aux pommes, six mousses au chocolat and a sorbet. OK?' Emma shouted through to the kitchen.

Alex nodded. He could barely believe this was the same girl who was always late at Bliss. And, of course, it wasn't.

Emma's problem, the one that ground her down in London, was that she always took on more than she could realistically handle. While she railed against the responsibilities she was loaded down with, she was simultaneously tossing more on the top. Even here, on holiday in New York, she couldn't resist saving the day. She had taken one look at that bride's expression and sprung into action. Emma had gone behind the bar and not only filled all the existing orders, she had given it a bit of a polish too.

While Alex and Frank looked on in amazement, Emma had whipped them into shape. In the space of an afternoon, she had reorganised the kitchen and bar so that it ran more smoothly. And she'd enjoyed it. It felt familiar – not the restaurant bit, but the getting-everyone-organised bit. It reminded her of her job and her home and it made her feel satisfied. She was good at running things – a home, an office – and Emma liked knowing she was good at something. And other people seeing she was good, of course. She was aware of Alex's admiring glances, the ones he shot her between cooking the food.

They'd started at lunchtime and run right through to dinner. It was almost over. Just the desserts to do and the coffee. Emma was winding the bar down. She went back to the kitchen to see if Alex wanted a hand. 'You OK?' she asked.

Alex stopped spooning sorbet into a bowl. 'Sorry you didn't get your lunch,' he said. 'Or drinks. We seem to be jinxed foodwise, don't we?'

'It doesn't matter,' Emma said, picking up a couple of plates of apple tarts. 'Another time.' She walked out into the restaurant.

When they finally closed up for the night, Frank ordered them a cab. He clapped them on the back, offering effusive thanks and the prospect of permanent jobs. Emma and Alex accepted the former, while laughingly declining the latter. Then the taxi took them back to the Majestic, Alex paid and they got out.

'So, it's, um, been . . .' Emma began.

'Knackering?' Alex suggested.

'I was going to say fun,' Emma said.

They were standing on the steps of the hotel. There

was one step between them, Alex above and Emma below. They both felt awkward.

'Well, it's late . . .' Emma said, breaking the silence.

'Yeah, you better, you know . . .' Alex added.

Emma put out her hand. 'Thanks,' she said.

'What for?' Alex asked, surprised, but taking her hand.

'I've enjoyed myself today,' she said.

'Really?'

'Yeah,' Emma laughed. 'Really.'

Alex still had hold of Emma's hand. He loosened his grip and slid his right hand round her back, then placed his left one on her shoulder. He went to kiss her. Emma panicked; expecting him to kiss her on the cheek, she turned her head. Alex kissed her ear. He stepped back and looked at the ground. Emma blushed a deep grape-juice red. She felt clumsy. She didn't know what to say. Had she ruined everything? Without looking at Alex, Emma turned and ran up the steps. 'Bye,' she shouted over her shoulder.

The doorman opened the door and Emma escaped inside.

Gill lay in Max's arms, her head against his damp chest. He was sleeping, but she couldn't. Not yet. She was listening to the sounds of the London night. She was remembering the night she'd spent in Chloë's hospital room. She'd listened to the night then too. And she'd made a resolution, hadn't she? To change her life. Well, it had changed, all right. The problem was, it wasn't her life. It was Emma's and, sooner rather than later, she was going to have to give it back to her. Charlotte and Gordon were due home later in the week. She had her deadline.

Chapter Twenty-One

Gill signed for the letter on her doorstep. The bike messenger handed it to her, climbed on his machine, and roared away. Gill looked down at the envelope. It was addressed to Emma Chancellor and had the Smith & Taylor stamp on the front. She carried it down to the kitchen, ripping the envelope as she went. Unfolding it by the kitchen table, she sat down and read.

'Dear Emma . . .' it began.
Following recent serious misconduct on your part, you have been placed on gardening leave. It is felt that this will offer you a period for reflection. However, as part of our ongoing motivational strategy, it has been decided that you should be given the opportunity to prove your worth to Smith & Taylor. Please see attached.

Gill turned over the letter to see a note stapled to the back.

Zoltar Paintballing Xperience!
Energise your staff and your business in this
fun environment.
(Round the corner from Finsbury Park Tube.
Formerly QuickSpend supermarket.)

There was a date scrawled on the top. It was today! Gill tore up the stairs to get changed. If she hurried, she might still be able to get Emma's job back.

'So what happened then?' Chloë asked. 'And before you answer, remember the second rule of the sisterhood.'

'I didn't sleep with him,' Emma said.

'Well, you were back jolly late. What were you doing?'

Emma smiled. 'Working behind a bar, actually.'

'Sorry? You were working behind a bar? What kind of date is that?'

'It wasn't a date.'

They were lying on Chloë's bed. The phone next to it rang. Chloë picked it up. 'Oh, hello, Alex,' she said. 'Gill?'

Emma shook her head violently. She was still embarrassed by the kissing débâcle.

'Yes, yes, she's here.'

Chloë handed the phone to Emma, who scowled. 'Hi,' she said.

'Hi,' Alex echoed. 'Sorry about yesterday. Not a great way to spend your holiday.'

'No, I told you, it was fine,' Emma said.

'Well, um, I just wondered . . .'

'What?' Emma asked. Chloë had her head very close to Emma's trying to hear the phone call. Emma batted her away.

'There's something I'd like you to see,' Alex said hesitantly. 'Can I pick you up in an hour or so?'

'I'm intrigued.'

'See you later, then.'

Emma put down the phone.

'Don't tell me,' Chloë said. 'You're going out. Well, if he doesn't try to sleep with you today, he's gay.'

'He is not gay!'

When Gill arrived at Zoltar Paintballing Xperience! some of the Smith & Taylor staff were already there. They were split into two groups. The younger male middle managers were excited, climbing into their jumpsuits and strapping on their canisters of paint with gusto. The older women, many of whom would clearly never have willingly put on a jumpsuit of any kind, let alone an orange one, were more glum. Gill joined the queue. She saw Jeanette walking up the hall, but there was nowhere to hide.

'Hello, Emma, how are you?' Jeanette said, overly loudly. She was behaving like an MP getting his picture taken with someone in a wheelchair. She clearly wanted to show everyone else what a lovely human being she was by agreeing to speak to Gill, the company leper.

'Fine,' Gill answered.

'Well, this should be fun,' Jeanette continued. 'A bit of an executive stress-buster, I'd say. Not, of course, that I'm under stress. But then, I'm not juggling other responsibilities, am I? How are Mike and the kiddies?'

'It's Max, and Saskia is not a kiddie. She's sixteen.'

'Oh, Emma, you don't look old enough to have a SIXTEEN YEAR OLD, does she?' Jeanette shrieked, turning to the rest of the queue. 'Not old enough at all.'

It was Gill's turn to put on her jumpsuit. She took her shoes off and put them in a locker and replaced them with rubber boots. Then she zipped herself into the all-in-one over her clothes. Finally, helped by a member of staff, Gill slipped her hands through the straps connected to the paint canister which sat on her back. The straps clicked shut at the front. A tube ran from the canister to a paint gun. Finally, she was given a helmet and goggles.

When they were all dressed, they were led into the cavernous space that had once been the supermarket. Suddenly, a large figure turned to greet them. He was wearing a jumpsuit and his goggles made it difficult to make out his features. But then he pulled the goggles off and he was greeted with a round of applause. It was Dino. He acknowledged the clapping and then handed over to a member of the staff who began distributing tabards, blue and red. Gill was handed a blue one, as was Jeanette. Then she saw that Dino had a red one. As Gill watched, Jeanette tore a red tabard out of a man's hand and put it on. The man protested lightly, but in the end put on the blue instead.

The object of the 'game' as everyone else insisted on calling it, was to hit an opponent from the other team in the head or chest with paint. If you were hit, you had to lie down and a sort of referee would come and assess your 'injury'. A direct hit to the head would mean instant death and you'd have to sit the rest of the game out. How this was supposed to improve management performance, Gill had no idea.

The two teams gathered in opposing huddles to discuss tactics. The blue team, it was decided by some of the younger, keener men, was going to 'blast the hell out of the reds'. That was about as much of a plan as they could come up with, such was their enthusiasm for just getting out there and firing the guns.

The room was balconied like an old-fashioned prison. Walkways ran round the sides of the room with multiple doors off them into small rooms. Some were connected. Some weren't. In daylight, it looked simple enough. However, as the red team took up positions on the floor above, the lights went down. It was almost totally dark and, at first, until Gill's eyes adjusted, she was blind. They'd been told not to move until they heard a klaxon.

Blaa! it sounded.

Gill heard a thundering above and looked up. Something exceedingly heavy was lumbering up a walkway. She squinted. It was Dino. He moved with all the elegance of a Woolly Mammoth – on dry land. He saw her and pointed his gun down. 'Take dat! Mother-fucker,' he yelled.

Gill dodged backwards, flattening herself against a wall. The paint shot past her, landing with a thud on the floor. She looked at it. Some game this was turning out to be.

The noise was deafening. In one corner of the room, someone was sawing plasterboard. Two other builders were up ladders, drilling holes for the electrics. In another corner, a circular saw was set up. Through the dust Emma could see sparks flying as metal tubing was cut. When Alex had said he had something he wanted to show her, Emma hadn't thought he meant a building site, but she followed him in anyway.

'Hey, guys!' Alex shouted, to absolutely no effect. He tried again. 'Guys! Guys!' Still nothing.

Alex put his fingers to his lips and emitted a high-pitched whistle. Immediately there was silence. The men up ladders turned, drills in hands. The man sawing froze and even the bloke with the circular saw tipped it into the off position and pushed his ear defenders back.

'Take five,' Alex ordered.

The builders shrugged, and shuffled off outside.

'Sorry about that,' Alex said. 'I know it's a bit of a mess.'

'Well . . .'

Alex started to lead Emma round the room. She had to climb over breeze blocks and bits of wood. Electrical cables dangled from the ceiling like stalactites in a cave. The lighting wasn't much better. 'Mind your head,' Alex had to say on more than one occasion.

This building site was going to be his new bar and restaurant, he explained. The ground-floor room had windows along one wall. The floor was sunken along one side. This was where the restaurant tables would be. He pointed up at the ceiling, telling her about the lights and the music system and the air con. Emma had no interest in air con and yet Alex made it sound like the most fascinating thing in the world.

They went downstairs, their feet crunching on grit and dust as they went. The basement was even darker. The only light was from a skylight set into the ground floor. 'Over there is where the other bar is going to be,' Alex said, waving his arms in the general direction of a pile of rubble. 'We'll put a dance floor over there and . . .'

Emma barely listened to his words. She was watching his face. It was lit up, despite the darkness. He was excited and wanted to excite her. This was his passion. He was standing directly under the skylight. He beckoned her over. 'If you look up, you can see right through to the sky,' he said.

Emma looked up. The skylight led to another in the ceiling above. The blue sky was visible at the very top. 'It's beautiful,' she said.

'Isn't it?' Alex agreed.

They were both aware of how close together they were standing. Emma could feel Alex's chest against her shoulder. He could sense her breathing, which had quickened. She knew it and tried to stop her chest from going in and out at such a rate. She looked down, embarrassed that her body was giving her away. Alex stepped back. 'Anyway,' he said, clearing his throat.

Emma was confused. Maybe Chloë was right. Maybe he was gay. She didn't have time to consider the question fully. Alex was speaking.

'So what do you think of it? All of it?' he asked.

'I told you. It's beautiful,' she answered. 'When does it open?'

'A month, six weeks tops – I hope,' he said. 'Sort of depends.'

'On what?'

'Partly on you.'

Gill was surrounded by shouts and screams and splats. Paint and people were flying in all directions. Following a relatively decorous start, some members of Smith & Taylor had let rip. Perhaps that was what they meant about unlocking your potential, but certain individuals had transmogrified from normal, law-abiding people into poster-paint commandos. Jeanette currently had Nigel from floral displays in a prone position at her feet. Her foot was on his head. 'Beg, scum, beg,' she was shouting.

Nigel sort of burbled.

It was only when the referee, plus another member of staff, took hold of Jeanette's gun that she let herself be prised off this poor bloke. He was sent home.

The contestants were gradually being whittled down. Gill, aching, and trying to remain out of the firing line, had survived, as had two other members of the blue squad. For the reds, there were just Dino and Jeanette. Dino's survival wasn't so much down to expertise as the fact that no one dared hit him, lest it affect their career prospects.

A man in a blue tabard who Gill didn't know approached. 'Cover me,' he shouted into the half darkness.

'What is this, *Gunfight at the OK Corral* or something?' Gill replied.

He looked blank.

'You know, *Gunfight at the . . .*' Gill studied him. He was about twenty. He had probably never seen *Gunfight at the OK Corral*. '*Tomb Raider*,' Gill tried. 'Do you think you're in *Tomb Raider*?'

'Yeah. You're Lara Croft,' he said excitedly.

The man leapt up some nearby stairs. Gill shrugged. She heard a creak overhead. She looked up. It was Dino. He was moving backwards along the walkway. A little further along, a figure Gill recognised as Jeanette was also going backwards. Without knowing it, they were closing in on one another.

The *Tomb Raider* man now arrived at the top step. He paused, aiming his gun, and then, with a war cry, he let out a volley of paint. There was confusion as Dino and Jeanette turned and fired at him and at each other. Paint landed on the front of their goggles and they collided. A grapple ensued as more paint was shot. Most of it landed on the floor, which made it slippery. As Gill watched, Dino lost his footing and went sideways, hitting the rail along the side of the walkway. It buckled and then broke under his weight. Dino and Jeanette sailed over the edge and fell, clasped together like lovers, with a horrifying thump on to the ground below.

'So, do you accept?' Alex asked. He looked nervous.

'It's a fantastic offer, running this place, but what makes you think I could do it?'

'I saw you at Frank's. You were brilliant.'

'Thanks.' Emma smiled. 'But, you know, that was a one-off.'

'It doesn't have to be. New York is such an exciting city. I could get your green card for you and —'

'Move here?' Emma exclaimed.

'Well, yes, you couldn't run it from London, could you?' Alex pointed out.

'But . . . but . . .'

'You don't have to give me an answer now. Just think about it. Please,' he begged. 'Just think about it.'

* * *

The ambulance came almost immediately. It took the two paramedics twenty minutes to get Dino into it, however. He was struggling and shouting and cursing all the way. Most of his foul temper was directed at Jeanette, whose fall he had broken. She didn't have a scratch on her, but Dino had a suspected broken leg, a dislocated shoulder and a severely bruised nose.

Jeanette kept apologising, but it was no good. Even without the broken bones, Dino's pride was hurt. He had been humiliated in public and there was no way to make up for that. When the photographer from the local paper arrived to snap him as he was being hoisted into the ambulance, Jeanette's fate was sealed. Dino was furious. Indeed, the photographer had to assure the newspaper's art director that he hadn't messed up with his exposure: Mr Marconi really had been that funny colour, his complexion was such a virulent pink.

'I'm so sorry, Dino,' Jeanette wailed as they shut the ambulance doors.

'It's Mr Marconi to you,' Dino shouted from the back.

'But I thought you said we should use first names because it built team spirit,' she sobbed.

'Fuck team spirit. You're sacked,' Dino bellowed as they drove him away.

Emma clicked the aeroplane seatbelt shut and began to pull things out of her bag and transfer them into the pocket in the back of the seat in front. Magazine, book,

Diet Coke . . . Chloë was taking more time to take her seat on the plane. She had multiple carrier bags to stow away overhead. Three days of time to kill had resulted in a lot of shopping. Fortunately, she had managed to chat up the steward at check-in and he'd let her bring her purchases as cabin baggage. Chloë dropped into the seat next to Emma.

'How much did that lot cost?' Emma asked. 'Or are you going to open the credit card bill with your eyes closed?'

'Who said I open them?'

Emma shook her head. 'At some point, you'll have to pay the piper.'

'Actually, I don't think I bought one of those,' Chloë laughed. 'Anyway, maybe Bob will settle the bill for me.'

'Bob Beresford? You saw Bob Beresford!' Emma exclaimed.

'Sshh, do you want everyone to hear? He is married, you know,' Chloë said.

'Well, exactly.'

'It seemed only polite, after he paid for the tickets. Anyway, I was at a loose end, remember.'

'Sorry.'

'What about you? You haven't told me what happened with Alex.'

'He showed me round a bar.'

'And then he threw you across it, right?'

'No.'

Chloë shrugged. 'I told you he was gay.'

'He is not gay. He's just . . .' But what was Alex? Emma didn't know. To be honest, she was surprised he hadn't made a pass. Maybe he didn't fancy her. Maybe he really did only want her to run his bar. Emma was disappointed – and then told herself not to be so silly. She was married and shouldn't have been thinking about whether another man fancied her anyway. It had been an enjoyable fantasy, her and Alex, and that was all. 'Actually . . .'

The plane began to move, slowly and awkwardly at first. It trundled over the tarmac with all the grace of one of those tartan shopping bags on wheels being negotiated over a tricky piece of pavement. The wings swung round; the plane paused and then began to pick up speed as it headed down the runway, faster and faster until, finally, Emma felt the sensation of weightlessness as the wheels left the ground and it soared upwards.

'Yes?' Chloë said.

'He wants me to run it for him.'

'He wants you to do what?' Chloë was incredulous.

'Run his new bar.' Emma's face was flushed. 'He wants me to come and live in New York and run the bar.'

'What about a visa?'

'He said he'd sort that out. Doesn't seem to think there'll be a problem.' Emma's voice was breathy with excitement.

'So, are you going to do it?'

The plane intercom sparked into life. 'Good evening, ladies and gentlemen. This is Charlene, your cabin services manager, speaking. A member of the onboard team will shortly be passing through the cabin with the drinks trolley. We have a full range of alcoholic and non-alcoholic beverages available . . .'

'Well?' asked Chloë, now as excited as Emma. 'Are you going to take the job?'

Emma's face fell. 'It's a nice idea, but . . .'

'What do you mean, a nice idea? It's a *fantastic* one.'

The drinks trolley's arrival next to Chloë interrupted them. A stewardess in a red jacket and matching cap (which was obviously supposed to look as if it had been set at a jaunty angle but actually appeared to have been put on when she was drunk), looked enquiringly at them. 'Anything to drink?' she said. 'Wine, beer or we have a full range of cocktails for those in the party mood. Tequila Sunrise, Black Russian, Zombie . . .'

'What about a New York State of Mind?' Chloë said, looking at Emma. 'It's like a Long Island Iced Tea, but you only get the chance to drink it once in a lifetime.'

Chapter Twenty-Two

When Emma and Chloë landed in London, it was early morning. It was one of those winter mornings that seem more like the middle of the night. The sun was thinking about rising but appeared to have decided on five more minutes under the duvet. Emma and Chloë carried their bags from the tube and past the cashpoint. For once it was free of people sitting cross-legged asking for money. They didn't get out of bed this early. Nor did many other people, by the looks of things. The street was practically empty when they walked up it. The sound of their footsteps on the pavements seemed as loud as gunfire. There was no traffic noise to mask it. Emma stopped and pulled Gillian's Afghan coat around herself and did up another button. She and Chloë had barely spoken since they got off the plane. They were tired and PHD – Post Holiday Depression – had kicked in.

Everything seemed greyer, dirtier, duller than it had before they left. The rubbish in the gutter that Emma would not normally have noticed was suddenly overwhelming. The graffiti that was ordinarily simply part of the landscape seemed to scream from every wall. Chloë put her key in the lock and they climbed the stairs to the flat, dragging their bags up the steps behind them. They did it slowly and in convoy, like a glum Wild West wagon train, leaving a big gap between themselves to allow for the bags.

Bump, bump, bump, went the bags as they pulled them up the stairs.

At the top, Chloë abandoned her luggage and her pile of carrier bags. 'Coffee?' she said.

'Yeah,' Emma answered. 'What time do you have to be in?'

'A couple of hours,' Chloë said from the kitchen.

Emma could hear her filling the kettle. She slipped off her coat. As she did so, something fell out of her pocket. It was her mobile. She hadn't switched it on since she got off the plane. She sat down on the sofa, pressed the top and put it on the coffee table. Almost immediately, it began to hop across the glass as it vibrated. Emma sighed deeply, but picked it up anyway. 'Hello?' she said.

'Can you talk?' whispered Gill from the other end.

'Oh,' Emma answered, shocked. 'Yeah, hang on while I go in the other room.'

Chloë had appeared with two mugs of instant. 'Lover boy?' she said, amused, as Emma walked out of the room.

Emma shut the door to her bedroom and sat down on the bed. 'OK, I'm on my own now. So, what's the, um, problem?'

'There's no problem,' Gill said quickly. 'I just called because, you know, it's been a few days since we last spoke and I wanted to hear how you were getting on.'

'Oh, fine. You know. What about you?'

'Yes, yes. Absolutely fine.'

Normally, Emma and Gill could talk for hours. But the ability to make small talk had deserted them. They both had something to hide and it gave their apparently casual comments a stiltedness.

'So,' said Gill. 'How are things at Bliss?'

'Oh, I haven't been there for a few days. I've been in, um, New York.'

'New York! What were you doing there?'

'I went with Chloë.'

'You and Chloë!' Gill felt jealous, as if they were children again and Emma had taken a favourite doll of hers. Chloë was *her* friend, not Emma's. Emma had no right to be going to New York with Chloë. Deep down she was already wondering if Chloë now preferred Emma to her.

'Yeah, well, she got the tickets.'

'So she paid!'

'They were a present, sort of. A present to her from, you know, some guy,' Emma explained.

'Some guy?'

'You know Chloë – there's always some guy.'

'Where did you stay?'

'The Majestic.'

'Jesus!' Now Gill was really jealous. The swapping plan hadn't included stays in New York at the Majestic. And certainly not with her best friend. 'Does it look like it does in the magazines?' she asked.

'Well, the Penthouse Suite —'

'You stayed in the Penthouse Suite!'

Emma realised how it sounded. Even if she hadn't been Gill's twin she could have read the envy in her voice. She decided to change the subject. 'Anyway, what about you? How did the fashion show go?'

Any envy on Gill's part disappeared, the flame extinguished by fear. 'Oh, fine,' she said in an unnaturally high voice. 'Liberty Honeywell came.'

'Really?' Emma was impressed. 'I suppose Dino was fawning all over her. Are they new best friends?'

'Well, I think there have been a few notes back and forth since, yes.'

This was the moment when Gill could have come clean about having been put on gardening leave by Dino. But she didn't. Gill was still feeling upstaged by Emma's trip to New York. It sounded like Emma was making a huge success of the single life; she wasn't about to admit that her attempt at being Emma wasn't going quite so smoothly.

'And Max, how's he?' Emma asked.

Gill's throat went tight. 'He's, well – you know Max.'

'Yeah, I've been married to him for thirteen years. I just wondered how he was this week.'

There was silence. Gill was trying to work out what to say.

'Nothing wrong, is there?' Emma asked.

'No, no. Nothing wrong,' Gill said finally. 'Actually, he's taken a few days off.' She winced as soon as she'd said it. Still smarting from Emma's New York revelations, she was now engaged in some sort of pathetic one-upmanship with her sister. My best friend might go on holiday with you, but your husband, your famously workaholic husband, has taken time off to be with me!

'Max, taking time off!' Emma was incredulous. 'He never takes time off.'

'Well, a big case finished and he was really knackered and . . .'

It was Emma's turn to be angry. Gill wasn't Max's wife, she, Emma, was. If Max was knackered it would be Emma who was the cause of it. No, that wasn't right. What she meant was . . . Emma pulled herself together.

'So, has Saskia come out of her room yet?'

'Well, she came to Brighton with us.'

'Us?'

'Me, Max and Kevin.'

'You took Kevin out of the house?'

'He's OK when you get to know him, you know.'

'Believe me, I know what Kevin is like. Dominique has brought him round enough. He's destroyed half my house.'

'All he needs is a little love.'

'Thank you for that Hallmark moment. Shame it hasn't worked on Saskia.'

'Well . . .'

'Oh, for God's sake. Don't tell me. She's turned into the perfect daughter. I left the Munsters back at my house –'

'Now, that's no way to talk about Max,' Gill laughed.

Emma didn't join in. 'I left the Munsters and I'm coming back to the bloody Partridge Family.'

There was silence between them.

'You did agree to this swap, you know, Em,' said Gill. 'You persuaded me, remember?'

'I know,' said Emma. 'It's just I never expected you to be so good at being me. I mean – it's taken me thirty-eight years to practise being me. You've managed it in a few weeks.' And for Emma, that was hugely depressing. The only way she and, indeed, Gill had coped with being twins was by assuring themselves that they were unique. Others might confuse them, but they knew there were fundamental differences between them. They each had special skills and qualities. That Gill could apparently step into Emma's shoes shredded that little hot-water bottle for the soul to ribbons.

'I don't know,' Emma continued. 'I was sure you'd fail.'

'Well, thanks for your faith in me.'

'I'm sorry. I thought you'd be a disaster, lose me my job or something.'

'Oh, yeah.' Gill laughed hoarsely. 'Yeah, right.'

'It's depressing though, isn't it, to think we're so inter-changeable. I thought someone would rumble us,' said Emma.

'Well, there's still a bit to go yet. Are you still OK for Saturday?'

Saturday was Gordon and Charlotte's golden wedding anniversary. With her trip to New York, Emma had lost track of time. It suddenly seemed very close.

'Yeah,' Emma said. 'I suppose we'd better do the swap back before the party on Saturday. Friday night, maybe. Have you had all the RSVPs and stuff?'

'Yeah. It's all organised. Max has been really helpful.'

After all the years she'd tried to get Max to help with things, Gill had him housetrained in a jiffy. Emma's hackles rose again. 'So, I'll see you Friday then,' she said crisply. 'Six o'clock?'

'Yeah,' said Gill.

Emma pressed the end call button and sat slumped on the bed. Gordon and Charlotte's golden wedding anniversary. Fifty years. It was a long time to be married. It was a long time to do anything. Fifty years of eating Hula Hoops, or driving a Ford Transit, or brushing your hair every morning. She reckoned she should get a medal for half a century of doing the washing-up. Would she and Max manage that long?

Beep, beep.

Someone had texted her. She picked up the phone and pressed a few buttons: 'how r u? A x'

Alex. What was she going to do about Alex?

Gill slid back into bed without waking Max. With Dino in hospital, a decision on her future at Smith & Taylor hadn't been made. Max was still off too, so with neither of them working, they could afford to stay in bed a bit longer. She rolled over to face Max. Her cheek formed a little hollow in the pillow.

'E-mma! E-mma!' Kevin was awake upstairs.

Oh, God. What had she just been saying to Emma about him, that all he needed was love? All he needed was a new body clock, set to go off two hours later in the morning.

'E-mma!' he shouted again.

Gill heard the creak of footsteps on the stairs. 'Oi, monster,' Gill heard Saskia hiss. 'Can the noise or you'll wake the whole house.'

There was a clunk as the door closed. It was Saskia. She had got up to see to Kevin. But Saskia hated Kevin. A terrible thought occurred to Gill. Had Saskia gone to smother Kevin with his own pillow? She wouldn't put it past her. She wouldn't put anything past Saskia. Then she heard laughter, which reassured her that Kevin was at least breathing. The door upstairs opened again.

'Coco Pops! I want Coco Pops!' Kevin shouted.

'All right, Coco Pops,' said Saskia.

'And Rice Krispies.'

'OK,' laughed Saskia. 'And Rice Krispies.'

'And Weetabix.'

'Hey, kid, don't push it.'

Their footsteps had reached the bottom of the stairs. Their voices disappeared into the kitchen. Maybe that Hallmark moment was right. All either Kevin or Saskia needed was a little love – from each other. Gill decided not to go down. She'd leave them together.

'What do you mean, you're not coming in? You've been away for three sodding days already!'

Emma was breaking the news to Gus that she needed the night off and he wasn't taking it well. This wasn't unreasonable, given that she had just come back from a rather glamorous trip to New York. Still, the fact she couldn't tell him why she couldn't work tonight didn't help.

'We all know you're not the best waitress in the world, especially recently –' Gus said.

'Thanks.'

'Well, it's true. But the temporary waitress we've had was crap. I need you tonight, Gill.'

'I'm sorry. If I could, I would, only what with my dad being ill . . .'

'What's he got again?'

'Heart trouble.'

'I thought you said it was a possible minor stroke?'

'Yes, um, well, they don't know what it is at the moment. Anyway, gotta go.'

Emma put the phone down, feeling incredibly guilty. She was taking her dad's health in vain – or was it for granted? What if she had now tempted fate and he did get ill? She told herself not to be ridiculous. She needed the night off tonight and that was all there was to it.

The squeal of the smoke alarm was deafening.

'Have you got the battery out yet?' shouted Gill from the bottom of the ladder.

'Well, obviously not,' Max shouted back from the top of it. He was jabbing at the alarm with a screwdriver. 'Remind me what the point of these is again?' he asked.

'They're to stop us being burned to a cinder,' Gill replied. 'Here, try this.' She handed him a broomstick. Max began bashing the alarm with the end of the handle, at first, relatively gently; he gradually became more manic.

'Think I'd prefer the cinders option to being sent stark, staring . . .' the noise suddenly abated '. . . mad.'

'Thank Christ for that!' Gill said.

'Christ! Christ! Christ!' Kevin squealed delightedly. 'Put the noise on again, Uncle Max.'

'No,' Max said firmly, coming down the ladder.

'P-lease.'

'It was only a bit of toast,' Saskia said, sullenly.

Perhaps it had been a tad optimistic to expect Saskia and Kevin to bond and cook breakfast at the same time. Saskia hadn't so much as switched on the grill for five years, ever since she declared cookery and housework a patriarchal plot to enslave women. That this meant that another woman – Emma – had to prepare all Saskia's food didn't seem to impinge on her argument.

'Look, let's all go out for brunch. My treat,' Gill said. 'Call it a sort of last supper.'

Gill was acutely aware that her days as woman of this house were numbered. In three days she would be saying goodbye to Max, Saskia and Kevin. Only she wouldn't be allowed actually to say goodbye. She would simply have to drift out of their lives. Worse, she would have to hover on the periphery afterwards. Never far enough away to forget them, but not near enough to do or say anything. She would have to become a ghost.

It felt like the last day of the summer holidays as a child, when Gill and Emma had tried to stretch the daylight hours for as long as possible. There always came the point when their mother would make them come inside to assemble their school things for the next morning: pencil case, pen, pencil, rubber, protractor . . . Gill had consoled herself with the thought that half-term would be with them in six weeks and then there was Christmas. However, there was to be no reprieve for her this time. Gill was counting the hours, but she hadn't meant to give herself away.

Max frowned. 'Last supper? Are you going somewhere?'

The pile of clothes on Gill's bed had grown from a slight hillock into a towering mountain of fabric. For the last twenty minutes, Emma had been trying on every item of Gill's clothing. Perhaps she'd have felt more confident if she could have worn something of her own. Everything felt unfamiliar. Tonight, she was meeting Alex. Emma had gone back and forth over whether to accept his offer or not. She knew it was lunacy, but she also knew it was the sort of chance she would never get again. She could start afresh in a new country, possibly with a new man.

Emma loved Max, but the relationship had never been a clean slate. Saskia meant part of the script of Max and Emma's life together had already been written when she entered stage, left. They had never had the chance to be reckless, to consider just upping sticks. They'd always had to consider the effect on Saskia. Emma had accepted that, but as the years had gone on, she had begun to yearn for change. Maybe it was an early mid-life crisis, but Emma's job at Smith & Taylor no longer scintillated her. Conscientious Emma, sensible Emma had hung on in there. Until now.

Emma was being given the opportunity to turn her life totally upside down and she was tempted, so tempted. The only thing stopping her was Max. Could she really leave him? Did she really want to? The weeks she had spent away from him had been hard in one sense. She missed him. But perhaps that was just habit. They'd been together so long, she had grown to accommodate him like ivy wound round an apple tree.

Emma's time as Gill had proved to Emma that she

could survive on her own. She felt empowered. It had also reminded her of an existence not weighed down with the responsibility of caring for others. As Gill, she hadn't had to think about whether Max had any clean shirts, whether Saskia had turned up for lessons or whether Kevin was eating a balanced diet. She only had herself to worry about. It was such a bloody relief. But more than all of this, there was Alex. Emma told herself it was just infatuation. She barely knew him. But the attraction was so strong. She could close her eyes and trace every contour of his face with her imagination. His blue eyes, his aquiline nose, his full lips . . .

Emma looked at her watch and realised that if she didn't get a move on she'd be late. She grabbed a black top and trousers and cantered down the stairs. 'See you later,' she called to Chloë as she went.

Chloë's head appeared at the top of the stairs.

'Good luck!' she shouted down.

Chapter Twenty-Three

Emma was lucky with a cab. She arrived at Alex's house on Connaught Square a few minutes early. She paid the taxi and stared up at the building. She'd known he was well off, but hadn't realised he was this wealthy. The house was magnificent; it was probably so heavily listed you'd have to get planning permission to change a lightbulb. Emma looked at the house and imagined herself living there, hosting chic dinner parties in the first-floor drawing room perhaps. She glanced up a floor to what she supposed was the master bedroom. As the mistress, she would be the one opening the curtains in the morning. Or maybe they'd have staff to do that and they'd bring her coffee and an ironed newspaper on a tray.

Emma's *Upstairs Downstairs* fantasy was interrupted by the taxi driver shouting, 'Your change. You forgot your change.' He was waving a ten-pound note.

Emma blushed and took the money. She was being ridiculous. She loved Max. She did. She looked at her watch. She was ten minutes early, but she couldn't very

well loiter. This was definitely not the sort of neighbour-
hood in which loitering was encouraged. They'd think
she was here to burgle the place – a challenge, given her
3-inch heels. She walked up the front steps and pressed
the bell. She felt the flutter of her stomach as footsteps
approached it from the other side and prepared herself to
meet Alex. She needed to prepare. She was so nervous, it
took conscious thought to arrange her features into what
she hoped was an even semi-relaxed expression.

The door swung open.

'Hello? Oh, I thought it was . . . Who are you?'

Instead of Alex, a woman stood on the threshold to
Emma's dream. She was very blonde and very thin and
had a baby balanced on one hip. She was Joelly Childs.
The baby gurgled. It was clutching a suede monkey. The
toy was soft and brown and had ears like Prince Charles.
It was also very familiar. Emma's heart flipped over. It
was the same suede monkey that Alex had bought at FAO
Schwarz with her in New York. She'd cradled it on her lap
and she'd thought how sweet it was of Alex to choose
such a cute gift for a child. She hadn't realised it was for
Joelly Childs's baby. Her heart sank. Suddenly, it all
began to make sense. The reason Alex hadn't made a pass
was that he lived with Joelly Childs and they had a baby.
But how could Alex have concealed this from her! Emma
felt betrayed. More than that, though: she felt humiliated.

Emma was a fool. She'd built this whole life on a lie.
She couldn't blame Alex. He'd never actually said he was

single, he didn't have a child or that they had a future together. He'd offered her a job. That was all. It was Emma who had hoped for more. Maybe he'd been tempted. There had been that clumsy kiss. However, the truth of his situation was standing in front of Emma holding her baby.

'I said, who are you?' Joelly Childs repeated.

'It doesn't matter,' Emma asked.

Joelly Childs frowned and very obviously looked Emma up and down. Emma felt heffalumpy next to the human pipe cleaner. 'Have we met?' she asked.

The baby started to cry. Joelly transferred it to the other hip. As she did so, the monkey fell on to the ground. Emma picked it up. It felt familiar in her hand. She gave it back to Joelly. The baby was calmed, but only for a minute. Its discreet wails soon turned into full-blown bellows. 'Trust Alex to go out when the baby needs feeding. Can I give him a message?' Joelly said.

'No, no,' Emma said, turning and starting to walk down the stairs. 'It doesn't matter.'

Emma walked back down the steps and down the street as quickly as she could.

Gill looked round the bedroom. She stroked a hand over the duvet and rearranged Max's book on the bedside table. She still had three days to the party but her bereavement had already begin. She was saying goodbye, but secretly. She felt like a convict on the run. She was going to have to leave silently, without bidding anyone goodbye or even looking back. That was the deal.

She walked to the window. Outside in the garden, Saskia and Kevin were sitting on the swinging seat. Saskia was swinging it, then stopping it with her feet, leaving them at an angle. Kevin was laughing and begging her to swing it again. Gill smiled and watched, a ghost at the window. Max appeared, carrying a tray with glasses of juice and a plate of biscuits. He sat down next to Saskia and put the tray on the ground. Kevin climbed on to his lap. They tipped gently backwards and forwards. Kevin put his thumb in his mouth and Saskia and Max stared serenely into the distance.

Then Kevin started shouting. Gill could hear a muffled echo of him through the window. 'Juice! Juice!' he shouted.

Max bent down and picked up a glass and handed it to him. As he took it, the seat tipped and some of the juice slopped on to Saskia. She and Kevin began to quarrel, but even the bickering couldn't spoil the scene for Gill. Gill felt just the way she had in Brighton. They were a real family: not a perfect one, but a real one. Max calmed Saskia and Kevin down and they went back to swinging the seat. None of them had the slightest idea they were being watched.

It was the end of the day. The light was low and weak. Gill sat down on the edge of the bed and watched as it gradually dropped so that she could no longer see the figures on the seat. She heard voices, a peal of childish laughter, but finally it was dark and they were gone.

"Scuse me love, is that machine free?'

Emma nodded and went back to watching someone else's clothes being tossed about in a tumble dryer. The man who had spoken to her put his bag on the floor, unzipped the top and began loading his stuff into the spare washer. Emma had not exactly chosen the launderette. It had simply been the first place she'd seen after leaving Alex's that was open. She had stumbled into it in a daze and slumped on a bench, which is where she'd been for the last twenty minutes.

She berated herself sharply for falling for Alex. How could she have been so stupid? Even up to the moment she had got in the cab to go to meet him, she hadn't known whether she would accept his offer, but now that it had been whipped away from her, she knew that she would have. She would have taken one look at Alex and said, 'Yes.' She would have thrown away thirteen years of marriage – and for what? For a man who never really wanted her at all.

Now, Emma felt empty. She felt stripped of all her dignity. She'd seen Alex's house. He was wealthy, attractive; he could probably have any woman he wanted. He already had Joelly Childs. Why on earth would he want Emma? At the same time as tearing chunks out of herself, Emma couldn't help remembering the almost-kiss on the steps of the Majestic. Had she really read the signs so wrongly? It had felt so real. His emotion – and hers – had felt genuine. She couldn't wipe out the memory of that moment, and a part of her didn't want to. Maybe, for that one minute, it hadn't been a lie? He had felt what she had?

But you can't build your life on maybes. Emma felt a sudden rush of relief. She hadn't thrown her marriage away. Perhaps meeting Joelly was a blessing. It had shown her how much she had to lose. She was lucky to have Max and Saskia and, yes, even Kevin. She couldn't wait to see them and hug them.

The man with the bag of washing was hovering. 'Sorry to trouble you again, love, but do you have a pound coin? I don't have the right change.'

'Oh, I'm sure I can help,' Emma replied, feeling warm about everything and everyone, including him, at that moment. She got out her purse and searched through it. Then she gave him a pound coin. He went to hand her some change in return.

'Forget it,' she said. 'I'm in a good mood.' Then she picked up her mobile. Never mind waiting another three days, she was going to call Gill now. Emma wanted to be back in her own home with her own husband. She dialled the number. Gill picked up immediately.

'Hello, Gill. I know we've got till the end of the week, but how do you fancy calling it a day now? It's been fun and everything but, you know . . .'

There was no answer.

'Gill, are you there?' Emma asked.

There was still no answer.

'Gill?'

'I'm not swapping back,' Gill announced quietly.

Emma frowned. 'What do you mean?'

'I'm not coming back. I'm staying.'

'Staying where?'

'Here.'

There was silence. Emma was trying to make sense of what she was being told.

'I don't want to swap back,' Gill said. 'I'm staying here.'

Emma was at a loss. 'But you can't. We agreed.'

'I know, but I've changed my mind.'

'But it was just an experiment. You know we only said we'd do it for a few weeks. The deadline is Saturday.'

'I know,' Gill said, quietly but firmly.

Emma began to panic. 'Do you need a bit more time? Another few days maybe?'

'No,' Gill replied.

'Shall I come and pick you up?'

'No.'

'I don't understand.' Emma's voice was starting to crack. 'I'm coming home. That's what's supposed to happen. That's what we agreed.'

'Oh, Em, I'm sorry, but I can't come back. I belong here.'

'No, you don't,' Emma shouted. 'You belong here. This is your life.'

'Not any more.'

'You can't do this. I won't let you.'

'You don't have a choice.'

It had never occurred to Emma that Gill might be the one who wouldn't want to swap back. She had been so caught up in her own crisis with Alex that she'd been oblivious to any notion that Gill might also be reassessing her life. She was shocked. But she was more than that. She was angry. She had put aside her hopes for a new life for herself with Alex. Emma felt she'd made a sacrifice, even if it had been forced upon her. Having given up her chance of a fresh start, she was not about to have Gill negate her sacrifice by stealing her old life out from under her. 'I'll tell Max,' she declared.

'He won't believe you.'

'Yes, he will. We've been married for thirteen years. He knows the difference between us.'

'He didn't know the difference last night.'

'What do you mean?' Emma asked, rattled.

Gill didn't answer her.

'My God! You've slept with him, haven't you? You bitch!'

'It wasn't like that. I didn't mean it to happen.' Up to now Gill had been calm, almost emotionless in fact. It was the only way she could cope with this conversation: cutting off all her emotions. But hearing the devastation in Emma's voice, she crumbled. 'Don't hate me, Em,' she sobbed.

'What do you expect? You've stolen my husband,' shouted Emma.

'You can't steal people.'

They both said nothing for a moment.

'You weren't happy, Em,' Gill said.

'Well, thank you, Oprah Winfrey,' countered Emma.

'But you weren't. You remember all the things you said to me about wanting to run away to an olive farm?'

Of course Emma remembered them, but she didn't want to be reminded now. 'We could have worked it out,' she said. 'We still can if you leave me and Max alone.'

'I can't,' Gill said.

'But you're stealing my whole life.'

'You can start again.'

'I don't want to start again. I want my old life back.'

'Do you? Do you really? Max and I are happy. And Saskia and Kevin. You should see them, Em. They're blossoming.'

'Spare me. I can't believe that my own sister, my *twin* would do this. You must be really evil.'

'But you know I'm not,' Gill said. 'That's what makes this so hard. I love you, Em.'

'You've got a funny way of showing it.'

'I do love you. This is so hard.'

'Am I supposed to feel sorry for you?' Emma asked sarcastically.

'No, no . . .' The misery Gill was feeling was clear in her voice. 'Just remember that I didn't do this to hurt you.'

'Well, that's what you're doing.'

'I know.'

Emma put her hands over her face and let out a low wail. 'Max will find out the truth, you know. And when he does he won't want anything to do with you.'

'Or you,' Gill pointed out. 'Remember, you agreed to this swap. How do you think Max is going to feel if he knows you deliberately walked out on him and Saskia? If he does find out, he's going to hate you for that.'

Emma knew Gill was right. She felt hopeless. 'Gill, I'm begging you. Please don't do this. We've still got time to swap back.'

'I'm sorry,' Gill answered, before switching the phone off.

Emma sat stunned for five minutes, then the anger boiled up inside her. So Gill thought she could get away with it, did she? Emma took a piece of paper out of her handbag. It was an email from her father: a picture of Gordon and Charlotte holding cocktails. They looked tanned and happy, the very image of the contented retirement couple. If Gill thought she was going to play Happy Families with Max then she had better think again.

Emma had three days until the party – and this was one bash that no one would forget in a hurry.

Chapter Twenty-Four

The Willow Lodge Hotel had definitely come up in the world since Gordon and Charlotte spent their honeymoon there. For a start, it was now called the Willow Lodge Hotel and Spa, the spa being a Swiss-style chalet bought through *Exchange & Mart* and pitched at the bottom of the garden. Sound-proofing remained a problem. As Gordon and Charlotte's golden wedding anniversary guests arrived they could hear the distant strains of dolphin squeaks wafting towards them from the CD player in one of the 'relaxation suites'.

A couple of Gordon's older friends who had served in the Navy were especially intrigued. They enquired of the receptionist whether there was an aquarium in the vicinity. 'Jolly useful chaps, dolphins,' one announced. 'Bloody excellent mine-clearers.'

When Gill, Max, Saskia and Kevin arrived, there was quite a throng already in the lobby. Men in navy blazers with shiny gold buttons; women in smart skirt suits or printed two-pieces with matching handbags and shoes. Charlotte's wasn't just the last generation of the nuclear family, it was also the last which saw the importance of fully co-ordinating accessories. They weren't giving up on either without a fight.

'If you'd just like to go through and join the other guests by the Japanese water feature,' the harassed receptionist said, pointing through an open door to one side of the bar.

Gill, Max and the others all milled through the doorway.

'Japanese water features are quite the thing these days, aren't they, Joy,' one lady in head-to-toe sage green proclaimed.

'It's all to do with Fing Sui, Olivia,' another in spriggy pleats added.

'Chop suey?' interrupted a lady in fawn.

'Feng shui,' bellowed the green lady at a volume that could have been heard in a saw mill. 'Are you wearing your hearing aid?'

'Yes, yes,' protested the lady in fawn.

'Well, turn it up, then.'

Gill wondered if anyone wore fawn any more. If they did, they'd call it biscuit.

When they got outside, they immediately sank into gravel. Most of the garden had been gravelled, apart from one side where lead flashing had been used to construct a rill to run water from the Japanese water feature into a large square pool.

'Must be lovely for the kiddies and their boats,' another lady with a huge cleavage and lots of pink beads said.

Gill noticed a large sign. 'No children'.

'What is that?' Max whispered, pointing at the pond.

'I think it's all to do with fing sui,' she giggled.

'Not chop suey?' Max giggled back.

'Let's get a drink,' Gill suggested and they moved towards a bar set up underneath an arbour to one side of the garden.

Gill looked round as she went, nervously searching the crowd for Emma. They hadn't spoken since she'd told Emma she wasn't switching back. Emma's silence was ominous. Still, so far there was no sign of her. Maybe she wouldn't come. Gill felt both a sense of doom and slightly high. She had done the unthinkable and, having done that, everything else seemed inconsequential. She was strong, all powerful. At the same time, she felt as light as a feather: if Max blew hard, she would float away like a helium balloon.

'Hello, you two.' It was Charlotte. She was beaming. Gill put her arms round her and gave her a big hug.

'Hello, Mum. Did you have a good trip? You look wonderful. Had your hair done?'

'We can have more of a chat later,' Charlotte said, touching her hair. 'But yes, the hair. Do you like it?'

'Very chic, Charlotte,' said Max, also kissing her. 'Happy wedding anniversary. What is it? Five, ten years?'

'You know very well it's fifty,' Charlotte said, blushing with pleasure.

'But it can't be. You don't look old enough,' Max said in full charm mode.

437

Charlotte smiled and batted him playfully. At that moment, she did look like a young bride.

Saskia was hovering nearby. Gill had hoped she might manage to get her out of baggy black layers and even achieve a semblance of a smile for this occasion, but there had been a bit of a retrenchment on the cheerfulness front ever since Gill had refused to let her dig a hole for her and Kevin to sleep in last night. She'd wanted to construct some kind of New Age shelter, but Gill had put her foot down, hence the scowl now. It just went to prove that Saskia may have been better but she hadn't undergone a personality transplant. It wasn't like she'd joined the Moonies or anything.

Kevin was looking at his reflection in the pool. He had also managed to secure a vol-au-vent from somewhere and was floating it round making *choo, choo* noises.

'Ah, there's your father with your sister,' Charlotte said, smiling and waving. 'Cooee! Over here!'

So Emma had come. What was she planning? Gill panicked. She had to get away, but she couldn't leave Max behind. Goodness knows what Emma would say to him with her not there. She looked round desperately. Her eye fell upon a series of copper balls, graduating in size from tennis ball to watermelon. They were lined up on top of a low brick wall.

'Come and look at these, Max,' she said, grabbing him by the shoulder and pulling him away from Charlotte.

'What, what,' Max stuttered, spilling most of a glass of

438

champagne down him as he was shunted away from Charlotte. He dabbed his shirt with the cuff of his jacket. 'What's the matter?'

'Nothing. I just wanted you to see these,' Gill said, pointing at the metal orbs. 'I wondered, you know, whether we could do something similar in the garden at home.' She glanced over her shoulder. Through the crowd she could see Emma talking to Gordon and Charlotte.

'But you hate gardening!' Max exclaimed.

'I thought I might get into it,' Gill protested.

'Anyway, I think we should congratulate your father. We haven't done that. And don't you want to say hello to Gill?'

'Um, yes, yes, of course,' Gill said. 'Just want to have a look at that shrub over there. Come and see.' She took hold of Max by the elbow of his jacket. He was propelled across the garden to the farthest corner.

'It's a box hedge,' Max said when they got there.

'Yes, well, it's been, um, clipped very well, hasn't it?'

'Not especially,' Max said. 'Can we get back to your parents now?' He started to walk back. Gill looked round for something, anything to delay him.

'Oh, look, Max. A robin! Is that a robin?'

'Where?' he said, suspiciously.

'Up there,' Gill said, pointing to the branches of a tree.

Max took a couple of steps back and stared upwards. 'It's a sparrow,' he said.

'No, it's not, it's a —'

'It's a sparrow. Now come on.' Max would not be dissuaded. He marched purposefully across the garden.

Ding, ding, ding. Gordon rang the side of a glass with a spoon. 'Would you all like to come inside now? Lunch is being served.'

They filed inside, back into the hall, and were guided up a wide wooden staircase into a first-floor dining room. The restyle hadn't got as far as this room, which remained firmly rooted in the 1980s. Dried hops as dry and dusty as a bowl of cheap muesli hung from the ceiling. The chairs were covered in gold-coloured brocade which matched the gold and burgundy floral wallpaper.

A long table had been arranged in a horseshoe shape in front of the windows looking on to the garden. Gordon and Charlotte had taken their places in the middle. 'Come and sit down, dear,' Gordon was saying to Emma, beckoning her into Gill's seat.

Gill hung back. 'Interesting picture. Is it an original?' she asked.

'What, *The Hay Wain*? I doubt it, don't you? Hadn't we better sit down?' Max said. He led the way through the crowd towards the two seats next to Charlotte. On the way, Gill said hello to one or two of the friends of her parents she recognised. Others she didn't know pointed her out to each other.

'That's Emma and her husband Max. She's done very well,' they said. 'There was an article about her in the newspaper, you know.'

440

When they had walked round to the far side of the table, Max leant over and shook Gordon's hand. 'Congratulations,' he said. 'You'd have got a shorter sentence for manslaughter.'

Gordon chuckled on cue. 'Quite so,' he said.

'Tell me about the trip later,' Max said.

Gordon nodded. 'Got a few snaps with me,' and he tapped his inside pocket, where there was an ominously large lump.

Gill sat down as quickly as possible and pulled Max down beside her, so as to block Emma's view of her. She studied the menu card in front of her minutely, all the while aware of Emma peering round Gordon in her peripheral vision.

'Where's Saskia?' Charlotte enquired.

'And Kevin,' Max added, frowning.

They all turned to look out of the window. Saskia and Kevin were in the garden. Kevin was piling gravel up on top of the copper balls and watching it slide down again. Saskia was sitting beside him, stroking his hair. And talking to him. Gill saw that Emma was looking. She wanted to shout: 'See! I was right. They're happy!'

Emma turned her head and, for the first time since their telephone conversation, they locked eyes. Emma's gaze was fierce with hatred. Gill looked away quickly. She'd never seen that look before. It frightened her.

Lunch was served by a phalanx of waitresses in black skirts and with aprons tied over the top. Asparagus mousse with a passion-fruit sauce, followed by poached salmon with a tiane of spinach and leek. Dessert was bread and butter pudding. Gill barely touched hers. She noticed that Emma's plate, too, was taken away still piled with food.

Gordon leant across. 'You girls and your diets,' he said. 'Always been the same,' he added to Max. 'Whatever one does, the other has to do, too. Like two peas in a pod. Couldn't separate them. Still can't.'

Gill thought what a lie that was now. She and Emma were sitting a few feet from one another, but they might as well have been in different rooms, cities, continents. For thirty-eight years, they had indeed been inseparable. Now, after two months' experiment they'd been torn apart. And no one but them noticed the difference. All the other guests were stirring sugar cubes into their coffee and deliberating whether to have another chocolate off the plates that were circling, as if nothing had happened.

Emma also was thinking how much things had changed. She watched Max and Gill together and it could have been her. Everyone thought it was her, even Max. She felt invisible. She wasn't anyone. She wasn't Emma. She wasn't Gill. She was in limbo.

Gordon got to his feet and rang his glass with his spoon again. 'I shall keep this brief,' he said, 'because you don't want to hear an old duffer like me going on.'

There was polite laughter from around the room.

'When Charlotte and I got married fifty years ago' – clapping erupted from the guests – 'we had no idea that we'd be here all these years on with our two beautiful daughters, twin daughters, all grown up.' He looked at Emma and Gill, smiling with pride, then transferred his gaze to his wife. 'All I can say is Charlotte is more beautiful now than the day I met her and why she's put up with me all these years I can't imagine.' He bent down and planted a kiss on Charlotte's lips. She kept her head tipped back and smiled indulgently.

'But then, when we said our vows, they were for life,' Gordon continued. There were nods and murmurs of agreement from all around. Gill felt Max's hand on top of hers. He gave it a squeeze. She looked up at him. He bent his head to her and kissed her. At that moment, Gordon raised his glass. 'So, could we all be upstanding for a toast?' he announced.

Gordon leant back to pull Charlotte's chair out as she stood. As he did so, he offered a clear view of Max and Gill to Emma. Max and Gill scrambled to stand up, but too late to prevent Emma seeing them kiss. She gasped.

'To marriage,' Gordon declared.

'To marriage,' everyone repeated, lifting their glasses and taking a sip.

'To Gordon and Charlotte,' Max said.

'To Gordon and Charlotte,' came the refrain, followed by more mass sipping.

The whole room was on its feet. Walking sticks were

being leant on, Zimmer frames shuffled, girdles were starting to pinch. There was the tiniest of pauses while people wondered whether to sit down again. Into this crevice in the proceedings, Emma inserted herself. 'I'd like to make a toast,' she said.

'Oh, would you, dear? That's nice,' Gordon said.

'Oh fuck,' Gill whispered.

Emma turned to face Gill and Max. She raised her glass. 'To the woman who stole my husband.'

'To the woman who . . .' the crowd began to repeat before petering out halfway through. There was a confused silence.

'Sorry, dear, what was that?' Charlotte asked, bewildered.

'Her. Gill. She's stolen Max.'

'But you're Gill, dear.'

'No, I'm not. I'm Emma.'

'This is one of those after-dinner games, isn't it?' said Gordon. 'Animal, vegetable or mineral?'

People had begun sitting down now. There's only so much support a pair of surgical stockings can provide. They were whispering.

'Do you know what's going on?'

'No, do you?'

Emma tipped the rest of the glass down her throat. She took a bottle of wine out of an ice bucket in front of her and poured herself another glass, before necking that too. 'We did a swap,' she said. 'Gill and I. We agreed to pretend to be each other and then that bitch —'

'Sit down, dear, and stop being ridiculous. You know what you're like when you've had too much wine,' Gordon said, placing a hand on her shoulder.

'No, no,' Emma said.

'No one's listening. You're not impressing anybody, young lady,' said Gordon, as if she was three and having a tantrum in the supermarket.

'You don't understand,' Emma said, struggling back to her feet. 'I am Emma and she is Gill and she's stolen my husband.'

Gordon looked angry now. 'Why do you have to spoil your mother's special day?'

'But I'm not. You have to believe me. This isn't my fault. It's her . . .' She flung an arm in Gill's direction a little too violently. She knocked over a vase with a single rose in it.

'Now look what you've done,' Gordon said.

'It's all right, dear,' Charlotte said, using her napkin to mop up the water. 'Remember your heart. You're not supposed to get overexcited.'

'Always apologising for them, aren't you, Charlotte? Well, there comes a point, there really does.'

'But I'm not lying. It's true. I'm Emma. Max! Max! You can see it's me,' Emma wailed.

During all this, Max had said nothing. He hadn't reacted in any way. Now he calmly put an arm round Gill's shoulder. 'I know it's you, Em. I've known all along,' he announced.

Gill and Emma's mouths dropped open in shock. When Emma had recovered herself enough to speak, she said, 'But how?'

'Do you honestly think I can't tell the difference between you? How stupid do you think I am? A quick dye job and I was supposed to be completely taken in? Oh, come on, Em. I decided not to say anything because I was wondering how long you could keep it up.' Max turned to Gill. 'But I got used to you being around . . . and then you got sacked.'

'I got sacked!' Emma shouted.

'I can explain . . .' Gill said.

'I mean, I'd suspected from the beginning, but it was only when you got sacked and you didn't fight it that I knew. Emma would have fought back, but you didn't. And then, well . . .' He smiled tenderly at her.

'And then you fucked her!' Emma shouted. 'That's what happened, isn't it, Max? You fucked my sister!'

The crowd, even those who were saving the batteries of their hearing aids, had no trouble following this part of the proceedings. 'It's better than *Kilroy,*' one said.

Gordon Chancellor surveyed the crowd. 'Perhaps we should sit down,' he said. 'And you had better mind your language, young lady.'

They all sat down.

'You make it sound so sordid, but I'm in love with your sister,' Max said.

'You can't love her. You love me!' Emma wailed.

'No, I love her.'

'But how could this happen?'

'She's different from you. She's not always doing something. It was exhausting being married to you. I felt like I was messing up the living room just by being in it. Besides, we never saw each other.'

'You were as much to blame for that as me. I wasn't the only one who worked hard.'

'I know but I never really wanted that. I wanted a housewife.'

'A what!'

'See, you hate the whole idea, but Gill's at home and she likes it, don't you, Gill?'

'Well, um . . .'

'When I come home from work, I want my wife to be there. Maybe not with a hot meal ready, though that would be nice. But I can't deal with the stress of her life as well as my own. Home needs to be a sanctuary, not a place to swap horror stories.'

'God! You sound like something out of the nineteen fifties. Do you want your slippers put next to the fire, too?'

Gordon and Charlotte had been listening mute to this conversation. Now Gordon intervened. 'You know, Emma, maybe he's got a point. A man likes to come home to a happy house.'

'Yes, dear. Your father and I never had a cross word.'

'Oh, p-lease. If he wanted a walkover, then he married the wrong woman.'

'Yes, well, maybe I did,' Max said. 'Maybe I married the wrong twin.'

At that moment, there was a commotion at the other end of the room. Every head in the room swivelled as if they were watching a match at Wimbledon.

'You haven't got a glass of champagne, have you?' said Dominique, walking towards them. 'I'm absolutely parched.'

'Dominique!' Gill and Emma exclaimed together.

'What are you doing here?' Max asked, when the shock had waned. 'I thought you and Denzel were in Marbella?'

'We're finished,' Dominique screeched. 'Is this a clean glass?' She picked up a champagne flute and poured herself a glass of bubbly. Then she turned to the assembled throng, all of whom were silent. 'Not very lively, is it?' she said. There was no response, so she tried again, this time shouting: 'Not very lively –'

'It's OK,' Max said. 'They can hear you. It's just you've arrived at a tricky moment.'

'Sorry, but how did you know we were here?' Gill asked.

'I called Max. He told me.'

'Max?'

'Well, I thought you knew. Look, it doesn't matter now. There are more important things to worry about'.

'Why? What's going on?' asked Dominique. As self-obsessed as ever, she had failed to notice the atmosphere when she came in. It was soupy with emotion, but she was oblivious.

'It'll take too long to explain now,' Max said.

'Oh, all right then. I'll just pick up Kevin and go. You'll give me a lift, won't you, Max? I paid off the cab.'

Gill got to her feet. 'No,' she said.

'It's only a cab, darling,' Max said.

'I don't mean that. I mean Kevin. She can't have him. He's staying with us.'

'Don't you think you've done enough stealing for one day?' Emma said acidly.

Gill looked Dominique up and down. Her lip curled in disgust. 'You are a disgrace as a mother. You think you can have kids and when you get bored of them you can just dump them on someone else. Children aren't like old handbags. You can't get a new one when you're tired of the old. You did it to Saskia and almost destroyed her. I will not allow you to do it to Kevin.'

'But he's my son!' Dominique cried.

'Oh, you finally noticed, did you? A cat with a litter of kittens has more maternal instinct than you.'

'This from the woman who's never been a mother till a few weeks ago,' Emma said.

Dominique looked confused. 'Sorry,' she said. 'Am I mixing you two up?'

'No,' they said together.

'Look, this is ridiculous. I'm going to get my son. Where is he?'

Emma and Gill glanced behind them to the garden. Kevin was still playing happily with Saskia.

'Oh, he's out there, is he?' Dominique said. She turned and began walking out of the room. Gill scrambled up on to the table and jumped to her feet. Then she ran down it, kicking vases and glasses off as she went. The sound of breaking glass was accompanied by startled shrieks from the diners as a pair of feet thundered past. Once Gill was at the other end, she launched herself off it and caught Dominique in a rugby tackle. Both of them came crashing down.

'What are you doing?' Dominique squealed, shocked.

'You're not taking him. I won't let you. I'm his mother now.' Gill had Dominique pinned down on her back. She was sitting on Dominique's chest with a hand clamped round each of Dominique's wrists.

Dominique saw her manic expression and quailed. 'Emma, you're mad,' she said, horrified.

'I'm not Emma. I'm Gill.'

Meanwhile, Max had been making his way behind the other diners to join them. 'Perhaps everyone would like to go downstairs,' he said, brightly.

'Not likely,' said the lady in fawn. Charlotte and Gordon's guests were dug in for the duration.

Dominique looked up at Max pleadingly.

'She is Gill,' he said.

'But why?'

'They were playing a joke, only it doesn't seem so funny now, does it, Em?'

She shook her head.

Gill looked up at Max. 'Tell her she's not taking Kevin,' she pleaded.

Max said nothing.

'Max, tell her,' Gill repeated.

'Kevin is hers,' Max said finally.

'But she doesn't care about him. She'll dump him again when the next boyfriend comes along. You know that. Kevin's been so happy. We've been so happy.'

'I know,' Max said. 'But . . .' He trailed off. He was used to being caught between Emma and Dominique. This situation had now become a triangle. He struggled to find a way out of his predicament. In Max's terms, this translated into finding a way to avoid having a scene with any of the three women and definitely with all three of them together. Gill was bitterly disappointed. Unlike Emma, she hadn't had thirteen years of Max folding in front of his ex-wife. She still saw Max through idealised eyes.

Emma, who was still sitting at the table, gave Max a surprise way out. She said, 'Why don't you let Kevin choose?'

'What?' said Gill, not releasing Dominique's arms, but looking up.

'Let Kevin choose who he wants to live with.'

'But he's only three!' Gill protested.

'Well, if you don't think he'll choose you . . .' Emma said.

Gill thought for a moment. 'OK,' she said.

'Dominique?' Max asked.

She nodded.

Gill loosened her grip and Dominique struggled free. They both stood up. Then they walked to the door and began the long trek downstairs. Emma, Max, Charlotte and Gordon went to the window and looked out on to the garden. There was a mass scraping of chairs as anyone who was even faintly able-bodied joined them. It was like the road to Lourdes as guests hobbled, shuffled and dragged themselves across the room to the window. They watched as Dominique and Gill emerged on to the gravel. At first, Kevin was so engrossed in his game with Saskia he didn't notice their arrival. Saskia ignored Dominique and nodded at Gill. Then Kevin sensed the change of atmosphere. He had a stick in one hand, with which he had been tracing circles in the dusty top of a wall; he dropped it and turned uncertainly.

Gill and Dominique separated. Dominique put her arms out. 'Kevin, come here. It's Mummy,' she ordered.

Gill dropped to her haunches. She too put her arms out. 'Kevin, sweetie, come and give me a cuddle,' she pleaded.

'This is obscene,' said Charlotte. 'Do something, Gordon. He's only a child.'

Gordon sighed. 'I think we have to let it run its course now,' he said.

Watching the awful scene unfolding below, Emma too was horrified. She wished she'd never suggested it. She had wanted to hurt Gill, but now she was ashamed that they were using Kevin to do it.

Kevin looked first at his mother and then at Gill.

'Kevin!' Dominique ordered.

'Sweetie,' Gill wheedled.

Everyone held their breath. Kevin started walking and then running towards Dominique. 'Mummy!' he giggled happily.

Dominique patted Kevin's head less in affection than in triumph. 'You know who your mummy is, don't you?' she said.

Gill rocked back on to her heels and sat down on the gravel, her knees pulled right up to her chin. She wrapped her arms round her shins and sobbed. Kevin, seeing her crying, broke free of his mother and scampered over to her. 'Don't cry, Aunty Emma,' he said. Then he frowned, looking for a phrase that might banish her tears. His face lit up. 'You can have all my toys in the bath, if you like. AND you can put the plug in!'

Gill lifted her head and smiled. 'Thanks,' she said.

Kevin put a hand on one of Gill's knees but it was more to humour her than anything else. Within a few seconds he had returned to Dominique. He reached up with his hand and slipped it into hers.

'Are you taking me home?' he said, his eyes wide with expectation.

'Yes,' said Dominique, beginning to lead him away.

'Are we going on a bus?'

Dominique wrinkled her nose in disgust. 'Of course not. Uncle Max will drive us.'

'*Brrm, brrm, brrm*,' Kevin said.

Dominique hadn't actually secured an agreement from Max on that point, but she assumed he would accede to her wish and she was right. Upstairs, in the dining room, he patted his pocket to make sure his car keys were there. They were. He was actually hugely relieved to have an excuse to make a quick exit from the fray. Max looked at Charlotte and Gordon. 'Well, I'll just . . .' he began.

Gordon nodded.

Max walked out of the room. Emma followed him. As he went down the stairs, she called after him, 'So that's it, is it? After thirteen years, you're just giving up on us, then?'

Max stopped at the bottom, put a hand on the newel post and turned. 'I think it was you who gave up on us, wasn't it?'

Emma stopped halfway down. She was chilled by Max's emotional coldness and didn't feel able to go any nearer. 'It was an experiment, that's all,' she said.

'Well, I'd rather not be experimented on,' he said.

'But it's over now.' Emma risked a few steps further.

'It's too late.'

'It can't be.'

'It is.'

'You didn't really mean that thing about marrying the wrong twin, did you?'

'Maybe.'

'But you always said you didn't fancy Gill.'

'Get real, Em, you're identical. If I fancied you then I was bound to fancy her too. You look the same.'

'We do not!'

'Look, I'm not saying I had any great fantasy about her before . . . well, you know. I put it out of my mind. You have to when you're married to a twin. It's off limits, isn't it?'

'It's supposed to be, yes,' Emma said dejectedly.

'You were the ones who did the swap. You brought this on yourself, remember. Play with fire and you're going to get burnt. Look, I've got to go.'

Max turned and began to walk across the lobby towards the back door into the garden. Emma threw herself down the last steps and pelted after him. She ran into the sunlight, which almost blinded her after the gloom of the stairs. 'Max! Max!' she said, squinting.

Dominique was standing holding Kevin's hand. Gill was still crouched on the ground and Max was midway between them all.

'Don't go,' Emma said, walking up to him and burying her head in his chest. Her arms slipped round him and she hugged him tight. He felt warm and familiar. She really had missed him. She breathed in his smell, a mixture of sweat and soap. She felt the relief flood through her. She nuzzled her cheek into his shirt. 'Oh, Max,' she whispered.

Then Emma realised that Max's arms were hanging

limply at his sides. His chest was stiff. She looked up at his face. To her horror she saw he was embarrassed. 'Dominique's waiting,' he said.

Emma didn't move, so Max took her hands and tried to undo them, as if picking at a tricky knot in a piece of string. She struggled. 'No, no,' she wailed.

'Come on, Em,' he said quietly.

Emma looked into Max's eyes and it was clear that he had made up his mind. Now he was trying to be kind, which was worse than anything. 'Please,' she begged, as he forced her hands from round his neck.

Max held Emma's hands in front of her as if he were about to put on handcuffs, only it was the opposite of that. He was trying to compel her to flee. Emma could see that her battle was lost, but clung to the hope that there might still be some way back for her. She fell to her knees and wrapped her arms around his legs. 'Max, you can't. I love you. Give me another chance,' she said.

'I have to go,' he said, disentangling himself from her clutches more roughly now. Once free, he walked quickly over to Kevin, picked him up and he and Dominique walked back into the hotel.

Emma was kneeling on the gravel. It was sticking into her flesh, but she welcomed the pain. It was more tangible than all the other pain she was feeling.

'You OK?' It was Saskia. Emma and Gill had almost forgotten she was there. She walked over to Emma, put out a hand to help her up, then did the same for Gill.

They dusted gravel off themselves. 'Well, that went well,' Saskia said.

It was black humour, but welcome all the same. They smiled at each other, then they looked up at the window to the dining room. A crowd of faces was staring down at them.

'Shall we get out of here?' Emma suggested.

'Not without me, I hope?' said a male voice.

Chapter Twenty-Five

'Alex!' Emma exclaimed. 'How did you know I was –'

'Gus told me.' He pointed at Gill. 'You didn't tell me there were two of you.' He frowned, looking from one to the other. 'So you're twins.'

'No, we're just really good friends, so good I had cosmetic surgery so I could look just like her!' Gill said with considerable hostility. She only knew Alex as her boss, the one who couldn't remember her name, and his presence was unwelcome.

There was a pause.

'Jesus! It was a joke. Of course we're twins,' Gill spat.

'So, which one of you works for me?'

'We both do,' Gill said.

'What?'

'We did a swap,' Emma explained. 'Anyway, what are you doing here?' She was uncomfortable in Alex's presence. He had a palpable physical effect on her and she didn't want him or anyone else to see that.

'I've come to see you,' he said, then, turning to Gill: 'I think I have. Apart from the hair colour, you're identical.'

'That's why they are called identical twins,' Saskia said drily.

'It's me you've come to see,' Emma said. 'You think I'm Gill. I'm not, but you think I am.'

Alex still looked confused.

'I was the one in New York,' Emma explained.

'But I thought you went with Chloë,' Gill said.

'I did. Look, it's complicated.' She looked at Alex. 'Right, you wanted to say?'

'Yeah,' said Gill. 'What are you doing here?'

'I've come to ask for a decision,' Alex stated.

'About what?' said Gill.

'He's asking me, not you,' said Emma.

'Well, will someone, either of you, give me an answer?' Alex said in exasperation.

'Perhaps you ought to consult your wife,' Emma replied curtly.

'Wife? I haven't got a wife,' he said, frowning.

'Really.'

'Yes, really.'

'What about Joelly Childs?'

'What about her?'

'So you don't even deny it? I saw the baby holding the monkey.'

'What monkey?' Gill and Saskia said together.

'The monkey he bought in New York,' Emma explained.

'How did you get it though customs?' Saskia asked suspiciously. 'Monkeys are an endangered species.'

'It wasn't a real monkey,' Alex explained. 'But we're getting off the point here.'

'The point being?' Saskia asked.

'He lives with Joelly Childs,' Emma said. 'No use denying it. I've met her.'

'I don't deny it. I live with Joelly at the moment, yes. She's my sister.'

'Sister!' Emma exclaimed.

Gill was incredulous. 'Didn't you know? I'm sure I told you, that time we saw her in the kids' shop. And you thought they were an item! Don't you read *Heat* magazine?'

'I don't have time to read the cooking instructions on the back of a microwave meal,' said Emma.

Saskia was frowning. 'You said you wanted an answer. To what?'

'I offered Gill – I mean . . . oh, whatever,' Alex said, pointing at Emma. 'I offered her a job. I wanted her to come and run a bar for me in New York.'

'New York! Wow! I'll go,' Saskia said.

'He's not asking you. He's asking me,' Emma chided her.

'Well?'

Emma looked at Alex. He appeared punch drunk, but then she and Gill tended to forget the effect they had on people. Talking to them together was like wearing funny glasses. You saw double.

'I don't know,' Emma said. 'I'm confused. Look, I'm

going to say this and then really regret it, but I have to . . .'

'Yes?' Alex said.

'Well, remember when we almost kissed on the steps of the Majestic and then we didn't? I thought maybe that was because you were married and now I know you're not and I'm really confused and are you gay?'

Alex laughed. 'No, I'm not gay.'

'So why haven't you . . .'

'Made a pass?'

Emma nodded.

'Well, there was Bob to think about.'

'Bob? Bob who?'

'Bob Beresford.'

'The talk show guy?' Saskia exclaimed.

Alex nodded.

'What the hell has Bob Beresford got to do with this?' Emma asked.

'You were with him in the Winchester. I just sort of assumed you two were . . . you know.'

'Me and Bob Beresford! Of course not. He's married!'

'Yeah, well, that doesn't stop Bob.'

Now it was Emma who laughed. 'So you thought I was Bob Beresford's bit on the side, did you?'

'Hey, don't knock it!' Chloë was standing by the doorway from the hotel, holding a glass. Gus was with her.

'What are you doing here?' Emma and Gill asked in unison.

'Gus called and said Alex had been into the bar to find you and –' Chloë began.

'We couldn't have missed this, could we? So where have we got to?' said Gus.

Saskia stepped forwards. 'Since I'm obviously the only sane one here, let me,' she said. 'For a start, Gill is Emma and Emma is Gill.'

'Right,' said Chloë and Gus, uncertainly.

'Now, he . . .' Saskia pointed at Alex, 'wants her . . .' she pointed at Emma, 'to run his bar in New York. Oh, yeah and she . . .' she pointed at Gill, 'has been sleeping with my dad. Dominique also turned up but she's gone now and taken Kevin with her.'

'Well, that's all as clear as mud,' Chloë said.

Gill suddenly spoke. 'If it was me, Em, I'd take the job. It's the chance of a lifetime.'

'Then you go,' Emma said. 'Ah, but I forgot. You're a bit busy shacking up with my husband, aren't you?'

Gill looked down. She was serious. 'No,' she said quietly.

'What do you mean?' Emma asked incredulously.

'I thought he loved me, but, well, when the chips were down, he backed Dominique, didn't he?'

'Don't feel bad. It wasn't you. A child will always go to his mother. It doesn't matter how crap she is. It's an inbuilt thing.'

'No, it's not that. I mean, I really wanted Kevin, but it's the fact that Max didn't back me. If he'd stood with me on it, Dominique might have given in. She doesn't really want him. Not really. But Max didn't back me. He seems to think that I would be willing to give up everything for him, not least you, Em, but he wouldn't do this one thing for me. You know, I don't think he wanted me at all. He wanted a fantasy of me, or of you really. He wanted us, but with all the difficult bits removed. But that's not you or me, is it, Em?'

Emma shook her head.

'I can't come second to someone else – Dominique – for the rest of my life,' Gill said.

'So what are you saying?' Emma asked.

'It's over.'

'Over?'

'It never really began. I was just playing at being you. Give me a month and I'd have been dying to get pissed on Bloody Marys and stay out till four in the morning. And, let's face it, I didn't make a great success of your job, did I? You're on gardening leave, by the way.'

'I hate gardening.'

'So do I.'

They smiled at each other.

'So,' Gill said. 'What about you and Max?'

'You said it yourself. You don't want to spend your life coming second to his ex-wife. Well, maybe I've spent too long doing that already. He doesn't want me, anyway.'

'But maybe you could try counselling or something?'

'What, sit in someone's spare room in Tufnell Park

while a stranger deconstructs our marriage? I don't think so. No, you were right. Things haven't been right for ages. We just stayed together for . . . Saskia? Where's Saskia?'

Emma and Gill looked round the garden. They spotted her at the far end by the low box hedge Gill had so admired.

'Come on,' Emma said.

Emma and Gill jogged across the garden.

'Hello!' Alex said as they went. 'I am still here, you know. What about an answer?' Then he turned to Gus. 'Bliss not open then?'

'Well . . .'

Saskia was sitting picking leaves off the box hedge. 'You might find a Strimmer does a quicker job,' Gill said as they reached her.

Saskia didn't answer.

Gill and Emma sat down each side of her. 'What's the matter?' Gill said gently.

'Nothing,' she hissed.

'There must be something,' Emma coaxed.

Silence.

'You can tell us,' Gill tried again.

'Which one of you?' Saskia said, looking up. 'I mean, how am I to know which one of you is going to pretend to be my mother this week? What are you going to do, flip a coin? Or maybe you'll draw straws and the short one gets me.'

'Sask . . .' Emma said, putting an arm round her shoulder.

Saskia stood up and faced them. 'No. Your little game might have been fun for you, but what about me? Does anyone actually want me? The old cow doesn't. Oh, she wants Kevin, but not me. She couldn't wait to get out of here with him.' A tear was running down her cheek. She brushed it away with the back of her hand angrily. It was a sign of weakness and she hated it. 'What is so wrong with me that no one wants me?'

Emma stood up. 'There's nothing wrong with you. Your father and I both love you.'

'No, you don't. You wanted to marry my dad and you got me as part of the deal. But you never wanted me. You just put up with me.'

'Is that what you think?' Emma said. 'Oh, Saskia, I'm sorry. I never wanted you to feel like that.'

'So why did you leave me too?'

'What do you mean?'

'First the old cow goes and then, when you did your swap with Gill, you didn't just walk out on Dad, you know, you walked out on me too.'

'I . . . I . . .' Emma didn't have an answer. At least not a good enough one. She had left Saskia. There was no getting around that.

'It was only meant to be for a while,' she tried.

'Is that supposed to make me feel better?'

'I'm sorry.'

Gill intervened. 'We had a good time, didn't we?'

Saskia said nothing.

'Em needed a break. It's not easy being a working mother, you know.'

'Oh, spare me the juggling balls speech, please.'

'It's true, though.'

'But it's not even as if she' – Saskia indicated Emma – 'is a real mother. If you liked children so much, why didn't you have any of your own kids with my dad?'

'Oh, well, you know . . .'

'No, I don't actually.'

Emma bit her lip. 'It was never the right time and, well, we had our hands full with . . .'

'Me! You didn't have any kids of your own because of me,' Saskia shouted. 'No wonder you hate me.'

'I didn't say that. I don't hate you. There were a lot of factors.'

'God. How you must hate me!' Saskia gasped.

Emma stepped forwards and pulled Saskia towards her. 'But I love you, don't you see? You may be the most irritating child –'

'I am not a child.'

'OK, irritating young woman alive, but I love you. You are my daughter and if occasionally I'm not a very good mum –'

'You are a good mum,' Saskia sobbed. 'I'm a rubbish daughter.'

'Well, maybe we could all do better,' said Gill, who had joined them. Emma put out an arm and all three hugged.

'Can anyone join in this hugging thing? I'm not being kinky. It's just bloody freezing out here.' Alex was standing a few feet away, slapping his arms across his chest.

'Sorry,' Emma said. 'I haven't given you an answer, have I?'

'No.'

Emma looked at Gill and Saskia.

'The thing is,' Emma said, 'it does sound like an awful lot of work.'

'You're not asking for a pay rise already, are you?'

'No, I just thought . . .' Emma winked at Gill. 'Two pairs of hands might be better than one.'

Alex laughed. 'Well, it might be a good marketing gimmick. Twins running a bar.'

'Just so long as we don't have to wear the same clothes,' Gill said.

'There is one more thing . . .' Emma said.

'What now?'

'What are the schools like in New York? Saskia hasn't done her A levels yet.'

Saskia began whooping. 'New York. We're going to New York!'

Gus and Chloë heard and raised their glasses.

Gill turned to Emma. 'Are you sure? I mean, I don't want to cramp your style.'

'Of course,' Emma whispered. 'I haven't decided what I'm going to do about Alex yet. Maybe I should just give men a complete rest.'

'Oh, come on, this is me, Em, I can see you fancy the pants off him.'

'I've just thought of something,' Alex said. 'You two, you're like one of those special offers. Buy one, get one free.'

'Do you want to hit him,' said Gill to Emma, 'or shall I?'

Now you can buy any of these other bestselling
Headline books from your bookshop or
direct from the publisher.

FREE P&P AND UK DELIVERY
(Overseas and Ireland £3.50 per book)

A Married Man	Catherine Alliott	£6.99
Olivia's Luck	Catherine Alliott	£6.99
Cuban Heels	Emily Barr	£6.99
Amazing Grace	Clare Dowling	£6.99
Pure Fiction	Julie Highmore	£6.99
Azur Like It	Wendy Holden	£6.99
Falling For You	Jill Mansell	£6.99
Nadia Knows Best	Jill Mansell	£6.99
A Compromising Position	Carole Matthews	£6.99
The Sweetest Taboo	Carole Matthews	£6.99
Right on Time	Pauline McLynn	£6.99
Too Good To be True	Sheila O'Flanagan	£6.99
Dreaming of A Stranger	Sheila O'Flanagan	£6.99

TO ORDER SIMPLY CALL THIS NUMBER

01235 400 414

or visit our website: www.madaboutbooks.com

Prices and availability subject to change without notice.